Praise for
Long Spoon Lane

"One can always count on Anne Perry's elegant Victorian mysteries."

—*The New York Times Book Review*

"The plot of *Long Spoon Lane* is neatly put together and works out like a clever contraption with no loose ends."

—*Los Angeles Times*

"There is much to love in *Long Spoon Lane*. The characters are subtly many-layered. Fans of the series, with its amazingly well-drawn historical details, know the delight of time traveling back to Victorian England. . . . An altogether intriguing and enjoyable mystery."

—Bookreporter.com

D0029773

LONG SPOON LANE

ANNE PERRY

LONG SPOON LANE

A CHARLOTTE AND THOMAS PITT NOVEL

BALLANTINE BOOKS TRADE PAPERBACKS • NEW YORK

Long Spoon Lane is a work of fiction. Names, characters, places, and incidents are the products of the author's imagination or are used fictitiously. Any resemblance to actual events, locales, or persons, living or dead, is entirely coincidental.

2011 Ballantine Books Trade Paperback Edition

Copyright © 2005 by Anne Perry

All rights reserved.

Published in the United States by Ballantine Books, an imprint of
The Random House Publishing Group, a division of Random House, Inc., New York.

BALLANTINE and colophon are registered trademarks of Random House, Inc.

Originally published in hardcover in the United States by Ballantine Books,
an imprint of The Random House Publishing Group, a division of
Random House, Inc., in 2005.

Library of Congress Cataloging-in-Publication Data
Perry, Anne.
Long Spoon Lane : a novel / Anne Perry.
p.   cm.
ISBN 978-0-345-52372-3
eBook ISBN 978-0-345-49086-5
1. Pitt, Thomas (Fictitious character)—Fiction.   2. Pitt, Charlotte (Fictitious
character)—Fiction.   3. Police—England—London—Fiction.   4. London
(England)—Fiction.   5. Police spouses—Fiction.   6. Anarchists—Fiction.   I. Title.
PR6066.E693L66 2005b
823'.914—dc22
2004060898

Printed in the United States of America

www.ballantinebooks.com

2   4   6   8   9   7   5   3   1

In memory of my mother,
H. Marion Perry,
with gratitude,

January 30, 1912–January 19, 2004

LONG SPOON LANE

CHAPTER

ONE

THE HANSOM CAB lurched around the corner, throwing Pitt forward almost onto his knees. Victor Narraway, his companion, swore. Pitt regained his balance as they gathered speed towards Aldgate and Whitechapel High Street. The horse's hooves struck hard on the cobbles and ahead of them traffic was scattering out of the way. Thank heaven this early there was little enough of it: a few costermongers' carts with fruit and vegetables, a brewer's dray, goods wagons, and one horse-drawn omnibus.

"Right!" Narraway shouted at the driver. "Commercial Road! It's faster!"

The driver obeyed without answering. It was fifteen minutes before six on a summer morning and there were already laborers, hawkers, tradesmen, and domestic servants about. Please heaven they would be in Myrdle Street before six o'clock!

Pitt felt as if his heart were beating in his throat. The call had come just over half an hour ago, but it felt like an eternity. The telephone had woken him and he had gone racing downstairs in his nightshirt. Narraway's voice had been crackly and breathless on the other end. "I've sent a cab for you. Meet me on Cornhill, north side, outside the Royal Exchange. Immediately. Anarchists are going to bomb a house on Myrdle Street." Then he had hung up without waiting for a reply, leaving Pitt to go back upstairs and tell Charlotte before he scrambled into his clothes. She had run downstairs and fetched him a glass of milk and a slice of bread, but there had been no time for tea.

He had stood a cold, impatient five minutes on the pavement outside the Royal Exchange until Narraway's cab arrived and slithered to a halt. Then the driver's long whip snaked out and urged the horse forward again even before Pitt had fallen into the other seat.

Now they were charging towards Myrdle Street and he still had very little idea what it was about, except that the information had come from Narraway's own sources on the fringes of the seething East End underworld—the province of cracksmen, macers, screevers, footpads, and the swarming thieves of every kind that preyed on the river.

"Why Myrdle Street?" he shouted. "Who are they?"

"Could be anyone," Narraway replied without taking his eyes off the road. Special Branch had been created originally to deal with Irish Fenians in London, but now they dealt with all threats to the safety of the country. Just at the moment—early summer 1893—the danger at the front of most people's minds was anarchist bombers. There had been several incidents in Paris, and London had suffered half a dozen explosions of one degree or another.

Narraway had no idea whether this latest threat came from the Irish, who were still pursuing Home Rule, or revolutionaries simply desiring to overthrow the government, the throne, or law and order in general.

They swung left around the corner up into Myrdle Street, across the junction, and stopped. Just up ahead the police were busy waking people up, hurrying them out of their homes and into the road. There was no time to look for treasured possessions, not even to grasp onto more than a coat or a shawl against the cool air of the morning.

Pitt saw a constable of about twenty chivvying along an old woman. Her white hair hung in thin wisps over her shoulders, her

arthritic feet bare on the cobbles. Suddenly he almost choked with
fury against whoever was doing this.

A small boy wandered across the street, blinking in bewilder-
ment, dragging a mongrel puppy on a length of string.

Narraway was out of the cab and striding towards the nearest
constable, Pitt on his heels. The constable swiveled around to tell
him to go back, his face flushed with anxiety and annoyance. "Yer
gotta get out o' the way, sir." He waved his arm. "Well back, sir.
There's a bomb in one o' . . ."

"I know!" Narraway said smartly. "I'm Victor Narraway, head
of Special Branch. This is my associate, Thomas Pitt. Do you know
where the bomb is?"

The constable stood half to attention, still holding his right
hand out to bar people from returning to their homes in the still,
almost breathless morning air. "No sir," he replied. "Not to be
exact. We reckon it's gotter be one o' them two over there." He inclined his head towards the opposite side of the street. Narrow,
three-story houses huddled together, doors wide open, front steps
whitened by proud, hardworking women. A cat wandered out of
one of them, and a child shouted to it eagerly and it ran towards
her.

"Is everyone out?" Narraway demanded.

"Yes, sir, far as we can tell—"

The rest of his answer was cut off by a shattering explosion. It
came at first like a sharp crack, and then a roar and a tearing and
crumbling. A huge chunk of one of the houses lifted in the air then
blew apart. Rubble fell crashing into the street and over other
roofs, smashing slates and toppling chimneys. Dust and flames
filled the air. People were shouting hysterically. Someone was
screaming.

The constable was shouting too, his mouth wide open, but his
words were lost in the noise. His body staggered oddly as if his legs
would not obey him. He lurched forward, waving his arms as people stood rooted to the ground in horror.

Another blast roared somewhere inside the second house. The walls shivered and seemed to subside upon themselves, bricks and plaster falling outward. Then there was more flame, black smoke gushing up.

Suddenly people started to run. Children were sobbing, someone was cursing loudly, and several dogs burst into frenzied barking. An old man was swearing steadily at everything he could think of, repeating himself over and over.

Narraway's face was white, his black eyes like holes in his head. They had never expected to be able to prevent the bombs going off, but it was still a searing defeat to see such wreckage strewn across the road, and terrified and bewildered people stumbling around. The flames were getting hold of the dry lath and timber and beginning to spread.

A fire engine pulled up, its horses sweating, their eyes rolling. Men leapt out and started to uncoil the big, canvas hoses, but it was going to be a hopeless task.

Pitt felt a stunning sense of failure. Special Branch was for preventing things like this. And now that it had happened there was nothing comforting or purposeful he could do. He did not even know if there would be a third bomb, or a fourth.

Another constable came sprinting along the street, arms waving wildly, his helmet jammed crookedly on his head. "Other side!" he shouted. "They're getting away on the other side!"

It was a moment before Pitt realized what he meant.

Narraway knew immediately. He twisted on his heel and started back towards the hansom.

Pitt galvanized into action, catching up with Narraway just as he swung up into the cab, barking at the driver to go back to Fordham Street and turn east.

The man obeyed instantly, snaking the long carriage whip over the horse's back and urging it forward. They went to the left, crossed Essex Street barely hesitating, and glimpsed another hansom disappearing north up New Road towards Whitechapel.

"After them!" Narraway shouted, ignoring the morning traffic of delivery carts and drays, which swerved out of their way and jammed together.

There had been no time to ask who the bombers might be, but as they slewed around the corner into Whitechapel Road, and past the London Hospital, Pitt turned his mind to it. The anarchist threats so far had been disorganized and no specific demands had been made. London was the capital of an empire that stretched across almost every continent on the earth, and the islands between, and it was also the biggest port in the world. There was a constant influx of every nationality under the sun—recently in particular immigrants had arrived from Latvia, Lithuania, Poland, and Russia, seeking to escape the power of the tsar. Others from Spain and Italy, and especially France, had more socialist aims in mind.

Beside him Narraway was craning forward, his lean body rigid. His face turned first one way then the other as he sought to catch a glimpse of the hansom ahead. Whitechapel had turned into Mile End Road. They passed the huge block of Charrington's Brewery on the left.

"It makes no damn sense!" he said bitterly.

The cab ahead of them turned left up Peters Street. It had barely straightened when it disappeared to the right into Willow Place and then Long Spoon Lane. Pitt and Narraway's cab overshot and had to turn and double back. By that time there were two more cabs slithering to a halt with policemen piling out of them, and the original cab had gone.

Long Spoon Lane was narrow and cobbled. Its gray tenement buildings rose up sheer for three stories, grimy, stained with the smoke and damp of generations. The air smelled of wet rot and old sewage.

Pitt glanced along both sides, east and west. Several doorways were boarded up. A large woman stood blocking another, hands on her hips, glaring at the disturbance to her routine. To the west one door slammed, but when two constables charged with their shoulders to it, it did not budge. They tried again and again with no effect.

"It must be barricaded," Narraway said grimly. "Get back!" he ordered the men.

Pitt felt a chill. Narraway must fear the anarchists were armed. It was absurd. Less than two hours ago he had been lying in bed half-asleep, Charlotte's hair a dark river across the pillow beside him. The early sunlight had made a bright bar between the curtains, and busy sparrows chattered in the trees outside. Now he stood shivering as he stared up at the ugly wall of a tenement building in which were hiding desperate young men who had bombed a whole row of houses.

There were a dozen police in the street now and Narraway had taken over from the sergeant in charge of them. He was directing some to the other alleys. Pitt saw with a cold misery that the most recent to arrive were carrying guns. He realized there was no alternative. It was a crime of rare and terrible violence. There could be no quarter given to those who had committed it.

Now the street was oddly quiet. Narraway came back, his coat flapping, his face pinched, mouth a tight, thin line. "Don't stand there like a damn lamppost, Pitt. You're a gamekeeper's son, don't tell me you don't know how to fire a gun! Here." He held up a rifle, his knuckles white, and pushed it at Pitt.

It was on Pitt's tongue to say that gamekeepers didn't shoot at people, when he realized it was not only irrelevant, it was untrue. More than one poacher had suffered a bottom full of buckshot. Reluctantly he took the gun, and then the ammunition.

He backed away to the far side. He smiled with a twist of irony, finding himself standing behind the only lamppost. Narraway kept to the shadow of the buildings opposite, walking rapidly along the narrow shelf of footpath, speaking to the police where they were taking as much cover as there was. Apart from his footsteps there was no other sound. The horses and cabs had been moved away, out of danger. Everyone who lived here had vanished inside.

The minutes dragged by. There was no movement opposite. Pitt wondered if they were certain the anarchists were in there. Automatically he looked up at the rooftops. They were steep, pitched too sharply to get a foothold, and there were no dormers to climb out of, no visible skylights.

Narraway was coming back. He saw Pitt's glance and a flash of humor momentarily lit his face. "No, thank you," he said drily. "If I send anyone up there, it won't be you. You'd trip over your own coattails. And before you ask, yes, I've got men 'round the back and at both ends." He took a careful position between Pitt and the wall.

Pitt smiled.

Narraway grunted. "I'm not waiting them out all day," he said sourly. "I've sent Stamper for some old wagons, something solid enough to take a few bullets. We'll tip them on their sides to give us enough shelter, then we'll go in."

Pitt nodded, wishing he knew Narraway better. He did not yet trust him as he had Micah Drummond, or John Cornwallis when he had been an ordinary policeman in Bow Street. He had respected both men and understood their duties. He had also been intensely aware of their humanity, their vulnerabilities as well as their skills.

Pitt had never set out to join Special Branch. His own success against the powerful secret society known as the Inner Circle had contrived an apparent disgrace, which had cost him a position in the Metropolitan Police. For his safety, and to provide him with some kind of job, he had been found a place in Special Branch to work for Victor Narraway. He had been superseded in Bow Street by Wetron, who was himself a member of the Inner Circle, and now its leader.

Pitt felt uncertain, too often wrong-footed. Special Branch, with its secrets, its deviousness, and its half-political motives, re-quired a set of skills he was only just beginning to learn. He had too few parameters by which to judge Narraway.

But he was also aware that if he had gone on to further promotion in Bow Street he would soon have lost his connection with the reality of crime. His compassion for the pain of it would have dimmed. Everything would have been at secondhand, particularly his power to influence.

His situation now was better, even standing outside in a chilly lane with Narraway, waiting to storm an anarchist stronghold. The moment of arrest was never easy or pleasant. Crime was always someone's tragedy.

Pitt realized he was hungry, but above all he would have loved a hot cup of tea. His mouth was dry, and he was tired of standing in one spot. Although it was a summer morning, it was still cold here in the shadow. The stone pavement was damp from the night's dew. He could smell the stale odor of wet wood and drains.

There was a rumble on the cobbles at the far end of the lane, and an old cart turned in, pulled by a rough-coated horse. When it reached the middle of the lane, the driver jumped down. He un-harnessed the animal and led it away at a trot. A moment later an-other, similar cart appeared and was placed behind it. Both were tipped on their sides.

"Right," Narraway said quietly, straightening up. His face was grim. In the sharp, pale light, every tiny line in it was visible. It seemed as if each passion he had experienced in his life had writ-ten its mark on him, but the overwhelming impression he gave was of unbreakable strength.

There were half a dozen police now along the length of the street. Most of them seemed to have guns. There were others at the back of the buildings, and at the ends of the lane.

Three men moved forward with a ram to force the door. Then an upstairs window smashed, and everyone froze. An instant later there was gunfire, bullets ricocheting off the walls at shoulder height and above. Fortunately no one staggered or fell.

The police started to fire back. Two more windows broke.

In the distance a dog was barking furiously, and there was a dull rumble of heavy traffic from Mile End Road, a street away.

The shooting started again.

Pitt was reluctant to join in. Even with all the crimes he had investigated through his years in the police, he had never had to fire a gun at a human being. The thought was a cold pain inside him.

Then Narraway sprinted over to where two men were crouching behind the carts, and a bullet thudded into the wall just above Pitt's head. Without stopping to think about it, he raised his gun and fired back at the window from which it had come.

The men with the ram had reached the far side of the street and were out of the line of fire. Every time a shadow moved behind the remains of the glass in the windows, Pitt fired at it, reloading quickly after. He hated shooting at people, yet he found his hands were steady and there was a kind of exhilaration beating inside him.

Higher up the street there was more shooting.

Narraway looked over at Pitt, a warning in his eyes, then he strode across the cobbles to the men with the ram. Another volley of shots rang out from an upstairs window, cracking on the walls and ricocheting, or thudding, embedded in the wood of the carts.

Pitt fired back, then changed the direction of his aim. It was a different window, one from which nobody had fired before. He could see the shattered glass now, bright in the reflected sunlight.

There were shots from several places, the house, the street below it, and at the far end of the lane. A policeman crumpled and fell.

No one moved to help him.

Pitt fired upward again, one window then another, wherever he saw a shadow move, or the flash of gunpowder.

Still no one went for the wounded man. Pitt realized no one could, they were all too vulnerable.

A bullet hit the metal of the lamppost beside him with a sharp clang, making his pulse leap and his breath catch in his throat. He steadied his hand deliberately for the next shot back, and sent it clear through the window. His aim was getting better. He left the shelter of the lamppost and set off across the street towards the constable on the ground. He had about seventy feet to go. Another shot went past him and hit the wall. He tripped and half fell just short of the man. There was blood on the stones. He crawled the last yard.

"It's all right," he said urgently. "I'll get you safe, then we can have a look at you." He had no idea whether the constable could hear him or not. His face was pasty white and his eyes were closed. He looked about twenty. There was blood on his mouth.

There was no way Pitt could carry him because he dared not stand up; he would make a perfect target. He might even be accidentally hit by a ricocheting bullet from his own men, who were now firing rapidly again. He bent and picked up the constable's shoulders, and inching backwards awkwardly, pulled him over the cobbles, until at last they were in the shelter of the carts.

"You'll be all right," he said again, more to himself than anyone else. To his surprise the man's eyes flickered open and he gave a weak smile. Pitt saw with heart-lurching relief that the blood on his mouth was from a cut across his cheek. Quickly he examined him as much as he could, to find at least where he was hit, and bind it. He kept on talking quietly, to reassure them both.

He found the wound in the shoulder. It was bloody but not fatal. Probably hitting his head on the cobbles as he fell had been what had knocked him senseless. Without his helmet, it would have been worse.

Pitt did what he could with a torn-off sleeve to make a pad and press it onto the site of the bleeding. By the time he was finished— perhaps four or five minutes later—others were there to help. He left them to get the man out, and picked up his gun again. Bending low, he ran over to the men with the ram just as the frame splintered and the door crashed open against the wall.

Immediately inside was a narrow stairway. The men ran up ahead of him, Narraway on their heels, Pitt right behind.

There was a shot from above them, raised voices and footsteps, then more shots in the distance, probably at the back of the house.

He went up the stairs two at a time. On the third floor up he found a wide room, probably having originally been two. Narraway was standing in the hard light from the broken windows. At the far end, the door to the stairs down towards the back was swinging open. There were three police cradling guns, and two young men standing still, almost frozen. One had long dark hair and wild eyes. Without the blood and the swelling on his face he would have been handsome. The other was thinner, almost emaciated, his hair red-gold. His eyes were an almost too pale greenish-blue. They both looked frightened and trying to be defiant. Simply and violently, two of the police forced the manacles on them.

Narraway inclined his head towards the doorway where Pitt was standing in a silent instruction to the police to take the prisoners away.

Pitt stepped aside to let them pass, then looked around the room. It was unfurnished except for two chairs and a bundle of blankets crumpled in a heap at the farther end. The windows were all broken and the wall pockmarked with bullet holes. It was what he had expected to see, except for the figure lying prone on the floor with his head towards the center window. His thick, dark brown hair was matted with blood and he did not move.

Pitt went over to him and knelt down. He was dead. There was even more blood on the floor. A single shot had killed him. It had gone in the back of his skull and emerged at the front, destroying the left side of his face. The right side suggested he had been handsome in life. There was no expression left but the remnants of surprise.

Pitt had investigated many murders—it was his profession—but few were as bloody as this. The only decent thing about this death was that it must have been instant. Still, he felt his stomach tighten and he swallowed to keep his gorge from rising. Please God it was not one of his bullets that had done this.

Narraway spoke softly from just behind him. Pitt had not heard his footsteps. "Try his pockets," he said. "Something might tell us who he is."

Pitt moved the man's hand, which was in the way. It was slender and well-shaped, with a signet ring on the third finger, expensive, well-crafted, and almost certainly gold.

Pitt turned the ring experimentally. It came off with only a little effort. He looked at it more closely. It was hallmarked on the inside, and there was a family crest on it.

Narraway held out his hand, palm up. Pitt gave it to him, then bent to the body again and started to look through the pockets of the jacket. He found a handkerchief, a few coins, and a note addressed *Dear Magnus*. Most of the rest of the paper was missing, as if it had been used for a further message.

"Dear Magnus," Pitt said aloud.

Narraway was looking at the ring, his lips pursed. In the hard morning light his face was troubled and weary. "Landsborough," he said as if in answer.

Pitt was startled. "Do you know him?"

Narraway did not meet his eyes. "Seen him a couple of times. He was Lord Landsborough's son—only son." His expression was unreadable. Pitt did not know whether the heaviness in it was sorrow, anxiety for trouble to come, or simply distaste for having to break such news to the family.

"Could he have been a hostage?" Pitt asked.

"Possibly," Narraway conceded. "One thing for certain, I don't know how he could have been shot through the window, in the back of his head, and fallen like that."

"He wasn't moved," Pitt said with certainty. "If he had been, there'd be blood all over the place. A wound like . . ."

"I can see that for myself!" Narraway's voice was suddenly thick, emotion crowding through it. It could have been pity, or even sheer physical revulsion. "Of course he wasn't moved. Why the hell would they move him? He was shot from inside the room, that's obvious. The question is why, and by whom? Maybe you're right, and he was a hostage.

"God Almighty, what a mess! Well, get up off the floor, man! The surgeon will come and get him, and we'll see if he can tell us anything. We must question these two before the police muddy everything up. I hate using them but I have no choice. That's the law!" He swung around and strode to the door. "Well, come on! Let's see what they have at the back!"

Downstairs the sergeant on duty was defiant, as if Narraway accused him of having let the murderer past.

"We didn't see 'im, sir. Your man came down the stairs, yellin' after 'im, but 'e din't go past us! You must 'ave still got 'im somewhere."

"Which man of mine?" Narraway demanded.

" 'Ow could we know, sir?" the sergeant asked. " 'E just came runnin' down the stairs shoutin' at us ter stop 'im, but there weren't no one ter stop!"

"We found two anarchists alive and one dead," Narraway said grimly. "There were four men in that room, maybe five. That means at least one got away."

The sergeant's face set hard, his blue eyes like stone.

"If you say so, sir. But 'e din't come past us. Maybe 'e doubled back on the ground floor and went out the front, while you was upstairs, sir?" It was said with an insolent edge. Some police did not like being seconded to do Special Branch's arrest work, but since Special Branch had no power to do it themselves, there was no choice.

"Or went out and straight back into one of the other buildings?" Pitt suggested quickly. "We'd better search them all."

"Do it," Narraway said curtly. "And look everywhere, in every room, in beds, if there are any, cupboards, under rubbish or old clothes, if there are lofts, even if it's only space enough to crawl. And up the chimneys, such as they are." He turned and strode along the length of the alley, staring up at the other houses, at the rooftops and at every door. Pitt followed on his heels.

Fifteen minutes later they were back at the front door on Long Spoon Lane. The full daylight was cold and gray and there was a sharp edge to the wind down the alley. No anarchist had been found hiding anywhere. No policeman from the front admitted to having seen anyone or having chased them inside the building, and no one had emerged at the front. The sergeant at the back did not change his story by so much as a word.

White-faced and furious, Narraway was forced to accept that whoever else had been in the house where Magnus Landsborough lay dead, he, or they, had escaped.

"Nothing!" the young man with the dark hair replied with contempt. He was in the cell at the police station, sitting on a straight-backed wooden chair, his hands still manacled. The only light came from one small, high window in the outer wall. He had said his name was Welling, but he would give no more. Both Pitt and Narraway had tried to glean from him any information about his colleagues, their aims or allies, where they had obtained the dynamite or the money to purchase it.

The man with the fair skin and red-gold hair had given his name as Carmody, but he too refused to say anything of his fellows. He was in a separate cell; for the moment, alone.

Narraway leaned back against the whitewashed stone wall, his face creased with tiredness.

"No point in asking anymore." His voice was flat, as if accepting defeat. "They'll go to the grave without telling us what it's all about. Either they don't know the point of it, or there isn't one. It's just mindless violence for the sake of it."

"I know!" Welling said between his teeth.

Narraway looked at him, affecting only the slightest interest. "Really? You will go to your grave, and I shall not know," he continued. "That's unusual for an anarchist. Most of you are fighting for something, and a grand gesture like being hanged is rather pointless if no one knows why you go to it like a cow to the abattoir."

Welling froze, his eyes wide, his lean chest barely rising or falling with his breath. "You can't hang me. No one was killed. One constable was hit, and you can't prove that was me, because it wasn't."

"Wasn't it?" Narraway said casually, as if he neither knew nor cared if it were true.

"You bastard!" Welling spat with stinging contempt. Suddenly his pretense of calm was gone, and the anger exploded through him. His face was slicked with sweat, his eyes widened. "You're just like the police—corrupt to the bone!" His voice shook. "No, it wasn't me! But you don't care, do you! Just so long as you have someone to blame, and anyone will do!"

For a moment Pitt was merely aware that Narraway had provoked Welling into response, then he realized what Welling had said about the police. It was not the accusation that stung, but the passion in his voice. He believed what he was saying, enough to face them with it, even now when it could cost him the last hope of mercy.

"There's a lot of difference between incompetence and corruption," Pitt said. "Of course there's the odd bad policeman, just as there is the odd bad doctor, or . . ." He stopped. The scorn in Welling's face was so violent that it distorted his features grotesquely, like a white mask under his black hair.

Narraway did not interrupt. He watched Pitt, then Welling, waiting for the next one to speak.

Pitt breathed in and out slowly. The silence prickled.

"Don't tell me you care!" Welling made it a stinging accusation.

"Neither do you, apparently," Pitt replied, forcing himself to smile. That was not easy. He had been a policeman all his adult life. He had devoted his time and energy, working long days, enduring emotional exhaustion to seek justice, or at least some resolution of tragedy and crime. To place a slur on both the honesty and the ideals of the men he worked with robbed from him the meaning of a quarter of a century of his past, and his belief in the force that defended the future. Without police of integrity there was no justice but vengeance, and no protection but the violence of the powerful. That truly was anarchy. And this smug young man in front of him would lose as much as anyone. He could survive to plant his bombs only because the rest of society obeyed the laws.

Pitt let his own contempt fill his voice when he answered. "If the police were largely corrupt, you wouldn't be sitting here being questioned," he said gratingly. "We'd simply have shot you. It would be easy enough to make an excuse afterward. Any story would do!" He heard how harsh and on the edge of control he sounded. "You sit here to face trial precisely because we keep the law you break. It is you who are a hypocrite, and corrupt. You not only lie to us, you lie to yourself!"

Welling's anger blazed. "Of course you could shoot us!" he said, leaning forward. "And you probably will! Just like you shot Magnus!"

Pitt stared at him, and realized with rising horror that Welling really was afraid. His words were not bravado; he believed them. He thought he was going to be murdered here.

Pitt turned to Narraway, who addressed the prisoner. "Magnus Landsborough was shot from behind," he said carefully. "He fell forward, with his head towards the window."

"He wasn't shot from outside," Welling responded. "It was one of your people coming up from the back. As I said, as corrupt as hell itself."

"You've proved nothing," Pitt countered. "And it's only just happened, so it could hardly be motive for bombing Myrdle Street. Why Myrdle Street, anyway? What did those people ever do to you? Or doesn't it matter who it is?"

"Of course I don't have proof of corruption," Welling said bitterly, straightening his body again. "You'll cover it up, just like you do all the rest. And you know why Myrdle Street."

"All the rest of what?" Narraway asked him. He was standing elegantly, leaning against the wall, his thin body tense. He was not a big man. He was shorter than Pitt and much lighter, but there was a wiry strength in him.

Welling considered before he replied. He seemed to be weighing the risks against the values of talking. When he finally did, he still gave the impression of being in the grasp of anger rather than reason.

"Depends where you are and who you are," he said. "What crimes you get caught for, and what gets overlooked—if you put a little money the right way." He looked from one to the other of them. "If you run a string of thieves, give a proportion of your take to the local police station and no one'll bother you. Have a shop or a business in certain places and you won't get robbed. Have it somewhere else and you will." His eyes were hot and angry, his body stiff.

It was a massive charge he was making, hideous in its implications.

"Who told you all this?" Narraway inquired.

"Told me?" Welling snapped back. "The poor devils who are paying, of course. But I didn't expect you to believe me. You've a vested interest in pretending not to. Ask around Smithfield, the Clerkenwell Road, and south to Newgate or Holborn. There are scores of alleys and back streets full of people who'd tell you the same. I'll not give you their names, or next thing they'll have to pay twice as much, or have the police all of a sudden find stolen goods in their houses."

Narraway's face reflected open disbelief. Pitt did not know if it was real, or a mask put on precisely to provoke Welling to continue talking.

"Go ask Birdie Waters up the Mile End Road!" Welling charged. "But he's in the Coldbath Prison right now. Doing time for receiving, except he didn't even know he had the things. Silver, from a robbery in Belgravia." His voice hurt with rage. "Birdie's never been to Belgravia in his life."

"Are you saying the police put it there?" Pitt interrupted whatever Narraway had been going to say.

"That's only one of a dozen," Welling retorted. "Good, decent people are being robbed, injured, frightened into giving up their honor and their business, and the police look whichever way suits them best." He was close to tears with frustration. "The whole government wants throwing out, destroying, before it twists us all so tight we have nothing left to fight with. We need to make a clean sweep, start over." He jerked his head violently. "Get rid of them all, the greedy, lying, corrupt . . ." He stopped suddenly, his body sagging as if the spirit had gone out of him. He turned away. "But you're government—police," he said helplessly. "Everything you want, your money, your power, it's all tied up in keeping things as they are. You're all part of it, whether you know it or not. You can't afford to escape!" He gave a wild laugh. "Where would you go?" He held his chin high, eyes blazing, but without hope.

Pitt's mind was racing. Many of the streets Welling had spoken of were within the Bow Street area, policed by his own old station, men he had worked with, commanded. Now it was under Superintendent Wetron, who was of the Metropolitan Police—and the Inner Circle. But Pitt refused to believe that he could have changed things so dreadfully in little more than a year.

Welling was staring at him, understanding of his defeat in his face already. He gave a jerky little laugh, as if to protect his vulnerability from showing. "You don't dare believe it, do you!" he said wretchedly.

"Why Myrdle Street?" Pitt asked again, going back to the unanswered question. "They're just ordinary people."

The sneer twisted Welling's face again. "Police," he said the single word with a snarl.

"Police?" Pitt questioned.

"As if you didn't know!"

"I don't! I'm Special Branch."

Welling blinked. "The house in the middle was Grover's. He's Simbister's man! Cannon Street."

"And that is worthy of a death sentence?" Narraway inquired icily.

Welling was defiant, his eyes filled with hate. "Yes! If you'd watched him, seen him hurt and humiliate people . . . yes, it is!"

Narraway straightened up away from the wall.

"You are not judge, jury, and executioner, Mr. Welling. You take rights that are not yours."

"Then you do it!" Welling shouted at him. "Someone has to!"

Narraway ignored him and turned to Pitt. "I shall go to inform Lord Landsborough of his son's death. It will be necessary for him to identify the body." His voice was perfectly steady. "You go back to Long Spoon Lane and examine everything again. I should like to know for myself who murdered Magnus Landsborough, and if possible why. It seems peculiarly pointless, but then I suppose anarchy is pointless by definition."

"You murdered him!" Welling spat, tears on his white face. "Because he was our leader. Can't you understand that when you cut one of us down, another will rise up to take his place! Over and over as many times as it needs. You can't kill everybody. After all, who would do the work then? Who would you govern?" His voice shook with passion. "Can't have a government unless there's someone to hew the wood and draw the water, someone to take the orders and do as they're told."

Narraway did not look at him. "And I should like to demonstrate to Mr. Welling that one of his own people is responsible for the death of his leader," he added. "We don't shoot people we need to get rid of. We hang them." With that he turned and walked out of the room leaving Pitt to follow him. Welling stared after them, his eyes scalding in tears of helplessness.

NARRAWAY HAD TO make several inquiries and it took him until the middle of the afternoon before he walked up the steps of the Atheneum at 107 Pall Mall to speak to Lord Landsborough. Narraway was a member, or of course he could not have entered, Special Branch or not.

"Yes, sir," the steward said quietly, his voice little more than a whisper. "Shall I inform his lordship you are here?"

"A private room," Narraway instructed him. "I am afraid I have very bad news for his lordship. You might see that there is a decent brandy and glasses on the table."

"Yes, sir. I'm very sorry, sir." The steward conducted him along the silent corridor to such a room as he had requested, and left him there. Two minutes later another steward brought a silver tray with Napoleon brandy and two delicately engraved balloon glasses.

Narraway stood in the middle of the Aubusson carpet and tried to compose his thoughts. This was the heart of the most civilized place in Europe: a gentlemen's club where impeccable manners were observed at all times. Voices were not raised. A man could sit here and discuss art and philosophy, sport or governments of the earth, exploration of the Empire and beyond, the history of the world itself, and meet with intimate wit and disciplined intelligence.

And he had come here to tell a man that his son had been murdered in an anarchist gun battle a handful of miles away.

Pitt might have been better at this. He was used to it. He might have some form of words that made it at least dignified. He had children himself. His imagination would lend an eloquence to his pity. Narraway could only struggle after it. He had no wife, no children, not even a younger sibling. His job had taught him how to survive alone even more than fate had dictated for him. He lived in his mind, his brilliant, subtle, instinctive brain, caring but never caring too much. Deliberately, he had no hostages to fortune.

The door opened and he found himself standing rigidly, gulping air. Lord Sheridan Landsborough came in and closed it softly behind him. He was a tall man, a trifle stooped now. He looked past seventy, with a wry, gentle face, which must have been handsome in his youth, and still held unusual charm and intelligence.

"Mr. Narraway?" he said courteously.

Narraway inclined his head in a slight bow of acknowledgment. "My lord. Perhaps you would like to sit down?"

"My dear fellow, I am not as fragile as all that! Or is the news you have brought so very terrible?" There was already a shadow in his eyes.

Narraway felt himself color slightly.

Landsborough saw it.

"I'm so sorry," he apologized. "Of course it is. You would not have come personally were it something trivial." He sat down, but more to oblige Narraway than because he felt required to. "What has happened?"

Narraway sat also, to avoid looking down at him. "There was an anarchist bombing in the Mile End area this morning," he said quietly. "We were warned of it, and arrived in time to pursue those who caused it. We ran them down in Long Spoon Lane and laid siege to the house. There was a brief gun battle before we took it. When we went in we found two anarchists alive, and the body of a third. He had been shot. We don't yet know by whom, except that it was from inside the room, not outside." Looking at Landsborough's face he could see that he already knew what Narraway would say next. "I'm sorry," he continued gravely. "The signet ring on his hand, as well as the statements by one of the men we caught, identify him as Magnus Landsborough."

Landsborough might have been half expecting it, but still the color bleached from his face leaving his skin almost gray. He hesitated a long, agonized moment, fighting to control his voice, then he answered. "I see. It was considerate of you to come in person. I suppose you wish me to identify . . ." He was unable to continue. His throat simply closed up and he gasped to draw air into his lungs.

Narraway felt utterly helpless. He had just inflicted appalling pain on a man, and was obliged to sit by without even averting his eyes as Landsborough struggled to maintain his dignity.

"Unless there is a close relative you would prefer to send," he offered, knowing Landsborough would not accept, even were there such a person.

Landsborough tried to smile, and failed. "No." His voice cracked. "There is no one else." He did not say that he would not ask it of Lady Landsborough. Such a thought would not enter his mind.

Narraway wanted to apologize again, but to do so would only require Landsborough to wave it away. Instead he used the moment to ask the painful question he was obliged to. It was still just possible that Magnus had been some kind of hostage, although he did not believe that. Welling had said he was their leader, and for all his naïveté, his passionate, ignorant, and one-sided philosophy, Narraway felt that Welling was speaking what he perceived to be the truth.

"What were Mr. Landsborough's political ideals, my lord?" he asked. "As far as you know."

"What? Oh?" Landsborough thought for a moment, when he answered there was a softer tone to his voice, on the edge of self-mockery, and tears. "I am afraid he followed some of my own liberal ideas, and took them rather too far. If you are trying a little delicately to ask me if I knew he had espoused more violent means of persuasion, I did not. But perhaps I should have expected it. Had I been wiser, I might have done something to prevent it, although precisely what escapes me."

Narraway was wrenched with an unexpected pity. Had Landsborough railed against fate or society, or even Special Branch, it might have been easier. He could have defended himself. He knew all the reasons and the arguments for what he did, the necessity of it. Most of them he actually believed, and he had never allowed himself to care whether others did or not. He could not afford to. But the silent, uncomplaining wounds of the man opposite him struck where he had no armor prepared.

"We cannot force other men to adopt our convictions," he said quietly. "Nor should we. It is always the young who rebel. Without them there would be little change."

"Thank you," Landsborough whispered. Then he coughed several times and took a few moments to master himself again. "Magnus felt passionately about individual liberty, and he said he believed it to be under far more threat than I did," he continued. "But then I have seen tides of opinion ebb and flow more than he has. The young are so impatient." He climbed stiffly to his feet, using the armrests of the chair to propel himself upright. He seemed a decade older than when he had sat down less than ten minutes earlier.

There was no answer for Narraway to make. He followed him out of the door, retrieved their hats from the steward, and went to the front steps where there seemed always to be a hansom waiting. He gave the driver the address of the morgue where the body had been taken, and they rode in silence. It was not that Narraway was ignoring Landsborough, or even did not know what to say; rather he wished to allow him to grieve without the necessity of having to disturb himself to find the words to be courteous.

And yet at some point Narraway would have to ask him more about his son: questions of associates, of money, names, places that might lead to other anarchists that he could not afford to let pass, however painful.

The morgue had the smell of wet stone, carbolic, and the indefinable odor of death familiar to Narraway but perhaps alien to Landsborough. Most people died at home, and a sick room, whatever the illness, never had this cloying, overscrubbed dampness to it. This building was not designed for the living.

The attendant met them with a professional mask of solemnity. He knew how to conduct himself in the presence of overwhelming pain without intruding upon it. He took them along the corridor to the room where the body was lying on a table. It was covered by a sheet, even the head.

Narraway remembered how damaged the face was, and strode over ahead of Landsborough, interposing his body between him and the table. He pulled up the side of the sheet exposing the dead man's hand. The signet ring had been replaced and would be sufficient for Lord Landsborough to identify the body.

"Is he really so badly disfigured?" Landsborough said with faint surprise.

"Yes." Narraway diverted his gaze to the hand.

Landsborough looked down at it. "Yes, that is my son's ring. And I believe that is his hand. I would still like to see his face."

"My lord . . ." Narraway started to protest, then changed his mind. He was being foolish. Without looking at the face it was not a full identification. He stood aside.

"Thank you," Landsborough acknowledged the gesture. He picked up the sheet and looked in silence at the features—shattered on one side, almost peaceful on the other. Then he replaced the sheet. "That is my son," he said in a whisper. His voice jerked, as if he had meant to speak aloud, but his body would not obey him. "Is there more you require of me, Mr. Narraway?"

"I'm sorry, sir. There is." Narraway turned to lead the way out along the corridor, thanking the attendant briefly, and went outside into the warm air of the street.

"The anarchists must have had money to finance their arms," he said as the traffic clattered past them. "Dynamite has to be paid for. If we could trace their purchases we might find the rest of them, before they blow up more people's homes." He spoke of the destruction deliberately, ignoring the wince of pain that tightened Landsborough's face. "We need to find them," he emphasized. "We need to know Mr. Landsborough's associates, anything of his movements lately."

"Yes, of course you do," Landsborough agreed, blinking a little in the sun as if its light were suddenly harsher than before. "But I can't help you. Magnus was seldom home. I was aware of his convictions—although I admit, not of their depth—but I did not know his friends." He bit his lip. "And as for money, he had a small annuity, but it was not sufficient to buy arms, merely to feed and clothe himself. I paid the rent of a set of rooms for him, off Gordon Square. He wished to be independent."

"I see." Narraway was not certain of how entirely he believed Landsborough, but he was quite sure that it would be pointless to press the issue any further at the moment. "We will require to look at the rooms in Gordon Square, in case he left anything there which could lead us to them."

"Naturally. I shall send my man to give you the address and my keys to it." Landsborough straightened his shoulders. "If that is all, Mr. Narraway, I should like to return to my home. I must inform my wife of what has happened."

PITT RETURNED TO Long Spoon Lane with a sense of foreboding. It was still guarded by police and he was stopped by a constable, who took a moment to recognize him before snapping to attention.

Pitt did not blame him. He did not look like an officer at all, let alone a senior one. He was tall, and walked with the loose-limbed practical grace of a countryman who was accustomed to covering great distances over heath and woodland. His father had been a gamekeeper on a large estate, and as a boy Pitt had gone through the woods or over the heath with him at times. Even now, decades later, Pitt still tended to stuff his pockets full of objects that might one day be of use: handkerchiefs, odd bits of string, coins, sealing wax, a box of matches, pencil stubs, paper, a couple of bull's-eye sweets in wrappers, two paper clips, a pipe cleaner, half a dozen keys, and odd buttons.

"How's the man who was injured?" he asked.

"Oh, he'll be all right, sir," the constable assured him. "Bled a bit, but it's nothing that won't heal. He was lucky. You'll be wanting to see the sergeant."

"Yes. And I need to go back into the building and see the room where the young man was killed. Who was at the back stairs first?"

"I dunno, sir, but I'll find out. Can you make your own way inside, or would you like someone to go with you?"

"I'll make my own way."

"Yes, sir."

Pitt walked across the cobbled lane, in through the broken door, and up the stairs. It was only a matter of hours since he had come in here, his heart pounding. The shots were still ringing in his ears. Now it seemed oddly desolate, as if no one alive had been here for weeks. It was not that it had a sense of settled dust, or even the staleness of closed air, but a feeling as if whoever had left it would never return. There were no personal belongings anywhere, nothing valued or intimate: only a broken bottle, the lower half of a cocoa tin, a couple of rags too discolored to be identifiable.

At the top, in the main room, light streamed in through the broken windows. The dust and grime on the shards still left in the frames made them look almost like frosted or painted glass. The pool of blood where Magnus Landsborough had lain was congealed now and smeared because the body had been moved. Other than that it was exactly as when Pitt had first arrived. The police and the surgeon had been very diligent.

Pitt leaned over and looked at it long and carefully, studying the outline of the body where it was indicated by footprints, dried blood, and the scuffing of men lifting something heavy and awkward. Magnus had lain full length on the floor. Pitt had a measuring tape among the numerous items in his coat pocket. He took it out and stretched it from the top of where the head had been down to the farthest mark of the feet. Allowing for a little crumpling, the man must have been a trifle over six feet tall. It was not possible to be more accurate.

What was absolutely certain was that he had fallen forward when the shot had struck the back of his head. There was no way at all in which it could have come from the street below and caused him to fall as he had. Added to that, the shot had struck him in the back of the skull, and emerged through the general area of his left cheekbone. The street was narrow and two stories down. Had it come from below it would have been at a sharp upward angle, in at the back of the neck, and out through the brow. And he would have to have been standing facing the room, looking away from the gunfire.

Was it possible Welling was speaking the truth, and the first constable up the back stairs had shot him? But why? Rage? Fear that Landsborough had a gun and posed some immediate danger to him? There had been no gun beside the body.

He heard footsteps on the stairs and a moment later a uniformed sergeant stood in the doorway. He was fresh-faced, probably in his late twenties, and at the moment very sober in demeanor.

"Linwood, sir," he said stiffly. "You wanted to see me?"

Pitt straightened up. "Yes, Sergeant. Were you the first into this room when we broke in?"

"Yes, sir."

"Describe what you saw, exactly."

Linwood concentrated, looking down at the floor. "There were three men in here, sir. One was standing in the far corner, with a gun in his arms, a rifle. He had gingery hair. He was looking straight at me, but not holding the gun to fire. I reckon it could have been empty by then. They'd shot plenty out of the window."

That sounded like Carmody, from the description. "Who else?" Pitt asked.

"Dark man, lots of hair," Linwood said, screwing up his face in concentration. "He looked pretty shocked. Standing just about there." He pointed to a place less than a yard from where Pitt was.

"Beside the body on the floor!" Pitt said in surprise.

Linwood's eyes opened wide. "Yes, sir. He had a gun, but he couldn't have shot him. The bullets had to have come from over there." He indicated the door at the farther end of the room, going towards the stair to the back, down which the police had pursued the man who had shot Landsborough, and presumably escaped.

"What else?" Pitt asked.

"The dead man on the floor," Linwood answered.

"You're sure? How was he lying—exactly?"

"Just as you found him, sir. That shot killed him outright. Blew his brains out, poor devil."

Pitt raised his eyebrows. "Poor?" he questioned.

Linwood's mouth curled down. "I pity any man shot by his own, sir, whatever he believed in. Betrayal turns my stomach."

"Mine too," Pitt agreed. "Are you sure that's what it was?"

"I don't see what else it could have been, sir." Linwood stared straight back at him. "I heard a shot when I was at the bottom of the stairs. Ask Patterson; he was straight behind me, and Gibbons behind him."

"And Welling and Carmody were standing where you said?"

"Yes. So either one of them shot him, and the other is lying to protect him, or it was one of the ones who escaped," Linwood replied. "Any way you look at it, it was one of his own."

"Yes," Pitt agreed grimly. "Welling says it was us."

"He's a liar."

"Not someone in uniform."

"We were all in uniform, sir," Linwood said stiffly. "The only ones in plainclothes were you and your boss from Special Branch."

"I don't think Welling was lying," Pitt said thoughtfully. "I think it was someone he didn't know, or didn't recognize."

"Still one of his own," Linwood's face was hard, anger making his voice cutting. "He was shot in the back."

"I know. Looks as if anarchy's an even uglier business than we thought. Thank you, Sergeant."

"Yes, sir. Is that all?" Linwood stood to attention, or close to it. He did not consider Special Branch to be real police.

"For the moment," Pitt replied.

Linwood left, but Pitt stood still in the room, picturing in his mind the sequence of events. He had come up the stairs behind Narraway and the three policemen. He had been one flight up when he had heard the shot from the room above, and the shouting.

When he had got there, seconds after the police, they had been standing still to this side of the gunman. The far door had been swinging. Someone else had just gone out of it. No one had mentioned seeing him, so he must already have disappeared when the first man came in at the front.

Welling and Carmody were refusing to name anyone else, but they insisted the police had shot Magnus Landsborough. From the angle of the bullet and the way Landsborough was lying, the shot had to have come from the door to the back stairs. Presumably the man had escaped that way, Welling and Carmody assuming him to be police, and the police at the back mistaking him for one of the police with Special Branch from the front, in hot pursuit of an anarchist. They must have let him go right past them!

The mechanics of it were beginning to make sense.

Had the police at the back been careless and let at least one man through, perhaps more? Or corrupt, and intentionally allowed them to escape?

Who was the man who had shot Landsborough from behind

the door, and then raced downstairs pretending to be a policeman? Had he seized a chance suddenly presented to him by fate, or had he waited in the building in Long Spoon Lane, knowing that after the explosion the bombers would return here?

Why? An internal rivalry, one group against another? A clash of ideals, a war for territory? Or a fight for leadership within one group?

Or something else altogether?

Pitt walked slowly across the room and out of the door to the back stairs, the way the killer must have gone. Outside in the street he found another constable, but he could tell him nothing more.

CHAPTER

TWO

Pitt closed the front door quietly, took off his boots and walked along the passage towards the lights and the sounds of laughter in the kitchen. It was nearly eight o'clock, and although it was a mild evening, he was shivering cold with exhaustion, not so much of body as of mind.

He pushed the door open and was engulfed with the warm smells of hot pastry, vegetables, and the dry, delicate odor of clean linen on the airing rail above. The gaslight shone on the blue-ringed china on the dresser and the pale, scrubbed wood of the table.

Charlotte swung around to smile at him. Her hair was still pinned up, but wisps of it were coming loose, and she had an apron on over the sweep of her skirt.

"Thomas!" She moved quickly towards him, then looked at his face and frowned. "There was a bomb! What happened? Are you all right?"

"Yes, I'm just tired," he answered her. "No one was hurt in the blast. One policeman was shot in the siege, but it was just a flesh wound."

She kissed his cheek quickly and pulled away. "Have you had anything to eat?" she said with concern.

"No," he admitted, pulling out one of the hard-backed chairs and sitting down. "Not since a ham sandwich at about three o'clock. But I'm not really hungry."

"Bombs!" Gracie said with a snort of disgust. "I dunno wot the world's coming ter! We should put the lot of 'em on the treadmills down the Coldbath Fields!" She turned around from the stove and regarded Pitt with proprietary disapproval. She was far more than a maid, and her loyalty was passionate.

"Well, a bit o' apple pie won't do you no 'arm. An' we've some cream, thick as butter, it is. Could stand yer spoon up in it, an' all." Without waiting for him to accept or decline, she swept into the pantry, swinging the door wide open.

Charlotte smiled across at Pitt, and got him a clean spoon and fork out of the drawer. Just then, eleven-year-old Jemima came racing down the stairs and along the passage.

"Papa!" She threw herself at Pitt and hugged him with enthusiasm. "What happened in the East End? Gracie says the anarchists should all be shot. Is that true?"

He tightened his arms around her, then let her go as she remembered her dignity and pulled away.

"I thought she said to send them to the treadmill?" he replied.

"What's a treadmill?" Jemima asked.

"A machine that goes 'round and 'round pointlessly, but you have to keep walking in it or you lose your balance and it bruises you."

"What use is that?"

"None at all. It's a punishment."

"For anarchists?"

Gracie returned with a large wedge of apple pie and a jug of cream and set it on the table.

"Thank you," Pitt accepted, helping himself. Perhaps he was hungry after all. Anyway, it would please all of them if he ate it. "For anyone put in prison," he answered Jemima's question.

"Are anarchists wicked?" she asked, sitting at the other side of the table.

"Yes," Gracie answered as Pitt had his mouth full. "O' course they are. They bomb people's 'ouses and smash things up. They 'ate people who've worked 'ard and made things. They want ter spoil everything that in't theirs." She filled up the kettle and set it on the stove.

"Why?" Jemima asked. "That's stupid!"

"Usually because nobody will listen to them otherwise," Charlotte answered her daughter. "Where's Daniel?"

"Doing his homework," Jemima replied. "I've done mine. Does smashing things up make people listen? I'd just get sent to bed without any supper." She looked at the apple pie hopefully.

Charlotte controlled her smile with an effort. Pitt saw it in her eyes, and looked away. The warmth of the kitchen was unknotting the pain inside him; violence was retreating from his thoughts to some dark place beyond the walls. The pie was crisp-crusted and still had some of its heat, the cream thick and smooth.

"Yes, you would," Charlotte agreed with Jemima. "But if you were certain something was unjust, you'd be terribly angry, and you might not stay silent or do as you were told."

Jemima looked at Pitt doubtfully. "Is that why they broke things, Papa? Is something unjust?"

"I don't know," Pitt replied. "But bombing ordinary people's houses isn't the answer."

" 'Course it in't!" Gracie added forcibly, stretching up onto her toes to reach the tea caddy off the shelf. "If summink's wrong, we 'ave police and laws ter put it right, which most times they do. Adding another wrong don't 'elp, an' it's wicked." She kept her small, square-shouldered back to the room. She opened the teapot lid with a snap. She had grown up in the back streets, begging and stealing to survive. Now that she was respectable, she was yielding to no one on the rule of law.

Charlotte, who was well-born, schooled to be a lady—before she had been wild enough to fall in love with a policeman—could afford a more liberal outlook.

"Gracie's quite right," she said gently to her daughter. "You can't hurt innocent people to make your point. It is wicked, no matter how desperate you think you are. Now go upstairs and let your father have his supper in peace."

"But Mama . . ." Jemima began.

"We'll have no anarchy in this house," Charlotte told her. "Upstairs!"

Jemima made a face, slipped her arms around Pitt's neck again, and kissed him. Then she went out the door and they heard her feet lightly along the corridor.

Gracie warmed the teapot and made the tea.

Pitt ate the last of his apple pie, and sat back, letting the brightness and the warmth anchor him for now.

PITT LEFT EARLY in the morning, and Charlotte sat at the breakfast table alone looking at the newspapers. They all reported the bombing in Myrdle Street, but with varying degrees of outrage. Some were full of pity for the families who had lost their homes, and showed pictures of frightened and bewildered people huddling together, faces hollow-eyed with shock.

Others were angrier, calling for punishment for the criminals who would cause such devastation. The police were criticized; Special Branch even more so. Naturally there was much speculation as to who was responsible, what their aims might be, and if there would be further atrocities of the same kind.

The siege in Long Spoon Lane was mentioned, and the capture of two of the anarchists. Bitter questions were asked as to why the others were still at large.

Magnus Landsborough's death was mourned in many ways. The *Times* was discreet, writing more about Lord Landsborough's distinguished career as a Liberal member of the House of Lords, and extending sympathy to him and his family on the loss of his only son. Little question was raised as to what his son had been doing at Long Spoon Lane, but the possibility of his having been a hostage was not ruled out.

Other papers were less charitable. They assumed that he had been one of the anarchists himself, simply unlucky enough to have been the only casualty in the gun battle that had ended the siege. The injured policeman was mentioned as well, with commendation for his courage.

It was the last newspaper that troubled her. It was edited by the highly respected and influential Edward Denoon, and he had written the leading article himself. She read it with an increasing sense of unease.

Yesterday morning while the residents of Myrdle Street were preparing for another day of labor, the police interrupted their meager breakfast to tell them that anarchist bombers were about to strike. Old men shuffled out into the street, women with frightened children at their skirts grasped the few belongings they could carry, and fled.

Minutes later the shabby row of houses erupted in flames. Bricks and slates flew like missiles, crashing into the windows and through the roofs of neighbors streets away. Black smoke gushed into the morning air and terror and destruction struck scores of ordinary people, ruining homes, lives, and the peace that citizens of England have a right to expect.

The men responsible were pursued and hunted down and cornered in a tenement in Long Spoon Lane. Police laid siege to them and there was a gun battle in which twenty-two-year-old Constable Field, of Mile End, was shot down, but owing to the courage of his comrades was rescued from death.

Magnus Landsborough, the only son of Lord Sheridan Landsborough, was less fortunate. His dead body was found in an upper room. It is not known at present what he was doing there, whether taken as hostage, or with the anarchists of his own will.

Then we must ask ourselves what manner of barbarian commits such atrocities? Who are they, and what conceivable purpose do they imagine it may serve? Surely it can only be intended to terrorize us into submission to some dreadful rule, which we would not submit to otherwise? Does this act of violence stem from foreign soil, the first wave of conquest from another country?

This newspaper does not believe so. We are at peace with our neighbors near and far. There is no intelligence, however discreet, to implicate any other nation. Rather, we fear it is a political ideal of such a twisted nature that men would impose their ideal of society by destroying all that we have worked for through centuries of growth and labor, through the civilizing arts and sciences and the inventions that improve the comfort and welfare of mankind. Then on the ashes of our lives they hope to build their own order, as they think it should be. They may call themselves socialists, or anarchists, or whatever they will. They are savages, by any name, criminals who must be hunted down, arrested, tried, and hanged. That is the law, and it is there to protect us all, the strong and the weak, the rich and the poor alike.

But these madmen who would destroy our lives are powerful, and all too obviously they are well-armed. Our police, who are the soldiers of this civil army, to defend us, must be well-armed also. It is they who risk their lives, and sometimes lose them, to form the shield between us and the chaos of violence and anarchy. We cannot afford to send them into battle without weapons, and it would be morally indefensible for us to try.

Not only must we provide them with adequate guns in their hands, but also we must legislate to give them the weapons of law they need in order to find among us the wicked and the mad who wish our destruction. The law requires proof of crime, as it should. That is the defense of the innocent. But a policeman who is prevented from searching the person or the property of someone he suspects of criminal intent can only wait helplessly until the act is committed, and then avenge the victim. We need more than that. We deserve, we must have, a prevention of the crime before it occurs.

She put the paper down and stared across the kitchen in disquiet.

Gracie came in from the back step and looked at her. "Wot's 'appened?" she said anxiously. "Summink bad?" When she had first come to Charlotte, she could neither read nor write. Now, with Charlotte's help, she was quite good at both. She made it a habit to read at least two articles in the newspaper every day. Now she looked at Denoon's paper skeptically, and at the cold tea in Charlotte's cup. "There's never bin another bombing?" she said with disbelief.

"No," Charlotte answered quickly. "It's the editor calling for more guns for the police, and more rights to search people's houses."

Gracie set down the vegetables on the draining board of the sink. "Well if people 'ave got bombs an' guns, police can't fight 'em wi' sticks," she said reasonably. Then she frowned. "Mind, I wouldn't like ter think o' Mr. Pitt wi' a gun. Can't 'ave it in the 'ouse—they in't safe!" The downward tone of her voice reflected her distaste for the entire idea. "Why 'ave some people always got ter be making trouble?"

"It's usually only trouble that makes us change things," Charlotte replied. That was true, but it did not answer what Gracie was asking. "If somebody tips rubbish out in your street," she went on, "or makes a noise late at night, if you don't complain, they'll go on doing it." She smiled as she saw the temper flare in Gracie's eyes. She had chosen the subject of rubbish deliberately.

Gracie realized it and grinned; then the laughter vanished and profound gravity took its place. "But if I went an' shot the stupid little article wot's leaving it out there, I'd be put in jail, an' right thing too. I give 'er a piece o' me mind, but I never touched 'er." The grin of triumph returned. "She won't go do it again, mind!"

"Of course," Charlotte conceded. "Anarchy is wrong, and it's ridiculous. But I'm not at all sure that giving the police guns is the solution. And I'm quite sure that giving them more power to go into people's houses looking for evidence, unless they have a good reason to believe it's there, is only going to make everyone angry, and even less likely to help."

"Is that what Mr. Pitt says?" Gracie asked, doubt flickering in her eyes.

"Actually he was too tired to say anything," Charlotte admitted. "And he hasn't seen this yet. But I think it's what he will say."

LADY VESPASIA CUMMING-GOULD sat at her breakfast table looking at the same newspaper, also with feelings of distress, but hers were caused by different aspects of the tragedy. The name of Lord Landsborough had caught her eye immediately, and sharp, sweet memory flooded in from the past. They had first met over forty years ago, at a reception at Buckingham Palace. Both had been married ten or twelve years and were restless and a trifle bored with the same social round, the same gossip, and the same opinions.

Landsborough then had been an idealist, a believer in the innate decency of people, and filled with optimism that great good could be accomplished if more government were given into their hands, more freedom to decide their own destiny. He had been elegant, effortlessly well-dressed, and possessed an easy charm that concealed a greater sensitivity than he allowed most people to know.

His wife, Cordelia, was darkly beautiful, ambitious, and, in Vespasia's view, colder than a winter night. They had taken an instant and well-founded dislike to each other, and concealed it with icy good wishes and the most meticulous courtesy. Neither ever made a social mistake, or was caught less than perfectly dressed, jewels blazing, every hair exquisitely in place.

Vespasia herself had found her marriage not uncomfortable, but neither was her husband the love of her life. That had been Mario Corena, the Italian patriot and hero of the '48 revolution in Rome. Happiness between them had been impossible for reasons neither could overcome, but the memory of his idealism, courage, and sacrifice—and of one dazzling season of hope—had never faded.

Then last year they had met again, briefly, when Mario had deliberately given his life to foil Charles Voisey's plot to overthrow the throne of England. It had been a beautiful and terrible decision. Vespasia had had her revenge upon Voisey, but at a cost she would never forget.

But all those years ago when she had met Sheridan Landsborough, his gentle humor and his wry radicalism had appealed to her. He had shown a moderation, a tolerance, and an almost innocent trust in decency. And her wit, her regal and lonely beauty had awoken something in him. Cordelia had been striking, but Vespasia had turned heads and stirred hearts in every court in Europe. She had had the passion, the intelligence, and the courage to dare anything.

Now she sat alone in the early-morning sunshine in her breakfast room and read that Sheridan had lost his only son, and she felt an intense sadness for him. The years since their last meeting vanished, and even Cordelia's dislike seemed irrelevant. She must write and convey her sympathy. In fact, merely sending a letter through the post was inadequate. She would take it personally.

She rose and walked to the fireplace beside which hung the bell rope to summon the maid. She pulled it and remained standing until it was answered.

"Gwyneth, please put out black for me," she requested, then changed her mind. "No, that is too severe: dark gray. And tell

Charles I shall require the carriage at ten o'clock. I shall be calling upon Lord and Lady Landsborough to offer my condolences."

"I'm sorry, my lady," Gwyneth replied. She had not heard the news and had no idea to what Vespasia was referring. "Will the dark gray silk be right? And the hat with the black ostrich feather?"

"Excellent. Thank you. I shall write a letter, then I shall be up."

"Yes, my lady."

Gwyneth withdrew, and Vespasia walked across the hall to the morning room where her escritoire held pen, ink, and paper.

It was always difficult to know what to say in such circumstances. For Cordelia the most formal of expressions would be correct, but for Sheridan, whom she had known so well, it would sound stilted and absurd, in a way worse than nothing at all.

She sat at the escritoire in the cool, green light of the room. The sun beyond the curtains was filtered by leaves.

> *My dear Sheridan and Cordelia,*
>
> *I heard today of your loss and I am dismayed at the pain you must feel. I wish I could offer help, words of comfort and assurance, but I know that grief has simply to be endured. But if faith and friendship can give you anything of worth, now or in the future, please call upon me. I shall always be at your service.*
>
> *Sincerely,*
> *Vespasia Cumming-Gould*

She folded it, placed it in an envelope, and sealed it. She did not reread it or wonder if it was elegantly or appropriately phrased. It was honest, and that was all she could attempt. If she weighed what Cordelia might make of it, she would never send anything.

Upstairs, she changed into the dark gray silk and surveyed herself in the glass.

"You look beautiful, my lady," Gwyneth said from behind her.

She was right. Vespasia was tall and still slender. Her aquiline features and fine, pale skin were flattered by the cool colors. As always she wore ropes of pearls around her neck, complimenting the silver crown of her hair. The dress itself was in the latest cut, narrow at the waist, full sleeved at the shoulder, slender at the hip but flaring more widely at the knee and to the ground. The jacket had the fashionable very wide lapels.

Gwyneth set the hat upon her head and offered her the gray kid gloves, which were softer than velvet. A small, gray silk reticule carried a handkerchief, a few calling cards, and the letter.

IT WAS A SHORT journey, no more than fifteen minutes to the Landsborough's house in Stenhope Street near Regents Park. Vespasia alighted from her carriage and went to the front door, the letter in her hand. It was opened within moments and an elderly butler regarded her with courteous inquiry. He recognized the coat of arms on her carriage door, and greeted her by name.

"Good morning," she replied. "I am sure the family is not receiving callers, but I prefer to pass my letter of condolences to you rather than send it through the post. Would you be good enough to tell Lord and Lady Landsborough that they have my deepest sympathy?"

"Of course, my lady." He held out the silver tray and she placed the envelope on it. "Thank you. It is most gracious of you to come in person. If you would care to step inside, I shall pass your letter to Lady Landsborough. She may wish to acknowledge it." He stepped back.

"I do not wish to put her to trouble." Vespasia remained on the step.

"It would be no trouble at all, my lady," he answered. "But if you are previously engaged, then . . ."

"Not at all," she said honestly. "I came out only for this purpose." It would now be rude to decline. She followed him inside. There was black crepe in the hall. The long-cased clock had been stopped, the mirrors had been turned to the wall. She was shown into the morning room, where no fire had been lit. There were white flowers on the table, ghostly in the half-light through lowered blinds.

There was nothing to do but wait until the butler should return and convey Cordelia's thanks; then she would be free to leave. She did not wish to sit down; it seemed inappropriate, as if she expected to stay. One did not make oneself comfortable in such circumstances.

She looked around idly, trying to remember if it had been just the same all those years ago when she had been a frequent visitor here. The bookcase had been here then, the glass reflecting back so the titles were unreadable. The picture of Venetian canals over the mantel was the one she knew. She had always thought it a genuine Canaletto, but had never been frank enough to ask. She could not imagine Sheridan Landsborough having anything less.

The house was very quiet, as if its usual business of cleaning and errands had been suspended. The sound of horses' hooves in the street outside was audible.

The door opened and she turned, expecting the butler, but it was Cordelia herself who stood there. She had changed little since the last time Vespasia had seen her, perhaps a couple of years ago. There was a hint of more white in her dark hair, but in broad, handsome streaks, not a fading to pepper and salt. Her features were still strong. She was less firm of jaw; the skin of her throat had withered and even a high-necked gown could not completely hide it. Shock had bleached her face today, and naturally she wore unrelieved black.

"It was good of you to come, Vespasia," she said, instantly establishing a familiarity that had not existed between them for years. "It is a time when one needs one's friends." She glanced around. "This room is chilly. Would you prefer to come into the withdrawing room? It faces the garden and is far pleasanter." She was allowing Vespasia the opportunity to excuse herself, and yet after such a plea to friendship, that would be a deliberate rebuff.

"Thank you," Vespasia accepted.

Cordelia led the way across the hall and into a warmer, far more agreeable room. It still carried all the marks of mourning, but it was several degrees warmer, and the sunlight coming through the half-drawn curtains made bright patterns on the wine-and-blue carpet.

Vespasia's mind was racing as to why Cordelia had asked her to remain. They had never been friends, nor was she a woman to confide either joy or sorrow in someone else.

They sat on huge, soft sofas opposite each other in the flickering sunlight. It was Cordelia who broke the silence.

"Sometimes it takes a tragedy of this magnitude to make one realize what is happening," she said gravely. "One sees things eroded little by little, and each step is so small it hardly registers in one's mind."

Vespasia had no idea what she was referring to. She waited patiently, her face a mask of polite interest.

"If you had told me ten years ago that police would be having gun battles with anarchists in the streets of London," Cordelia continued. "I should have said you were mad. Indeed, I would have said you were a political alarmist, almost certainly with some purpose of your own in trying to frighten people." She took a deep breath. "Now we are forced to admit that it is the truth. There are madmen in our society who are bent upon destroying it, and the police need all our support, morally and materially."

Vespasia thought of Pitt, whom she had known since her great nephew had married Charlotte's sister Emily. George had been killed, and Emily had married again, but the friendship had continued and grown stronger. "Yes, indeed," she said aloud. "Theirs is a difficult and frequently thankless task."

"And dangerous," Cordelia added. "A young policeman was

shot in the battle. But for the courage and quick-thinking of his fellows, he would have bled to death there in the street."

"Yes." Vespasia had read the account in two newspapers. "But it appears he will recover."

"This time," Cordelia conceded. "But what of the future?" She looked at Vespasia earnestly, her face grave, her back ramrod stiff. "We need more police, and they must be better armed. We must not handicap them with antique laws framed for a more peaceful age. London is now teeming with foreigners of all sorts, men with wild ideas of revolution, anarchy, even socialism. And to institute their own insanities upon us they have made it plain that they intend to destroy what we have, and terrorize us into accepting their will." Her eyes were brilliant with grief and rage. "As long as I draw breath, I will not let that happen! I will fight with every influence I have to see that we uphold and assist them to protect us and all we believe." She watched Vespasia intently.

Vespasia felt a vague shadow of discomfort. It was so nebulous she could not be sure if it was something Cordelia had said, or the embarrassment of not being able to say anything that would address the real issue of her grief. Cordelia had had only one child, and yesterday he had been killed. Vespasia had several children and they were all alive and well. They were all married; she saw them seldom, but she kept a warm correspondence with each. It was absurd to feel guilty because she had so much more than this furious woman opposite her. Cordelia was trying to come to terms with her pain by turning it into anger, and a crusade, which would occupy her mind and her energy, and perhaps blunt the raw edge of her emotions with exhaustion.

Or if she were honest, Vespasia's guilt was more truly for the sweetness and the intensity of friendship she had shared long ago with Sheridan Landsborough.

Cordelia was still waiting for some response to her words. Vespasia was not at all certain that she wished for a police force with more guns, but this was not the time for her to say so.

"I am sure after this tragedy we will find many people determined that our police will have every assistance we can give them," she agreed.

Cordelia forced herself to smile. "We must see to it," she agreed. "There need to be some changes made. I have scarcely had time to think of details, but every energy I have will be directed to that end. I am sure I can ask you to use your influence also." She assumed agreement, and yet her eyes searched Vespasia's as if she still required an answer.

Vespasia took a deep breath, doubtful of her own motives for being reluctant. Was it some genuine reason of political uncertainty, or her old dislike of Cordelia intruding? The latter would be shameful, and she felt the blood burn up her cheeks. "Of course," she said too quickly. "I have not had time to think either, I admit. But I shall do. It is an issue that concerns us all."

Cordelia sat back a little, and was about to resume the conversation on some other topic when the butler came in, stopping discreetly just inside the door.

"Yes, Porteous?" Cordelia asked.

"Mr. and Mrs. Denoon are here, my lady. I have informed them that his lordship is out, and they asked if you wished to see them, or would prefer to leave it until another time."

"Ask them to come in," Cordelia replied. She turned to Vespasia. "Enid is my sister-in-law, as I am sure you remember, although, as I recall, you did not know her well." She gave a tiny, stiff shrug. "I am not particularly desirous to face her. She is bound to be terribly distressed. She and Sheridan have always been close. It will be difficult. If you would prefer to excuse yourself I shall understand." Her words made it perfectly acceptable for Vespasia to leave, but her expression left no doubt that she would find it easier were Vespasia to stay.

Morally speaking, Vespasia had no choice, nor did she have the opportunity to do more than accept before Porteous returned, followed by Enid Denoon and her husband. Vespasia had actually forgotten her, but seeing her again brought back what could have been friendship in other circumstances.

Enid was tall, like her brother, slender but with squarer shoulders and the upright carriage of a woman who still sat a horse superbly. Her figure had survived the years better than Cordelia's. There was no thickening of her waist or heaviness in her hips. Her fair brown hair had lost much of its color, but her face was not greatly changed, her high cheekbones and well-defined nose had kept their lines, and her skin had a bloom many a younger woman might have envied.

Behind her Denoon was darker, heavier, his hair still thick and almost black. He was imposing rather than handsome. All Vespasia remembered of him was that she had not liked him, possibly because he had an odd mixture of high intelligence and an almost total incapacity for laughter. He did not see the joy of absurdity, which she adored. It was one of the sanities of life. Without it, the world of fashion, wealth, and political power would have been suffocating. She had been married irretrievably, with a certain degree of companionship, but without passion. To laugh was the only alternative to weeping. Denoon's gravity had seemed then to be without delicacy or tenderness.

Enid was clearly surprised to see her, yet she did not look displeased. But then, she would be too carefully schooled in good manners to show it, even if she were.

"How do you do, Lady Vespasia," Denoon responded to Cordelia's introduction. "It is very good of you to take time to call in person on this sad occasion." He was just short of expressing surprise.

"Like us, Lady Vespasia recognizes that we must lend all our support to action," Cordelia intervened, looking at Denoon intently. She did not even glance at Enid.

Denoon's eyes met Cordelia's with a strange mixture of understanding and an emotion Vespasia could not read, but the power of it remained in her mind. Then he turned back. "How farsighted of you, Lady Vespasia," he said quietly. "Indeed we are in times more dangerous than I believe most people are aware. The tide of chaos is rising, and yesterday marked a steep increase, to our tragic loss. I am so sorry." This last remark was addressed again to Cordelia.

"King Canute was a wise man," Enid said to no one in particular.

Cordelia blinked.

Vespasia looked at Enid in surprise, and saw her eyes far away, sad and angry.

Denoon swung around irritably and glared at his wife. "He was a fool!" he snapped. "Any man who imagines he could turn back the tide is an idiot! I spoke figuratively. We do not have to await the movement of the earth or the moon in order to alter social trends, or hold up our hands helplessly because things are happening that we do not like. We are masters of our own fate!" He looked back at Cordelia, impatient at Enid's lack of understanding.

Cordelia started to speak, but Enid overrode her. "Canute was not trying to hold the tide back," she contradicted him. "He was demonstrating that even he could not. Human power, even of kings, is limited."

"That is obvious!" Denoon said tartly. "And completely irrelevant. I am not attempting to alter the course of nature, Enid, but to prompt people into understanding the laws of the land so we can defend ourselves from the tide of anarchy."

"Not the tide of anarchy," Enid corrected him. "The tide of change."

This time he ignored her, but there was a dull flush of anger in his cheeks. "Cordelia, in spite of appearances, we came to say how deeply grieved we are for your loss. If there is anything we can do to comfort or help, we are here, and shall remain so. Please believe me, these are not idle words."

"Of course they're not!" Enid said, her voice suddenly so choked with emotion it seemed to cost her an effort to speak. "Cordelia knows that!" She shot a burning look at her sister-in-law, which seemed more filled with hatred than sorrow. Vespasia was chilled by it, until she remembered that many people's grief is so threaded with anger that the two become inextricable.

Cordelia reacted as if she had barely heard her. She continued looking at Denoon with a hard, chilly smile. "Thank you. It is a time for families and friends to draw together, at least all those who are like-minded and perceive the tragedies and the dangers with the same courage and resolve. I am grateful to you, and Vespasia, for seeing things as I do, and realizing that this is no time to indulge private emotions, no matter how deep, while we allow history to overtake us." She did not specifically exclude Enid, but Vespasia had the strong feeling that she meant to, and that Enid was acutely aware of it.

She also would like to have removed herself from the sentiment. Denoon was outspoken about increasing the power of police to intervene in people's lives when crime was suspected, before the proof. She was considerably more cautious, afraid of the possible abuses, and of the public backlash.

Cordelia and Denoon were still talking. The name Tanqueray was mentioned, a meeting suggested, and other names.

Vespasia looked at Enid Denoon, who appeared not even to be listening. Her face in repose had a vulnerability to it that was startling, as if pain were familiar to her. She could not have been aware of her expression, or she would have been more guarded, although neither Cordelia nor Denoon gave her a glance.

There were footsteps across the hall outside. A moment later the door opened. They all turned as Sheridan Landsborough came in. Vespasia had expected to see grief in his face, and yet she was still shocked to see the parchmentlike tone of his skin and the sunken cheeks and hollows around his eyes.

"Good morning, Edward," he said coolly, then he forced a smile. "Enid." He barely looked at his wife before turning to Vespasia. His eyes widened and a fraction of the color returned to his cheeks. "Vespasia!"

She took a step towards him. The formal words were in her mind, but they died before they reached her lips. "I'm so sorry," she said quietly. "I cannot think of anything more dreadful."

"Thank you," he murmured. "It was good of you to come."

Almost as if unaware of doing it, Enid moved closer to him. Standing side by side the resemblance between them was subtle but perfectly clear. It was not in their features so much as the shape of their heads, their way of standing, their weary but effortless grace, which was so innate as to be impossible to cast off, even at a time like this.

Cordelia stared at him. "I assume the arrangements are complete?"

There was no softening of his expression as he looked at her. "Of course," he answered. "There is nothing to choose, nothing to decide." His voice held no intonation. Perhaps this total control was all he could bear. To have allowed any emotion through might have broken the dam and brought it all. Dignity was a kind of refuge. Magnus had been their only child. Vespasia thought the distance between them was perhaps a safeguard also. Each might have touched the one unbearable wound in the other.

She was aware of an electricity in the air like that before a storm, and it made her conscious of her intrusion. She turned to Cordelia. "Thank you for receiving me," she said with a slight inclination of her head. "It was extraordinarily gracious of you."

Cordelia made no move to accompany Vespasia to the door. "Your help is invaluable," she said. "Now, of all times, we must fight for what we believe." She took a deep breath, the extreme pallor of her skin accentuated by her dark eyes. "You are a true friend."

Vespasia could not agree. Cordelia was as aware as she was that they were anything but friends. "I could not do less," she murmured, hearing the irony in her words.

Sheridan turned to Vespasia. "May I call your carriage?" He reached for the bell cord a few feet away.

"Thank you," she accepted. The atmosphere in the room prickled with tension. Enid looked from her brother to her sister-in-law, but Vespasia was not sure if it was anger or apprehension in her face. Her shoulders were stiff, her head high, as if expecting some old pain to return that all her courage would not offset.

"Piers will be most distressed," Denoon said abruptly.

Vespasia remembered that Enid had a son. He must be almost thirty now, roughly the same age as his cousin Magnus.

Cordelia acknowledged the remark.

"Perhaps we should leave also," Enid observed, more to Denoon than to Cordelia. "Discussions of law reform can surely wait a day or two. They will take months to enact anyway, if not years."

"We don't have years!" Denoon said angrily, his face flushed. "Do you imagine the forces of anarchy are going to sit around and wait for us to thwart them?"

"I imagine they will be quite happy to watch us thwart ourselves," she replied.

"Don't be absurd!" Denoon said, almost under his breath, as if she embarrassed him and he were uncertain how to deal with it in front of Vespasia and Landsborough.

Landsborough stiffened, moving closer to his sister, and away from his wife. He drew in his breath between his teeth.

Vespasia was acutely uncomfortable. She felt compelled to intervene, before the situation became worse.

"If we react too swiftly, or too drastically, we may well do harm," she said, glancing at Enid, and then away again. "We do not wish to provoke criticism that we are as repressive as they say, or to turn sympathy from us by heavy-handedness. At the moment all hearts and minds will be in our favor. Let us not lose that."

There were several seconds of tense silence, then Landsborough spoke. "Yes, of course. You are quite right." He moved out into the hall. Vespasia followed him. A footman was sent to inform her coachman that she was ready to depart, and the Denoons' coachman similarly. Cordelia made a remark about the weather. Vespasia replied.

The green baize door opened from the servants' quarters and a footman in livery came through. He was young and moved with the grace of a man used to physical action and confident in himself. He looked only at Enid, ignoring everyone else, including Denoon himself.

"The coach is ready, ma'am," he said respectfully, standing a few feet from her. He met her eyes for a moment, then deliberately looked away.

Enid thanked the man, then took her leave of Landsborough with a quick placing of her hand on his arm. She nodded to Cordelia, smiled at Vespasia, and walked calmly to the door, leaving Denoon to follow.

The moment after, Vespasia's carriage arrived also. Landsborough offered her his arm in a discreet indication that he would like a moment of conversation with her, if not alone, at least out of earshot of his wife.

Vespasia bade Cordelia good-bye yet again, then accepted Landsborough's arm. Together they went out of the front door and down the steps towards the waiting carriage.

"Thank you for coming," he said quietly. "It was good of you, especially in the circumstances."

She was uncertain if he were referring to their past association or the way in which Magnus had died, and what might yet emerge about it. There might be storms of public blame or outrage to come.

"I grieve for your loss," she said candidly. "No doubt we shall have to face other things later, but just at the moment they all seem irrelevant."

He smiled very slightly. His face looked old, his skin papery thin, but his eyes were as she had always known them. "It will come soon enough," he agreed. "Magnus was always too much of an enthusiast. He espoused causes because he cared about injustice. He did not always look closely enough at them, or realize that sometimes bad people can preach a good crusade. I should have taught him more patience, and much greater wisdom."

"You cannot teach people what they do not wish to learn," she told him gently. "I seem to remember I was somewhat revolutionary when I was in my thirties. My only wisdom was that I did not pursue it in my own country. But I made Rome too hot to hold me. Fortunately I had England to return to."

He looked at her with an old tenderness she remembered with pleasure and guilt. "You never told me about it," he said. "Except for the heat, and the food. You always liked Italian food."

"One day, perhaps," she replied, knowing that she would not. That summer of 1848 was an island of time that could not be brought into the rest of her life, and she did not wish to share it, even with Sheridan Landsborough. But quite apart from that, it might hurt him, remind him of youth and fierceness of idealism and love that had slipped away from him now, but perhaps was reminiscent of the son he was mourning.

The carriage was waiting. She looked at him steadily and saw memory in his eyes, loneliness, and perhaps guilt as well. He might have been a revolutionary in his youth. He had cared about injustice and change, and had the courage to say so. That might have been the reason he had never held high office in government. How much might he have known about what Magnus was doing? Might he even have sympathized in the beginning, and prepared to defend his memory now?

"Good-bye," she said, and accepted his arm to step into her carriage.

She rode home still turning the questions over in her mind, and even through the afternoon her thoughts kept going back to the conversation between Cordelia and Denoon, and Enid's arguments against them. There had been a heat of emotion in her face, which was more than idealistic, and a pain so close to the surface it was almost beyond her control.

In the early evening Vespasia could no longer weigh the matter on her own, and she sent for her carriage to take her to Keppel Street.

CHARLOTTE WAS DELIGHTED to see her. She was no longer embarrassed by the modesty of her home. She had several years ago realized that Vespasia felt at ease in the kitchen in a way she never would have in her own, where she was mistress, servants answered her only when spoken to, and the gulf between them was unpassable. Vespasia lived in a house full of people, but she was in many ways alone. It had been so since her husband had died, and possibly before that. Children offered a different kind of love, not necessarily the kind that includes companionship.

"Aunt Vespasia!" Charlotte greeted her with unfeigned delight. "Please come in. Would you like to sit in the parlor?"

"Not in the least," Vespasia said candidly. "Is there something wrong with the kitchen?"

Charlotte smiled.

"Not more than usual. The laundry is dry, the cats are asleep in the wood basket, and Gracie is putting away the last of the dishes. But I can quite easily do that, and she can fold the clean clothes upstairs." She took Vespasia's cape and the silver-topped cane she carried, but never really used, then her hat.

As soon as they opened the kitchen door, Gracie rose from the bench where she was drying the supper dishes and became instantly very formal. She made a wobbly curtsy.

"Good evening, Lady Vespasia!" she said breathlessly.

"Good evening, Gracie," Vespasia replied, ignoring the curtsy as if she had always managed it with such style. "I have had a very disturbing day. Would you be kind enough to make me a cup of tea?"

Gracie flushed with pleasure, and caught her elbow on the crockery as she swiveled around to obey. She only just saved it from falling to the floor.

Charlotte glanced at Vespasia and hid a smile. "I'm sorry," she said quickly. "What happened today?"

Vespasia sat in one of the kitchen chairs, her back as ramrod straight as it had been since she was a schoolgirl and her governess had poked it with a ruler every time she slouched. She had learned to walk with a pile of books upon her head—dictionaries, nothing as frivolous as novels—and the habit had never left her. Without thinking she adjusted her dark gray skirts to sweep about her without getting in the way of others.

"I went to express my condolences to Lord and Lady Landsborough," she said without prevarication. "I expected merely to leave a note, and was amazed to be received." She saw Charlotte's eyes widen. "I do not like Cordelia Landsborough, nor does she like me, for good and sufficient reason we do not need to discuss."

Charlotte bit her lip, and made no comment.

"I believe she received me because she wishes to use my political influence in her crusade to have a bill passed in Parliament that will allow the police to carry firearms," Vespasia continued. "And to have far greater power to invade the privacy of ordinary people, in the pursuit of their duty, however they see it. It disturbs me greatly."

Gracie dropped a spoonful of tea leaves on the floor, and bent to sweep them up, moving silently so as not to interrupt the conversation.

Charlotte glanced at her, then back at Vespasia, her eyes grave, her face faintly puckered with anxiety. "Is she not speaking from grief?" she asked. "She must be distraught, poor woman." Her lips tightened, and the muscles of her throat, as if she were thinking of her own son upstairs, who was presumably studying his schoolbooks before going to bed. He was a child, still governable, still willing to listen. A mere handful of years and he would be so different, full of passion and self-will, certain he knew the ills of the world and how to address them. At least he would if he had any of the fire or the courage of youth.

"She will work through her pain by driving herself to act," Vespasia replied. "Through exhaustion or tears, through everything that you or I might feel."

Charlotte considered for a moment before responding, but her face was gentler, lost in thought rather than the difficulty of understanding Vespasia's feelings.

"Would you help her to have such a change made in the law?" she asked, dismayed at the thought.

Gracie was standing with her back to the sink, not even pretending that she was uninvolved. Her eyes moved from one to the other of them with rapt attention. She did not dare to interrupt, but the subject was very obviously something about which she had profound feelings.

"No," Vespasia replied. "I would not."

Gracie drew in her breath sharply.

Charlotte smiled, relaxing a little in her chair. "I can understand why they feel as they do," she conceded. "The violence is very frightening, and we must do all we can to prevent it."

Her moderate tone was the last straw for Gracie. Because it was Charlotte who was speaking, not Vespasia, she did not feel obliged to keep silent anymore. "It's ordinary people wot's blown up!" she said desperately. "They may not 'ave any power nor money, but they're the ones wot police and government is meant to protect! It's 'orrible. I saw pictures in the newspapers o' wot they done. Where's those people going ter sleep now? Their 'ouses is all gone, everything they got. 'Oo's going ter replace all that, eh?"

Charlotte colored with embarrassment in case Vespasia was offended.

Vespasia looked at Gracie with seriousness. Gracie went white, but she did not lower her eyes.

"It is an extremely difficult question," Vespasia said quietly. "I shall do what I can to see that money is raised to help those who have been made homeless. I give you my word. But the reason I will not help Mr. Denoon is that I do not trust him to be moderate in his response. I fear he will react so strongly he will make the problem worse rather than better."

Gracie blinked. "Would yer? I mean 'elp 'em? Really?"

The kettle boiled and no one took any notice.

"I have said so," Vespasia answered gravely. "Your comments are very fair. We are too willing to indulge our anger at the destruction and think how we can punish those who have inflicted it, rather than make any effort to help those who have suffered."

None of them had heard Pitt close the front door, nor his soft footsteps down the hall.

"Thank you, Aunt Vespasia," he said gravely. She had given him permission some time ago to address her thus. He walked into the room, acknowledging her first, then Charlotte and Gracie. He sat on the third hard-backed chair.

"There is a backlash, Thomas," Vespasia told him. "Edward Denoon intends to press for arming the police and increasing their powers to search people, and their homes." She had no need to explain to him who Denoon was.

"I know," he said somberly. "Do you think he will succeed?"

She looked at the anxiety in his face, and the need for hope. She had never lied to him, and she could not afford to begin with this. "I think he will be difficult to stop. Many good people are very angry, and very frightened," she said.

He looked tired. "I know. Perhaps they are right to be. But arming the police with guns is not going to make it better. The last thing we need is pitched battles in the streets. And if we search people without real cause, or go into their homes, the one place they feel any sense of being master, we shall lose their willingness to help. And it has taken us thirty years to earn that."

Gracie looked deeply confused. He had his back to her and did not see the consternation in her face.

Charlotte saw it. "We must fight them," she responded. "What is it best we do? Have you any idea who they are, or at least what they want?"

"I know what they say they want," he replied wearily.

Charlotte sensed another emotion in him, more painful than anything that had emerged before. "What?"

"An end to police corruption," he replied.

Charlotte froze. "Corruption?"

Pitt pushed his hands through his hair. "I don't know if it exists in the degree they say, but I shall have to find out. People need to believe in the law before we can expect them to honor it."

Vespasia felt a chill take hold of her, and a sense of loss far broader than the death of one man, however violent or tragic. "Then perhaps we have a battle," she answered him. "We must draw up our lines."

CHAPTER

THREE

IN THE MORNING, Pitt went back to try again to see if he could learn anything from the two anarchists in jail. He found Welling hollow-eyed and exhausted. He looked as if he had been up all night pacing the floor, and now he was too distraught to think coherently. He did not dare trust himself to speak to Pitt.

Carmody was different. He was an idealist burning to speak about the oppression of government, the exploitation of the poor, and the inherent evils of property and rules. The energy danced in him; he could barely keep still.

"We're old!" he said, staring fiercely at Pitt and jabbing his thin fingers in the air. "Tired! We need a new start. Get rid of the mistakes of the past, sweep them all away." He gestured wildly with both arms. "Begin again!"

"With new rules?" Pitt asked bitterly.

"There you go, doing it too!" Carmody accused him. "You can't even think without rules. You pretend to be listening, but you're not. You're just like all the others, trying to impose your will on everyone else. That's it: power, power, power all the time. You don't hear a thing I'm saying. No rules! You're suffocating people, killing them slowly. Can't you see that? You're killing the whole country."

"Actually I think your real complaint is exactly the opposite,"

Pitt replied, shifting his weight from one foot to the other. The air in the cell was close and musty.

Carmody was exasperated. Pitt's apparent stupidity defeated him. "Get out!" he shouted suddenly. "I'm telling you nothing! You killed Magnus—we didn't. Why would we? He was our leader."

"Maybe somebody else wanted to be leader?" Pitt suggested without moving.

Carmody regarded him with total contempt. "Is that what you do?" he asked. "You want promotion in your police, so you kill the man above you?"

Pitt pushed his hands into his pockets. "Wouldn't work," he answered. "There are rules against it."

Blind fury touched Carmody's face for an instant, then he realized he was being laughed at. "And of course you always obey the rules!" he said sarcastically. "I've seen a bit of that, down Bow Street way."

Pitt had been about to retort, trapping him in his own need for rules, but the jibe about Bow Street cut him more sharply than he was prepared for. He cared intensely for its reputation, even now when it was Wetron's responsibility, not his. Some of the men there were those he had worked with, especially Samuel Tellman, who had resented him so bitterly when he had first taken over. Tellman had thought him unfit for command, a man jumped up beyond his ability. Command belonged to gentlemen, ex-army or ex-navy officers who understood the merits of experience and did not interfere. He did not approve of those who rose from the ranks. It had been a long and often uncomfortable journey for both of them until they reached the place of mutual trust, before Pitt's expulsion. Then it had been Tellman's loyalty that had saved Charlotte's life in Devon.

A look of triumph slowly lit Carmody's face as Pitt did not answer him, and he realized that his shot had found its mark.

"If you don't want any rules," Pitt replied at last, "why are you complaining that some of the men in Bow Street don't keep them?"

"Because you're hypocrites!" Carmody spat. "You abide by rules well enough when it suits you!"

"Don't you?" Pitt asked. "Isn't that your point? Do what you like, no rules, even about keeping the rules."

Carmody looked momentarily confused.

Pitt leaned forward. "Look," he said gravely. "I want to know who killed Magnus just as much as you do, maybe more. Whoever did it broke my rules. You say that you don't believe in rules, but that's rubbish. You're angry with me because you think I'm lying to you . . ."

"Aren't you?" Carmody accused.

"So you have rules about lying!" Pitt observed.

Carmody drew in his breath sharply.

"And you think one of us shot Magnus," Pitt went on. "Which makes you angry, because you don't expect police to kill people in cold blood. So you have rules about murder. What about betrayal? Do you have rules about that too?"

Carmody stared at him.

Pitt waited.

"Yes," Carmody admitted at last, his eyes careful, hurt.

"Whoever shot Magnus could just as easily have shot you and Welling as well," Pitt observed. "Why didn't he?"

Carmody blinked.

"Well, if he was a policeman, wouldn't it make sense?" Pitt pressed his momentary advantage. "Why leave a witness? What's the difference between one anarchist and another?"

"Magnus was our leader," Carmody answered without hesitation. "Makes sense to kill the leader."

"If it wasn't one of your own, how would he know that?" Pitt said.

Carmody was silent, and he watched Pitt with absorption. The affectation of boredom had vanished.

"If we'd known anything about you, we would have arrested you long before you blew up Myrdle Street," Pitt pointed out. "It makes us look incompetent. And of all the police in London, why Grover?"

"Because he ran all the dirty errands for Simbister at Cannon Street," Carmody replied.

Pitt felt a tightening in his own chest. "How did you know?" he asked.

Carmody gave a grunt of impatience. "If you knew Magnus, you wouldn't doubt it."

"I didn't know him."

"He was careful. He collected times and places, amounts. He knew exactly who was paying and how much, who was making the threats and who was carrying them out. He even paid debts for some people." There was pride in his voice and he stared at Pitt with a rage for helpless pain and the injustice of it, which he could not redress.

Pitt believed him, but he needed more information—and he could not expect Carmody to trust him. He tried to keep his own emotions from his face. "And you know this for certain?"

"Yes, I do!" Carmody leaned forward a little. "And you believe me. You know damn well I'm telling the truth. You can get me hanged for Magnus's murder, if you lie enough, and get your men to lie too, but you'll not silence all of us. There's proof, and you'll never find it. Whoever killed Magnus won't stop his work from going on."

"What did Magnus want?" Pitt asked. "Apart from chaos, no rules, no safety to grow food, or move it to the cities, no transport, no heat or light, no protection for the weak . . ."

"No, of course he didn't want that!" Carmody said in disgust. "None of us wanted real chaos, just an end to oppression." He shifted position a little. The air in the cell was clammy. "You can mock us all you like, but Magnus was a reformer, not a revolutionary. You asked me who would want to kill him? Not us. We believed in what he was doing and we were prepared to give every-thing we had to help. We still are!" He jabbed his finger towards the steel door. "Ask who has something to lose—motive. Isn't that what detectives are supposed to look for? Who was Magnus going to hurt? Corrupt police. There's your answer."

"In Cannon Street?" Pitt said quietly.

"And Bow Street, Mile End, Whitechapel."

"Who has the proof?" He did not expect an answer, but he had to ask.

Carmody snorted. "You think I'd tell you? If you really don't know, start with Myrdle Street, and work west. Try Dirty Dick's Tavern, at Bishopsgate. Or Polly Quick up at the Ten Bells by the Spitalfields Market."

Pitt accepted that he would get no more than that, no matter how long he pursued the subject. He was compelled to prove or disprove it by following the trail of accusations.

He straightened up. "I will," he answered.

"They're all over the east end of the city," Carmody added, a strange, naive note of hope in his voice. "If you want to, you'll find them."

PITT WENT BACK TO Keppel Street again before he followed Carmody's directions. If he were going to learn anything in the East End he needed to be less conspicuously dressed. He kept clothes at home that were frayed at the hems, mud-spattered and ill-fitting, and boots that were scuffed and resoled several times, much to Charlotte's distaste.

It was while wearing these that he arrived at Bishopsgate at about midday, mixing in with the peddlers, clerks, and laborers in the street. In this area men, women, and children worked all their waking hours to scrape enough to survive by making cheap furni-ture, weaving baskets, stitching clothes, trading in anything peo-ple would buy. The streets were crowded, noisy, and dirty. The smell of refuse, old soot, and close-pressed humanity clung in the nose and throat. A few gaunt cows and pigs rooted among the market refuse for anything edible. Dogs sniffed around hopefully and cats followed the trails of vermin.

Pitt had already removed anything of value from his pockets, and he walked up Bishopsgate without concern for petty theft. He passed Camomile Street, Wormwood Street, and then Hounds-ditch till he came to Dirty Dick's. During the reign of Louis XVI of France, the tavern had been known as the Gates of Jerusalem. It had definitely come down in the world.

The door was open and a thickset man with hair plastered across his head was wheeling a barrel over the pavement to the trapdoors opening on the cellar.

Pitt stopped next to him.

The man looked up. "There's someone inside ter serve yer," he said with a nod.

"I don't want ale," Pitt answered, remaining where he stood.

The man straightened his back slowly. " 'Oo are yer?" His voice was heavy with suspicion. He looked Pitt up and down, his eyes narrowing. "I in't seen yer 'round 'ere before." It was almost an accusation.

Pitt decided on at least something of the truth. "I haven't been here much. Usually work up the Bow Street area."

The man swore viciously, but there was as much despair in his voice as anger.

Pitt waited. Something was wrong, but he did not understand what it was.

The man's face was bitter. "Well, I in't givin' yer nothin'! I paid already this week, an' I in't got no more. Close me down, then! Go on! Then yer get nothin'! Yer stinkin' bastards!"

"I didn't ask you for anything," Pitt said slowly. "What made you think I wanted money?"

The man's face was ugly with contempt, his lips twisted showing yellow teeth. "Yer stand 'ere, blockin' me way. Yer don't want ale. Yer think I'm stupid? Well, I in't. An' I in't payin' yer neither. Do yer worst! I in't got no more."

Pitt's stomach turned cold. The man thought he had come for more protection money, just as Carmody had said. "Nobody can pay more than once," he agreed. "Better not to pay at all . . ."

"An' get me 'ead beat in?" the man said savagely. "An' 'oo's gonna 'elp me, eh? Police?" He spat on the ground at Pitt's feet, but he was close to weeping with frustration. He choked on his words. "Go on, get out of 'ere!" He stood with his fists clenched, his shoulders tight, as if he were on the edge of losing control and lashing out.

"Tell me who's taking the money, and I'll . . ." Pitt started, then realized the futility of it. He was the enemy, no matter how much he worked to deny it. As far as this man was concerned, it was the truth. "Look . . ." he started again.

The man took a step towards him, head down, muscles bunched, ready to swing his fist.

Pitt moved back, then turned and walked away. He had not handled it well, and he had learned nothing that was of any use. The man believed his tormentors were policemen, but Pitt needed names, accounts, times of collection, something he could prove. He must do a great deal better than this.

He went up Bishopsgate and turned left past the bootlace seller on the corner of Brushfield Street towards Spitalfields Market. Three women were standing on the curb arguing. A child wailed. A chimney sweep's boy passed by, soot-stained, round-shouldered. Half a dozen urchins played a game of bones on the pavement, tossing them up in the air and catching them again while they moved others as counters, absorbed in the skill of it. It was good for nimble fingers, training them for picking a pocket swiftly, unfelt.

He passed houses that were shabby now but had once been the homes and workshops of silk merchants who had fallen on much harder times. A costermonger's cart trundled by, then a brewer's dray, wagons of coal and timber being moved down towards the docks.

At the Ten Bells tavern, he went inside and asked for a pint of cider. He let the clean taste of it wash away the sour flavor of the streets, at least for a few moments.

He was aware of the landlady watching him covertly, because he was a stranger here. She was small and buxom, with fair hair falling out of its pins. All the time she smiled, as she greeted most people by name. She was doing a good trade.

He walked over to the bar and ordered a second pint of cider, and a portion of bread and cheese. She passed it to him, the smile still curving her mouth, but her eyes were wary. Closer to, he noticed that her white neck was sagging a little and there were fine lines on her skin.

"Thank you," he took the tankard and the plate. "You keep a good house here, mistress. A lot of trade."

She stared at him. He knew in that careful look that she was already certain in her own mind that he was going to cause her trouble. He loathed doing this, but he had to have the information.

"Enough," she said, keeping up the pretense of welcome.

"Enough to share the profit a bit," he replied, making it a statement rather than a question.

The warmth in her face died. "I already pay," she said coldly.

"I know!" he cut across her protest. "Can't pay twice. I know that. Just pay me instead. I'll take care of it. Pay me, and pay less, just see it's regular."

"Oh yeah?" she said bitterly. "An' wot about 'im wot comes, then, eh? I'm just gonna tell 'im 'e don't get nothin', an' 'e'll jus' go away, peaceful-like?"

"No, you're going to tell me when he comes, and what he looks like, and I'm going to take care of him."

Her eyebrows rose. "Yeah?" She looked around. "You an' 'oo else? There's 'undreds of 'em! There's the 'ole bleedin' police force!

Take one out, an' two more'll fill 'is place. 'Ow many is there o'
you, then?"

He thought only a moment before he answered. "Don't you
worry about that. Just tell me who he is, when he comes, and what
he looks like and I'll get rid of him. Then you pay me."

She looked wary and frightened. There was knowledge of defeat in her eyes. Pitt felt a surge of fury so savage that the look of it
in his face made her back away. Then he wanted to apologize, but
that would undo all he had achieved. "Name?" he said aloud.

"Jones," she replied. "We call 'im Jones the Pocket."

"What does he look like?"

"Sharp nose, black 'air," she said, her mouth puckering up.
"Not very tall. 'Ard ter tell if 'e's thin or fat 'cos 'e wears a big coat,
summer an' winter. Could be anythin' under it."

"Does he come regularly?"

"Like taxes an' death."

"When?"

"Every Wednesday. Middle o' the arternoon when there's
'ardly anyone 'ere."

"Then next Wednesday will be his last," Pitt said with acute
satisfaction.

She mistook his pleasure for the greed he had expressed earlier.
She lifted her shoulders very slightly. "Makes no odds ter me. Pay
'im, pay you, it's all the same. Can't pay twice or I got nothin' ter
pay the brewer. Then we all got nothin'."

Before he relented and tried to offer her some encouragement
that soon it would all end, Pitt turned away and walked across the
sawdust floor and out into the street.

BY DUSK THAT EVENING he was standing in the entrance of
the alleyway across from the house where Samuel Tellman lodged,
waiting for him to come home. The wind was colder and it smelled
like rain. He shifted his weight from one foot to the other. He had

turned the problem over in his mind, and there was no other solution that made sense. Tellman worked in Bow Street. If anyone could have seen or heard who was behind the corruption, without being part of it, it would be he.

The wind was rising chill with coming rain. Pitt turned up the collar of his coat and stood a little closer to the wall. Doubt began to eat into him. Perhaps the anarchists were not naive at all, but were manipulating his loyalties on purpose. Their prime motive was chaos. What better way to achieve it than to turn Special Branch against the police, sowing suspicion between them? Perhaps they were also doing exactly the same thing in reverse. Someone might even now be suggesting to the police that Narraway was responsible for the bombing and the murder of Magnus Landsborough, in order to carve out his own little kingdom of power. Pitt did not believe it for an instant, but he would not be able to prove it to anyone else. He was amazed how little he really knew of Narraway.

An old man with white hair poking out from under a bowler hat walked briskly through the pool of lamplight and away again. Then the moment after, Tellman himself appeared—lean, lantern-jawed, his shoulders stiff.

Pitt left the shadow of the alley and strode across the cobbles to catch up with him just as he reached his own door. Tellman looked around in surprise.

"I need to talk to you," Pitt explained by way of apology. "As privately as possible." He did not feel free to ask to go into Tellman's rooms. He was seeking a favor, and it was extremely important that they were not observed together, otherwise he would have suggested going to any of the nearby taverns.

Tellman looked suspicious. He glanced at Pitt's disreputable clothes, but he knew him well enough from their days together to realize why he was wearing them. "What's happened?" His body was rigid. "It's not to do with Gracie, is it?"

Pitt felt a stab of guilt for not having said so to begin with. He had watched their slow, tender, and awkward courtship and seen how intense was the caring. "No," he said quickly. "It's police business."

The fear ironed out of Tellman's face. "Come in. I've got a better room now, bigger." He did not wait for agreement but opened the door with his key and led the way inside. The hall was narrow and linoleum-floored. Framed samplers adorned the wall. A pleasant aroma came from the back of the house, strongly pungent of onions. It reminded Pitt that he was hungry.

Tellman went up the stairs to the first floor and opened the door of the room overlooking the street. It was spacious, with a brass bed in one corner, a table and chair by the window, and two upholstered armchairs near the fireplace where the coals were already burning nicely. He invited Pitt to sit, then after loosening his bootlaces and taking off his jacket he sat in the other.

Pitt did not waste time. "The bombing in Myrdle Street," he said without preamble. "Anarchists. One dead, we have two of the others. Another one, maybe two escaped."

Tellman waited. He knew Pitt would not be asking police help in finding them.

"I've been questioning the ones we have," Pitt went on. "They're young, naive; they feel violently about social wrongs. In particular police corruption." He watched Tellman's face to see if there would be any anger in it, any leap to deny it. It was not there. He simply looked guarded, waiting for Pitt to explain.

"My first thought was 'Why Myrdle Street?'" Pitt went on. "There didn't appear to be any answer other than random violence. Then I learned that the central house that was destroyed belonged to a policeman from Cannon Street named Grover."

Tellman nodded very slowly. "I know him."

"What can you tell me?"

"Big man, about forty-five, heavy-built," Tellman was visualizing him as he spoke. "Been in the force since he was twenty or so. Worked his way up to sergeant but never seemed to want to go any higher. He knows the streets like the back of his hand, and most of the people in them. There isn't a screever or a fence he couldn't name, and tell you his business."

"How do you know?"

Tellman's lips thinned. "Reputation. If you want to know anything going on in the Cannon Street patch, ask Grover.

"I see. According to at least two sources, some policemen are collecting protection money from pubs around the Spitalfields area," Pitt went on. "I checked it myself, at Dirty Dick's and the Ten Bells. A man they know as Jones the Pocket comes for the money every Wednesday, midafternoon."

"You sure he's in the police?" Tellman asked unhappily.

"No, I'm only sure the pub owners think he is. I have to know. I want him arrested, and I'll take his place."

"What for? He may connect with Grover eventually, but you'll have to prove it. You don't know who he reports to, first," Tellman pointed out. "And he's not going to tell you."

"No," Pitt agreed. "But if I have the money, someone will make it their business to find me."

Tellman winced, his face grim. "Probably with a knife!"

"Not till they have the money from me, and know if I'm working alone." But Pitt was perfectly aware of the danger, and he would much rather have found another way to the same end, but he could not think of one.

Tellman drew in his breath to argue, just as there was a knock on the door.

"Come in," he said, then stood up as his landlady entered. She was a handsome woman, between fifty and sixty, carrying a warm, savory smell of the kitchen with her. A stiff, white apron covered most of her cotton dress.

"You want me ter keep yer dinner, Mr. Tellman?" she asked.

She stared at Pitt. "There's enough fer yer caller, if 'e'd like it. Just bangers and mash, an' a spot o' cabbage, but yer welcome."

Tellman looked at Pitt.

Pitt accepted warmly, and Tellman asked her to bring it as soon as she could. They waited until it was carried up on a tray, and the landlady duly thanked, before continuing with the conversation between mouthfuls. It was plain food, but it was well-cooked and generously portioned.

"Spitalfields is in the Cannon Street area," Tellman said unhappily. "That's Simbister's patch. Wetron's got pretty close to him lately. He seems to be making alliances all over the place, more than I've ever seen others do. Usually there's a kind of . . ." he looked for the right word, "rivalry . . . but not now. It's different. It feels . . . different."

Pitt knew what he was thinking. The Inner Circle was a web of secret alliances, promises, and loyalties between men who on the surface had no connection with one another. Outsiders did not know who they were, just that some people succeeded when others failed. Certain business deals went one way rather than another. Some men were promoted above rivals who had more skill. But if Wetron, now the head of what was left of the Circle, were making alliances with potential rivals from the most senior police command in the country, it was cause for anxiety.

"Simbister?" Pitt said aloud.

"And others, but him the most," Tellman answered through a mouthful of sausage. "If it's men from Cannon Street who are taking extortion money, it'll be more than two or three. You won't be able to count on anyone!"

"I know." Pitt felt a chill, even sitting in this warm room, and with the food inside him. "That's why I need you, and someone you can trust, to arrest Jones, when I find him. I have to know if what the anarchists say is true." He did not explain why. It was not only to find who killed Magnus Landsborough, it was far bigger than that. At issue was the whole morality of the force they had both served and believed in all their working lives.

Tellman nodded, then finished the last of his meal without pleasure. The silence stretched on after they had swallowed their final mouthful and the tea in the pot was getting cold.

The hurt was naked in Tellman's thin face. He came from a poor but fiercely respectable family. His father had worked all the hours he was awake in order to keep them clothed and fed. His mother was energetic, angry, and scrupulously fair, and loved them with a defensiveness that bordered on violence. She scolded them for laziness, deviousness, too much laughter, for telling lies or minding other people's business. But let anyone else find fault with her children, and they'd have their ears burned by her defense. Their achievements were considered to be no more than their duty to perform while their faults were addressed with a whirlwind of discipline. She loved them all, but she was proudest of Samuel, because he fought for what was right. She embarrassed him furiously by holding him up as an example to his younger siblings, and yet next to Gracie's approval, hers mattered more to him than anyone else's.

To see his own force tainted cut him to the bone, perhaps even more than it did for Pitt.

"I want to know too," he said quietly. "I have to. If it's in our patch as well, our men taking protection money, then it's down to me to stop it. If I don't, then I'm part of it too." He stared at Pitt, defying him to argue.

"Be careful!" Pitt warned impulsively, knowing how easily Tellman could be falsely disgraced, or even killed.

Police officers were sometimes killed in the line of duty. It would be a hero's death. Wetron himself would eulogize him. Pitt would be helpless to prove otherwise. And he realized with a tightening of his stomach, a weight inside him, that in spite of Tellman's belligerence, his odd, stiff vulnerability, his prejudices and his doggedness, Pitt liked him more than anyone else outside his own family. It would be more than guilt for involving him that he would suffer, it would be a loneliness, a searing and permanent loss.

IN THE MORNING, Pitt went to Narraway, who was sitting in his office, a pile of papers on the table in front of him, a pen in his hand.

"Yes," he said abruptly, looking up as Pitt closed the door.

Pitt sat down without being asked to. It was the first time he had done so. He was still very aware of Narraway being his superior, and while his position was not officially insecure anymore, the feeling of uncertainty had never left him.

"I looked around yesterday at the corruption Welling and Carmody are accusing the police of," he said bluntly. "I wanted to prove them wrong."

"And you didn't," Narraway replied, still holding the pen.

Pitt was jolted. "You know!" He felt oddly betrayed that Narraway had not spoken of the charge of corruption, as if he did not trust him to be loyal to his principles above his past associations.

Narraway gazed at him steadily. His face was tense, deeply lined in the sunlight that came in through the window to his left. His eyes were nearly black. His hair had once been just as dark, but now it was liberally streaked with gray at the temples.

"No, Pitt, I did not know," Narraway replied wearily. "I can see it in you. You signal the magnitude of it like a ship's beacon." He smiled bleakly. "What is it? A little fencing of stolen goods, a blind eye here and there, favor for favor?"

"Worse than that," Pitt replied, thinking of the landlady at the Ten Bells. "Intimidation on a large scale, regular collection of part of the takings from more or less honest businesses."

Narraway looked somber. "Not our job. And hardly enough to provoke a man like Magnus Landsborough to anarchy. But I'll speak to the commissioner. Looks as if he has a little housecleaning to do. I'm sorry. It's unpleasant to find corruption in your own patch." He looked down at his papers again, then, when Pitt did not move, he raised his eyes. "Is that why Myrdle Street was bombed?"

"Yes. Man from the Cannon Street station—named Grover— lived in one of the houses. Carmody said he was connected to the extortion. Have you found a link between Landsborough and any foreign anarchists?"

"No. We know where the most active anarchists are, and the most competent." His mouth twisted wryly. "The incompetent ones blew themselves up and are either in hospital or dead. As far as I can tell, Landsborough had no European connections. If Welling and Carmody are examples of his recruitment, they are naive social reformers who haven't the patience to do it through the usual ways, and imagine that if they destroy the system, they can build a better one in its place. Which is patently absurd, but without the bombs, we might consider them saints."

Pitt studied him, trying to measure the emotion lying behind his words. Was there pity there, a mourning for the tortured inno- cence that had driven those young men to rage at injustice and dream of changing it? Or was he simply making a professional judgment so he could act accordingly, and perhaps weigh Pitt a lit- tle more closely at the same time?

"That isn't what bothers me," Pitt told him, and was rewarded to see a flicker of surprise in Narraway's face. "I went to see Samuel Tellman yesterday evening. In his own rooms, not Bow Street," he added quickly, seeing Narraway's sharpened gaze. "I told him about Grover, and Carmody's accusations, and what I had found."

"Don't dance around it, Pitt!" Narraway snapped.

"Tellman believed it," Pitt said. "Without proof. And he knows it must go higher."

"That's obvious," Narraway retorted curtly. "What is your point?"

Pitt felt his body tighten. He loathed having to tell anyone this, and Narraway was not making it easier. "Tellman says Wetron is making alliances with men who would normally be his rivals for promotion. Specifically, with Simbister of Cannon Street."

Narraway let out his breath slowly. "I see. Is Simbister in the Inner Circle?"

"I don't know. But if he isn't now, I imagine he soon will be."

"And Wetron's purpose in this?" Narraway's fingers were gripping his pen and he moved it up and down very slowly, but with a tension as if he would not be able to stop.

"Power," Pitt answered simply. "Always power."

"Using Simbister?" Narraway's voice rose very slightly. He found it hard to believe.

"It seems so."

"How is a corrupt police force in his interest?" Narraway questioned. "If he wants to be commissioner, he needs to be seen to be not only highly competent but also above suspicion. If he isn't, Parliament won't sustain him, even if he's as rich as Croesus. Men in power want stability; above all they want the streets safe. If property isn't safe, the voters are unhappy." There was a faint challenge in his face, as if he expected Pitt to argue with him.

"I don't know," Pitt admitted. "Are you prepared to take the chance that he isn't?"

Narraway did not bother to answer. "What did you ask Tellman to do?"

Pitt hesitated. He had not wanted to tell Narraway about his plan to have Jones the Pocket arrested, and then take his place, but perhaps he should have realized he would have to. Now it was unavoidable. He did so as briefly as possible. There was no need to explain why he needed Tellman's help. Special Branch had no power of arrest themselves, and he could hardly trust any man from Cannon Street.

"Be careful, Pitt," Narraway said with surprising urgency. All the irony was gone from his face now. He leaned forward a little in his chair, all pretense of interest in his papers forgotten. "You don't know who is involved, or how many. It's not just greed you have to consider; it's old loyalties. God knows, you should understand that!"

"I know," Pitt said quietly.

"Do you?" It was a challenge. "And any association with you will make Tellman a marked man. I assume you realize that? Wetron is nobody's fool, least of all yours. You gave him the chance to destroy Voisey and take over leadership of the Inner Circle, but he knows you are its most powerful and most successful enemy. He won't ever forget that, and neither must you."

Pitt felt cold. He had known it already, but here in this quiet room it seemed more real. He had been careful to go to Tellman's rooms to see him, and at dusk when the streets were busy and half-lit. There was no one else he could trust, especially at Bow Street. War does not allow you to spare your friends and send only strangers into battle.

"I know that," he said aloud. "And so does he."

"Then get on with it," Narraway said quietly. "I want to know who was behind this bombing. Was Landsborough the leader? Where did the money come from for the bombs? And above all, now that Landsborough's dead, who's the new leader? By the way, who did kill Landsborough?"

"I don't know," Pitt replied. "Carmody and Welling behave as if they believe it was one of us, which suggests it was someone they don't know. A rival anarchist? One of Simbister's men?"

"Which means one of Wetron's?" Narraway said almost under his breath. "Find out, Pitt. I want to know."

PITT SPENT THE rest of the day in the bombed-out ruins of Myrdle Street. He made several more inquiries about Grover, but no one was willing to say much about him beyond verifying that he had lived in the center house, and of course was now homeless, as were they all. Yes, he was a policeman. Their faces had closed expressions, defensive, and he thought also that there was fear. No one spoke ill of him, but there was a coldness in their eyes, without sympathy. It tended to confirm rather than disprove what Carmody had said.

Deep in thought, walking along the Thames Embankment, he was pleasantly half-aware of the steamboats on the river, which were crowded with people enjoying themselves, wearing hats with streamers and waving to the shore. There was a band playing somewhere just beyond the curve where he could not see them. Street peddlers were selling lemonade, ham sandwiches, and various kinds of sweets. It was all exactly as London should be late on a summer afternoon. The breeze carried the smell of salt with the incoming tide, the sounds of laughter, music, horses' hooves on the cobbles, and the faint, background surge of water.

"Good evening, Pitt. All looks very normal, doesn't it."

Pitt stopped abruptly. He knew the voice even before he turned. Charles Voisey, knighted by the Queen for his extraordinary personal courage in killing Mario Corena and saving the throne of England from one of Europe's most passionate and radical republicans. Now he was a member of Parliament as well.

What Her Majesty did not and would never know was that Voisey had then been the head of the Inner Circle, on the point of achieving his ambition to overthrow the monarchy and become the first president of a republican Britain.

However, it was Mario Corena who had precipitated that act intentionally, forcing Voisey into killing him in order to save his own life. It had offered Pitt the chance to make Voisey seem the savior of the throne, and thus the betrayer of his own followers. For that Voisey would never forgive him, even though he had crossed sides brilliantly, almost without hesitation, using his new-found status as royal favorite to stand for Parliament, and win. Power was the prize. Only the Inner Circle had ever known his republican goal. To everyone else he was a brave, resourceful, and loyal man.

Now Pitt looked at him standing on the footpath, smiling. He remembered his face vividly, as if he had seen him only minutes ago. He was distinguished but far from handsome. His pasty skin splashed with freckles, his long nose a trifle crooked. But as always, his eyes shone with brilliant intelligence, and he also seemed mildly amused.

"Good evening, Sir Charles," Pitt replied, surprised to find his breath catching in his throat. This meeting could not be by chance.

"You are not an easy man to find," Voisey continued, and as Pitt started to move again, he fell into step beside him, the breeze in their faces. "I imagine the bombing in Myrdle Street has you considerably exercised."

"Did you follow me along the embankment to say that?" Pitt asked a little testily.

"It was a preamble," Voisey replied. "Perhaps unnecessary. It is the Myrdle Street bombing I wanted to talk to you about."

"If you are trying to recruit me into backing a drive to arm the police, you are wasting your time," Pitt said curtly. "We have guns now, if we need to use them. And we don't need any more authority to search people, or houses. It's taken us decades to get even as much cooperation as we have; if we start being heavy-handed, we'll lose it. The answer is no. In fact, I shall do whatever I can to fight against it."

"Will you?" Voisey turned half a step ahead and turned to face him, his eyes wide.

Pit was obliged to stop in order to answer. "Yes!"

"No chance of you changing your mind, under pressure, for example?"

"None at all. Were you intending to exert pressure on me?"

"Not at all," Voisey answered him with a very slight shrug. "On the contrary, I am very relieved to hear that you will not be changed, regardless of threats or pleas. I had expected as much of you, but it is still a relief."

"What do you want?" Pitt demanded impatiently.

"To have a reasonable conversation," Voisey said, dropping his voice and suddenly intensely serious. "There are issues of urgent importance upon which we agree. I am aware of things which possibly you are not."

"Since you are a member of Parliament, that is unarguable," Pitt observed tartly. "But if you imagine that I will share Special Branch information with you, you are mistaken."

"Then be quiet and listen to me!" Voisey snapped, his temper suddenly giving way, his face flushed. "A member of Parliament called Tanqueray is going to propose a private bill to arm the London police and give them wider power of search and seizure. As things stand at the moment, he has a very good chance of getting it passed."

"It will set the police back years." Pitt was appalled.

"Probably," Voisey agreed. "But there is something far more important than that."

Pitt did not bother to hide his impatience, but already a sharp needle of curiosity was pricking him. Voisey must want something, and he must want it very much to have swallowed his loathing of Pitt sufficiently to follow him and speak like this. "I'm listening," he said.

Voisey's face was pale now, a small muscle ticking in his jaw. His eyes held Pitt's as they stood facing each other on the pavement by the embankment in the wind and the late sun. They were oblivious of passersby, the laughter, the music, and the splash of the rising tide on the steps below them.

"Wetron will use people's fear to back the bill," Voisey said quietly. "Every further outrage plays into his hands. He will allow crime to mount until no one feels safe: robbery, street attacks, arson, perhaps even more bombings. He wants people so afraid that they will be begging him to get weapons, new men, more power, anything to make them feel safe again. And when he is given them he will quell crime almost overnight, and emerge the hero."

"And you want him stopped," Pitt realized aloud, knowing

how intensely Voisey must hate the man who had so brilliantly taken over the position from which he had been driven.

"So do you," Voisey said softly. "If he succeeds he will be one of the most powerful men in England. He will be the man who saved London from violence and chaos, who made it safe to walk the streets again, to sleep undisturbed in one's own bed without fear of explosions, robbery, losing one's home or one's business. The commissioner's office will be his for the asking." His voice was thick with fury and loathing too powerful to conceal anymore. "And he will be in command of a private army of policemen, with guns and the power of search and seizure that will ensure no one dislodges him. He will continue to take tribute from organized crime, payment for being able to continue their extortion unmolested. If any ordinary man disobeys, or protests, he will be stopped in the street, or his house will be searched, and they will find he was in possession of stolen goods. Next thing he will be in prison, and his family destitute."

An open landau passed by on the road, young women in pale dresses, parasols aloft, laughing and calling out to friends going the opposite way.

"No one will come to his aid," Voisey continued, oblivious to them. "Because those with the power to will long since have been silenced. The police will not trust anyone because half of them will be Wetron's anyhow, but no one will know which half. The government will look the other way, grateful for law and order. Is that what you want, Pitt? Or do you hate the idea as much as I do? It doesn't matter what your reasons are."

Pitt's mind raced. Was it possible? Wetron's ambition knew no bounds, but had he really the imagination and the nerve to try something so appalling? He knew the answer even as the question formed in his mind. Of course he had.

Voisey saw it, and slowly he relaxed, the panic dying out of his eyes. "Then ally with me," Voisey said softly. "Help me prove what Wetron is doing, and stop him!"

Pitt hesitated. The hatred between them was like a razor-sharp blade.

"What is more important to you?" Voisey asked. "Your love of London and its people, or your hatred of me?"

Along the embankment a band played a dance tune. People below them on the river were laughing and calling out to one another. Somewhere in the distance a hurdy-gurdy was churning out a popular song. A girl's hat blew off in the wind, ribbons flying.

"Hate is irrelevant," Voisey said drily. "I trust you—to be predictable, anyway. Think about it. I have a seat in Parliament, and I know the Inner Circle. We can do better together than either of us can alone. Think what it is you want, Pitt. Remember, 'the enemy of my enemy is my friend'—at least until the battle is over. Think about it. Meet me tomorrow and give me your answer."

Pitt needed more time. The whole idea was preposterous. Voisey was a dangerous man who hated Pitt and would destroy him at the first chance. It was only what Pitt knew—and had proof of, a carefully kept secret—that prevented Voisey from harming his family. Voisey had used his own sister, the only person in the world he loved, as his tool in a murder.

But the thought of Wetron using the anarchist threat to rise to power was too real to ignore. He knew it, and Voisey understood that.

"Day after tomorrow," he said. "Where?"

Voisey smiled. "There's no time for self-indulgence. Make it somewhere nice and public," he replied. "How about midday, in the crypt of St. Paul's, by Nelson's tomb."

Pitt drew in a long breath. He met Voisey's eyes, and saw that he already knew Pitt would agree. He nodded. "I'll be there."

CHAPTER

FOUR

Pitt did not feel his usual pleasure as he let himself in at the front door in Keppel Street. Voisey had spoiled that. If Pitt as much as mentioned his name, Charlotte would remember all the misery and violence of the past. It would be a self-indulgence to tell her of his meeting with Voisey, simply so he did not have to weigh his decision alone.

He stepped inside and unlaced his boots without calling out to tell her he was home. There was no point in saying anything about Voisey if he decided not to ally with him. And if he accepted his offer, it would be far easier for Charlotte if she did not have to know. He told her the things that mattered; he always had. They had first met because of a murder. She was observant, wise, and she understood women as he never would. What was often more important in his investigations, she understood her own social class in a way that he, as an outsider, did not. Many times it had been her observation that had shown him some vital point, an anomaly, a motive, a pattern of thought.

Still, he protected her from some things, and the need to work with Voisey must be one of them. Not that he had made up his mind. He wanted to refuse. Every instinct was against it.

He walked softly down the corridor to the kitchen. The lights were on and he could hear the chink of crockery.

But every time he was on the brink of dismissing the idea of working with Voisey, Wetron's smooth, passionless face came into his mind, and he knew that Voisey might be right about him. He might be playing for the ultimate police office, holding the law in his own hands, with the power to corrupt almost limitless. And perhaps allying with Voisey was the only way to defeat him.

He could never trust Voisey, of course! But could he use him, just for this one purpose? The gain was worth the risk. Or perhaps more honestly, the loss would be too great not to try.

He opened the kitchen door and went in.

All through supper he did not mention it, nor did he say anything about police corruption. Charlotte would hear the pain in him and it would hurt her too. She would know that all the words, the holding him in her arms, the gentleness and the trust would not alter the reality he still had to face.

When the meal was over and the plates cleared away he leaned back in his armchair in the parlor and watched her as she sat with her head bent. The lamplight on the side of her face cast the shadow of her lashes on her cheek. Her slender hands pulled the needle through the linen she was mending, and he was glad he had not disturbed her peace.

There was no sound in the room but the slight tick of her needle against the thimble as she stitched. The sight, the near silence but for the needle, and the faint whicker of the flames—it was uniquely, perfectly comfortable. It was safety, companionship, the kind of unspoken ease that was the real prize at the end of each day, more than food or warmth, more than time in which to do whatever he wished. It was the certainty that it all mattered. Whether they agreed or differed, they were on a crusade for something they both cared about. Victorious or defeated, full of energy or too tired to think, she was there with him.

It was stupid to frighten her with the prospect of working with Voisey, or the ugliness of police corruption. And anyway, if he thought about it carefully, with judgment, weighed all the possibilities, he might find another, better solution.

Jack Radley would be the person to ask. He was Pitt's brother-in-law, the husband of Charlotte's sister Emily. He was a member of Parliament also, and gaining in experience. Pitt would go to the House of Commons in the morning and ask him. Tonight he put the matter out of his mind, and let the warmth deepen inside him, driving out everything else.

"TANQUERAY," JACK SAID with an edge to his voice. He had chosen to meet Pitt not in his office, where he might be interrupted by clerks, Parliament officials, and other members, but outside on the terrace overlooking the river. With their backs to the great Gothic palace of Westminster and the tower of Big Ben, they would look like anyone else, and might largely escape recognition.

"Is it true?" Pitt asked quietly. A couple of elderly men walked past behind them and he caught a whiff of cigar smoke on the breeze. The sun was bright on the water. Strings of barges were making their way upstream on the tide.

"Oh, yes," Jack said with feeling. "And he has a lot of backers. In fact, it's the backers who matter—Tanqueray is merely the spokesman. That's one of the many things that worry me. I don't really know who's the moving force behind it."

"His bill is not a response to the bomb in Myrdle Street?" Pitt asked.

Jack smiled with a downward twist of his mouth. "They are using it, certainly, but they are far better prepared than anyone could be in a day or two. The bill still needs drafting, but they have all their promises and the main arguments to support them. They are testing opinion, but there's a lot of agreement already. Crime in the street has been increasing over the last year or so." He looked sideways at Pitt, his eyes narrowed against the sun. "Everyone knows somebody who's been robbed, or experienced a nasty incident, or even simply preferred to go the longer way home because of the threat of violence. Perhaps, being in Special Branch instead of the police, you haven't noticed it."

"And police corruption," Pitt said softly. "I hadn't noticed that either."

"Corruption?" Jack asked, frowning. "Where? How do you know?"

"The two anarchists we caught," Pitt answered, beginning to walk slowly. "That's presumably why they bombed Myrdle Street. They meant to destroy only the center house—it belongs to a policeman from Cannon Street. They're apparently not very skilled with the dynamite. They took away three houses at least, and damaged five more so badly they'll have to be demolished."

Jack raised his eyebrows. "And you believe them?" He kept pace with Pitt.

"I didn't at first. I did a little investigating myself. At least part of it is true."

"And the rest?"

"I don't know."

"How high does it go?" They reached the end of the terrace and turned to go back again.

"To the top," Pitt replied.

Jack was silent for several minutes because there were some M.P.s walking behind them, closely enough to overhear. Two or three spoke to Jack and he replied briefly. He did not introduce Pitt.

"Who do you mean?" he asked at length when he was perfectly sure there was no one within earshot.

"Wetron in Bow Street," Pitt replied. "Simbister in Cannon Street. Don't know who else, but it's Wetron that matters."

Jack did not ask why. Pitt had previously told him that Wetron was head of the Inner Circle.

"The police are saying that they can't protect us from theft or random violence unless they have more men." Jack stood still, staring out across the wind-riffled water. "And now they want more guns, as general protection for their men, and the argument for it is powerful. We haven't had many police killed in the line of duty yet, but it will happen. We can't ask them to protect us if we won't give them the means. When the next policeman gets badly injured there is going to be an uproar. Not to mention that more police will leave the force. People are frightened, Thomas, and they have reason to be."

"I know." Pitt leaned on the wall beside him, watching a ferry boat passing under the arches of Westminster Bridge. "But giving us guns isn't going to help; it will only escalate everything. We already have them if we face a really bad situation, like the siege in Long Spoon Lane. If we have too much power then sooner or later some of us will abuse it. We'll separate ourselves from the people we're supposed to be part of."

Jack chewed on his lip. "There's worse to come," he said unhappily. "I don't know what, not yet."

"Worse?" Pitt was jolted. "What could be worse than corrupt police with guns and the power to go wherever they want, to search whomever they want simply because *they* say they have a reason, but don't have to prove it? It's license for a private army!"

"I don't know. It's only a rumor of an addition to the bill, something no one will specify. But I believe it exists. Or at least, let us say, I fear it." He straightened up and turned to face Pitt. "There's a lot of fear around, Thomas. Fear of change, fear of violence, fear of apathy allowing us to lose what we have. It's a bad motive for doing anything. We react without taking account of the consequences."

Pitt smiled bitterly, thinking of Welling and Carmody, and Magnus Landsborough, whom he had never known. "Like the anarchists, who want to bomb things without considering how they can replace them."

"Is that what they said?" Jack looked curious.

"That surprises you?"

"I suppose it depends. The old theory of anarchy isn't very practical; at least I don't think so. It relies too much on the inherent good nature of mankind. It believes that wise men should learn to rule their own behavior, away from the interference of governments." He smiled a little bitterly. "Trouble is, who is to decide who is wise and who isn't? And what do we do about those who are lazy, or inadequate, or simply don't want to contribute to the general welfare? There are always going to be the sick, the old, the foolish, not to mention the rebellious. Who is going to take care of them? Who is going to curb the bully or the liar, or the thief? It needs to be done by common consent, and so we're back to government again."

"And police," Pitt agreed. "There's something else. Yesterday, on the embankment, I met Voisey."

Jack stiffened. "Voisey!"

Pitt told him what Voisey had said of Wetron's ambitions to rise until he effectively governed the whole city.

"God in Heaven!" Jack said violently. Then he deliberately lowered his voice, aware of drawing attention to himself from a group of men passing by. "He's mad! Isn't he?" he asked incredulously. "What does Victor Narraway think?"

"I don't know," Pitt admitted. "I haven't told him yet."

"And exactly when are you intending to do that?"

"When I leave here."

"Don't trust Voisey!" Jack said with intense urgency. "He'll forgive nothing and forget nothing. He wanted to be president of Britain, and it was largely you who stopped him, with Lady Vespasia's help, and he won't have forgotten that either."

"I know," Pitt assured him. "I'd be head of Bow Street, not Wetron, if Voisey hadn't had me thrown out. Does any of that make the charge against Wetron untrue?"

Jack stared at him, his face pale. The wind was rising, whipping at his hair. "No," he said reluctantly. "No, I suppose it doesn't.

What does Voisey want? He didn't tell you without wanting something."

"He wants me to work with him to prevent Wetron from succeeding," Pitt answered.

"You can't!" Jack was appalled. "Thomas, you can't work with Voisey! He'll stab you in the back the first chance he gets. For God's sake, you know that!"

"Yes, I do." Pitt turned up his coat collar. "But I also know that he could be right, and if he is, Wetron would end with virtual control of London, and the heart of the whole Empire."

Jack did not answer. They stood in silence thinking over the enormity of the possibility.

"And there is another thing," Pitt said at last, starting to walk back the way they had come. "What if Wetron is not quite as clever as he thinks, and he is betrayed from within the Circle, perhaps by someone with foreign sympathies. Is the conspiracy confined to England? I don't know. But even if it is, some men can be bought for money, or power, or any of a dozen other things. An Inner Circle member could be a traitor to England quite easily. It has been torn apart by factions before, and the leadership changed. That is how Wetron got rid of Voisey. It could happen again."

Jack's eyes were dim cast, his face furrowed in unhappiness. "You don't think Voisey is simply making this up so he can use you to destroy Wetron?" he suggested, but with no belief in his voice. "He must hate him even more than he hates you. What could be more satisfying than to pit your enemies against each other? No matter who loses, you win, and the survivor may well be sufficiently weakened that you can finish him off too."

"I know that." Pitt did know it, with a sickening certainty that knotted in his stomach. "Can we afford to stand apart from it?"

Jack waited a long time before he answered. They were nearly at the doorway to go back inside the palace and towards his office. "No," he said softly. "But be careful, Thomas, for heaven's sake, be careful. Don't trust him with anything, not even for a moment."

Pitt said nothing.

"What do you want from me?" Jack asked him.

Pitt looked at him steadily. "The answer you gave me. Tanqueray's going to go ahead with his bill, and you think it might well get passed. If it does, it will give Wetron the power to impress his rule on London. I can't let that happen if there is any way to stop it, whatever the risk."

PITT ENTERED NARRAWAY'S office, tense even before he broached the subject. Narraway was standing, staring out of the window, his back to the door, the gray in his hair catching the light. He turned as Pitt came in, his face expectant. "You're late," he said bluntly. "What else have you learned about Magnus Landsborough? I need to know before they regroup and find another leader." He was impatient. "Where was the money coming from? Who else is involved? I've spoken to all my sources of information, and I've heard of no connection to any foreign group. The East End is littered with Poles and Jews, Frenchmen, Italians, Russians, anything and everything you can think of, but no one was interested in blowing up Myrdle Street."

"I don't think there's a foreign connection," Pitt replied, remaining standing also. He was too stiff and shivery to sit anyway. Better to come to the point straight away. It was not as if he could avoid telling Narraway. "I'm late because I was at the House of Commons, talking to Jack Radley. He says Tanqueray's bill has a good chance of passing."

Narraway swore viciously and with a suppressed violence that spoke of intense emotion.

Pitt found that instead of shocking him, it was oddly comforting. It betrayed a humanity that bridged the gulf he so often felt between them. Narraway seldom allowed anything but his intellect to show.

"I have an offer of help that I am going to accept," Pitt told him. "Because the situation may possibly be worse than we thought, and Jack believes it is going to deteriorate even further."

"Oh? And what are they going to blow up next? Buckingham Palace?" Narraway said sarcastically.

"Sabotage by corruption," Pitt answered. "The police force could become Wetron's private army, if this bill is passed."

Narraway drew in his breath sharply, then suddenly he understood. His shoulders relaxed and he breathed in very deeply, his eyes bright. "Wetron seizing the chance," he said softly. "Brilliant! Then he won't want us to catch the anarchists. He'll want them to strike again, so everyone is frightened enough to give him the power he's after. Then he'll reverse the corruption he's encouraged. It won't be hard for him to arrest all the men because he already knows who they are—God help them, he put them there! What made you see that, Pitt?" There was a gleam in his black eyes that could have been admiration.

There was only one possible answer, and that was the truth. "Charles Voisey," Pitt answered. "He caught up with me in the street yesterday evening. He wants me to work with him to prevent the bill."

"Does he indeed? And what did you tell him?"

Pitt forced himself to be calm. "I told him I would consider it. I'm meeting him at St. Paul's. But I am going to do it."

Narraway's voice was very soft, almost like an animal's purr. "Oh, are you!" It was more of a challenge than a question.

Pitt answered it as such.

"I can't afford not to. And you can't afford that I don't. We need police cooperation in order to succeed at our job. With Wetron as commissioner, and the Inner Circle against us, not to mention the police seen as a public enemy, we'd be blocked at every point. We would be able to do only what Wetron allowed us to."

"You believe this?" Narraway asked. "It hasn't occurred to you

that Voisey could have made it all up in order to use you to destroy
Wetron and get himself back in control of the Inner Circle?"

"Of course it has occurred to me," Pitt replied bitterly. "And
I'm sure Voisey knows that it has. But it doesn't alter Tanqueray's
bill, or the police corruption that Wetron has not prevented,
whether he knows about it or not."

Narraway nodded. "And who killed Magnus Landsborough?"

"I don't know," Pitt admitted. "I need to speak to Welling and
Carmody again, but it's getting harder to get anything useful out of
them. They're both idealists who see largely one vision: a corrupt
authority that can only be got rid of by violence. They let off
bombs after giving the residents warning to get out." He tried to
put into words the innocence or essential futility of such tactics.
"They won't shed blood, which was the ultimate weapon, but they
were willing to destroy homes and possessions."

"They'll hang," Narraway said, looking at Pitt steadily. He put
his hands into his pockets. "I imagine they know that, but it might
have escaped them. No one died in the Myrdle Street bombing,
but one of them shot at a policeman and hit him. If you hadn't
gone to him and stopped the bleeding, he might have died. They
can be charged with attempting to murder a policeman while in
the course of committing a very serious crime."

Pitt knew it was pointless to argue with Narraway. Actually he
had no idea what Narraway believed about hanging, or what he
felt about anything else deeper than the surface pleasures or irrita-
tions of the job. Narraway was meticulous in his clothes and habits
and untidy with paperwork. He ate sparingly, but he liked good
pastry and good wine. He read voraciously: history, biography, sci-
ence, and poetry. Pitt had not seen him with a novel except in
translation from other languages, especially Russian. But what
stirred his emotions, what hurt him, or woke his dreams, Pitt had
no idea at all.

"Offer them amnesty." Narraway's voice cut across Pitt's
thoughts. "In return for information to stop police corruption, more

bombings that will kill people, any way you want to phrase it that will work."

Pitt was astounded. "Amnesty?" he said incredulously.

Narraway widened his eyes. "You know, I rather thought that would please you! Not that that's why I'm doing it, of course. Five years' prison, instead of the rope. But don't sell it cheap."

Pitt's spirits surged upward. "Who do you have to ask? When will you know?"

Narraway put his hands into his pockets. "I know now, Pitt." The faintest flicker of amusement crossed his eyes. "Go and see what you can get for it."

FIVE MINUTES BEFORE NOON Pitt went across the black-and-white stone floor of St. Paul's Cathedral, and down the flight of steps to the crypt. He walked through the arches quietly, trying to keep his footsteps from disturbing the near-silence. There were only two other people down here that he could see, an old man with thin hair and a mild, dreamy face, and a young woman concentrating intently on a piece of paper in her hand. Neither of them looked at him as he passed.

There were many plaques on the walls commemorating the famous dead from great battles of the past. He was startled to notice how many of them were naval captains who had fallen at Trafalgar. It was a stark reminder of just how dark England's future had seemed then, with Napoleon conquering Europe and poised on the shores to take Britain as well. It had seemed as if nothing could stop him.

He saw the central pale-arched ceiling where the colonnades met and under it, in the heart of the crypt, the great memorial tomb of Horatio Nelson. Voisey was standing in front of it. Was he in silent contemplation of heroism, sacrifice, the fortunes of war that could change history in the outcome of one battle? And could the leadership of one man with vision, skill, courage, eccentricity, control that? Nelson's signal to the fleet before the attack had passed into history, and perhaps into all that it meant to be English: "England expects that every man will do his duty."

Why had Voisey selected this tomb, among all those in this great cathedral? There were a score of other places to meet, as easily found. And why was he early? Was that his first and startling tactical error? Pitt had expected him to be about ten minutes late, not long enough for Pitt to leave, but enough to make him feel anxious and at a disadvantage, as if he were the petitioner, not Voisey.

Pitt stopped, to see if Voisey would turn in a moment or two to look for him. He did not. Was he more confident than his earliness would suggest? Or could he see Pitt reflected in the black marble surface of the tomb?

In case that was so, Pitt smiled and moved forward. He would not spoil his advantage by seeming to measure it, as though it mattered to him.

"Morning, Sir Charles," he said, using both the correct form of address and the one that would remind Voisey that in their greatest clash it had been Pitt who had won. He would prefer not to have been the one to approach, but to avoid it would have made it even more obvious. It would have signaled that he was walking soft-footedly on purpose. The realization of how much thought he had given it, even before they entered any conversation, before Voisey himself said anything at all, was discomforting.

Voisey turned slowly. He was smartly and soberly dressed, almost as if he had come here to contemplate the heroes of the past rather than to discuss the political battles of today. "Good morning, Pitt," he replied. "You are a trifle late. Is it the first time you have been to St. Paul's? If you can keep your attention on the business in hand, perhaps you would like to walk around? I can show you some of the other notable tombs, although of course there is nothing to rival this for sheer"—he hesitated—"spectacle."

Pitt looked at the magnificent monument. It was ornate, resplendent, a nation's tribute to a man who was not only the archi-tect of their greatest naval victory but a hero personally loved, who had died at the moment of his supreme triumph. Pitt thought it to-tally fitting, and he was filled with a deep pride as he stood in front of it, for a moment unaware of Voisey beside him.

"We lost nearly forty officers and five hundred men," Voisey's words interrupted his thoughts.

"In Trafalgar?" Pitt was surprised. It sounded very few for such a battle.

"In the British fleet," Voisey replied, irony in his face, his eyes bright. "That doesn't include the French, Spanish, of course."

Pitt said nothing, feeling a little foolish.

"They lost over a hundred officers, and eleven hundred men," Voisey went on.

Again Pitt did not answer.

"Funny little man," Voisey continued. "Seasick at the begin-ning of every voyage."

He was referring to Nelson. "I know," Pitt said.

"And he liked fat women, who smelled," Voisey added.

Pitt had no idea whether that was true or not, and he did not wish to know. He glanced at Voisey, and away again quickly. He knew why he had mentioned it, it was a matter of class. He was re-minding Pitt that he was a gentleman and Pitt was not. He was using the aristocrat's ease with the fallibility of heroes, and the earthier side of nature, compared with working-class prudency. He was testing, trying to find the place of offense.

"Really?" Pitt said casually. "How many ships did we lose?"

"The French and Spanish lost twenty-one from the combined fleet."

"How many ships did we lose?" Pitt repeated.

"The French lost eight, the Spanish thirteen."

"And us?"

Voisey nodded towards the tomb. "We lost Nelson."

"And ships?" Pitt persisted, refusing to think of men, lives, passions. Stick to the measurable.

"None. We lost no ships. Every last one made it home." Voisey blinked, as if his own emotion had caught him off-guard. "It was the greatest victory in the annals of our naval history. We were saved from invasion. And the fleet returned to England with flags at half mast, as if it had been a defeat." His voice was thick and he looked away from Pitt for a moment. "Did Jack Radley tell you that Tanqueray's bill will pass?" he asked.

Pitt concealed his jolt of surprise that Voisey knew already that he had spoken to Jack. "Yes," he replied. "Also that there is very little organized resistance against it. We shall have to be much cleverer than we have been so far to turn the tide." He had used the naval metaphor unintentionally.

A faint flicker of amusement touched Voisey's mouth, but his hands were clenched at his sides, their powerful knuckles white. "That sounds like defeat," he remarked. The heavy symbolism of where they were was not lost on either of them. This too was what Voisey had intended.

"It should sound like caution," Pitt replied. "I think we are also outnumbered and outgunned, at least at this point. It takes more than bravado to win, and unfortunately, more than a just cause."

Voisey's eyebrows rose fractionally. "We need a Nelson?" A tiny smile touched his mouth. "Do you think Narraway's up to the task?"

"I'm not sure how much I intend to consult him," Pitt answered.

"I rather thought you liked him! Am I mistaken?"

"It's irrelevant," Pitt said a little tartly. Voisey's amusement stung him. "I can work with people whether I like them or not, if I believe their goal is the same as mine, and that they are competent at what they do. I had rather assumed you knew that!"

"Good," Voisey approved very softly, almost under his breath.

"If you had said you trusted me, I should have known you for a liar, and a poor one at that. But you appreciate that my goal is the same as yours. That'll suffice."

"One step at a time," Pitt replied. He did not question whether Voisey trusted him. That was Voisey's advantage and they both knew it. Pitt was bound by his own rules. Voisey was bound by nothing.

"What is this Tanqueray like?" Pitt asked.

"A jam tart of a man," Voisey replied. "Attracts those with more appetite than sense, and you come away licking your fingers and looking for somewhere to wash yourself. Somehow a napkin never does it."

Pitt smiled in spite of not wishing to. "Why did they choose him?"

Voisey's eyebrows rose. "A guess? Because we have a lot of members who think there is nothing more innocent or innocuous than a jam tart! Offer them a rum baba or a brandy cream éclair, and they know you want something."

Pitt saw his point. "And who else can they rely on?"

"Too many," Voisey said ruefully. "Dyer is the most powerful. Unctuous beggar. Looks like a defrocked priest. I wouldn't trust him with the party funds, or my god-daughter, if she was under twenty. Lord North used to say of Gladstone that he didn't mind him having the ace of trumps up his sleeve, he just objected virulently to his claim that it was God who put it there. Dyer's the same, holier than the pope!"

Pitt turned away to hide the amusement that betrayed him. He did not want to like anything about Voisey. He started to walk away from the tomb, back the way he had come in.

"Who killed Magnus Landsborough?" Voisey asked.

"Why do you care?" Pitt responded. "Isn't police corruption your interest? That will be your chief card to play against them in Parliament."

"Precisely. Are you certain they are not the same thing?"

"No, I'm not. I think they may be."

"I will need better than that," Voisey answered. "I want proof of corruption on a systematic basis, or at least enough that far more must be assumed."

"Oh, I can see what you need, and why," Pitt agreed. "I could get it and as easily give it to Jack Radley." He turned to look at Voisey. He could not resist seeing if the mention of Jack's name, with its memories of past defeat, galled him. The momentary hatred appeared in Voisey's face, bitter as bile. Pitt had known it was there. Seeing it undisguised for an instant chilled him, but it should not have. It was a reminder. He should be grateful for it. It was too easy to forget. "What are you giving me that he could not?" he asked.

"Knowledge of the Inner Circle," Voisey answered. "Names, details, who owes what and to whom." It could be the ultimate betrayal of all his oaths, payment for those who had turned against him and chosen Wetron. He would be taking an irretrievable step, breaking bones for which the penalty was death. Pitt must never, for an instant, forget that he too had waited just as long for his revenge on Voisey.

"And how much of this information are you prepared to use?" Pitt asked quietly, guarding against being overheard by passersby, any of whom could be one of that secret brotherhood.

"All of it," Voisey replied. "Until it is as dead as the men whose bones lie in all this marble and porphyry."

"I see."

"No, you don't," Voisey answered. "But you will. I will send you a message if I have anything to tell you about what happens in Parliament. Otherwise, meet me here again in three day's time. Now go. We are not together. We simply happen to be at the same place at the same time, by chance."

Pitt swallowed. His mouth was dry. He wanted something cutting and final to say, but there was nothing in his mind except the knowledge of Voisey's corroding and irreversible hatred. He turned and walked away, back towards the stairs and upward into the vast cathedral, and the rest of the world.

AT HOME IN THE evening Pitt was grateful for the children's pleasure in seeing him at the dinner table. He welcomed their incessant questions, deliberately not meeting Charlotte's eyes when she turned to intervene and keep some sort of order.

"What are anarchists, Papa?" Daniel asked with his mouth full. "Mrs. Johnson says they are devils. Is that true?"

Charlotte started to admonish him to eat his vegetables, but Pitt interrupted.

"No. People are not devils," he said. "But they can do bad things, for all kinds of reasons. Anarchists don't believe in order. They think they would like no rules, no government."

"Why?"

Charlotte rolled her eyes, hiding a smile. She was not going to help.

Pitt was tempted to make a flippant reply, but he looked at Daniel's serious, rather worried expression and changed his mind. "They think it would be better if we all did whatever we liked."

Daniel waited.

"Do you remember when we went to Piccadilly in a hansom?" Charlotte said gently. "Do you remember one person's carriage wheel getting caught in someone else's and coming off, and everybody went in different directions to get around it, and ended by making it all worse?"

Daniel nodded, satisfaction close to laughter lighting his face.

"Well, that was what it would be like," Charlotte replied. "It was quite funny for a little while, but it wouldn't be if you were in a hurry, or you were very tired or cold, or not feeling well. If there are rules then we all get where we are going . . . eventually."

Daniel turned to his father. "Why would anybody want a mess? It's stupid!"

"Some people are stupid," Jemima ventured. "Dolly Jones is stupid. My cat has more sense."

"Cats are very practical," Charlotte agreed. "Finish your carrots and don't call people stupid."

"Cats don't eat carrots," Jemima tried her luck.

"No," Charlotte conceded. "Would you prefer a mouse?"

Jemima let out a howl of disgust, and ate the rest of her carrots in two mouthfuls.

Pitt was not alone with Charlotte until nearly nine o'clock. Then he could no longer evade the issue, not because he felt compelled to broach it but because she did.

"I visited Emily today," she said, ignoring her sewing folded up beside her on the small table next to her chair. Both children were upstairs, and Gracie had taken the rest of the evening off.

"How was she?" Pitt asked, both from courtesy and because he was genuinely fond of his sister-in-law, even if he was also exasperated by her at times.

"She is concerned," Charlotte replied.

Pitt was happy to talk about Emily's concern. Presumably it had something to do with her children, or some other domestic matter. It would save him from struggling with his guilt over not sharing his own feelings with Charlotte. He could not tell her that he was going to work with Voisey. Every time he was half an hour later home than she expected, she would be filled with fear, visions of violence and betrayal tearing through her mind. "What about?" he asked.

She looked at him very directly. "About the bill to arm the police," she replied. "She is afraid that men like Wetron, whom we know is the head of the Inner Circle, will get members of Parliament, like Tanqueray, who's a fool, to force the bill through. And then Wetron will end up with even more power. We don't know who is with him, and who is against. Perhaps Charles Voisey will come back into the Circle again, maybe even buy his way back by helping with the bill."

"No, he won't," he said immediately, then wished he had not been so emphatic. "At least . . ." he stopped. She was staring at him with her brows furrowed.

"How do you know that, Thomas?" It was not a challenge. She had seen that he did know, and she was asking him to explain it. Now he had either to tell the truth or take the vast step of deliberately lying to her.

"Thomas?" she asked. "How do you know that Voisey won't do that?"

She would be terrified for him if she knew what he was going to do.

"Wetron doesn't need him back in the Circle," he answered. That was true. "And he'd be a fool to trust him." There was a corroding irony in that! Was anyone a fool to trust Voisey?

"Would you trust him?" she asked. It was a blank question, honest.

"I would trust him to act in his own self-interest," he said. "To follow his chance for revenge, if you like." He was making it worse. Now he had backed himself into a corner where it was impossible to tell her that he was going to work with Voisey, and yet neither was he prepared to sacrifice as much of himself as he would have to in order to lie. He wanted to retreat into simply asking her not to pursue it. But that evasion would only make the fear worse.

"Voisey's involved in this, isn't he." She made it a statement, but there was a pleading in her face that he would deny it all the same.

"Of course he is," he admitted. "He'll do everything he can to thwart Wetron, and if he succeeds I shall be delighted. But if you are asking me if I know what he plans to do, then no, I don't."

"But he'll do something!" she insisted.

"I believe so. I'm expecting it."

She let out her breath in a sigh. "I see."

He wanted to lean forward and touch her, take her in his arms, but the awareness of his evasion kept him back.

He slid a little farther down in the seat, as if he were exhausted, and smiled at her. He meant it far more than she would ever know. "I'll be careful," he promised. "I haven't forgotten what he did, any more than you have, or Vespasia."

CHAPTER

FIVE

THE MORNING THAT Pitt went to St. Paul's to meet with Voisey, Charlotte telephoned Emily to say that she was coming, and the matter she wished to discuss was of some importance. Emily obligingly canceled her proposed errands to her milliner and her dressmaker, and was at home when Charlotte arrived.

She received her in her private sitting room with the big floral-patterned cushions. The embroidery frame stood with the basket of silks below the painting of Bamburgh Castle outlined against the sea.

Emily was wearing a morning dress of fine muslin in her favorite shade of pale green. It was actually last year's cut, but no one would have noticed it unless they were a devotee of the minutiae of fashion.

The years had been extremely kind to Emily. In her mid-thirties, she still had a slender figure—she had had only two children rather than the half dozen or so that many of her friends had had—and her skin had the alabaster delicacy of the naturally fair. She was not quite beautiful, but she had elegance and character. Best of all, she knew exactly what flattered her and what did not. She avoided the obvious, choosing the cool colors, the blues and greens of water, the grays and cold plums of shadow, for all important occasions. She would not have worn red even if freezing had been the only alternative.

When it came to fashion, Charlotte was limited by finances. There had been many occasions when, if she wished to move in society, she had been obliged to borrow clothing either from Emily, which was awkward because she was a couple of inches taller, or from great-aunt Vespasia.

"Charlotte!" Emily met her at the sitting room door, her face full of animation. She hugged her quickly, then stepped back. "What is it? Something has happened, or you would not be here at this hour. Is it one of Thomas's cases?" There was a note of urgency in her voice, almost of hope.

Charlotte remembered the time when the two of them had involved themselves in Pitt's investigations. These had usually been murders, driven by personal greed and hunger, or by fear of the exposure of some private sin. Together they had done things in the name of detection that now seemed outrageous, and yet she was not ashamed. They had uncovered truths and obtained at least some kind of justice, even if there had been tragedy as well. She also missed those times, even though much of what had made such exploits impossible now were Jack taking his career in Parliament too seriously for Emily to risk a wild indiscretion, and Pitt's move to secret and more dangerous work in Special Branch. Jack's move was good; Pitt's was unavoidable; and therefore it was foolish to grieve over either.

"In a sense it is related to Thomas's work," she answered the question. She followed Emily into the room and sat down. "It is to do with this anarchist bombing in Myrdle Street, where Magnus Landsborough was killed," she finished.

The light went out of Emily's face. "Oh, that's appalling! I mean it's awful for the destruction, of course, and Magnus Landsborough's death, although one wonders what on earth he was doing with such people! But there is a group in Parliament who are trying to bring in a bill to arm the police and make it possible to search people's homes at the drop of a hat. Jack is afraid it will undo years of goodwill, and far from helping the police, it will actually make their day-to-day work much harder." Her eyes were now deeply shadowed. "I'm not sure that it matters as much as he says, but nothing I can do persuades him not to fight against it."

Charlotte looked at Emily, sitting hunched forward on the elegant sofa. Her hands were stiff, her face tight with anxiety. For all the sunshine and the colors around them, the bowls of flowers and the scent of cut grass blowing in through the half-open window, there was fear in the room.

"You don't want him to?" Charlotte asked. Surely after all the wasted years of Jack's youth, Emily should be proud of him for taking up a battle, even relieved that he had such a sense of purpose. She had wanted it long enough, fought, cajoled, and persuaded him.

Emily's delicate mouth tightened impatiently. "It's an ugly battle, Charlotte!" she said tersely. "A lot of people care about it very much. They're frightened, and fear makes people dangerous. Tanqueray is nobody in particular, but he's only the spokesman. There are powerful interests behind him, and they are not going to have patience, or mercy, with anyone who tries to block them."

"Do you know who else is involved?" Charlotte asked, avoiding the subject of danger until she was certain her own anger would not show through.

"I could give you a dozen names!" Emily responded immediately. "Some of them are in very high office, and quite willing to ruin Jack, or anyone else who stands in their way. What does Thomas think? Does he want guns for the police? Jack said he wouldn't, but perhaps after the gun battle in Long Spoon Lane he might feel differently."

Charlotte bit her lip. She had not intended to confide her sense of exclusion to Emily, but she found it almost impossible to hold it secret any longer. She understood Emily's fear so very well. They should not be separate even in this.

"He doesn't," she said quietly, meeting Emily's eyes. "There is something troubling him far more than he is telling me, and I think it is not only a danger, but something that he is both sad and ashamed of, which is why he won't discuss it."

"Thomas?" Emily said in surprise. "Ashamed?"

"Not for himself," Charlotte corrected the error defensively. "For the police. He has mentioned corruption, but I think it is worse than he is saying. There's hardly anyone he can trust."

"Corruption!" Emily said sharply, the last vestige of ease vanishing from her face. "No wonder Jack hates the thought of them having guns. If he could show that, then—"

"No!" Charlotte put out her hand as if she could physically stop her. "Remember, Wetron is in charge in Bow Street. That could mean the whole of the Inner Circle might be involved, which could mean Parliament, or at least some of it."

The muscles in Emily's face tightened. "The Circle wanted Jack to become a member, you know? He refused." She swallowed. "Sometimes I wish he hadn't won a seat. Then he could have followed some other profession with an easy conscience, and been safe." She bit her lip, embarrassed at the confession.

"Do you? Is that who you want him to be?" Charlotte asked. Then she smiled, halfheartedly at her own weakness. "I wish that too, sometimes. If Thomas could have stayed in the police, just doing what somebody else told him to, as a constable, he wouldn't have had to make any decisions that other people might not have liked, and he wouldn't be in much danger. Poorer of course. And if Jack had stayed in a junior position, that wouldn't affect you, because of the money you inherited, but it would affect Jack. He'd hate it."

"I know. I know," Emily surrendered, lowering her eyes. "And what we would have liked doesn't matter anyway, it's what we have that we must deal with. There are some good people against the bill—Somerset Carlisle, of course. He would be." She named half a dozen other members of Parliament with wry, slightly disparaging comments. "And of course several of their prosperous constituents are crying out for peace in the streets and safety in the home, a return of the rule of law, and so on. They are saying the police are ineffectual because we don't give them the power or the weapons they need." She looked very steadily at Charlotte. "One of the most serious opponents of the bill, and best speaker against it, is Charles Voisey."

"Oh." Charlotte's mind raced. She remembered a dark night on Dartmoor, fleeing the rented cottage with Gracie and the children; Tellman helping them; then long evenings alone in Keppel Street because Pitt was in Whitechapel and she had no idea when he would be home, or even if he would be at all. He had had to live there in lodgings, walk the alleys in the failing gaslight and the shadows. It was all Voisey's doing, his guilt and his hatred. It made most perfect sense that he would fight this battle, even if only to thwart Wetron. "Not the ally I would have chosen," Charlotte said aloud, smiling ironically. "But perhaps better than none."

"I would rather look for others," Emily said curtly. "By the way, his sister, Mrs. Cavendish, is back in society, you know. There is even talk that she may marry again, and well. But that is by the way. I shall have to learn what more I can about the members. You know, sometimes I wish women did have the vote, then perhaps people would be obliged to listen to us with more attention."

"We can hardly afford to wait for that!" Charlotte retorted. "But by all means let us think whose aid we might enlist now."

They considered it for some time, making suggestions and adopting or abandoning them. Working together on a plan was something Charlotte had missed, and there was a warmth to it, in spite of the gravity of the subject. It was almost time for luncheon when they heard Jack's footsteps outside, and the moment later he stood in the doorway. He looked harassed, and surprised to see Charlotte.

Emily turned towards him, then stood up quickly. There was a solicitude in her manner that was not characteristic, and Charlotte knew her well enough to read her fear in it. She greeted Jack; he spoke to both of them, but he looked as if he had anxieties on his mind; and was disconcerted not to find Emily alone.

"We were talking of the Police Bill," Charlotte said, by way of explaining her presence. "Thomas is very unhappy about it."

"Yes, I know," Jack agreed as he sat down. "He saw me earlier this morning."

Emily stood in the middle of the room. The sunlight fell in bright patterns on the carpet and the polished wood in the wide margins around it. The perfume of the late tulips was heady in the warmth.

"We were trying to think who else might be helpful," Emily said. "We have a few ideas."

Jack frowned. "I would prefer you did not involve yourself," he told her. "I appreciate your help, but not this time." He saw her body stiffen, and the mixture of anger and unhappiness in her face. "It's going to be ugly," he tried to explain. "People are frightened. Edward Denoon has stirred up all kinds of specters of violence, as if we were all in danger of being bombed, just because the police don't know who these anarchists are."

"They'll find them!" Charlotte said a trifle more sharply than she had meant to. Jack's remark had sounded like a criticism of Pitt. "You can't expect to solve a murder in a couple of days."

Jack looked tired, even though it was barely midday. "No," he agreed wearily.

Emily was very pale. She looked at Jack almost as if she could no longer see Charlotte. "Then if you can't win, don't ruin your career trying," she said with a gulp. "That's pointless. Don't speak for it, but don't speak against it either. Leave it to Somerset Carlisle, and Charles Voisey. I won't go to anyone for help, I promise!"

He said nothing.

"Jack!" She took a step towards him. "Jack?"

Charlotte felt a shiver of surprise, and alarm. For the first time she realized how truly afraid Emily was, and she wondered how long she herself had lived with fear that Pitt would be hurt, either emotionally or physically. She could see the urgency in Emily, because she was unaccustomed to such turmoil within. Emily was used to being safe. And she could read very clearly the anger in Jack, the knowledge that he was forced into something that frightened him, and yet from which he could see no escape. There was going to be pain, and a clash of wills in which she should not intrude.

Charlotte rose to her feet. "Perhaps we should leave this after all." She smiled at Emily, who was too consumed in her confrontation with Jack to notice.

"Charlotte's right," Emily said firmly. "And perhaps it isn't so bad anyway. The police have to stop crime. We all want that."

"That isn't the issue," Jack replied. "It's how they do it. And anarchy isn't the only crime."

"Of course it isn't," Emily agreed. "Everyone says that robbery, burglary, and arson are increasing as well. And violence in the streets, not to mention prostitution, forgery, and anything else you care to think of."

"That isn't what I meant." He looked unhappy, as if the entire discussion were against his will. "I have to oppose the bill, Emily. It's wrong. It's . . ."

"No, you don't!" she said hotly. "You can't win anyway. Just leave it for someone else. Let Charles Voisey do it, if he wants to. Who cares what happens to him? Or Somerset Carlisle, if he's stupid enough." She took a step towards him, touching her hands lightly on the lapels of his jacket. The sunlight sparked fire in the diamonds on her ring. "Please, Jack! You are worth far more than ruining your career fighting a cause that's lost anyway." She drew in her breath to continue.

"That isn't all, Emily," he said hurriedly.

He took her hands gently and eased them away from him.

"What else is there?" Emily was angry. "The police have guns anyway. They must have, or they couldn't have had a battle in Long Spoon Lane! Let them have more, if they need them. If they stop too many people in the street or search their homes, then Parliament can reverse the bill."

"You can't just turn the tide of feeling because you want to," he replied.

Charlotte stepped closer to him. "Jack, you said that wasn't all. What else is there?"

"It's only suggested," he said, but his face was heavy with the weight of it. "It might not happen, but I have to fight it as if it will." He looked back at Emily. "I'm sorry," he apologized. "There's no choice. They want to include the right for police to question domestic servants without the knowledge or permission of anyone else in the house."

Emily was astounded. "Question them about what? Stolen goods? Guns? What, for heaven's sake?"

"No one will know, will they?" The old, easy smile played about his mouth for a moment, then it was gone. "That's exactly the point. Who was here, how much money was spent, where your coachman took you, who you spoke to, who you wrote letters to, who wrote to you? What did they say? Everything!"

Emily shook her head. "But why? Why could they possibly care?"

Charlotte saw the enormity of it. But she was more familiar with the work of police and she felt Pitt's fear of corruption. "That would be a charter for blackmail," she said softly, her stomach tightening. "If you ask the right questions, you could imply almost anything. We'd all live in terror of whispers, misunderstandings. It's a kind of irony! In the past servants have lived in fear of losing their good character if a master or mistress should speak ill of them. Now I can see a glimpse of what that would be like. We would live in fear of them. A wrong word to the police, and we'd be the ones to lose our character. But surely such a bill couldn't pass, could it?"

Jack turned to face her, his eyes shadowed. "I don't know. Think of the power. All it needs is one dishonest policeman, even one who is indiscreet, one who wants a favor or thinks himself insulted. The possibilities are endless. It will begin as a law used only where anarchy or treason is suspected, then it will be used for robberies, suspected embezzlement, or conspiracy to commit fraud, or to blackmail the blackmailers. The police will have power to do almost anything, because everyone will be vulnerable."

"But we don't have anything to—" Emily began.

"Hide?" he asked, eyebrows raised. "Who says it will have to be about the truth? What about a disgruntled servant, one caught stealing, a lazy or impertinent one, one who drinks or gambles or keeps a mistress, or simply wants more money or more power?" His voice sharpened. "Or one who is simply frightened, or in love, or easily led? Or one who is related to someone in trouble, or—"

"All right!" Emily shouted. "I see! I see! It's monstrous. No Parliament in its right mind will pass such a law."

"Emily, it won't be phrased that way!" he said exasperatedly. "It will sound like a very reasonable right for police to question servants in private. The master or mistress won't know, in order to protect the servant in question from pressure to lie in order to keep his position."

"Can't they do that now?" Charlotte asked, puzzled.

"Of course they can question servants, or anyone else," he responded. "But not secretly. This could be living eyes and ears in your house, at your dining table, your kitchen, in your bedroom! It's the excuse to do it in the name of protecting everyone from anarchy that's the difference. They don't need to show any reason for it. Now you have to suspect someone of a particular crime, and question them openly. This would be secret, and without any reason shown. It would begin softly, and grow without our ever realizing it."

Emily lowered her eyes. "I see. I suppose you have to fight." There was resignation in her voice, acceptance.

"When did you hear of this?" Charlotte asked him.

"Just now. After Thomas left to . . . to go back to Special

Branch, I suppose. I'll tell him. He'll have to know. I'm sorry. I didn't want to burden you with it, either of you." He turned to Emily, his face creased with regret, his eyes gentle. "You see why I have to do it, whatever it costs? If I'd never known about it I could back out, but I do know."

"Who told you?" Emily asked.

"Voisey. But it's true. I've seen the draft."

"Voisey?" Emily said with fury.

He put both his hands on her shoulders, holding her tightly, but without hurting her, unless she fought him. "It's true. I'll take it to the top, to the prime minister if need be, before I react, and I'll be the happiest man in Westminster if it proves to be a lie, but it won't. The police have asked for it. They say Special Branch is incompetent to stop the anarchist violence and the rising crime." He gave a little shiver. "In order to protect the people, they have to have the power to use if they need it. It's a tiny thing, and they say they hardly ever will use it, but the point is that once they have the power we can't stop them, and we know that the very nature of power is that it corrupts, and we have built in no way to stop it."

Emily looked across at Charlotte, then back at Jack. "All right," she conceded. "But I'm still frightened."

"So am I," he said softly, moving his hand from her shoulder to touch her cheek. "So am I."

CHARLOTTE GAINED JACK'S permission to tell Vespasia what he had said. After luncheon she declined Emily's offer of the use of her carriage, and set out in the spring sunshine to walk the mile and a half or so to Vespasia's house. It gave her the opportunity to calm her racing mind and compose her thoughts into something sensible. The wind was fresh and warm, rustling the leaves as the trees shivered, dappling the shade. Open carriages passed her with women showing off the latest fashions, extravagant hats, quite small in themselves, but decorated with feathers and huge satin bows and frills. She barely noticed any of it.

She arrived just as Vespasia was dressed in lilac gray silk, about to leave on her afternoon calls, but looking at Charlotte's anxiety and disappointment, she canceled her arrangements.

"What has happened?" she asked bluntly as soon as they were seated. The quiet room overlooked the lawn and the roses; only the yellow climber that bloomed first was showing a touch of color in the flower bed.

"I have been talking to Emily about this bill to arm the police and give them greater powers," Charlotte replied. "Jack returned home from Westminster and told us of a new dimension to it that is far worse than anything I knew of before, and that was bad enough." She did not mince words with Vespasia. It would not only be unnecessary, it would be insulting. They knew and understood each other better than that. "It seems feeling is running high, and likely to get higher if there is any more crime reported beyond the usual."

"We may rely upon that," Vespasia said grimly. "But we too have resources. I imagine Jack will be firmly on our side. That young man is finding his feet rather well. And Somerset Carlisle we may rely upon also. He has always been a fighter against injustice of any sort, regardless of cost to himself."

Charlotte saw a shadow cross Vespasia's face. She waited. To ask its cause would be an intrusion.

"In times past I would have been certain that Lord Landsborough would have lent all his weight to oppose it," Vespasia went on, her voice quiet and sad. "And his influence would have been sufficient to sway two or three government ministers. But since it was his only son who was killed, he may have different feelings now, or at the very least feel like abstaining from the fight." She frowned.

"But you said there was something worse than you had thought. Has something new occurred?"

"Yes. It has not happened yet, but Jack has heard word of it, and he is deeply afraid." Charlotte could hear the fear in her own voice, sharp and rough-edged. "They plan to add a provision for police to be able to question any household servants, without the knowledge or permission of the master or mistress."

Vespasia froze. "Question them about what?"

"Anything. Seems it is to be done in secret, no one will ever know." Charlotte stared at her, watching the realization flood her face and the enormity of it as she understood what it could mean.

"Surely they cannot pass it?" Vespasia let out her breath slowly. "It would be a charter for blackmail. It would . . ." She did not bother to finish her sentence. "I suppose it is driven by fear, without thinking ahead to what it will become." She looked suddenly tired. "Sometimes I despair of how stupid people can be. Ask anyone who has dealt with servants; they are people like anyone else—good, bad, and indifferent. They have their passions and rivalries, greeds and ambitions, as we all do. And they can be manipulated, or at times do the manipulating. Some will say whatever you want, just to please you. Some will take any chance for attention, or to put down a rival."

"Perhaps the members' wives will persuade them not to be so idiotic?" Charlotte said, without any hope at all. "Isn't it strange what people will do if they are frightened? But I believe we have one ally."

"Who?"

Charlotte felt a chill in the sunlit room as she said it. "Charles Voisey."

Vespasia was motionless, her chin high, her eyes far away. "I see. And is that for love of liberty, I wonder, or hatred of the police, as represented by Superintendent Wetron?"

"Hatred," Charlotte replied immediately. "But it's not his hatred of Wetron that frightens me," she elaborated. "It is the fact that Thomas is involved in the issue, on the same side. He has said very little to me. In fact, he is being evasive, which is not like him at all. I did not press him because I could see that he was most uncomfortable. I might have forced him into a position where he had either to tell me something he didn't wish to, or else say something that was not true."

She needed to explain it to Vespasia, as if to herself. "He could even have had to break confidence, or else lie to me. And I don't want either of those. If he were to lie, it would open up a gulf between us we might never entirely bridge again. We should both remember it." She watched Vespasia's face to see if she understood. "So I let it go. But I know Voisey is involved. Thomas admitted that much, and I am afraid of what he will do. I don't know if Thomas even believes anyone could be as consumed by hate as Voisey is."

Vespasia nodded slowly.

"I know people like Voisey," Charlotte went on. "Thomas doesn't. He thinks gentlemen with a certain background also have certain qualities, acts to which they will not descend. That's not true." She looked desperately at Vespasia's steady eyes. "Thomas will almost always give people a second chance. He doesn't hate— not implacably, like the hatred I saw in Voisey's eyes when the Queen knighted him. He'd lose the world to be revenged on us for that."

Vespasia let out a soft sigh. "And I assume you have no idea what Thomas intends to do that might involve Voisey?"

"No."

"Then we need to find some ammunition that we could use against Voisey, should we need it. We do not know enough about him. We might do well to recall the story of David and Goliath . . ."

"Is he really a Goliath?" Charlotte asked miserably. "I know the Davids win in the Bible, but they very often lose in life. I suppose if they didn't there would be no point in the story." She smiled a trifle lopsidedly. "I am sure enough that our cause is God's cause, but I don't have such faith in our absolute righteousness that I want to go out in front of the entire Philistine army with nothing but a slingshot and a couple of stones. I lack faith, don't I? Or am I simply more modest, and realistic?" She was joking to cover the sharp, aching fear for Pitt that gnawed inside.

"I have no intention of facing Goliath alone," Vespasia replied with some asperity. "I was referring to the fact that he was clad in impenetrable armor, which, however, left his temples uncovered— a small but highly vulnerable spot to someone with an accurate aim. Where is Charles Voisey's vulnerable spot? We need to aim."

"I don't know!" Charlotte gulped and took a shaky breath. "I'm sorry, I think my fear is running away with me. Thomas is so upset that there is police corruption. At least some of it is in Bow Street, where he used to be. I hate to see him hurt like this."

Vespasia sighed. "I suppose with Wetron in charge, corruption was a great likelihood. I take it you are quite certain?"

"No, but it is an educated guess," Charlotte replied, thinking back to the evening before. "Tellman is courting Gracie . . ."

Vespasia smiled with sudden, genuine pleasure. "My dear, I am quite aware of that. You are going to miss her greatly."

"I am. I don't know what life will be like without Gracie's comments on it. I loathe the thought of having someone else in my house. And Daniel and Jemima will be devastated. But I know it must happen."

"What has it to do with corruption in Bow Street?"

"Two evenings in a row now Tellman has canceled his engagement to take her out," Charlotte replied. "That means he must be doing something of intense importance. He would not do it for less. He didn't explain to her, so we both assumed it was something for Thomas, and at the moment it can only be to do with anarchy, and corruption."

"I agree. It seems inescapable." Vespasia nodded. "The more urgently we need to find Voisey's weakness. There must be something he cares about that can be gained or lost, some passion or need. Thomas may feel himself bound by his own code of honor—"

"He does."

"Of course. And we both love him the more for it," Vespasia said unhesitatingly. "But whether we are required to use it or not, we must find a means of protecting him. What does Voisey wish to gain from this, do you suppose? Is it as simple as vengeance upon Wetron?"

Charlotte was about to say that it was, then she thought a little more deeply. "I don't know. Perhaps he intends somehow to use Thomas to destroy Wetron, and then replace him? We need a weapon, don't we! The trouble is, if I have a weapon, I am afraid I might use it." She stared intently at Vespasia, searching her eyes, trying desperately to see in them some comforting answer that would ease away the fear inside her.

"Of course you would," Vespasia replied unhesitatingly. "Any woman would if those she loves are in danger. Threaten a woman's husband or her child, and she will fight to the death, and only think of the cost afterwards, when it is all too late to undo. But even then, I doubt she will regret it. But we still need a weapon, for all that. Sometimes the knowledge of it is sufficient."

"Is it?" Charlotte said doubtfully. "Or would he call my bluff?"

"Bluff?" Vespasia said gently.

Charlotte chose to change the subject. "I am sorry for interrupting your afternoon. I hope I have not inconvenienced you a great deal, but I am so grateful you gave me the time. There is absolutely no one else I could have told."

Vespasia smiled. There was pleasure in her eyes. "I had no errands of importance," she dismissed the subject. "Please consider what you do regarding Voisey. Since he and Jack are in agreement about Tanqueray's bill, you have every excuse to take an interest in him. But do not for an instant imagine that he is foolish, or assume that he will necessarily underestimate you." Vespasia rose to her feet. "I am going to look much more deeply into the whole subject of anarchy, and why on earth a young man like Magnus Landsborough should be prepared to give up a very agreeable life in order to pursue it."

Charlotte rose also. "Thank you," she said softly. "I really am very grateful."

"FOR HEAVEN'S SAKE, don't say anything," Emily urged late in the afternoon as she and Charlotte took their seats in the Strangers' Gallery in the House of Commons. The debate was about to begin in which Tanqueray's bill would be discussed. Around them was the rustle of silks and repositioning by ladies to either side of them—wishing to see over the rail, all dressed in the extravagant height of fashion. Emily leaned forward. "There he is," she whispered eagerly.

Charlotte followed her gaze, but could not see Jack, whose handsome head would have been easily distinguishable. "Where?" she asked.

"Halfway along, just behind the front bench," Emily replied. "Sort of reddish-brown, like a rather faded fox."

"What?"

"Voisey, Charlotte! Not Jack," she hissed.

"Oh, yes. Which is Tanqueray?"

"I don't know. He's about forty-five, apparently, but I know nothing of his appearance."

They were only just in time. The Speaker in his wig and robes called for order. The Home Secretary mentioned the subject of anarchists and general violence in the East End, and that the government had given it careful consideration and would formulate its plans accordingly.

There were boos and hisses of contempt from Her Majesty's Loyal Opposition. A few moments of general insults and applause ensued, then a man with a soft, blunt face rose to his feet. The lights shone in his thick hair, which was winged with white at the temples. The Speaker recognized him as the honorable member for Newcastle-under-Lyme.

"That's Tanqueray," Emily whispered to Charlotte. "I recognize his constituency."

Tanqueray began by expressing the grief of the House in general for the fear and loss of property of the people in Myrdle Street, and then elaborated to include the whole of the East End. He then spoke of the implied possibility of anarchism progressing to the rest of London.

"Gentlemen, we must address this threat now!" he said fervently. All in the House waited with baited breath. Tanqueray outlined the measures he had in mind to make guns available to every police station. He further proposed that the law itself be changed to give police on patrol the right to stop whoever they wished and to search their persons or their homes or premises of business.

The floor of the House erupted in cries of approval, a ripple of applause and shouts of "Hear, hear!" Even the Opposition voiced no serious argument.

Charlotte stiffened, waiting for the added measure about questioning servants. She glanced momentarily at Emily beside her and Emily gave her a tiny, bleak smile.

In front of them a large woman in bombazine clutched the hand of the younger woman next to her. "There you are, my dear," she whispered fiercely. "I knew we should be protected."

Tanqueray detailed his plan, with many stories of the hardship suffered by ordinary people because of robbery, arson, and the threats of violence. Each one was greeted with murmurs of sympathy and outrage. "We must do all we can!" he finished. "It is our duty to the country to exercise every power and discretion we have. And I pledge that I will never rest until we have given our police every assistance possible, and every protection in the fulfillment of their task to keep us safe."

The moment he resumed his seat amid a tumult of applause,

Jack Radley demanded to be heard, and was backed vigorously by his own leader.

Emily smiled, but she drew in her breath. Charlotte saw her hands clench, pulling the fabric of her gloves tight across her knuckles.

"My honorable friend refers to the hardships of ordinary people," Jack began. "He quite rightly says that they must be protected in the pursuit of their business and their lives. Their homes and families must be safe. That is the prime duty of the police."

There were murmurs of approval. Tanqueray looked pleased with himself.

Voisey's face darkened.

"I believe this will not be served by refusing to give them the same rights of dignity and privacy that we ourselves wish to enjoy," Jack continued.

There was a stunned silence. People turned to each other in puzzlement. What did he mean?

"Is there any man here who is happy to have policemen searching his home?" Jack asked, gazing around at the members. "Reading his letters, looking through his belongings? Perhaps his personal clothes and effects, his bedroom, his study? Even his wife's gowns and petticoats and gloves, because that policeman might think you have hidden something among them that might be contrary to the law?"

There were murmurings of alarm rising to anger. Members turned to each other, looking for support, and to assess if there could possibly be agreement for such deeply offensive ideas.

Emily closed her eyes and gave a groan. Her shoulders were locked, hunched forward. Her hands gripped each other in her lap.

Charlotte could see that she was afraid. She knew how much of both social and political success were dependent upon patronage. Jack was on the brink of the promotion he had worked so hard to achieve, and here he was as if bound and determined to make enemies.

"If they can do this," Jack continued with dreadful clarity, as if determined now to seal his own fate. "What else may they do purely in the pursuit of curiosity? Might they read your wine merchant's bill? The letter from your tailor, your banker, your father-in-law . . . heaven forgive us, your mistress?"

There was a splutter of laughter, but it was a slightly hysterical sound, utterly without joy.

"And what will the servants make of it?" Jack asked, shrugging his shoulders deliberately.

Emily sat rigid, craning as far forward as she could.

"Police in the house, searching everyone's things will offer the cook the chance she has always been looking for to give notice!" It was a very real threat. No one with a good cook wanted to lose her. Their social success or failure too often depended upon it.

Charlotte gave silent applause in her mind. To have reminded people of their creature comforts and their popularity in one stroke was masterly.

Jack continued as soon as the mutterings died down sufficiently. He did not mention the issue of servants again. Instead he argued that the success of the police, who were drawn largely from precisely the class of people most likely to be stopped or searched, depended upon the support of the community. He gave moving examples, and ended by stating that he thought Tanqueray's bill was excessive and misjudged.

Two members argued in support of it, pouring into their speeches both emotion and logic.

Then Voisey rose. The rustles died away to silence. The woman in black beside Charlotte murmured something in approval. Charlotte had no idea whether the woman knew what Voisey was going to say, or not.

He began by praising Jack's words and his courage in saying them, at possible cost to himself. He was a man of principle not expediency. At this point Emily shot a rueful glance sideways. Charlotte met her eyes, then looked back at Voisey. No matter what he said, she must never forget that he was the enemy. She must study him until she found his vulnerability, personal or professional: a dream, a hope, a mistake, anything at all.

Voisey continued, not by adding to the weight of evidence but by questioning the wisdom of giving guns to men who habitually dealt with violent elements of society. Might that not end in more weapons falling into the hands of criminals, particularly anarchists? Might it not end with warfare on the streets, and a number of innocent members of the public finding themselves hostages, victims, the eventual losers in such battles. It would damage business, and ultimately cost votes. The argument was aimed at their least noble interests. Charlotte despised it. But it was clever! No one booed or hissed. It was greeted by troubled silence.

Charlotte and Emily remained where they were until the first convenient opportunity to leave. Then they excused themselves and made their way down to the main halls and outside.

"He is going to sacrifice his career for nothing!" Emily said furiously. She was referring to Jack, of course.

"You mean we should do the right thing only if it comes at no cost?" Charlotte said incredulously, barely even attempting to keep the horror out of her voice.

Emily glared at her. "Don't be so stupid!" she snapped. "I'm saying there is no sense in making a sacrifice you don't have to! It is far more practical to keep your shot and use it when you can do some good." She was walking so briskly that Charlotte had trouble keeping up. "Politics is not about making grand gestures, it is about winning!" Emily went on, her smart black-and-white skirts all but tripping her up. "You represent other people—and they did not elect you to play the hero strutting about with grand and pointless gestures, soothing your own conscience. They elected you to get things changed, not gallop at the enemy's guns like the Charge of the Light Brigade!"

"I thought they elected you to represent their views," Charlotte replied, ignoring the military simile.

"Represent them to some purpose, not to do it ineffectively. Any fool could do that!" Emily walked even more rapidly and Charlotte had to increase her pace yet again to keep up with her. Her skirts swung wildly and she nearly bumped into a young man going in the opposite direction.

"I'm sorry," she apologized.

"I suppose I can't expect you to understand," Emily responded. "You've never been in that position."

"I wasn't apologizing to you!" Charlotte said furiously. "I walked into someone!"

"Then you should look where you are going!"

"Do you think you are the only one whose husband ever places himself in danger in order to do what he thinks is right?" she demanded. "How incredibly self-centered you are!"

Emily stopped so abruptly that two men behind them nearly overbalanced. Only with great skill did they avoid colliding with them.

"That's not fair!" she protested, ignoring the men.

"It's perfectly fair," Charlotte responded. "I'm sorry," she apologized to the men. "She's very overwrought." She turned back to Emily. "And if you are honest with yourself, not to mention with me, you would not wish it otherwise. Were he to avoid the issue you would have no time for him at all. You might love him, but you would also despise him. And that kind of love does not last very long."

Emily looked appalled. In an instant her fury had evaporated.

"Charlotte, I'm sorry!" she said with total contrition. "I'm just terrified he is going to get into terrible trouble, and won't know how to get out of it. And I don't know what to do to help!"

Charlotte knew exactly what Emily was feeling—the helplessness, the anger because it was unfair—but she should have expected it. She knew perfectly well how society worked, and if she thought about it, so did Jack. He had chosen his path because he wanted it—just as Pitt had done so many times.

"You can't help, except by believing in him," Charlotte said gently, wanting now only to help. "Don't let him doubt himself, and above all don't let him think you have no confidence in him, even if you are so frightened you could be sick."

"Is that what you're going to do?" Emily asked.

"More or less. No, less," Charlotte admitted. "I'm going to learn what I can about Charles Voisey, beginning right this moment. He must have some vulnerability, and I intend to find it. I shall report to you." She gave a little smile, then turned and walked away.

She had intended to watch Voisey, possibly even to speak with him. As it was, he spoke to her.

"Good afternoon, Mrs. Pitt."

She swung around to find him standing a couple of yards behind her.

"Good afternoon, Sir Charles." She caught her breath and had to clear her throat. She was annoyed with herself for being caught off-balance. "That was a very powerful speech you made."

His eyes widened so very slightly she was not sure if she imagined it. "You are interested in the issue of arming the police, Mrs. Pitt? Your husband is in Special Branch now. Surely he can carry a gun any time he believes the occasion warrants it?" His voice dropped a little. "As in the siege in Long Spoon Lane. You must be very relieved he was not hurt. Unpleasant affair." His eyes were hard, acutely self-aware. The hatred flared for an instant, and he knew he had not hidden it.

"Indeed," she said, her voice very nearly level. "But it is the job of Special Branch to deal with unpleasant matters, and therefore very often also with unpleasant people." She forced herself to smile at him, not because she imagined he might believe she meant it, but to show him that she was more in command of herself than he was. "I am so glad that you believe it is unwise, and unnecessary, to give the police more weapons or greater powers to search people without showing a proper cause for it. You are absolutely right in your conviction that the cooperation of ordinary people is the best help of all. That would serve everyone's interests."

He was studying her to read in her face if she had a deeper meaning or not. He was uncertain whether Pitt would confide in her, and for an instant she saw it in him.

"Not everyone's, Mrs. Pitt," he said quietly. "Yours and mine, perhaps. But there are others whose ambitions are different."

"I am sure there are," she agreed, then hesitated, not sure whether to let him know how far she understood.

He saw it, and smiled back at her. "Good afternoon, Mrs. Pitt. An unexpected pleasure to have seen you." He excused himself and walked away briskly, leaving her with a strange feeling of being at a disadvantage, and the memory of the instant's naked hate burned into her mind.

VESPASIA RACKED HER BRAINS for an acceptable excuse to call upon Cordelia Landsborough again. They had never liked each other, and no one of the least sensitivity visited the newly bereaved unless they were invited. There was only one issue that could offer acceptable pretext, and that was Cordelia's desire to be pivotal in seeing that Tanqueray's bill was passed.

The carriage was passing through quiet, residential streets. Elegant Georgian-fronted houses faced onto trees new with leaf. There were few pedestrians, mostly women, their skirts ruffled by the breeze, parasols up against the sun.

Vespasia thought of Charlotte and the fear she had heard in her voice when she spoke of having a weapon to use should Voisey threaten Pitt. It was not being hurt that frightened her, it was her own power to injure, and the knowledge that she would use it.

And then the idea was there in Vespasia's mind. By the time she reached the Landsborough house and alighted, she knew exactly what she was going to say, should Cordelia receive her. Indeed, she was prepared to make it difficult to be refused.

In the event, she was ushered through the somber hall and into the withdrawing room immediately. She found Cordelia standing by the window, looking out onto the lawn and the early summer flowers.

"How kind of you to come again so soon," Cordelia said, without any waspishness in her voice, or in her pale, exhausted face.

For an instant Vespasia was sorry for her. Her harsh good looks showed grief more dramatically than softer, more feminine features would have. There were shadows under and around her eyes, deep lines cut from nose to mouth, and her lips looked bloodless. She had never resorted to paint; her brows were naturally black, and now they looked like gashes above her hollow eyes.

"It may appear intrusive," Vespasia said gently. "I hope it is not. I have been turning over and over in my mind the issue of anarchist violence, and the terror it must inspire in all manner of people. It is something against which we have to fight, and I admire your courage and selflessness in doing so at such a time of personal loss." Oddly, that was true. Much as she had always disliked Cordelia, and thought her at times both cruel and self-indulgent, at this moment it was her strength that was uppermost in Vespasia's thoughts.

Perhaps Cordelia heard an honesty in her. "Thank you," she acknowledged it. "I appreciate that you do not mistake my composure for indifference to my son's death."

"Of course not! The thought is absurd and offensive," Vespasia said with heat. "One weeps alone, not before the world. I came because in my consideration of precisely what we should do to battle such things, some of the dangers occurred to me, and I know that we cannot afford to wait until circumstances are more comfortable. We have enemies, not personal but of the cause. They will strike while we are perceived to be at our most vulnerable."

Cordelia turned to look at her, her expression curious, aware of intense irony. But she chose to concentrate on subjects Vespasia had raised. "Enemies in Parliament?" she asked.

"We are bound to have, for many reasons," Vespasia enlarged on the subject. "Some will sincerely believe that to give police more power is unwise, others will have their own sympathies and ambitions. And I fear, of course, there will always be those who pursue personal enmities wherever they lead. We cannot afford to be ambushed by any of them."

"Ambushed?" Cordelia repeated the word uncertainly. "I assume from the fact that you are here, sword in hand, so to speak, that you have a plan for our defense?"

"I think so. But not without your assistance," Vespasia answered. They stood side by side before the window, their skirts touching. She had come for information. "I am certain you know far more than I do, but apart from that, we must work together."

Cordelia hesitated. Such an idea was revolutionary, given their past relationship with each other. She was not going to be easily beguiled.

Vespasia waited. She must not defend herself too quickly or she would give away her own vulnerability. Pity should not blind her to the reality of Cordelia's nature, however deep or genuinely she might feel it. She smiled very faintly. "At least in this," she conceded.

Cordelia relaxed. "Would you care for tea?"

"Thank you," Vespasia accepted. "That would be most pleasant."

Cordelia reached for the bell.

After the instructions were given, they both sat down, settling their skirts with almost identical movements, and Vespasia began in earnest. She had made the alliance, now she must justify it.

"Those who are against us will attack our motives," she began. "We must be certain we have the most acceptable and logical reasons, and that we give only those. Too much explanation looks like excuse."

Cordelia did not look impressed.

"They will not be able to criticize you, or Mr. Denoon," Vespasia made an intense effort to keep the impatience out of her voice. "And possibly not Mr. Tanqueray, although I do not know enough about him to be certain. But what of our other allies? It is an obvious tactic to fire at the most vulnerable and pick off the supporters one by one."

A sudden flame of intelligence lit Cordelia's face. "Yes, of course it is," she acceded. "And it works in reverse also. We would be well advised to learn who will stand against us."

Vespasia controlled her eyes, her voice, the hands lying loosely in her lap. She was playing a dangerous game, and she was well aware of it. "Precisely," she agreed. "Somerset Carlisle will be one of them. He is eccentric, but he is well liked. Others have tried to defame him, and met with little success. There is also Jack Radley, I believe. He has a distant connection to my family, but he is very minor in Parliament. I do not believe attacking him will be perceived as anything but a desperate action, and we do not wish to appear either spiteful or driven to a last resort."

"They seem negligible so far," Cordelia agreed. "Is there anyone about whom we should concern ourselves?" There was mild amusement in her eyes, but she was listening. She knew Vespasia would not have come without a purpose.

"Sir Charles Voisey," Vespasia answered, hoping to heaven she was wise in drawing him to Cordelia's attention. "He has far more influence than it might appear."

Cordelia's black brows rose questioningly. "Really? I had not heard of him until that extraordinary business to do with the republicans, and his shooting that Italian and apparently saving the Queen. I never know how much of that sort of thing to believe."

Vespasia felt her heart lurch, and the sharpness of loss as if it had been yesterday. The Italian that Cordelia referred to so condescendingly having been the greatest love in Vespasia's life.

Vespasia looked down at the hands in her lap. She could not afford to have Cordelia meet her eyes. "Voisey has associations," she replied quietly. "Friends and enemies in many places. Men contract obligations you know, and acquire certain pieces of knowledge."

"You mean—" Cordelia began.

She was prevented from completing the sentence by the arrival of the parlor maid, who announced the arrival of Mr. and Mrs. Denoon. Should she ask them to wait in the morning room, or show them in here?

Cordelia had no choice but to welcome them. She masked her appearance that her conversation was thus interrupted, and told the maid to show them in.

Enid was naturally in black also, but she had relieved it a trifle at the throat with a cameo brooch of extraordinary beauty, and her fair hair gave her a delicacy, almost a sense of life, that Cordelia lacked. She greeted Vespasia with interest little short of amazement.

Denoon himself looked grim. He was civil, but did not pretend to be pleased to see a relative stranger at what he had apparently assumed would be a family occasion.

Cordelia lost no time in explaining Vespasia's presence. She did not prevaricate or concede to niceties once the customary greetings had been exchanged. "Lady Vespasia has our concerns very much at heart," she said bluntly. "She has just warned me of the importance of guarding not only ourselves from political attack, but our allies as well."

"Considerate of you, Lady Vespasia," Denoon said coldly, condescension clear in his face. "But quite unnecessary. I am more than aware of such currents. One can hardly run a newspaper if one is utterly naive."

Cordelia's temper flared, perhaps because she wanted Vespasia's help and he had been undisguisedly rude to her. "If you were aware of Sir Charles Voisey's secret associations, it would have been more fortunate if you had thought to inform me," she said icily.

Denoon stiffened. "Voisey?"

Vespasia looked at him, watching the muscles in his neck, the slight alteration in the way he stood. In that instant she felt certain that not only was he allied with Wetron with full intent, but that he was also a member of the Inner Circle, and acutely aware of all that Voisey had been, before it had been torn apart. It was what she had come to learn.

"Yes," she said smoothly, her face almost expressionless. "Apparently he does not support the bill, and will make his feelings known with some force."

"How do you know this?" he challenged her.

She raised her eyebrows delicately. "I beg your pardon?"

"How do you . . ." he stopped.

It was Enid who spoke. "Is he an apologist for anarchy?" she inquired, then sneezed fiercely. "I'm sorry." She fished in her reticule for a handkerchief. Her clear, pale eyes were beginning to water.

As a matter of courtesy Vespasia effected not to notice. "I don't think so," she answered the question. "It would be an impossible position to maintain. I imagine he will say that the police already have all the weapons they need, and that information about subversive groups would be of far more value than the power to search people at random. The police are unlikely to obtain assistance from ordinary people if they are seen as oppressive, and prone to abuse their power."

Enid sneezed again. She seemed to be rapidly developing a cold in the head. Her eyelids were pink.

"A futile argument," Denoon dismissed it irritably. "If they had the powers necessary to obtain such information, as you suggest, they would have prevented the bomb in Myrdle Street. That seems to be self-evident."

Vespasia hesitated. If she pointed out that guns and searches would not have discovered Magnus Landsborough's part in it, it would be needlessly cruel, and could make her seem to be defending Voisey. It was an emotional game she was playing, as well as one of facts.

"I am not defending Sir Charles, or his point of view, Mr. Denoon," she said gently, with the tiniest touch of condescension. "I am concerned that we do not allow him to seem reasonable in Parliament, or in whatever newspapers that may choose to publish his opinions. I came merely to make you aware that he is likely to be a vigorous opponent of Mr. Tanqueray's bill."

Denoon let out his breath silently. "Yes, of course," he said more calmly. "Are you aware of the nature of his interest in the subject? Is it personal, or political?" He was watching her more closely than he pretended to be.

Enid sneezed again, and stood up from where she had been sitting on the large sofa. Her eyelids looked puffy.

Vespasia lifted her shoulders. The gesture was elegant, perfectly casual. "I have no idea," she lied.

Cordelia was impatient. "The two are probably the same," she said briskly. "He is an ambitious man. That much is obvious." She looked at Enid. "You had better sit in the other chair," she said without sympathy. "Edward, would you be so good as to open the window." It was an order, as to a servant, given without thought that he might not obey.

He frowned at her, not moving from where he stood.

"Enid is choking on the cat hair!" Cordelia snapped. "You know she is allergic to cats! For heaven's sake, Sheridan is just as bad. The wretched creature is supposed to remain in the servants' quarters, but obviously it got in here somehow. I shooed it out this morning, but it has left hair behind."

Denoon went reluctantly to the window and opened it unnecessarily wide, letting in the cool air and the smell of damp, mown grass.

"Thank you," Enid said, and sneezed again. "I apologize," she turned to Vespasia. "I like cats—they are very useful creatures—but we can't keep one. Both Piers and I are sensitive to them. All our family is, Sheridan as well." This last remark was directed at Cordelia.

"That is why it is restricted to the servants' quarters," Cordelia pointed out. "He never goes in there."

"Where is he anyway?" Denoon asked. "Is he expected home this afternoon? We could greatly use his assistance in the cause. He could speak more powerfully than anyone else. His weight behind the campaign would be superb. If he changes his mind from the liberal position he used to take, that would move more people than anything else I can think of."

"Of course he's going to be here," Cordelia replied. "He's late!" There was both anger and contempt in her face.

"I think we should continue our plans without him," Denoon said. "Inform him when he comes."

Vespasia turned slightly and caught a look of intense hatred on Enid's face as she stared at her husband. It was so virulent that it stunned her. Then an instant later it was ironed away, and Vespasia wondered if it had been her imagination or a trick of the shifting summer light through the window.

There were footsteps in the hall, voices. The door to the withdrawing room opened and Sheridan Landsborough came in. He glanced around the group and acknowledged them all—Vespasia with surprise and pleasure—but he did not apologize for being late. It was as if he were unaware that he had been expected. His face was pale, shadowed with grief, and there was no vitality in his eyes.

Enid looked at him with profound gentleness, as if she were aching with almost physical pain to reach out to him, but there was no comfort to give. His loss was untouchable, and she understood that.

There was no similar warmth in Cordelia. As happened so often, bereavement seemed to have driven them apart rather than brought them closer. Each nursed their pain in different ways: she was angry; he withdrew, holding himself even farther apart than before.

Denoon behaved as if he were not emotionally involved. "We

are discussing our best action to promote this bill of Tanqueray's," he said to Landsborough. "Lady Vespasia seems to think Charles Voisey is going to prove an adversary worthy of being taken seriously."

Landsborough regarded him with little interest. "Really?"

"For goodness sake, Sheridan!" Cordelia said fiercely. "We must give all the assistance we can now, while the atrocity is at the forefront of everyone's minds. It will not wait upon our bereavement."

"Quite," Denoon agreed, still looking at Landsborough. "You must know Voisey. What are his weaknesses? Where is he vulnerable. Lady Vespasia seems to think he is likely to be a nuisance. Can't see why, myself."

"He is likely to argue against the bill," Landsborough answered mildly. He remained standing, almost as if he wished to be able to leave at any moment. "From what I have heard, he believes reform will come about more effectively if done in a moderate manner, but that it is necessary in time, if we are to maintain a peaceful society."

"He's an opportunist," Denoon replied coldly. "You think too well of people, Sheridan. You are unrealistic."

Vespasia was furious. "You see that as an idealized view of Sir Charles's behavior?" she asked with chill.

"I think his protestations of drafting peaceful reform are self-serving," Denoon replied, his tone of voice suggesting that it should have been obvious, even to her.

"Of course it is self-serving," she retorted. "That is not the question. All that matters to us is what he will argue, not what he believes."

Denoon flushed a dull red.

"I had forgotten how frank you are, Vespasia," Cordelia observed with something close to pleasure.

"Or how wise," Landsborough added, provoking a smile from Vespasia.

"By all means, let me have the benefit of your opinion," De-noon said grudgingly.

Cordelia glared at him. "I am hoping that Vespasia will give us more than her opinion. Since she agrees with us about the urgency and the seriousness of addressing the violence in our midst, and doing something to make it possible for the police to curtail it, be-fore we are all overtaken by a tide of destruction, she may be of practical help."

For an instant the effort to control his arrogance was visible in Denoon's face, then he masked it. He looked at Vespasia blandly. "That would be excellent. I am aware that you have a great deal of social influence, perhaps among people whose support we shall re-quire, needless to say, your exercise of it would be invaluable."

The maid came in with tea and the discussion became practi-cal, naming other members of Parliament, editors of newspapers and political pamphlets, and how their assistance might be re-cruited, or if negative, how best countered.

Vespasia left as soon as it was courteous to do so. It was easy to plead other engagements. She excused herself and bade Cordelia and Denoon good-bye. Enid had left the room a few minutes ear-lier, without giving her reason. Vespasia asked to be remembered to her, and went out into the hall, accompanied by Landsborough.

The butler sent for her carriage, and while she was waiting she glanced towards the passage that led to a side door into the garden, and saw Enid talking closely with a footman. He did not wear the Landsborough livery, so presumably he was her own, and had come with her. He was a fine-looking young man, as was often required in his calling. However it was the expression on his face that caught Vespasia's attention and held her momentarily transfixed. His eyes were direct, intensely earnest, and he was looking at Enid as if she were giving him instructions for some complicated and profoundly important task. He stood to attention, and she, with her back to Vespasia, was speaking softly, closer to him than was customary, and she seemed, at least for the moment, oblivious of anyone else.

Then Landsborough returned and his footsteps on the hall floor shattered the moment. Enid broke off what she was saying. The footman took a step back and his differential manner was resumed. He accepted his instructions and turned away to fulfill them. Enid walked slowly back into the hall, moving naturally towards Landsborough.

Vespasia repeated her farewell. Enid acknowledged it and went back to the withdrawing room. Landsborough walked with Vespasia to her carriage.

"Do you really believe it will be a good thing if the police are given more arms?" he asked when they reached the pavement, his face puckered with concern.

She hesitated. He was looking at her with a puzzled honesty, expected candor in return. In the past they had said to each other many things that were perhaps kind more than they were true, but not in order to deceive. There was an understanding that it was a pleasant evasion, a blunting of the edges that would otherwise have cut. This was different; that part of their relationship was in the past, and events had long overtaken it. Grief and wisdom had replaced the old urgency, and loneliness was of a different nature, needing different healing.

What kind of truth could he bear now, amid such terrible pain?

A carriage clattered by on the street, the horse picking its feet up high, its harness gleaming in the sun.

"We need to deal with anarchists," she replied. "I am not yet certain how."

"An increase of police powers is not the right way," he said gravely. "Magnus told me quite a lot about the misuse of it already. The law must protect the innocent as well as catch and punish the guilty, or it is a license to oppress."

"I know," she searched his face, waiting to understand the

emotions behind his words. How much did he know of what Magnus had done? What could he bear to believe?

"Don't trust Voisey!" he said with sudden profound emotion thickening his voice. "Please! Whatever course you follow, Vespasia, take the greatest care in whom you confide. There is far more here than you know." Then as if he were aware of being watched from the curtained windows behind him, he bade her good-bye, and handed her up into the carriage, inclining his head politely as it pulled away.

CHAPTER

SIX

Tellman intended to find Jones the Pocket as soon as possible, but he knew that he must do it extremely carefully, and in his own time rather than from Bow Street. If anyone were to see him doing it, then he would have to account for his interest in a man whose crimes, if any, had not been committed in his area. Sooner or later it would reach Wetron's ears, and it would only be a matter of time before he put the facts together—probably a very short time.

The first evening he put on old clothes, something he hated doing. It reminded him of his youth when that was all he had. But it was necessary. He needed to be anonymous, and he knew his keen, lantern-jawed face was recognizable in far too many places. This was the one advantage to coming to the Cannon Street area, and farther east, but he dared not ask the help of any of the men stationed there. It would be reported back to Simbister first, and then to Wetron within hours. If Pitt was right and the corruption was as deep into the force as he feared, then he was working against them, not with them.

Tellman had been born in the East End. He knew the streets, the alleys, the courts and byways, the public houses and the pawnshops. He did not know many people there any more, but he knew what their lives were like. It was a strange, unpleasant feeling to be in such familiar places again, as if the smell had never left the back of his throat, and his feet still knew where the uneven cobbles were as he walked.

He had passed every one of these shops and houses before, trudging with boots that leaked, always a little hungry, uncertain of food or warmth, afraid of the future. If Jones the Pocket came from here, he would understand too much about him to be happy pursuing him. Grover was even worse. He could pity him for his knowledge of the life he was escaping, and hate him because he had betrayed the very path Tellman had taken out of it.

Grover would also have seen his mother struggle to feed and clothe her children, almost certainly losing some to weakness and disease. Tellman would never forget the silence, the fear, the smell of grief in the house. Old people could die; it was expected. But the grief was frightening and inconsolable, even after all these years, when it was a child. If he closed his eyes he could still see his mother's face the night it had happened, and taste his own help-lessness again.

Part of him hated Grover for leeching on his own. A large part of him understood that when you were hungry, when the despera-tion of survival drove you, you took when you could. You had to be strong, clever, or lucky not to be broken, sooner or later.

None of which in the slightest affected his determination to find Jones the Pocket, and arrest him. He simply had no joy in it.

During the course of the evening he went to every public house within two miles of Dirty Dick's and the Ten Bells. He watched the landlords, and familiarized himself with the easiest route from one to another.

THE NEXT DAY he dispatched the men who usually worked with him on errands that would keep them occupied for the rest of the afternoon. At midday he was back at the Ten Bells. According to what Pitt had told him, it was collection day, so he bought a beef sandwich and a mug of ale, and waited. He sat near the door and watched every man who came in.

He had come on the early side, to be sure. After he had waited over half an hour, a man with a long nose and flyaway hair came in, flirted with the barmaid, and then bought himself a hot pie and a pint of ale.

Tellman nearly missed the next man who came in. He had a sharp, pointed face, quick eyes, and he wore a loose coat that flapped around his legs as he moved. The blond landlady's face became suddenly expressionless. Without waiting for him to speak, she poured him a measure of gin in a glass and handed it to him across the counter. He took it and tossed it down in a swift movement, then replaced the empty glass on the counter. No money changed hands.

Tellman drank the last of his ale and stood up.

The landlady held out her hand, palm up.

The man in the coat fished out a coin and gave it to her.

Tellman felt foolish. He would have to sit down again. This was not Jones after all.

The landlady was stiff, uncomfortable. There was no smile on her face as she had had for Tellman, who was a stranger here. She went to the drawer where she kept her money, as if to find change. Instead she made a quick movement and put her hand into a separate pigeonhole and pulled out a bundle of coins tied up in a rag. She slammed the drawer shut, then turned around and gave the bundle to the man. He took it with a few words Tellman could not hear, and then placed it carefully into one of his vast inside pockets. The payment had been made, but to anyone looking less carefully than Tellman had been, it was an ordinary purchase, with change.

Jones had done his business. He left, and went out into the street, Tellman on his heels.

Tellman followed him but at a very considerable distance. He even allowed him to get out of his sight, because he knew where he was going. His only concern was that he might not deliver the money today. He still did not know where to find Jones again, except on the same route next week, and Pitt could not wait another seven days.

But by nearly six o'clock Jones had not passed the money to anyone, nor had he returned to any building that could reasonably be his home.

Finally Jones went into a public house in Bethnal Green, and ordered a meal. Tellman watched as the barmaid brought it to him without asking for any money. At first he leapt to the same conclusion as previously, but then he saw the woman laughing, and he realized there was no apparent anger in her. She walked easily, with a slight sway of her hips. In fact, she was self-confident, flirting a little with other customers as she passed them, catching an eye here and there and winking. She made a joke. A large man responded, and she pretended to be shocked. There was another bellow of laughter. Jones joined in.

The woman returned to the bar and made a little note on a piece of paper and put it in the drawer.

Jones was a regular here. He was not extorting from her, she was putting it on his account. He must eat here regularly. He probably lived within a few minutes' walking distance.

At last Tellman knew where to find Jones again. He left with life in his step. He realized he was hungry also, but he would eat somewhere else, not here, not in Jones the Pocket's tavern.

TELLMAN ARRIVED AT his lodgings in a spirit of triumph, but as he lay in bed thinking over his success, he realized that while he understood exactly what he had seen, he had no proof of any crime for which he could legally arrest Jones. Ironically, and he was fully aware of the bitterness of it, he could have used the new laws of search that were currently being suggested in Parliament. But the last thing on earth he wanted was a gun, and still less that police corrupted by Wetron and his like should have them.

He needed an excuse to arrest Jones and keep him long enough for Pitt to take his place—and his money—and wait for his masters to come in search of it.

Of course, if they assumed that Pitt was equally corrupt, which he would have to be, then Tellman's reasons for arresting Jones did not have to be honest.

But if they were not, and Wetron knew it, then Tellman would be hostage to that crime all the rest of his days.

He turned over and pulled the blankets with him. His pillow felt as if it were full of lumps. He was too hot one minute, and too cold the next.

Worse than hostage to Wetron, he would have dishonored himself. What would his mother have thought of him? He could taste her contempt as if it were already a fact, and, more bitter than contempt, her pain.

And Gracie. Gracie would be furious with him for not having been clever enough to have thought of something better. He would no longer be any kind of hero in her eyes.

What could he arrest Jones for, legally? He was guilty of extortion, but there was no way to prove it, because no one was going to say that they had paid him unwillingly; they did not dare to. Or the next thing they knew, they would receive a visit from the police, who would find stolen goods carefully planted in their houses, or forged money, or papers of some sort.

He sat up in the bed, cold air hitting his body through his nightshirt. That was it! He had not visited all the public houses in his area yet. There were more to collect from tomorrow. What if one of them paid Jones in forged money? That would be easy enough to arrange. There was nothing criminal in paying extortion with forged money. And Tellman could lay his hands on a few notes easily enough. There was at least one magsman in the Bow

Street area who owed him a favor and would be glad enough to acquit it. What did a forged note cost? Little enough in these circumstances.

He would have to do it carefully, of course. He would go around after Jones, make sure he took it, then arrest him. The bogus notes, whose forger he could never give away because he did not know him, would be grounds to hold him in prison for several days, even a week, quite long enough for Pitt to have an excellent chance to meet his masters.

Now Tellman was too wide awake to sleep, but his mind was made up. All that was still left to decide was who would he take with him to make the arrest. He dared not do it alone in case Jones fought, which he well might. In an area like Mile End or Whitechapel, there were enough dark alleys or closed-in courts for him to pull a knife on Tellman, and escape. No one would come to Tellman's aid, and he dared not look to the local police anyway. Any one of them could be as corrupt as Jones himself, could even be Jones's master, or a middleman between the two.

He lay down, and did eventually sleep fitfully, but woke up with his mind turned again immediately to whom he could trust to take with him.

IN THE EVENT HE had very little choice. It was either Stubbs or Cobham. Cobham was new, and disinclined to take orders easily. He tended to question, to want reasons for everything, and there was no time for explanations. It had to be Stubbs. All he knew about him was that, like Tellman himself, he was the oldest of a large family. He spoke occasionally of his mother but never his father. Perhaps he was dead. Stubbs might have ambitions or loyalties of his own, but that was true of everyone. Fear of that could stop Tellman from ever taking a step at all. That was one of the worst things about corruption, it crippled action, it blurred any decision until in the end you doubted everyone, even your ability to be right about yourself. It was a cool morning with a slight mist over the river and he set out very early to collect the forged note. By eight o'clock he had seen the landlord of the public house most likely to pay it on to Jones without giving him the slightest hint that there was anything unusual in this installment. But just to be as sure as possible, Tellman reminded him of the unpleasantness he would face were the operation to fail, as well as the advantages to his future if it succeeded.

By nine o'clock he was at Bow Street as usual, about his duties and keeping well away from Wetron's path. He decided not to risk telling Stubbs he would require him; instead, by lunchtime, he collected Stubbs from where he was writing up his paperwork in the ledger and said he had a job for him. Stubbs, who hated writing, was delighted to accept.

They went together and questioned a pawnbroker about a stolen silver urn and pair of candlesticks. It was something Tellman could perfectly well have done alone, and they went farther east as if to continue the search. They had an amiable lunch at the Smithfield Tavern, then walked quietly towards the public house where Tellman expected Jones to collect extortion money. He had considered picking him up earlier, closer to where he lived, and following him until he reached the one where the note was. However, if Stubbs were loyal to the Circle, or anyone in it, in debt to them, or afraid, or even simply careless, he might manage to get some warning to Jones.

So they were obliged to wait. The sky clouded over and occasional showers made them colder and left them shivering. Stubbs was growing steadily more puzzled, and less happy.

Tellman chose not to explain. It would involve too many details he was not willing to discuss.

Another shower drifted past. Momentarily, hailstones rattling against the windows of the shop behind them. Then Jones appeared, striding along the pavement, coat flapping, black hat jammed on his head. He went into the public house, and emerged ten minutes later, wiping the back of his hand across his mouth, and set out across the cobbles to the far side of the street.

"Come on!" Tellman said sharply. "He's the one we want."

"What for?" Stubbs asked, obeying with alacrity. He stepped into a puddle and swore under his breath. "Who is he?"

"Passer of forged money," Tellman replied.

" 'Ow do yer know?" Stubbs caught up with him as, ahead of them, Jones ducked into an alley to take a shortcut towards his next stop.

"It's my job," Tellman replied, crossing after Jones and going straight into the alley. He was reluctant to follow into a place he did not know, and where he could easily be ambushed, but he dared not lose Jones. Out of his sight for more than a moment or two, he could pass the money on and the whole arrest would fall through. The police corruption ate at Tellman like an ulcer in his flesh, and to fail in the battle against it for what amounted to cowardice would be unbearable. And he would have let Pitt down. That was almost as bad.

The alley was dark, the rain clouds graying the sky and making the shadows heavy between the high walls. Jones was ahead of him, rapidly approaching another man, who was thickset with a massive chest and short, slightly bowed legs. He had a powerful, hatchet-shaped face with deep-set eyes. He stood in the center of the alley, right across Jones's path, but Jones did not hesitate, and certainly made no move as if to turn or back away from him.

Tellman had no choice. Once the money passed hands he would have no excuse to hold Jones.

"We've got to take him," Tellman said quietly. This would put to the test beyond doubt which side Stubbs was on. Tellman's stomach knotted and his throat constricted so tightly for a moment he could barely breathe. He strode forward and lunged at Jones, grasping him from the back, twisting his arm around while keeping his body as a shield between himself and the other man. If he had a weapon of any sort it would be temporarily useless. He could hear Stubbs's feet on the cobbles behind him.

"Police, Mr. Jones," Tellman said very clearly. "I'm arresting you on suspicion of passing forged money."

Jones yelped, partly in surprise, but mostly in pain as he tried to wriggle away; Tellman's grip on his arm tightened. "You won't find nothin' on me!" he said in outrage.

"You're Bow Street," the hatchet-faced man said softly. His voice was quite light and his diction unusually clear. It did not match his image at all. "What are you doin' 'ere? My name's Grover," he went on. "From Cannon Street. Sergeant Grover."

"Sergeant Tellman. And I followed the money from the Bow Street area," Tellman replied.

"Liar!" Jones said indignantly. "I never bin nowhere near Bow Street."

"Are you sure o' that, Sergeant Tellman?" Grover asked, taking a step towards them. He was now only about three yards away.

Tellman stepped back, pulling Jones with him away from Grover and closer to Stubbs. "Yes, Sergeant, I am sure," he said. "Easy enough to see if he's got forged money on him. Let's take a look. Constable Stubbs!" He did not ask Stubbs to hold Jones. If he let him go, intentionally or not, it could then be three against one, and Tellman would have no chance. "Look in his pockets," he commanded.

For a long, aching moment no one moved, then Stubbs came forward.

Jones let out a snarl. "You'll find nothing forged on me!" he said angrily. "Sergeant Grover! You know me. This is your patch. What are you letting this Bow Street man get away with?"

"If you've nothing, I'll apologize," Tellman replied, tightening his grip even more and making Jones wince. "I'll even buy you dinner. Get on with it, Stubbs! What's the matter with you?" He was finding it harder to hold Jones, and he was aware of someone else at the far end of the alley, coming towards them from behind

Grover. Grover must have heard him because he swung around. Then he looked back at Tellman, his expression curiously uncertain.

The man from the far end came into the light. It was Leggy Bromwich, a petty thief Tellman had known for years. He had turned a blind eye to him once or twice when he was only getting his own back, so he owed Tellman a favor. Not that that counted for much.

"Hello, Leggy," Tellman said with a smile that was more a baring of his teeth. "Seen any good forgeries lately?"

"Yer got one, Mr. Tellman?" Leggy asked, his face brightening.

"I'm about to," Tellman replied, "when Constable Stubbs here gets to doing his job."

Leggy stopped just beyond Grover's reach, his eyes wide, a slight smile on his thin face.

Stubbs felt in Jones's pockets one after another, and picked out handfuls of money. "Just coins," he said expressionlessly.

Jones said nothing.

Tellman felt his heart sink. Had Jones passed the note to Grover already? Or had the publican betrayed Tellman and not given it to Jones at all? He could taste failure in his mouth like bile. "Try inside his shirt!" he said roughly.

"Oh now, Mr. Tellman!" Jones protested. "You can't do that! I'm an innocent man!"

Tellman twisted Jones's arm a little tighter. Jones yelled.

"Sergeant, you're out of your patch," Grover began warningly.

Stubbs glanced at Grover, then at Leggy. He put his hand inside Jones's shirt and pulled out two five-pound notes.

"Look at them," Tellman told him. "Look close."

Stubbs did so. Even at a three-foot distance Tellman could see they were not alike. At least one of them had to be a forgery, and only a moderately good one.

"Sergeant Grover?" Tellman said inquiringly. Now he was very glad Leggy Bromwich was here.

"Mr. Jones, I'm disappointed in you," Grover said with mock sadness. He took a step backwards. "It seems Sergeant Tellman is right after all. Careless, that. Very careless."

Tellman bared his teeth in another smile. "It is, isn't it," he agreed. "Not much use to anyone, a thing like that. I wouldn't like to have my debts paid by a handful of those! Constable Stubbs, handcuffs, if you please. We have to take Mr. Jones with us. Good day, Mr. Grover, Leggy!" And he jerked Jones around to face the way out of the alley and pushed him forwards, Stubbs beside him.

He walked out to the main street where with luck they would find a hansom soon. He did not look behind him to see Grover's expression, or the satisfaction he imagined on Leggy Bromwich's face. He would be wise not to cross Grover's path for a month or two at least.

THAT EVENING, AFTER having delivered his news to Pitt, Tellman stood in the street outside the Gaiety Music Hall beside Gracie. She was glowing with excitement. He had promised to take her for nearly three weeks now, and twice had had to put it off, on Wetron's orders or to pursue Pitt's request. Tonight he put all other matters out of his head and came here regardless. Gracie's shining face was sufficient reward to put the misery of suspicion out of his thoughts, at least until he was home again in his rooms and realization forced itself back upon him that he could afford to trust no one.

Of course it was possible the anarchists were mistaken about the degree of corruption. They were not exactly stable or rational men. Whoever heard of anything so totally idiotic as destroying all order so you could create justice again from the resulting chaos?

But the question of what Stubbs would have done if Leggy Bromwich had not been there nagged in his mind. And what would Stubbs tell Wetron? For that matter, what would Grover say to Simbister? Did he believe Jones had really dealt in forged money, or did he know perfectly well that Tellman had put it there himself? The one thing he was certain of was that Grover would not come out into the open and accuse the landlord of paying his extortion with forged money.

But if the rot was as widespread as Pitt feared, and they did not beat it, then Tellman faced a whole new problem. He realized with sick misery that he could not stay in the police. He would have to find some other profession to follow, but what? He knew nothing else. He had asked Gracie to marry him. What could he offer her if he had no work?

She was clinging onto his arm, largely to keep herself from being separated from him in the crowd surging forward as the doors were opened. It was a good feeling, warm and sweet. Heaven knows, he had waited long enough for her even to speak civilly to him! He remembered her original scorn towards him. She had swept by him with her chin in the air, which was an achievement, considering she barely made five feet and was as scrawny as a twopenny rabbit. But she had enough spirit for two women twice her size, and Tellman had been fascinated from the beginning. Admittedly, he had deceived himself for nearly a year that it was irritation with her meddling that moved him, nothing else.

They pressed forward with the crowd, and were shown to their seats. There was chattering and laughter as everyone arranged their skirts, complained about their neighbors, called out to people they knew, and generally made themselves comfortable.

It was an excellent bill: an acrobat, a juggler, two contortionists who worked together, a dancer, several singers, and two first-class comedians. He had bought Gracie chocolate and mint humbugs, and intended to buy her a lemonade in the interval. For three hours he could put everything to do with crime of any sort out of his mind.

The curtain rose. To bursts of applause the master of ceremonies announced the acts in the customary flowing and ornate language. Gracie and Tellman thoroughly enjoyed the jugglers

who were funny as well as clever, and the acrobat who was grace-
ful and something of a mime artist as well. They were happy to join
in enthusiastically with the singers, as was all the audience. The
first half of the show finished with howls of laughter at one of the
two comedians billed.

When the applause had subsided and the red plush curtain had
fallen, Tellman rose to his feet.

"Would you like a lemonade?" he offered.

"Thank you, Samuel," she said courteously. "That would be
very nice."

He returned barely ten minutes later. She accepted the glass
from him and sat sipping, a very slight frown on her face.

"What's the matter?" he asked anxiously. "Is it too sour?"

"It's lovely," she answered. "I'm just worried about Mr. Pitt."

"Why's that?" he said, wanting to reassure her. If she had seen
his anxiety, or the guilt eating at him because the force he had
served and believed in all his adult life was riddled with corruption, then he must help divert her from the truth, and find some
other explanation. "Special Branch is a hard job, you know," he
went on. "Not as straightforward as regular police."

"Course it isn't," she agreed, sipping again at the lemonade.
Her voice was very soft when she continued. The people next to
them could not have heard. " 'E's tryin' ter find out if them stupid
bombers is tellin' the truth about the police, or not. An' it in't
'ardly like 'e could ask anyone, is it? 'Oo could 'e trust?"

"Most of us are as honest as anyone in Special Branch!" he said
hotly. "And he knows that!"

" 'E knows *you* are," she corrected him. " 'E don't know about
nobody else."

"Yes he does. He knows . . ." He stopped, aware that he himself
was not sure whom he could trust.

She was looking at him, her eyes bright and sharp, seeing every
flicker that crossed his face. He felt the heat in his cheeks, and
knew he was coloring.

" 'E told you about it, din't 'e?" she said levelly, ignoring the lemonade. "Yer know wot it is as 'e's scared of, don't yer?"

Her friendship was too new, and far too precious to risk by telling lies, even half-lies. "I can't talk about police business," he said gravely. "Not even with you." If he told her it was to protect her from worrying she would be furious. He had tried it before, and been accused of talking down to her. She had treated him like a leper for two months afterwards.

"You don't need to!" she said stiffly. "I worked for Mr. Pitt for near ten years. I know as 'e won't let rottenness go by, whatever it costs 'im ter show it up. An' Mrs. Pitt might be so scared for 'im she can't barely see straight, but that won't stop 'im neither."

"Isn't that what you'd want?" he asked, hearing the fierce admiration in her voice, and seeing it in the brilliance of her eyes as she stared at him.

She hesitated, somehow caught in doubt.

He did not understand. "Well, isn't it?" He was certain he had not misread her emotion. Apart from knowing her, it was what he believed himself.

She looked away. "I know as 'e's gotter do it," she said so softly he only just heard her. Then she swung back, her eyes blazing, full of tears. "But you 'aven't! If they guesses wot yer doin', 'oo's gonna pull yer out, eh?" She gulped, her body stiff, shoulders square and tight. "Yer in the police all by yerself, an' if they catch yer 'e can't do nothin' ter 'elp, nor can nobody else!"

He opened his mouth to deny that he was doing anything dangerous.

"An' don't yer lie ter me, Samuel Tellman!" she said, almost choking on the words. "Jus' don't yer dare!"

"I wasn't going to lie," he said stiffly. Now he had no choice. If he allowed her to dictate to him what he was going to do, or not do, he would be making a rod for his back from which he would not be free for the rest of his life. No matter how he loved her, he was not going to have that. "I wanted to save you the worry of talking about it," he went on. "But you pushed your way in, I don't know how. I never told you, and I'm sure Mr. Pitt didn't either."

"Yer don't 'ave ter tell me," she retorted, still whispering fiercely. "I can work it out for meself! Them anarchists blew up 'ouses wot belongs ter a rozzer from Cannon Street, on purpose, like. Parliament's busy tryin' ter make laws ter give yer all guns, wot Mr. Pitt don't want, cos 'e says they'll just make policin' 'arder by puttin' everyone's back up agin yer. An 'is 'ole station o' Bow Street is run by a schemin' sod as we all know is 'ead o' the Inner Circle wot near killed Mr. Pitt before."

"Gracie!" he hissed warningly. "Keep your voice down! You don't know who's listening!"

She ignored him. "Lady Vespasia's all worried about it, and Miss Emily," she went on. "Yer can't go ter the music 'all cos yer too busy, an' when yer do, yer that tired yer got circles 'round yer eyes like someone's 'it yer! Yer think I can't work it out fer meself?"

He should have known better than to hope she would remain ignorant of at least the size of the trouble. But it made no difference to his duty.

"It seems you can," he conceded. "I hoped you would not need to know, so you wouldn't worry."

She snorted with contempt for the idea.

"But I'm still going to do all I can," he said firmly. "And don't ask me again, because I don't want to have to tell you not to, and I'm definitely not saying what's happening, not because I don't trust you, but so's you don't have to keep secrets from Mrs. Pitt, nor tell lies to her."

"She knows!" Gracie said with a gulp. "She can work it out too! We know they blew up that 'ouse cos the policeman wot lived in it's rotten!"

"Then it won't matter if I don't say anything," he responded. "Now there's an end to it, Gracie. That's how it's going to be, and you'd best get used to it." He sat very still and stared at her levelly, his face grave.

She looked furious, her fists clenched in her lap, small, white-knuckled, almost like a child's. She breathed in and out several times, as if her mind were racing for some answer to give him. He saw the fear in her eyes, wide, dark, and overwhelmingly real.

He almost wavered. What if she felt so shut out, so excluded, that she would not forgive him? He drew in his breath to say something gentler.

"Yes, Samuel," she said softly.

"What?" He was astounded. She was obeying him!

"Yer 'eard me!" Her voice was high and angry again. "I in't saying it twice fer yer! Jus' . . . jus' take care o' yerself, eh? Promise me . . ."

"I promise you!" he answered with overwhelming relief. He wanted to take her in his arms and kiss her, but she would be mortified if he were to do something like that in such a public place. People were beginning to take their seats again for the second half, skirts billowing and rustling, everyone standing on everyone else's toes. There were squeaks of protest and hasty apologies.

Gracie sat very stiff, her chin high. She was sniffing a little and fumbling for a handkerchief, but her face shone with pride and a kind of inner excitement. It had nothing to do with the contortionists who were the next act, or the comedian who would make her ache with laughter, or the singer who would top the bill, and have everyone in the house singing along with the rip-roaring songs.

Tellman found he was smiling so widely that the man next to him thought he had missed one of the best jokes, but he didn't like to ask.

THE NEXT MORNING all such pleasures vanished as Tellman reported to the police station at Bow Street and found a message ordering him to go to Wetron's office immediately.

"Yes, sir?" he asked, standing in front of Wetron's desk, his mouth dry.

Wetron looked up. He was an ordinary-seeming man, hair receding at the front. He was of average height and build, with nondescript features, until one noticed the hard brilliance of his eyes and the unyielding line of his thin mouth.

"Ah . . . Tellman." He leaned back a little in his chair. His desk was impeccably neat. "I wasn't aware that we had a forgery problem in our area, at least not more than the odd note here and there, usually badly made and wouldn't fool most people."

Tellman felt stiff, his face hot. "I don't think we have, sir. And I'd be happy to keep it like that."

"Cannon Street informs me that you made an arrest on their territory yesterday, but brought the man back here. Is that so?"

"Yes, sir. I had reason to believe the note came from our patch, so the crime was ours." That was in a way the truth. He must be extremely careful of what he said to Wetron. He had no idea what Stubbs might have told him already.

"A five-pound note?" Wetron lifted his eyebrows very slightly. His tone suggested how little it mattered.

Tellman was stung. He could not afford to let it show.

A faint shadow of amusement crossed Wetron's cold face. He said nothing.

Suddenly Tellman knew Wetron was waiting for him to excuse himself, to get away as quickly as he could, as if he were afraid, or guilty of something. Anger flared up inside him, and the knowledge that he must be intensely careful. Every word, every nuance, even the way he stood or the expression on his face, would be remembered. He would not retreat.

"I thought right at the moment, sir, that forgery might be particularly important," he said, straightening up a little to stand squarely in front of Wetron's desk. "Anarchists need money. It must have taken a fair bit of dynamite to blow up Sergeant Grover's house, and those on either side of it."

He was profoundly satisfied to see a moment's flicker of uncertainty in Wetron's eyes, as if he had been caught on the wrong foot. It was gone almost before he recognized it.

"Yes it must," Wetron agreed. "I didn't know you had such an interest in the matter. But then I suppose it's natural enough for you. You must still have some loyalty to Pitt." He let the ambiguity of his meaning hang in the air. "He is in charge of the bombing, isn't he!"

With a flood of relief, feeling like a runner recovering his balance, Tellman remembered that that fact had been in the newspapers. "Yes, sir, that's what the papers say," he acknowledged. "But my concern is that Sergeant Grover is one of us."

"I didn't know you knew him!"

"I don't, sir. But if it was him this time, it could be me next." He took a deep breath. "Unless, of course, there is something about Grover that I don't know."

Wetron's impassive face gave away nothing. Even his hands on the desk were motionless. "You think Sergeant Grover was the intended victim of those anarchists?"

"I've no idea, sir. But I wouldn't want to take any chances. It might be coincidence that a policeman's house was dynamited, sir," he said. "But Mr. Grover knows a lot of people in that area, and he must have offended a fair few of them because he's put them in prison, cut the rate of their business. Maybe they printed up a bit of money for the anarchists, and told them it would be a favor if they placed their dynamite in a certain street?" He was pleased with that. It made sense.

Wetron stared at him. "Is that what Mr. Pitt thinks, Sergeant?"

"I wouldn't know, sir. I imagine he's more concerned with catching them than whether they bombed Mr. Grover's house on purpose."

"He's not very quick, your Mr. Pitt, is he!" Wetron said with only the faintest derision in his tone. "The anarchists raise their own funds. Even I know that, just as a matter of keeping my ear to the ground. Seems he can't find it out, even by detection! Nor can you, for that matter."

Anger burned in Tellman's cheeks; he could feel the heat of it and knew Wetron must be able to see it. His instinct was to defend Pitt rather than himself. Perhaps that was what Wetron was trying to provoke him into. But if he did not rise to it, then Wetron would know he was being deliberately guarded. What did he expect? Bluff? Double-bluff?

Wetron was waiting, watching him. He must react now; any delay would betray his anxiety, and make him seem dishonest.

"Yes," he agreed. "Maybe being out of the police force means he doesn't get to hear things. And it seems we didn't tell him."

"Oh, I don't know," Wetron was still smiling. "I imagine he has his contacts, his informers, don't you, Sergeant?"

Tellman knew his voice was husky with tension, sounding unnatural. He resisted the impulse to clear his throat. "Well, sir, if you know that about the anarchists, and he doesn't, it would look like his informers aren't very good ones," he responded.

"It would, wouldn't it?" Wetron agreed. "He must be asking the ones their superiors, and their fellows, don't trust."

There it was, the precise warning. Tellman could report it to Pitt, and deliberately place himself in that category, or not tell him and be unworthy of his trust.

Wetron was oozing satisfaction. Tellman could almost smell it in the still air of the room.

"Very foolish, that," Wetron continued. "A policeman out on the streets, who doesn't have the confidence of the men he relies on, is in a very dangerous position. There are a lot of places in London where that could cost him his life."

Tellman thought of himself in the alley with Grover and Stubbs. Did Wetron know about that—from either of them? Only Leggy's accidental arrival had saved him from being at Stubbs's mercy, one way or the other.

"Yes, sir," he said aloud. "Should we inform Special Branch

about the anarchists' way of getting money, as a favor? It might be useful to have them in our debt."

"You think they will repay us one day?" Wetron said with surprise.

Tellman felt foolish. Pitt would, but Victor Narraway was another matter.

Wetron appeared to consider it. "We might trade it," he said thoughtfully. "If they are still floundering about, in three or four days, I'll see what they say."

Tellman could think of no answer, and he did not dare argue.

Wetron leaned back. "Are they investigating Magnus Landsborough's family?" he asked as if it were only mildly interesting.

Tellman was startled. "I have no idea, sir."

Wetron smiled again. "That's where they should look. His cousin, Piers Denoon, is the obvious place. Perhaps Pitt will work that out, eventually." He looked at Tellman, his eyes bright and hard, as if they could see right into his mind.

Tellman knew exactly what he was doing, just as Wetron did, and Tellman's dilemma amused him. Would Tellman repeat it to Pitt, and betray himself, or say nothing, and betray Pitt? It would place Pitt in an even greater shadow of failure than the Special Branch already was, with half London crying out that they had only two of the anarchists, and could not even name the rest, let alone capture them.

"Yes, sir," Tellman said quietly. He hardly dared trust his voice. Wetron had given one thing away irrevocably. If Tellman had ever imagined Wetron was a servant of the people, not of his own interests, that illusion was ripped apart. But then perhaps he knew that Tellman had not been deceived in that for years! He had lost nothing. "Is there anything else, sir?" he asked politely.

"No," Wetron replied, straightening up in his seat. "I just wanted to know why you were so interested in this forged five-pound note. It seems . . . trivial."

"I don't think there will be just the one, sir." Tellman smiled now, a very slight lifting of the corners of his mouth. "If someone's got plates, they can print as many as they like."

"And did this . . . Jones, give you any useful information?"

"Not yet, sir," Tellman said smoothly. "But there's time."

Wetron nodded slowly. He understood the battle lines between them, and he was sure that he would win. "Very well. You can go."

TELLMAN HAD ONLY ONE possible course open to him. However dangerous it was, he could not allow Pitt to remain ignorant of what might be a vital piece of information.

But first Tellman needed to discover for himself if what Wetron said of Piers Denoon was true or not. If it were not, and Pitt went seeking after him on Tellman's word, which Wetron would of course deny, then Pitt would make enemies he could not afford. Tellman needed to know for himself, and give that proof to Pitt, not simply the unsupported rumor. And of course he must pursue it in his own time.

It was two nights after his conversation with Wetron before he found the man he wanted. It had cost him both more time and more money than he wished. He ran him down in the Rat and Ha'penny, a public house on the corner of Hanbury Street, not far from where one of Jack the Ripper's victims had been found, her face disfigured and her stomach torn open, five years earlier.

The room was crowded, filled with raucous laughter and the smell of ale, sweat, and human bodies that had no means and no desire to wash. They sat opposite each other at a small table.

"Lunatic!" Stace said, puckering his mouth into a grimace. He picked up his glass and stared at it appreciatively. "Miserable enough ter cut 'is froat one minute, mad enough ter cut anyone else's the next. Talks more rubbish than anyone I know. In't scared o' nuffin', like 'e don't care if 'e's 'live or dead. Daft, I say. Got the money though. 'Eaps of it."

"What does he look like?" Tellman asked, pretending to be

only moderately interested, as if he were merely making conversation.

Stace shrugged. "Toff," he replied. "Wears dirt like it's painted on top of 'im. In't part of 'im, like them wot lives 'ere. Clothes fit 'im, an' 'is 'air's clean. Got dainty 'ands, like a man wot's never done a day o' work." He squinted sideways at Tellman. "But I wouldn't cross 'im, if I was you. Mad as a monkey, 'e is, an' clever as one too."

"Clever doing what?" Tellman took another swallow from his glass.

"I dunno, but some funny folks give 'im a lot o' time."

"What kind of funny?"

"Crazy people, wot blows up things," Stace replied, stuffing the last of his pie into his mouth and talking around it. "Always goin' on about doin' away wi' the law, an' I don't jus' mean the rozzers, I mean the 'ole Parli'ment an' everythin'. Blow up the Queen, if they could."

"Foreigners?" Tellman inquired innocently.

"Some of 'em, mostly as English as you or me," Stace said disgustedly.

"Or Irish, maybe?" Tellman suggested.

"All sorts," Stace gave an elaborate shrug. "Diff'rent ones. Move from one lot ter another. Like I said, 'e's daft as they come. Must be on the opium, or summink. Always lookin' over 'is shoulder like the devil was be'ind 'im. Don't stay in one place long enough ter sit down. Think 'is own shadder'd bit 'im. Wot about another pint, eh? An' I could manage another pie, if I was asked?"

Tellman obliged. The information was worth it. He fetched the pie and ale and returned to the table where Stace took them immediately.

"Daft, you say?" Tellman repeated.

"As a brush," Stace confirmed.

"Smokes opium?"

"Dunno. Not fer sure."

"Where does he get his money from?"

"Dunno. I said as 'e were daft." Stace took a large bite of his pie and swallowed it before he continued. " 'E is, but 'e in't stupid."

"Where could I find him?" Maybe it was too bold a question. The moment it was out of his mouth, he wished he had not asked.

"Dunno," Stace replied. "Wot's it worf?"

"If you don't know, it isn't worth anything," Tellman said frankly. "You said he had good clothes, and under the dirt he was clean."

"In't we all?" Stace grinned, showing broken teeth.

Tellman did not argue, but actually it was not true. It sounded as if Piers Denoon might return home to sleep, and possibly to eat, certainly to take a hot bath now and then. That might be the only place to find him. One could wander around the East End for months without running across him. They did not have months, quite apart from the obvious danger not only to Tellman himself, but to Piers also if the wrong people knew he was looking.

"Thank you," he said appreciatively. "Another glass?"

"Since yer ask, I don't mind if I do," Stace said generously.

Tellman did not find Piers Denoon that night, and the following day he had no opportunity to continue the search. He was tired and discouraged by the time he went home to eat, and change his clothes. It had been raining on and off during the day and his feet were sore, his trouser legs were wet, and he had not had anything hot to eat in two days. He began to think of Piers Denoon enjoying a steaming bath back in his parents' house in Queen Anne Street with a spirit of something close to bitterness.

He knew where the house was—he had taken the trouble to find out. The first night he had gone there and delivered a message. The footman had informed him that Mr. Piers was not at home.

He was not at home the second evening either, but Tellman had nowhere better to look, so he spent the latter part of the evening standing in the chill wind at the other side of the street arguing with himself as to how much longer he could endure it, and whether it was worth staying.

Twice he gave up and walked to the end of the road and was about to go down to Cavendish Square, and changed his mind, determined to give it another quarter of an hour.

It was half past ten when a hansom pulled up three doors along and a young man alighted and staggered uncertainly under the lamplight, almost bumping into it before he altered course. He was unshaven and looked very much the worse for wear. His clothes were dirty, but unmistakably well-cut and tailored to fit his slender, almost emaciated form. He passed into the shadow again, and Tellman did not move until the man started down the area steps of the Denoon house, as if to go in at the scullery door.

Tellman shot into action and sprinted across the street and down the steps. He caught up with the man as he fumbled to open the door to the back kitchen.

"Mr. Denoon!" Tellman said urgently.

Piers jolted as if for an instant he had almost cried out, then he swung around, his back pressed against the door. "Who are you?" he demanded.

Tellman already knew what he was going to do. "I came to give you a warning," he said quietly. "Not a threat!" he added. In the light above the kitchen door Piers Denoon looked haggard, every bit as tense and nerve-ridden as Stace had said. "The police looking into the Myrdle Street bombing know that you got the money for the dynamite," Tellman went on.

Piers stared at him, struggling not to believe him. Fear was so stark in his face that Tellman felt a twinge of guilt. But he could not afford mercy now.

"They've been questioning the men they caught, Welling and Carmody," he said urgently. "Someone must have talked. You've got to be careful, warn the people you get the money from!"

"Warn them?" Piers said, catching his breath. His eyes looked like hollow pits.

"Well, I can't!" Tellman said reasonably. "But don't delay. They're moving quickly." Was that enough? Would it send Piers Denoon to whoever was behind the anarchists? Would it give him the proof Pitt needed?

"I hear you," Piers said quietly. He looked ashen, sweaty, as if he were ill.

Tellman nodded. "Good. Do it." He turned away and climbed back up the steps into the street and walked away. He stopped half a dozen doors along, until he was out of sight should Piers be watching him. Then he crossed the street and went halfway down the steps of a house where no lights were on, and waited.

Forty minutes later he was rewarded by seeing Piers Denoon come up the steps again, this time looking clean, shaved, and dressed in fresh clothes. He walked briskly westward towards Cavendish Square. Tellman had to break into a run to catch up with him just as he stepped off the footpath into a hansom cab.

Tellman swore, and looked around for another. It was late and cold and the square was almost deserted. He sprinted along the footpath towards Regent Street, and was intensely relieved to see another hansom twenty yards away, ambling in the opposite direction. He ran after it. He did not dare call out until he was level with it, in case he drew attention to himself. He scrambled up, telling the driver to turn quickly and follow the first.

It was a hectic journey. Twice he lost Piers Denoon, but caught up with him eventually. He arrived twenty yards behind him when he alighted halfway along Great Sutton Street in Clerkenwell. Denoon paid the driver and after looking both ways along the footpath, rang the doorbell at number twenty-seven.

Tellman shouted to his driver to take him to Keppel Street, and found his voice was hoarse and his mouth dry. The sweat was running down his body and chilling, as if the air froze.

It was just after one o'clock in the morning.

CHAPTER

SEVEN

Pitt woke to hear Charlotte speaking urgently to him, her voice low and sharp with alarm.

"Thomas, there's someone outside the front door."

He struggled to escape the clouds of sleep. The room was dark, he could barely even make out her shadow, it was more a sense of the warmth of her near him. But he could hear the low, insistent knocking on the door below.

"I'll go," he said, reaching out to touch her shoulder and feeling the soft skin for a moment. Then he climbed out of bed and fumbled for the candle and struck a match. The flame burned up at least sufficiently to find his jacket and trousers. He would have to come back up and dress properly if he had to go out. He looked at his pocket watch sitting on the dresser. It was just after quarter past one.

The knocking had stopped. Whoever it was must have seen the glow through the chink in the curtains and realized they would soon be answered.

Pitt turned up the gas on the landing lamp then ran downstairs in bare feet and went to the front door. He unlocked it, and pulled it open to find Tellman on the step. In what light there was from the hall, he looked pale and exhausted.

"Come in," Pitt said quietly. "What's happened?"

Tellman did as he was told and Pitt closed the door. Inside,

Tellman looked even worse. His skin was pasty, his lean cheeks covered with faint stubble, and his eyes were hollow.

"What is it?" Pitt repeated. "Do I have to get dressed, or have we time for a cup of tea?"

Tellman was shivering slightly. "There's nowhere to go," he answered. "At least not now."

Without comment, Pitt turned and led the way along the passage to the kitchen. His feet were cold, but at least the wooden floor there would be warmer, and since it was relatively early in the night, he might be able to get the stove back to life without having to rake it all out and start again.

He lit the gas in the kitchen. "Sit down," he ordered Tellman. "I'll go up and tell Charlotte it's just you, then I'll make a cup of tea."

Tellman obeyed.

Pitt was back in a few minutes with a shirt and socks on as well. He riddled out the dead ash from the stove, put kindling on top of the warm embers, and watched till they caught. Then he added coal and closed up the front so it would draw. He filled the kettle and put it on the hob. In the basket by the stove the cats Archie and Angus stirred and stretched, rearranged themselves and went back to sleep.

"What is it?" Pitt asked, sitting down opposite Tellman. It would be several minutes before the water boiled.

Tellman seemed to relax a little. Perhaps this kitchen where Gracie worked, and where he and Pitt had sat so often, was as much home to him as anywhere since his childhood. However a deep misery haunted his face.

"I don't know how long they'll hold Jones the Pocket." He chewed his lip. "If it's as bad as we fear, they could lose the evidence against him. You'd better move quickly." He looked at Pitt with steady, miserable eyes.

"What's the charge?" Pitt asked, curious to know how Tellman had accomplished it. "And the evidence?"

"Passing forged money," Tellman replied, the very smallest lift of pride in his voice. "Which he did," he added. "With a little help. I took a constable along, so someone knows apart from me, but of course I don't know if I can trust him. He might develop a sudden blindness. Or worse, he might say I put the money there."

"Could you have?" Pitt was worried for him.

"No. I was careful not to go anywhere near his pockets. I held him, and had Stubbs search."

"How did the forged money get there?" Pitt asked.

"I gave it to one of the people he was going to collect from. He owed me a favor and was glad enough to earn a contribution to its repayment."

"Good. So what is it?" It was on the edge of Pitt's tongue to ask why Tellman was here at half past one in the morning, but he looked so wretched he forbore.

"Wetron called me into his office about it," Tellman replied quietly, staring at his hands on the kitchen table. "He was bound to hear, but it was quick! I don't know whether it was Stubbs who reported to him, or Grover from Cannon Street, who was with Jones when I arrested him." He raised his eyes to Pitt's. "Wetron crowed a bit, but he told me that the money from the anarchists is raised by Piers Denoon, Magnus Landsborough's cousin. He said everyone knows that, and Special Branch is pretty poor not to have found out. He's setting me up to see if I'll tell you."

"Yes . . ." Pitt agreed. He could hear the kettle begin to hiss. "Of course he is. You—"

"It's true," Tellman cut across him. "I found out for myself. I asked about him, and I got him at home and told him the police knew what he was doing. He went straight to report to his leader." His face was now almost gray, and behind Pitt the kettle was beginning to whistle.

Pitt ignored it. "Who?"

"Simbister."

Pitt felt the cold bite into him, and a faint sickness in his stomach. It should not have surprised him. It was what Welling and Carmody had implied. He tried once to evade it. "Of Cannon Street? Are you sure?"

"Yes."

"At his home? Are you certain?"

"Yes. Are you going to see Jones?" Tellman asked.

"No. I can't do it without running the risk that Wetron will hear of it. I doubt he'd tell me anything."

Tellman nodded unhappily.

"Thank you."

He stood up to take the kettle off the hob before it woke the rest of the house. "What do you know about Piers Denoon?" he asked, reaching for the tea caddy.

Quietly, Tellman told him.

First thing in the morning Pitt sent a message to Voisey, and at noon once again he walked down the steps to the crypt of St. Paul's, and along the same arched aisle as before. This time he went past Nelson's tomb to that of the great Duke of Wellington, successful against the Maratha Confederacy in India, commander of the campaign in the Peninsular War, and finally, of course, victor at Waterloo.

Voisey was standing at the far end of the tomb, moving his weight from one foot to the other. He turned as he heard the sound of Pitt's steps. A flush of irritation crossed his face at his own predictability. "I assume you have a damned good reason for this!" he said in a low voice as soon as Pitt was beside him. "I was about to have a meeting with the home secretary."

"Of course I have," Pitt replied tersely, glancing at the magnificent tomb. It was solemn and imposing as befitted the greatest military leader in British history, and yet still less ornate or individual than Nelson's. It spoke of glory and admiration, but not love. "Do you think I would send for you for anything less?"

Voisey ignored the "send for you" with difficulty and it showed on his face. "Well, what is it?" he demanded.

Pitt was certainly not going to tell him about the arrest of Jones the Pocket, or his plans to take his place. It was dangerous enough as it was, with little he could do to protect himself. Nor was he going to mention Tellman, for the same reasons.

"The anarchists are getting their funds through Piers Denoon, only son of Edward Denoon," he told Voisey. "He is an erratic, nervy young man, but apparently brilliant at raising money." He saw Voisey's face light with an interest too vivid for him to conceal. "When frightened into believing the police were aware of it," Pitt continued, "he reported immediately, at one in the morning, to Simbister, head of Cannon Street police."

Voisey swore, and let out his breath slowly. This time he did not bother to hide his emotion. His cheeks were flushed, almost hiding the blotchy freckles. "I knew it!" he said between clenched teeth. "The corruption goes all the way! Who told you about Piers Denoon? Wetron?"

"Indirectly," Pitt said.

Very deliberately Voisey glanced at Wellington's tomb. "Great tactician," he said, his expression now impossible to read, there was irony in it, amusement, anger. "Do you know about his 'scorched earth' policy? I don't think you would approve of it." The inflection in his voice suggested that his own opinion was different, and that the disagreement in Pitt was based on some kind of weakness, a failure of courage.

He looked again at the huge, imposing tomb.

Pitt was at a disadvantage, as was undoubtedly Voisey's intention. "I assume this scorched-earth policy has some relevance to Wetron, or Denoon, or you would not bother mentioning it now?"

"Of course it has, but he's not a lovable hero, is he!" That was a remark almost thrown away. "I imagine you prefer Nelson. They all adored him. And of course he had the exquisite good taste to die on deck at the height of his greatest victory. Who could question him after that? It seems like blasphemy. Whereas Wellington, stupid sod, had the poor judgment to come home safe and sound, and go on to be prime minister. Unforgivable."

Voisey flashed a brief smile. "He won in Vimiero early in the Peninsular War, then the year after chased the French army all the way to Madrid. But when they forced him to retreat, in 1810, he laid waste to the land behind him as he moved on. Ugly, but very effective."

"You admire it?" Pitt asked, then realized how he had betrayed his own revulsion.

Voisey savored the moment. "Do you want to separate the man from the campaign?" he asked with a lift in his voice. "Without Wellington, Napoleon might have won. Almost certainly he would have. He was a genius. Or don't you think so?" There was a challenge in his voice, undisguised.

"Of course he was," Pitt agreed. "A little ill-considered to attack Moscow! A wiser man might have learned from the scorched-earth policy in Spain. Maybe he didn't appreciate that scorched and frozen are essentially the same when it comes to feeding an army."

Voisey's eyes widened, a flash of humor in them. "You know, Pitt, I could almost forget myself and like you! Just when I think you are utterly predictable, you surprise me."

"Very arrogant to think you can predict someone," Pitt observed. "And arrogance is stupid, sometimes fatally so. We can't afford that."

"One moment you are pedestrian," Voisey went on as if Pitt had not spoken, but the sharp angle of his body betrayed his tension. "The next acutely perceptive, then complacent to the point of idiocy! Perhaps it comes from being half gamekeeper, half would-be gentleman."

Pitt forced himself to smile. The slur on his heritage stung. Why did Voisey feel a need to attack him so sharply that he could not govern it? What was it in Pitt that disturbed him so much that he did not hide it? "Does Wellington's scorched-earth policy in the Peninsular War have anything at all to do with Wetron and the anarchist bombs, or Simbister and Denoon?" he asked curiously. "Or did you just want to see if I knew as much military history as you did?"

Quite suddenly Voisey started laughing, openly and with apparently quite genuine humor.

Pitt had to remind himself that Voisey hated him. Voisey had caused the death of the Reverend Rae, a good and innocent old man, and he had killed Mario Corena himself, even if he had been forced into it. He was behind scores of other acts of greed and destruction. His wit and essential humanity, his power to laugh or to be hurt were irrelevant. His hate was all that mattered, and Pitt must never forget it. If he did, it could cost him all he had.

"Do you think Wetron is planning to scorch the earth if he's forced to retreat?" Pitt asked aloud.

"I think he'll burn it to a cinder," Voisey replied. "Don't you?"

"Only if he is sure he's lost. He is a long way from losing now."

Voisey was still watching him intently. If anyone else passed by the tombs of the famous, neither of them saw or heard. "I think he'll be happy to cast Sergeant Tellman into the flames," Voisey said softly. "And he could most certainly do it."

"Of course," Pitt agreed. "But he won't destroy a tool he believes he can use."

"Against whom?" Voisey raised his eyebrows. "He would hurt you far more by destroying Tellman than anything else he could do." There was a sharp, satisfied glitter in his eye. "You would miss him, but the guilt for using him, and putting him in the path of such danger, would corrode inside you forever." He stared at Pitt, trying to read his mind and touch the soft, vulnerable passions inside, to see where the center of pain lay. Was he speaking of Wetron? Or reminding Pitt that he too could do that if he chose?

Pitt looked away from Voisey and regarded the monument to Wellington. "He was a great soldier," he remarked almost casually.

"I suppose victors have certain things in common. One is that they don't go chasing personal vanities, petty issues of vengeance or justification, instead of the main cause." His eyes followed the name on the marble facade. "He would never have left the field of Waterloo to fight a duel with one man, whoever he was. He would have chosen his lieutenants for their ability, not because he liked or disliked them, or for favors owed or expected. He never lost sight of the real goal." He looked back at Voisey. "That's a rare quality, the ability to concentrate. I think Wetron has that, don't you?"

A flush of fury washed up Voisey's cheeks. They both knew Wetron had beaten Voisey to take over the leadership of the Inner Circle. It was the last thing he wanted to be reminded of.

"It isn't over yet," he said in a thin, hard voice. "Don't they say 'he laughs best who laughs last'? Don't be arrogant, Pitt." There was an edge of spite to that, a warning of how thin the veneer of wit or alliance was. "If you imagine because you beat him once that you can do it every time, you're more of a fool than I took you to be, and you're no use to me as an ally, except as cannon fodder!" He said the last words with immeasurable contempt.

"A soldier who won't face the cannons is not much use to anyone," Pitt pointed out. "So far the best attack from our side has come through Tellman. It is in both our interests to do what we can to keep him alive. If that means letting Wetron imagine he can feed information both ways, I'll do that. However, it seems that Piers Denoon is definitely linked to the anarchists, by providing money to them. When he felt threatened, he went straight to Simbister, at one o'clock in the morning. And he was admitted."

"The question," Voisey said slowly, "is how much is Edward Denoon behind the anarchists? And can we prove it? Or for that matter, how much did Sheridan Landsborough know about his son's activities?"

"It could be anything, or nothing," Pitt answered. "And while it is interesting, it doesn't help us fight against the bill. All it will tell us, at best, is which side they ally with. So far we know from his newspaper that Denoon is for the bill, and Landsborough has said nothing at all."

"What will he say?" Voisey asked softly.

"I don't know. He's lost his only son. I daresay he doesn't know either. But this new side of the bill may be a step too far. It could be a blackmailer's charter."

"The right to question servants without the master knowing?" Voisey said bitterly, his face tight with anger. "Of course it's a blackmailer's charter, for God's sake! Wetron could have the leaders of the nation in his hands. Is there any man in England whose valet doesn't know something about him that he would rather were not repeated? Even if it is only that he wears a corset to hold his belly in, or that his wife would rather sleep with the footman— although with luck she has more sense than actually to do it."

"Probably not," Pitt agreed. "But that is its weakness, not its strength. It means that no one will feel secure enough to vote for it."

Voisey closed his eyes. "You are beautifully naive! At least it would be beautiful, if it weren't so damn dangerous." His eyes opened wide. "They won't phrase it like that, you fool! There'll be all kinds of promises that it won't apply to the innocent. They'll swear it will only be used on those suspected of anarchist conspiracies. Every man in Parliament will know that he is either guiltless in that, or else he is already allied with Wetron, and imagines that protects him. And if he is in the Inner Circle, he is probably right. 'The guilty flee where no man pursueth,' " he quoted. "And all too often the innocent stand rooted to the spot imagining their innocence will save them. Until it is too late to run."

"Surely you have the skill, and either have or can acquire the knowledge to suggest to a few of your more articulate friends that there are issues in their private lives they would prefer no servant were pressured to speak of?" Pitt asked.

Voisey stood still for several seconds, a wry slow smile curving his lips. "Why, Pitt! You have quite a flair for blackmail yourself! How very interesting. I confess, I never suspected it of you."

"You have to have some idea of what the crime is before you can become successful at solving it," Pitt said drily.

Voisey pushed his hands into his pockets. "Now that much is obvious about Wetron," he remarked. "I wonder why I never realized it about you? I accept the criticism."

Pitt knew what he was doing. The comparison with Wetron was meant to hurt. "Because Wetron is head of the Inner Circle," he replied levelly. "You likened him to yourself."

The barb went home perfectly. He saw it in Voisey's face. Voisey winced very slightly, then surprisingly he shrugged. "I underestimated you, Pitt. If you don't lose your nerve, you could be really very useful. You have more intelligence than I thought you had. It's your rather erratic conscience I worry about."

Pitt grinned. "We all fear what we don't know."

Voisey gave a little grunt, but there was humor in his eyes. He started to walk slowly away from the tomb.

Pitt swung around and caught up with him. "You appear to have forgotten something," he said.

"Do I?" Voisey did not stop.

"You told me when you suggested this . . . collaboration . . . that you had particular knowledge to bring to it regarding the Inner Circle. It is time you offered some. To begin with, is Sheridan Landsborough a member?"

"No," Voisey said with hesitation. "Unless he has joined in the last half year, which I suppose is possible, but I doubt it. Rather high-flown ideals—that eccentric conscience again. Self-indulgent." His eyes caught Pitt's and flickered away. "Would never have left Waterloo to fight a personal duel, but he might well have left it to rescue a drowning dog, or something of the sort. Highly impractical. Now we would all be speaking French."

"I always thought anarchy was a little impractical." Pitt fell into step with him. "I like ideals, but only those that actually work.

And considering what will work, you must know several of the members of Parliament who are in the Circle, and know them well enough to be aware of what they would rather keep out of police hands. Remind them of the dangers."

"Inner Circle members do not betray one another," Voisey said as they approached the steps up into the main body of the cathedral. "That is one of its great strengths—loyalty above all."

"Yes, I know," Pitt agreed. "And the penalty for betrayal is death. I've seen it. Is Parliament planning that only those police in the Inner Circle are to have the power to question people's servants?"

Voisey turned and missed his step, catching his balance by gripping onto the rail. "Your point is well taken," he said quietly. "It is a weapon we must use. Next time we will make it Turner's memorial."

"Good," Pitt agreed. "I like Turner."

Voisey smiled. "Police must earn a better wage than I thought! Have you many Turners at home? Or do you have lots of time to go around to the galleries?"

"Robbery detail," Pitt replied with a smile. "Not much point in trying to recover a stolen painting you wouldn't recognize from a forgery."

"Fascinating," Voisey said drily. "Police work is obviously more complex than I thought." He continued up the steps towards the host of people who were gathering, staring around them.

"The house where I grew up had a Turner," Pitt went on. "I always preferred him to Constable. It's all in the use of light." He smiled at Voisey and walked away. It was true; the estate on which his father had been gamekeeper had had several fine paintings. But Pitt let Voisey make his own assumption.

PITT REPORTED TO Narraway briefly. He needed him to know about Piers Denoon and Simbister, not that he expected him to be surprised.

"So Denoon is running with the hare and hunting with the hounds," Narraway remarked, stretching out in his chair and regarding Pitt. "Or father and son are on different sides? Interesting. What about the Landsboroughs? Were they on different sides also? Sheridan Landsborough used to be extremely liberal in his youth. He had a considerable social conscience and deplored what he perceived as heavy-handed government. 'Interference' was the word he used. But then, as they say, every man with a heart is liberal in his youth, and every man with a head is conservative in his old age. What is he now, Pitt? Mature preserver of order, or senile tolerator of license?" He raised his eyebrows. "Wise politician, bereaved father, husband who wants peace in his home? Brother to defend his sister's son? Or simply a man confused, hurt, and out of his depth?"

"I don't know," Pitt admitted. "I've been too busy pursuing police corruption." He said it with defiance, not in anger in case he were attacked, but simply in a statement to Narraway that that was his priority. He cared very much who had killed Magnus Landsborough, but solving that crime would have to wait upon the larger issue. He did not even know if the murder had been personal or political. That was the next thing he intended to learn. He told Narraway about Jones the Pocket, and his plan to make the next collection of extortion money himself.

Narraway sat up straight. "I don't like it, Pitt," he said quietly. "I can't protect you—or Tellman. You've left him wide open."

"I know," Pitt admitted. It hurt and he was very aware of it.

"What about Voisey? What is his part in this?"

"Anything he can to curb the police bill, particularly the part about questioning servants in secret. He should know enough through his old Inner Circle days to frighten a few people."

Narraway regarded him soberly. "Any information would be in the hands of people like Wetron, anyway. He wouldn't use it to destroy his own. The Inner Circle has never turned on one another, except Voisey and Wetron, and Wetron will make damn sure that never happens again. Anyone who even thinks of such a thing will be torn to bits by the others. They survive through loyalty. You should have known that, Pitt."

"I do," Pitt replied, sitting down in the chair opposite him. "Do you think that any policeman who is given the power by the act of Parliament is going to pass it on to his superior, then quietly forget it? Most of them are honorable, but corruption begets corruption." He heard the bitterness he felt very clearly in his voice. "That's what I hate about it most, the contagion of it. Men who could have been good become tainted, and the more of it there is the harder it is to survive without being touched by it. If you give people power, sooner or later they are tempted to abuse it. It takes a very strong man not to, a man wise enough to see its price, brave enough to go against the tide, and he can pay dearly for it."

Narraway's face darkened and he sat up in his chair, no longer at any kind of ease. "Be careful of whoever is behind the extortion," he warned. "Remember, you play by rules, they don't."

Pitt knew Narraway was worried for him, but the warning still irritated him. "You sound like Voisey."

Narraway shot upright, scraping the legs of his chair on the floor. "For God's sake! You didn't tell him—"

"Of course I didn't!" Pitt said tartly. "I told him about Piers Denoon, nothing else. He patronizes me, as if I know nothing about crime. You'd think I was a country parson!"

"I've known a few country parsons. One of them in particular was more familiar with the ugly side of human cruelty and greed than anyone else I've met. He saw them when they were very small sins, but he recognized the hunger for dominion over others, the use of belittlements, countless small humiliations that destroy belief." He stopped suddenly, as if recalling himself to the present. "Get on with it, Pitt. Find out exactly what is happening in this anarchist group."

"Yes, sir. Have you learned anything that I ought to know?"

A ghost of quite real humor flickered in Narraway's eyes. "Are you asking me to report to you, Pitt?"

Pitt weighed his chances of getting away with candor. He chose to risk it. "Yes, sir, it might be helpful."

Narraway's eyebrows rose. "So far the likelihood of the Inner Circle being penetrated by any European power is extremely slight," he said. "However, there are certain men high in finance whose interests might not coincide with England's. You do not need to know more than that. Attend to the police corruption. It endangers us all."

PITT FOUND WELLING in a cell in Newgate Prison. He looked cold in spite of the fact that it was quite a pleasant day outside. The stone seemed to hold a dampness that ate into the flesh and touched the bones. His face was even paler and his hair more unkempt than last time. He sat on the cot, his shoulders hunched.

"What do you want?" he asked as Pitt came in and the warden closed the door behind him with the clang of iron on stone. "I told you before, I'm giving you no names and no places. Don't you believe me?"

"I believe that you mean what you say," Pitt answered. The air was stale in here. There was only one man living in it, yet it had the odor of many men, as if it had never been washed, or had clean air blown through it. The heaviness added to the sense of chill.

"So why are you wasting your time here? You haven't any idea who shot Magnus, have you?" Welling said with a sneer curling his lip. "Except it was the police, and you won't admit that! You're helpless."

"If it was someone in the police, I'd like to know who," Pitt responded.

"What difference does it make? You aren't going to do anything about it."

"Don't you want to know who it was?"

Welling slid a little farther down in the cot, his arms folded tight across his chest. "What for? They're all the same to me. And Magnus will be just as dead, and there'll still be no justice. I don't care a damn who."

Pitt felt the man's anger and fear as if there had been a drop in temperature in the air. It made him angry as well, for the futility of it and the blindness, but it also stirred a pity. He had known something very close to it when, as a child, his father had been accused falsely of poaching, a form of theft taken very seriously then. He could not prove his innocence. He had been deported, and Pitt had never seen him again.

He concentrated on the present. "How many policemen did he know?" he asked, controlling his voice with an effort.

"What?" Welling was startled.

Pitt repeated the question.

"None!" Welling said angrily. "The police are liars, corrupt oppressors, and thieves from the poor. Why would you ask such a stupid question?"

"Then why would a policeman kill Magnus?" Pitt asked.

"Because we know them for what they are! Are you stupid?" Welling snarled.

"Yes, it seems you do," Pitt agreed. "So why kill Magnus and leave you and Carmody alive? Or was Magnus the only one who was any danger to them?"

It was a second or two before Welling realized what he meant, then his face flooded scarlet with outrage. "How dare you? You filthy—" He stopped equally abruptly. Suddenly, like someone opening the door into a lighted room, he understood what Pitt was saying.

"Exactly," Pitt nodded. "Magnus was killed for a personal reason, not because he was an anarchist, you agree?"

Welling swallowed, his throat jerking. "Yes . . ." he said hoarsely. "But who would do that?"

"I don't know. Let's start with why."

Welling was staring at him as if he had seen a new horror, something that had never occurred to him before.

Pitt began to think, with surprise and a thread of pity, how naive these young men were. They spent their passion hating an enemy that was formed of a whole class of people, impersonal, without individual names or faces, personalities, lives. It was easy, in comparison. But when they were obliged to consider being hated for themselves, fiercely enough to kill, Welling, at least, was appalled.

"Did anyone want to take Magnus's place as leader?" he asked aloud.

"Of course not!" Welling was disgusted by the thought, it was clear in his wide eyes and twisted mouth. "That's your kind of belief, not ours. We don't want a morality where one person has to obey another, regardless of what their conscience dictates. We're not looking for power. The very idea of it is corrupt."

"Someone took a gun, hid behind a door, and shot Magnus in the back of the head," Pitt reminded him. "I don't know whether I would call that corrupt, precisely. But it is certainly against my law. Is it all right with yours? Or your lack of it?"

"No, of course it isn't! It's vile," Welling spat. "It's not only brutal, it's cowardly."

"It suggests he didn't want to be seen," Pitt amended. "Perhaps if you had seen him, you would have known his face."

Welling gulped again. "Maybe."

"We're back to someone Magnus knows," Pitt went on. "Not only that, but someone who knew where you would run to after the Myrdle Street bombing. We didn't know that. Who did?"

Welling stared at him, blinking slowly.

"Other anarchist groups?" Pitt asked.

"Why would they want to kill Magnus?" Welling said miserably. "We all want the same thing!"

"Do you? Is there only one kind of chaos? Perhaps they think there are several."

"We don't want chaos! You are ignorant . . . a stupid man!" Welling was growing increasingly annoyed, sitting upright again. "One minute you sound as if you can think and have some shred of understanding, then the next you go and say something so bigoted, so crass, you betray everything in you that would be worthwhile. Anarchy isn't about chaos, or violence." He chopped his hand in the air. He leaned forward towards Pitt, his eyes burning. "Anarchy is about getting rid of tyranny so all men can be free and be their better selves. Wise men, whole men, should be able to grow, become the best in themselves." His voice rose in enthusiasm. "Evolve into free men, away from the petty rules imposed by laws, courts, governments, the armies of small men who enslave the mind. There is only one true law: that of reason and the universal brotherhood of humanity. All else is a fear of imprisonment, an unrighteous dominion of one man over another. Let us all be equal, and free."

Pitt thought for a moment. "If you want an equal gift, then you must be prepared to pay an equal price," he said at last. "And I don't think all men are prepared. Some are lazy, and some are greedy. If there are no laws, and no one to enforce them, who will protect the weak?"

"You don't understand!" Welling accused.

Pitt leaned against the stone wall. "Explain it to me."

"Without oppression, we wouldn't need to protect the weak," Welling said at last. "No one would harm them."

"Except people who hid behind doorways and shot them in the back of the head."

Welling was very pale. "That wasn't one of us!"

"Yes it was."

"No it wasn't!" Welling shouted. "Maybe it was the old man? There was an old man who accosted him several times in the street. He seemed to know him, and I saw them arguing. It was pretty fierce, but Magnus wouldn't say who he was, or what it was about."

"Old man?" Pitt demanded. "Describe him."

Welling's eyes widened. "You think he could have killed Magnus?" His face lit with hope. "Why would he? It was just a quarrel. Where would he get the gun? He was far too old to be an anarchist."

Pitt smiled in spite of himself. "How old?"

"I don't know. Sixty, or more? He was tall and thin. He had white hair."

"And they quarreled?"

"Yes."

"What was his manner like?"

Welling froze, understanding in his eyes. "Gentle man," he said softly. "He wasn't dressed like one, but his voice . . ."

"His father?" Pitt asked, wishing it were possible for Welling to deny it. He could not help thinking of his own son, and far in the future wondering how he would feel were Daniel to espouse some extremist politics that turned him towards crime. What would he do to try to save him from what he saw as wrong? How would he comfort Charlotte? How much would he blame himself for whatever had gone wrong? It was easy to put himself in Landsborough's place.

Or was it? Had he been seeking to protect his son, or the political system he believed in himself? Or even the honor of his family, with all the comforts and privileges that gave them. His son would bring disgrace upon it?

That was a hideous thought, but honesty compelled him at least to consider it.

Welling looked at him. "Maybe. Magnus never said anything about it. But that old man wasn't the only one. There was a younger man too, well set up."

Pitt was puzzled. "And his voice?"

"No idea. He never spoke, that I knew of."

"A rival anarchist?"

"Looked like a servant to me, sort of discreet but there," Welling replied. Then his candor vanished. "I'm telling you nothing about any of us. Anarchists have that much loyalty."

"So you have," Pitt said with admiration in his voice. "It looks as if you are prepared to hang for each other." He saw Welling's skin pale. Perhaps he was more afraid than Carmody had been. Pitt continued. "You must be very sure that your ideals are the same. Which makes me wonder why one of you killed Magnus, and he did it from hiding."

There was a sneer on Welling's lips. "You can't hang me for shooting Magnus. There's no way even you can make it seem as if I did it. I was in the room when you got there, and nowhere near the door he was shot from. Everyone heard the man escape. Your own police heard him come down the back stairs, and let him go." His voice wavered as the realization came that they could lie, even if only to cover the fact that they had made such an error. He gulped. It was clear in his eyes that he believed Pitt would do that, and the rest of them also. "I wouldn't have killed him! You know that!"

"Yes, I do," Pitt agreed. "At least not personally. But you might have connived at it. You are keen enough to protect whoever did, so it's reasonable to suppose you are allies, or even that you paid him. . . ." He saw the horror in Welling's eyes, and in that moment knew his innocence. "But I was actually referring to the policeman in the street who was shot," he finished.

"He wasn't . . . dead . . ." Welling's uncertainty was naked in his face.

Pitt refused the temptation to imply that he was. "No, but that was lucky. You still tried to kill him."

"I . . . I . . ." Welling's voice died away. There was no argument that mattered.

Pitt waited while he considered it. Imprisonment would be harder than Welling would have any idea of, but there was a finality about the rope.

"Are you a religious man?" Pitt asked suddenly.

Welling was startled. "What?"

"Are you a religious man?" Pitt repeated.

The sneer came back to Welling's face, but it was more out of bravado than confidence. "You don't have to believe in God to have a morality," he said bitterly. "The Church has got the biggest hypocrites of the lot! Have you any idea how much they own? How many of them preach one thing, and do something quite different? They condemn people whose lives they don't begin to understand, and—"

"I wasn't thinking of morality," Pitt cut across him. "I've no more time for hypocrites than you have. I was thinking of there being anything to hope for after death."

Welling went as white as a sheet. Suddenly he found it hard to breathe.

"You're a young man," Pitt said more gently. "You don't have to give up your life, or all you can do in it, the good things and the mistakes, if you help me find out who killed Magnus Landsborough, and prove it. It was a wrong thing to do, by your morality and mine. I have the authority to give you amnesty for the shooting of the policeman, or anything else, if you help."

Welling licked his lips. "How do I know that? How do I know you aren't lying? Maybe the policeman did die!"

"No, he didn't. He'll be back on duty in a few weeks. The shot went through his shoulder. Didn't touch the artery." He pulled the piece of paper from his pocket with the promise Narraway had written for him and passed it to Welling, who took it and read it, blinking several times, his hands shaking slightly.

"What about Carmody?" he said at last. "I . . ." He had to clear his throat. "I won't save myself and let you hang him."

Pitt could only guess what it had cost him to say that. He admired him for it. "You won't have to," he promised. "The same offer goes for him, if he wants it. Now tell me all you know about

Magnus Landsborough, who'll be leader in his place—you can call him whatever you like—and the old man who spoke to him. How often, where, what time of day or night? How did Magnus react?"

Welling told him bit by bit, measuring every word so he was not tricked into betraying something he had not meant to. He could give no name to the man he believed would be the new leader, but his respect for him was clear. He shared Magnus's passion against unjust dominion of one person over another. He was infuriated by the helplessness of the poor, the disadvantaged in health or intelligence, in education, birthright, or simply position in society. Power without responsibility was for him the ultimate evil, the begetter of cruelty, injustice, every kind of abuse one person may inflict upon another.

Pitt discussed with him only the means with which he sought to address it. Perhaps Welling sensed something of that, because he began to speak with less contempt, and more cordially of his hope to achieve some greater balance.

Pitt did not argue with him that in his belief it owed as much to human nature as to any specific political system. It rose to his mind to do so, but the coldness of the cell, the stale odor of the air, reminded him of the immediate urgency of corruption today, and Wetron's power in the future.

Welling also told him of Magnus's meeting with the older man. It had happened perhaps half a dozen times, and that Magnus had seemed disturbed by it. He had refused to say who the man was, or what he wanted, but he would hear no ill of him, nor would he permit any of the others to approach the old man or warn him not to come again. The few of their conversations that had been observed were obviously arguments. The older man's feelings had run high, but no one knew enough to say what they had been, and Magnus refused to discuss it at all.

Pitt broached the subject of the source of the money, obliquely at first, but he gained no response. Welling became even more guarded.

"There's no need to protect him," Pitt said casually. "We know who he is. In fact the police know as well."

Welling smiled. "Then you don't need us to tell you," he said.

"No. I wouldn't mention it if there were any chance that you would warn him."

"Really." Welling's voice was back to its initial skepticism.

"Piers Denoon," Pitt told him, and saw the chagrin in Welling's eyes. Not that he needed any confirmation. It was on the edge of his tongue to ask if Magnus and Piers had quarreled. Perhaps Magnus had realized that Piers was a double player, both for the anarchists and the police, and had threatened to expose him. Then, just before he spoke, he thought of the danger to Tellman. Welling might testify in court to defend himself, and the information could get back to the police. He changed his mind. But the possibility remained. Maybe it was Piers Denoon who had killed Magnus, to safeguard himself.

IT WAS JUST AFTER NOON when Pitt began his round of the public houses, replacing Jones the Pocket. He had seldom performed any task he loathed more. Perhaps because he knew how much he would hate it, he dressed in old clothes as unlike his usual ones as possible, as if he were trying to divorce himself from the act. He had brought a tweed jacket that was patched in places, something he would never have chosen otherwise. It was prickly to touch, and too warm in the evening sun.

In every place he went to, he had to explain that Jones was temporarily indisposed, and until he returned, Pitt was taking his place.

"Sick, is 'e?" one landlord said hopefully. "Real sick?"

"Probably," Pitt replied. "And if he spends any time in the Coldbath Fields, he'll get sicker." He was referring to the London prison whose reputation was the worst.

"Wot a cryin' shame," the landlord said smiling broadly. Then the smile vanished and he glared at Pitt, "I 'ope it's catchin'!"

"Maybe," Pitt had already made up his mind what he intended to do. "But I won't get it so badly."

"Why's that then? You look jus' the same ter me!"

"I'm not as susceptible," Pitt answered. "Jones was hard. I want you to stay in business. I'll take half what he did. That'll be enough. Just keep it regular."

The man looked startled, then suspicious. "I don't want that bleedin' Grover comin' 'ere an smashin' up the place," he said warily.

"You don't think Jones kept anything for himself?" Pitt raised his eyebrows.

"Oh yeah? An' you're doin' it fer nothin'? Do I look like I came down wi' the last rain?"

"I have my reasons," Pitt answered. "Give me half, and get on to serving your customers. The longer you stand there arguing with me, the more you neglect them."

In the next place it was essentially the same, and so on around them all. He collected nearly sixteen pounds. That was as much as an ordinary constable on the beat would earn in three months.

He could neither keep the money nor risk losing it. There was only one place where it would be safe, and also keep him from the possible charge of having extorted it for himself. Wetron would be delighted to try that! It would be an exquisite irony.

"Sixteen pounds!" Narraway said, flinging it down on his desk as if its source tainted him even to touch it. "That's nearly fifty pounds a month, just from those few poor devils."

"I know," Pitt agreed. "And I only took half what Jones did."

"Jones took twice that? Why didn't you go to all of them?"

"I did. I just took half the money."

Narraway rolled his eyes, but allowed his expression to make his comment.

"Look after it," Pitt requested.

"Now what?" Narraway asked, his face creased, suddenly serious. "Someone will be expecting to receive this. You're playing a damn dangerous game, Pitt. What's to stop them cutting your throat, to make an example of you? Especially when you haven't got the money."

"Greed," Pitt answered. "Whoever comes after me will be getting a cut. They'll want it, and I'll offer them more. I'm no use dead."

"You haven't got more. You've got less!" Narraway pointed out.

"Since I haven't got it with me, they won't know that."

"They may not believe you've got it at all, you fool!" Narraway said, suddenly furious. "Do you think I've got men to spare tracking you around London until someone comes after you for this?"

"It won't be long," Pitt told him frankly. He was taking a risk, and he knew it. Please heaven he had judged Narraway accurately enough that he would back him now. "I went a little earlier than Jones would have, and I left two altogether. If I go back for them in an hour or two, someone'll be waiting for me. I'll need men just long enough for that. Please . . . please give me someone who won't hesitate to step in, if he's needed."

Narraway swore elegantly and viciously. "You try my patience, Pitt. But you'll have someone, and they'll be armed. And it will be someone who'll shoot if need be, I'll promise you that."

"Thank you, sir."

Narraway glared at him.

IT WAS DUSK WHEN Pitt walked slowly down the cobbled street towards the last public house to collect the extortion money. He was trying to judge the exact manner to display. If he looked completely unafraid he might arouse suspicion. He had robbed an organization of a considerable amount of money. If he were not afraid, it could only be because he believed he had greater strength then they did. If they saw that, then this whole exercise was wasted, and he could not start again. It would not work a second time.

He could hear no footsteps behind him, only the moving and

shifting in doorways of beggars half asleep, the scuttle of rats' feet in the side alley, and the drip of leaking roofs and guttering. Fifty yards away someone laughed. He sounded drunk. Please God that Narraway's man was close too, watching him, there to protect him when the time came. Narraway could not afford to lose him, he was essential to his war against Wetron. There'd be nothing left of Special Branch if Wetron became commissioner.

Pitt tripped over a loose cobble and nearly pitched over. Narraway could not be a member of the Circle, could he? Double bluff!

A man was crossing the road towards him, a big man with heavy shoulders. The streetlamps were not lit yet, but there was still enough daylight to see his face. It was broad, big-nosed, a scar over one cheek. His left ear was almost shapeless from bruising and tearing.

He stepped in front of Pitt. When he spoke his voice was soft with a faint burr to it.

"I wouldn't go askin' fer that if I wuz you. In't no point, cos' I got it, see?" He was Pitt's height, and they stood face-to-face on the narrow pavement, about two feet apart. Pitt could feel the sweat run down his body and freeze. He prayed that his voice would stay steady enough to hide the fear that rippled through him.

"Did you collect the usual amount?" he asked politely.

"Course I did! Wot 'appened ter Mister Jones?"

"You don't know?" Pitt affected surprise. "He got careless. Took a bit of flash paper instead of the real thing. Got caught with it."

The big man pursed his lips. "Jones is too fly for that. Wot really 'appened?"

"It was a good copy. He got careless."

"Did you make that 'appen, then?"

Pitt decided to take the credit. "I have plans," he said in reply. "I can make more out of this than he did. I have contacts. And what you'll like about it is that I can make more for you too. That is, if you like?"

"Oh yeah? An' 'ow's that, then?" the man asked skeptically. "Tell me why I shouldn't stick a shiv inter yer gut an' take it all, eh?"

"Because I haven't got it with me, of course!" Pitt responded. "Stick a knife in me now, and you'll never know what I plan, and more to the point, you won't have any money to take back to your . . . master." He invested the word with contempt.

"In't nobody's my master!" the other man snarled.

"Jones the Pocket was working for you?" Pitt damned the idea as idiotic by the laughter in his voice. "You're an errand boy, a carrier of messages. But you don't have to be . . . Mr.—?"

"Yancy." He was interested, in spite of himself, but he kept his right hand in his pocket, where Pitt guessed he had his fingers around the hilt of a knife.

"You happy with being a messenger, Mr. Yancy?" Pitt was shaking slightly, his heart was knocking in his chest. "Safe, is it?"

"What do you want then?" Yancy asked cautiously.

"Who do you give it to?"

"If I tell you that, you'll take my place!" Yancy spat. "Think I'm a fool?"

"Not your place, Mr. Yancy, I want far more than that! I want his place!" He saw the doubt in Yancy's eyes. He had not gone far enough. How much did Yancy know? It all hung on persuading him now. A word too much, a word too little, and it would slip out of his grasp. "There are people getting a bit above themselves," he said, his voice catching. He needed to cough, to clear his throat, but it would betray his nerves. There was no one else on the footpath except a couple of street women twenty yards away. If Yancy pulled out the knife, they would look the other way, see nothing, know nothing. "I can give you a bigger share because I'm getting rid of the middleman," Pitt threw a wild gamble. "I report to the top. Are you in, or out?"

"Gawd!" Yancy let out a long breath. "Mr. Simbister isself? Grover'd kill me!"

"Higher than that, even," Pitt replied with a smile. "Are you in?"

Yancy opened his mouth to reply, and there was a shattering roar from two streets away. It was so violent the ground shook, and on the roof above them, slates broke loose and slid off the eaves to shatter on the streets. There was another ear-splitting roar and a gust of flame shot into the air. Someone was screaming, over and over and over. The crash of masonry drowned out voices and the smell and heat of the fire filled the dusk.

CHAPTER

EIGHT

Pitt turned on his heel, Yancy forgotten, and ran to the end of the street, round the corner, and towards the flame filling the sky. Behind the jagged outlines of the roofs, ripped open and spewing fire, the belching smoke already caught in his lungs as he came closer. People were crying out, weeping. Some were standing motionless as if too stunned or confused to know what to do. Others were running one way then the other, some just stumbled about aimlessly. Rubble was still falling, with charred and burning pieces of wood, and flying glass, the shards bright like daggers.

As Pitt came to the end of Scarborough Street, the smoke caught in his throat and he felt the heat on his face. There were injured people lying in the roadway, some motionless, crumpled over like heaps of rags, their limbs twisted. Someone was screaming. There was blood, smoking wood, bricks, and shards of glass everywhere. A dog barked incessantly. Above it all was the sound of flames soaring up inside what was left of the last three houses. In the heat, wood exploded, and slates flew off like hurled knives, edges sharp as blades, dust and rubble poured into the air.

Pitt stood still, trying to quell the horror inside himself and to keep control. Had anyone sent for the fire brigade? Burning wood was already falling onto the roofs on the next street. What about doctors? Anyone to help? He moved forward, trying to find any sort of order in the terror and chaos. He could see clearly now in the glare of the fire.

"Has anyone called for the fire engines?" he shouted as another wall caved in. "Get the people out!" He took an old woman by the arm. "Go to the end of the street!" he told her firmly. "Away from the heat. Things will fall on you if you stand here."

"My 'usband," she said, blank-eyed. " 'E's in bed. 'E were drunk out of 'is skin. I gotta get 'im. 'E'll be burned."

"You can't help him now." He did not release her. A young man was standing a few yards away, barefooted, shaking uncontrollably. "Here!" Pitt called to him. He turned slowly. "Take her out of the way," Pitt told him. "Move everyone. Help me!"

The young man blinked. Slowly awareness returned to his eyes and he obeyed. Other people were beginning to react, trying to help the injured, picking up children and carrying them away from the heat.

Pitt went to the nearest body lying on the stones and bent to look more closely. It was a young woman, half on her back, her legs doubled under her. A single glance at her face told him that she was beyond help. There was blood in her hair and her wide eyes had already misted over. He knelt beside her feeling sick and twisted inside with rage. They should have been able to stop this. This was not any kind of idealism or desire to reform; it was madness, inhumanity driven by stupidity and hate.

Someone was moaning a few yards away. There was no time to spend in emotion now. It helped no one. He clambered to his feet and went over to the person moaning. It was getting hotter. He found himself blinking and turning his head from the flying ash. More slates were sliding off the roof and falling onto the road or the pavement. He reached the person: an older woman with a badly broken leg and a blood-pouring gash in her arm. She must have been in a lot of pain, but it was the bleeding that was frightening her.

"You'll be all right," he said with conviction. He tore a piece off her petticoat and tied up her arm. He was afraid it might be too tight, but he had to stop the blood gushing through. Surely someone would have gone for a doctor?

"There." He stood up, then bent and lifted her onto the good leg. She was heavy and awkward, and it took all his strength. He nearly lost his balance. "Lean on me, and I'll get you as far as the main road," he said.

She thanked him, and as he turned towards the street again he saw Victor Narraway outlined against the flames. He was lean, all tense angles, his hair wildly on end, his face smeared with soot and lit red in the reflection.

Pitt's first reaction was disbelief. "How did you get here?" he had to shout above the noise. "So soon? Did you know about it?"

"Of course I didn't, you fool!" Narraway snapped, coming closer to him. "I was following you!"

"You were?" Pitt could scarcely grasp it. "Why? Didn't you think I'd do it?"

Another house collapsed inward, sending fire belching upwards like the roar of a volcano. The blast knocked both Pitt and Narraway backwards, the heat searing their hair and faces. Pitt stumbled, tripping over timber and the dead body of a man. Only Narraway catching his arm and almost twisting it out of its socket prevented him from falling. He righted himself with difficulty.

The first fire engine arrived, its horses panting and rolling their eyes, the driver steadying them with difficulty. Another followed immediately behind, but a glance was enough to show them it was useless trying to control any of the fires here. Only in the surrounding streets was there any chance of trying to keep it from spreading.

A young man with a bag in his hand was picking his way through the rubble, and every now and then he bent down.

Narraway shouted something, but Pitt could not hear the words. He shook his head and started towards where the man, presumably a doctor, was assisting someone onto his feet, but the weight was too much for him.

Pitt worked for as long as there was anything more he could do. He was aware of Narraway coming and going. Several times they searched the rubble together, for more people still alive, tearing off timber and broken bricks and glass. Narraway was stronger than Pitt would have expected, looking at his lean body, but he knew how to balance himself, and his will drove him on.

Finally the flames died down and the noise of the crashing and falling abated. There were more people helping. There seemed to be vans and wagons taking the injured away, and perhaps the dead as well. Many times Pitt saw the red light glare on polished buttons or the familiar tall shape of a police helmet. It was not until he stood still at the outside edge of the wreckage that he realized with dismay that it was not as comforting a sight as it had been only a few weeks before.

He stood beside a cart with rubble piled high, and Narraway was a couple of yards to the other side. Wordlessly he held out a tin mug with water in it. Pitt tried to speak but the sounds were strangled. He took the cup and drank. "Thank you," he said at last. It was completely dark now, and all he could see was the red glow of the fires that were still burning in two of the houses. The fire brigade had soaked the roofs farther over, and it had not spread.

Narraway took the cup back and raised it to his lips. Pitt was startled to see that his hand was trembling. His skin was smeared with blood and ash, and for the first time that Pitt had seen, there was fear in his eyes.

It was not physical fear. Narraway was not foolhardy, but he had gone towards the flames without hesitation, even close enough to the crumbling and exploding walls, in order to pull people out. Pitt didn't need to be told that it was the escalation of violence that frightened him, and the reaction there would be to this destruction. Almost the whole street was damaged beyond any further use. It would all have to be demolished and the ground cleared, and then new houses built.

Far worse than that, there were at least five people dead, and another twenty or more injured, some badly. They might yet die. This time there had been no warning, and there had obviously been at least three times as much dynamite as in Myrdle Street. They had no idea who had done it.

Pitt looked at Narraway, exhausted and filthy. No doubt his body ached just as much, his skin stung, his head felt pummeled and his lungs were tight and sore every time he took a breath. Most of all he would feel a sick overwhelming knowledge of failure. People would expect him to have prevented this. They hadn't even captured anyone to show for it. They had not a clue or a thread to follow. Nowhere to start, nothing to say it would not happen again, and again, as often as the anarchists had a mind to do it.

Narraway looked back at him. Both of them wanted to say something, but the truth did not need words, and lies of comfort were pointless and stupid, a shattering of what little there was left.

Narraway drank some more water and handed the mug back to Pitt, who finished the last of it.

"Go home," Narraway said, clearing his throat. "There's nothing anyone can do here tonight."

Pitt could think of nothing to do even tomorrow, but he ached to be back in Keppel Street and the safety of it. He was suddenly overwhelmingly sorry for Narraway that he had no such place to go, no one who loved him with unquestioning certainty. He did not want Narraway to know that he had seen it. "Thank you," he accepted quietly. "Good night."

He had not realized it was so late. It was nearly midnight when he opened the front door. By the time he had closed it, Charlotte, still dressed, was in the passage, the light in the parlor behind her.

"I'm all right!" he said too loudly, seeing the horror in her face. "It's only dirt! It'll all wash off."

"Thomas! What . . ." she gasped, her eyes wide, her cheeks almost bloodless. "What happened?"

"Another explosion," he answered. He wanted to take her in his arms now, immediately, but he was filthy. He would not only stain her clothes but pass on the stench of the fire.

She gave the matter no such thought. She flung her arms around him and held him fiercely, and kissed him. Then she buried her head in his shoulder and clung to him as if he might escape her were she to let go her grip.

He found himself smiling, touching her more gently because he was safe, and she was in his arms. Her hair had fallen out of its pins. He pulled out the remaining few and dropped them on the floor. Her hair fell down over her shoulders and he ran his fingers through it, feeling the softness of it. It was cool, like loose silk, so slippery and smooth it could almost have been liquid. And it smelled sweet, as if all the burning and the rubble and the blood had been in his imagination.

He was sorry for Narraway, and, if he had thought about it, he would even have been sorry for Voisey.

In the morning he awoke with a jolt, the silence of his bedroom beating in his ears. Memory returned with its violence and pain. Charlotte was already up. Daylight shone bright behind the curtains, and a gold strip crossed the floor where they were not quite closed. He could hear horses' hooves and wheels in the street.

He got up quickly. Charlotte had laid out clean clothes for him on the chair. The old clothes from last night were in the scullery, keeping the smell out of the bedroom.

He shaved and dressed, and was downstairs within a quarter of

an hour. His muscles ached from his exertions the previous night
and he had more bruises and scratches than he could count, but he
felt rested. He had slept without the nightmares he had expected,
and he was hungry.

The kitchen clock said nine, and there were no newspapers on
the table. Charlotte turned from the sink where she was drying
dishes, and smiled at him.

Gracie came in from the pantry with a bowl of eggs and bade
him good morning. He allowed them to look after him before he
asked what the news was.

"Bad," Charlotte said at last, when he was finishing his third
slice of toast and marmalade and refilling his tea. She went to the
pantry and returned carrying three newspapers. She put them on
the table in front of him, and took the plates.

When he saw the headlines, he was glad she had hidden them
until he had eaten. Denoon's paper was the worst. He did not criticize the police; he conceded that they had an impossible task.
Even with more men, better arms, and the freedom to arrest people on serious suspicion, they could not be expected to prevent
atrocities like this. It required the right to gain information before
such things reached the stage of violence. They must know who
planned such mass murder and destruction, who held beliefs that
prompted such war against the ordinary people of London and, for
all anyone would say, of the whole land.

The editorial was passionate, simple, and rang with an outrage
that would find an echo in half the households in England. The
police, Special Branch, the government itself were helpless to tell
anyone where or when it would happen again, which row of houses
would be the next to shatter into a burning ruin. This was far
worse than Myrdle Street.

No one had been killed there. The warning had given people
time to evacuate. No such humanity had been exercised this time.
What would be next? More, worse: greater numbers dead, fires that
could not be put out? The fire brigades could not control anything

much larger. There were not enough men. There were not the resources, even the water, to hand. Whole areas of London could burn. What was there to stop it?

The possibility of such terrible devastation required extreme measures to prevent it. The government must have the power to protect those who had elected it, and the people had the right to expect that. If the laws were needed, then they must be passed, before it was too late. Honor, patriotism, human decency required it. Survival depended upon it.

Pitt had expected to read something of the sort, yet seeing it in print now gave it a reality that he realized now he had been refusing to face. Denoon had not specified in detail the provision to question household servants without the master or mistress's knowledge. Even if he had, it is likely that most people would have seen nothing sinister in it. Those with nothing to hide would have nothing to fear. The use of such a power was easy enough to justify. It was the measure of it that was the blackmailer's charter. It was the ability to question people without having to prove to any authority that there was just cause, and the fact that the man or woman whose actions were being spoken of, whose intimate lives, whose personal habits and belongings, whose correspondence, whose friendships were being discussed, would have no chance to deny or explain or disprove anything that might be said. A servant could be mistaken, have overheard half a conversation, have remembered facts inaccurately or merely be repeating gossip. Worse than that, they could be spiteful, dishonest, ambitious, or simply gullible and easily led. It placed in their hands the power to blackmail any master or mistress with the threat of a betrayal against which they had no defense.

And the secrecy of it made the possibilities almost endless; there would be no safeguard at all.

He looked up to see Charlotte watching him.

"It's bad isn't it?" she said quietly.

"Yes." He could see in her eyes that she understood the depth of it as far and as clearly as he did. "Yes, it is."

"What can we do?"

He forced a smile at the inclusion of herself. "I'm going to go back and question the anarchists we've got in jail, although I don't suppose they can help," he answered. "I really don't believe it is anyone in their group doing this. This time at least five people were killed. It may make them more willing to talk. You are going to do nothing, unless you go and give Emily a little support." He searched her face. "Jack is one of the few allies we can rely on. It may cost him dearly."

"His career?" she asked.

"Perhaps."

She smiled very bleakly; it barely reached her eyes. "Thank you for not pretending. I wouldn't have believed you if you'd said it wouldn't."

He rose from the table, kissed her lightly, and went to the front door to put on his boots. He knew she was standing in the kitchen, still watching him.

HE WENT TO SEE Carmody first, and found him pacing the floor, so tense he was unable to sit down. He swung around as soon as he heard the key in the big iron lock, and was facing Pitt when he came in. His hair was matted and his overpale skin with its rash of freckles looked almost gray.

"Who did it?" he said accusingly. "That's murder! Why didn't you stop them? What's the matter with you? Who are they? Irish, Russian, Poles, Spaniards? What?"

"I don't think so," Pitt replied as levelly as he could. "Who told you about the explosion?"

"It's all over the prison!" Carmody shouted, losing control of his fury. "The warders are counting the hours till we get tried and hanged. It's nothing to do with us. For God's sake, we told you, so

you would get everybody clear. We wanted to get rid of bloody
Grover, and police corruption, not kill a whole street full of people."

"All the evidence is that it's not foreign anarchists, from Europe or anywhere else," Pitt replied.

"It's . . . not . . . us!" Carmody roared at him, his voice shaking.
"Can't you hear me? It's not what we want, or what we believe. It's
bestial! There's nothing of freedom or the honor or dignity of man
in it. It's just plain murder—and we're not murderers."

Pitt believed him, but he was not ready yet to say so.

"Magnus Landsborough's dead," he pointed out, leaning against
the wall. "You and Welling are in prison. Has it even occurred to
you that the purpose behind the Myrdle Street bombing was to get
you out of the way?"

Carmody started to speak, then stopped. His face drained of the
last vestige of blood. "Oh, God!" he breathed. "You think . . . no!"
He started to shake his head, repeating the word over and over, but
there was no belief in it. It was himself he was trying to convince,
and his eyes never left Pitt's.

"Why not?" Pitt asked him. "Maybe there was someone else in
your group who wanted to follow a different plan, a more violent,
more decisive one. Somebody certainly does!"

"No!" But it was an empty word. Carmody understood, and
even as the seconds ticked by it made more and more sense to
him. He sat down suddenly on the cot, as if his legs had given
way.

"Someone you know killed Magnus," Pitt went on, speaking
quietly and firmly. "Someone planned it. They knew where you
would escape to after the Myrdle Street bomb went off, and they
were there waiting for you. They shot Magnus, and then escaped
out the back way. They went down the stairs and past the police,
who thought it was one of us from the front, in pursuit of one of
yours. That takes thought, care, and intelligence. It also takes a

good deal of knowledge about your plans. Why would any one of you want Magnus dead, except to get rid of him as leader, and take over yourselves?"

Carmody raised both hands up to his face and pushed his hair back so hard it stretched the skin of his brow and pulled his features. "This is a nightmare!"

"No, it isn't," Pitt said deliberately. "It's real and you won't wake up from it. The only way out is to tell the truth now. Who is the man to take over the leadership if anything happened to Magnus? And don't tell me you never thought of that. That would be stupid. There was always a chance that any one of you could get caught, or killed."

"Kydd," Carmody said in a whisper. "Zachary Kydd. But I would have sworn he believed the same as we did. I'd have put my life on it!"

"Looks as if you would have lost, like the people in Scarborough Street last night."

Carmody said nothing.

"Where will Kydd be now? Unless you want more like last night, we've got to get him."

Carmody stared at him, his eyes wretched. "You're asking me to betray my friend."

"You can't be loyal to your friend and your principles. You have to choose. Even remaining silent is a choice."

Carmody closed his eyes. "He has a place about half way down Garth Street, in Shadwell, down near the docks. I don't know the number, but it's on the south side, with a brown door."

"Thank you. Just one more thing. The old man who kept on speaking to Magnus Landsborough, tell me as much about him as you know."

Reluctantly, and with more emotion than he could mask, Carmody described Magnus's meeting with the man who could only have been his father, and the heated exchanges they had had. The

older man was begging for something, and being refused. Afterwards, Magnus was always quiet. He would not discuss it, it was
quite clearly something that pained him. Twice Carmody had also
seen a younger man some way in the distance, as if following the
old man, but so discreetly that Carmody was not certain. It clearly
distressed him to recall it, and when Pitt left he was quiet, drawn
into the pain of his own memories.

VOISEY HAD AGREED that the next time that he and Pitt met
it should be at the memorial to Turner, and as before, at noon.
Surely, after last night's bombing, Voisey would be there?

Pitt was five minutes late, and strode across the black-and-
white marble floor. When he saw Voisey looking unnaturally
around, fidgeting from one foot to the other, he was annoyed and
also very slightly amused to feel such an intense relief.

Voisey was expecting him to arrive from the opposite direction, and spun around to face him only at the last moment. His
eyes lit with relief. "Is it as bad as the newspapers say?" he demanded.

"Yes. In fact it will get worse."

"Worse?" There was a bitter edge to Voisey's tone. "What have
you in mind?" he asked sarcastically. "Two streets destroyed?
Three streets? Another great fire of London, perhaps? We were
damned lucky that it only went as far as it did. At low tide and
with only a little rain, we could have lost half of Goodman's Fields
last night."

"Wait until Parliament meets this afternoon," Pitt answered
him. "We won't need any more explosions to make them demand
immediate passage of the bill, together with the provision to be
able to question servants. Did you read Denoon's editorial?"

Voisey turned away and started to walk as if he could not bear
to stand still. "Yes, of course I did. This is his chance, isn't it?
They'll use this to get the bill through!" It was really more of a

statement than a question. He did not need Pitt's answer. He knew before he came, he had been avoiding acknowledging the fact of defeat.

Pitt needed to walk swiftly to keep up with him, as if he had a purpose.

"If they burn down half of London again, do you suppose we can produce another genius to rebuild it like this?" Voisey said grimly. "They began this in 1675, you know." He gestured at the vast cathedral around him. "Only nine years after the fire. Finished it in 1710."

Pitt said nothing. He could not imagine London without St. Paul's.

They had reached the plaque to Sir Christopher Wren. Voisey read from it. " 'Lector, si monumentum requires, circumspice,' " he said. "I don't suppose you know what that means." His voice was hushed, there was admiration and bitterness mixed in it. " 'Reader, if you seek a monument, look around you.' " There was pain and awe in his face; his eyes were bright.

Suddenly Pitt caught a different and startling glimpse of Voisey as a man aching to make a mark in history, to leave behind him something uniquely his. He had no children. He had inherited, but he would not bequeath. Was part of his hatred envy? When he died, it would be as if he had not existed. Pitt looked at his face as he stared upwards, and saw in it for a few moments a bone-deep and naked hunger.

It was an intrusion to see it, like catching a man in a private act, and he looked away.

His movement caught Voisey's attention, and the mask was replaced instantly. "I don't suppose you know anything about who placed the bomb?" he said.

"Possibly," Pitt replied. He could feel Voisey's hatred, it had a new depth to it, as if it were a palpable thing in the still air and the near silence. No one else was near them, and the slight murmur of footsteps in the distance was so soft it faded into the background. They could have been alone. "The man to take on the leadership if anything happened to Magnus Landsborough is called Zachary Kydd. It's possible it was he who killed Magnus."

"An internal rivalry?" The contempt in Voisey's face was scalding.

Pitt felt his own temper rise. "It was someone who knew him, one of the anarchists."

"Why?" Voisey was incredulous. "He didn't need to get rid of Landsborough in order to blow up Scarborough Street!"

"How do you know that?" Pitt asked.

"Why the hell would he? Landsborough was going to stop him?" His disbelief was scathing. "How? Warn the police, get them out in force? Are you suggesting that someone in their group trusted the police?"

Pitt allowed an exaggerated patience into his voice. "To set off explosions like that, you need a great deal of dynamite, and planning, and people prepared to risk their own lives. Maybe Kydd didn't know that, until he'd taken over Magnus's leadership."

Voisey struggled for a few moments. Pitt was right, and he knew it. He met Pitt's eyes and saw the understanding in them. If he denied it, he would add one error to another. He gave in quickly, while he had the chance. "Kydd," he said aloud. "Why did he do it? What does he want?"

"I don't know," Pitt admitted, smiling very slightly.

A shadow crossed Voisey's eyes.

Pitt waited.

"Wetron used the Scarborough Street bombing perfectly," Voisey said. "Nothing could have served his purpose better. Do you really believe that is coincidence?"

Pitt had a coat on, and it was not cold in the cathedral, but still he felt a chill inside. He would like to have escaped that conclusion, found at least one compelling reason why it could not be true, but he could find none. "Do you think he is behind it?" he said very quietly.

It was Voisey's turn to smile. "Your ability to think well of people never fails to surprise me, Pitt. It shouldn't do. In spite of all that's happened to you, to your father before you, your years of solving God knows how many murders, and now dealing with political fanatics, you are still naive. You refuse to look at the realities of human nature." His face darkened. "Of course Wetron is behind it, you fool!" he said savagely. "He put poor, stupid, essentially harmless Landsborough up to setting off the first bomb. He told the group no one would be hurt. Idiotic young anarchists, who have no idea what they're doing, except protesting against corruption, would easily agree to something like that. You caught at least some of them, which was doubtless what he intended, and the pump is primed. The second time it looks similar, but it's far worse. Everyone assumes, quite naturally, that it is an escalation of the same thing, and blames the same people. What will be next? Fear is ignited and Denoon fans the flames. If Wetron didn't do it, he is the most incompetent and the luckiest man alive. What do you think, Pitt? What does your police intelligence think? What does your Special Branch brain make of it?"

"Exactly the same as you do," Pitt replied. "But how much of it he used and how much he created doesn't really matter, as long as we can connect him to enough of it to stop him."

"Ah! Pragmatic at last! Thank God. And how do you propose we do that?" Voisey hesitated only a moment. "We have Tellman, of course. A man on the inside."

He looked at Voisey and saw in his face an exquisite awareness of all the emotions and the cost, and of Pitt's dilemma. He was waiting for Pitt to say he could not do it, and then his contempt would be complete. Either way he had entire control over it, and the relish of the power shone in his eyes.

Pitt ached to have some other solution, equally as good, which would offer him escape. But there was nothing.

"I'll ask Tellman to see if he can trace the money back to Wetron," he agreed reluctantly.

"Money!" Voisey said with contempt. "We know he's extorting money! You'll only trace it as far as Simbister, anyway. We need dynamite, connections that prove complicity, knowledge of what it was to be used for."

"First the money," Pitt said patiently. "Trace it to Wetron, then look for the purchase of the dynamite. If it tracks back to Simbister that's good enough, as long as we can tie Simbister to Wetron. I've followed the money as far as Simbister's right-hand man."

"Have you?" Voisey's eyebrows shot up. "You didn't say so."

"I've only just done it. I was in the process of doing it when the bomb went off in Scarborough Street. I was only a few hundred yards away."

Voisey froze. "You were there? You saw it?" He looked at him more closely, noting the scratch marks on his face and where his hair was singed. "You were there," he said with respect. He grudged giving it, but felt it in spite of himself. "I thought you had just been called afterwards."

"I spent half the night trying to get the injured and homeless out of the way," Pitt told him, trying not to let the memory swamp him. "I expect they're still looking for the dead. Believe me, you are no angrier with Wetron than I am."

Voisey breathed out very slowly. "No, I imagine I'm not. If there is anything that could snap that very elastic tolerance of yours, this would be it. Good. Connect Wetron to the dynamite, and let's see him hang!" He said the last word with a sudden passionate viciousness that Pitt knew had more to do with the Inner Circle than the dead of Scarborough Street.

"I mean to," he answered. "But carefully. What are you going to do?"

Voisey smiled; it was like sudden sunshine. "I am going to find more honorable members of the House who would not care to have their servants questioned in their absence, and remind them of the dangers of such a thing." He raised his hand in a tiny half-salute, and walked away.

TELLMAN WAS NOT SURPRISED to see Pitt waiting for him in the street outside his lodgings. It was the only place Pitt could be certain of finding him, except at the Bow Street station. There, not only would he be uncertain of what time Tellman would be in, he would also unquestionably be seen and recognized. It would be a matter of minutes before his presence was reported back to Wetron.

As it was, Pitt had to wait. Tellman came home at different hours every night, depending upon his case and its progress. Wetron would take it for granted that they were in touch; in fact, he had already proved that in his conversation with Tellman, when he told him of Piers Denoon. Even so, it was wiser not to be seen. Pitt remained in the shadow of the alley in the gathering dusk until Tellman reached his door.

They said nothing in the street. Pitt followed him inside and up the stairs to his room. Tellman drew the curtains before turning up the gaslight. The fire was already lit, taking the chill from the air. The landlady brought them both bread and hot soup and made no comment.

Tellman listened with growing horror as Pitt recounted what had happened in Scarborough Street. Although he had already heard about the bombing, it was different when told by someone who had been there. It changed from being a series of facts to an account of the blood, the violence, the noise and the pain, the smell of smoke and scorching flesh.

"Voisey believes Wetron actually caused it," Pitt finished bleakly.

Tellman felt sick. It was a degree of deliberate and planned evil he found hard to imagine. He had seen a certain ambition in men before, but he could not conceive of a hunger for power that would drive anyone to such human slaughter. Even picturing Wetron's bland face and cold, clever eyes, he found it was still too much to grasp.

But Pitt was prepared to believe it; it was there in his face, the sadness and the anger, and overriding it all was the desperate knowledge that there was no one else to battle it, apart from Voisey. Even Jack Radley did not know the full reach of the threat, and there was no purpose in telling him. He was already doing all he could.

"We must connect Wetron with the dynamite," Pitt said quietly. "Without proof, we have nothing."

"I'll try Jones the Pocket," Tellman said after a moment's thought. "We ought to be able to trace the dynamite to someone through the money, as you say. I can't think of anything else."

IN THE MORNING Tellman went straight to the prison where Jones was being held and asked to see him. The charge of passing forged money was very serious, if it could be proved, but it was not always easy to do. People made poor imitation of notes, never claiming they were real. It was known as flash money and was used in theaters, games, and tricks. That was distinct from counterfeit, which was intended to be taken as real.

Tellman had been careful to plant counterfeit money with the landlord who had passed it to Jones. Since Jones had taken it in extortion, he could not pass the blame to the landlord and therefore exonerate himself. Even so, he might well think up some other excuse and get his freedom within a reasonably short time.

He faced Tellman with a confusion of anger and the desire not to antagonize the police until he was sure exactly where his best chances lay.

"What d'yer want?" he said sullenly, when the cell door was closed.

Tellman looked him up and down. Without the large coat on, Jones was a far less massive figure, lean and slightly pot-bellied, his toes turned in, pigeonlike. But his dark face was not without strength, and a good deal of cunning, as he stared back at Tellman. He might be a tool of Grover's, but he was not a foolish or unwilling one.

Tellman considered trying to copy Pitt's easy manner, but he was too angry. It would be better to stay with his own sparse, slightly dour nature. "Something that would do you good, and me too," he answered.

"Yeah? Well I don' think as yer'd come 'ere jus' ter do me good," Jones said sarcastically. He might be of Welsh ancestry, but he had none of the music of Wales in his voice.

"You're in a spot of bother," Tellman observed. "Caught with a counterfeit five-pound note. Bad business, that."

"It ain't counterfeit," Jones contradicted him. "It's flash— nuffin' wrong in that. You made a mistake. You police is always makin' mistakes."

"No, it isn't flash," Tellman argued. "It looks real unless you know the difference. Paper's wrong, that's all."

Jones looked aggrieved. "Then 'ow was I ter know it weren't real. I got took! It's me as you should be sorry for. I'm the one wot was robbed 'ere!"

Tellman affected innocence. "Of what, Mr. Jones?"

Jones was indignant.

"A finny, o' course. You saw it! Took it off me. 'Ere was I think-in' it was the real thing. I bin 'ad!"

"Yes, it looks as if you have," Tellman agreed. "Who by, I won-der. Do you know where you got it? Maybe he's the one I should be talking to."

"Yeah! Yer should, an' all!" Jones agreed. "It were that thievin' landlord of the Triple Plea! I got it just afore yer nicked me. I dn't 'ad time ter look at it proper, or I'd a known!"

"And brought it to us," Tellman added, playing the game. "So we could go and speak to the landlord, and see where he got it, and if he knew it was forged."

Jones winced. "Don' use that word, Mr. Tellman, it ain't nice. I knowed o' forgers wot got crapped."

"Don't worry," Tellman soothed him. "We're not that free with the rope anymore. Keep it mostly for things like murder. Anyone killed, to do with this, was there? Then of course the rope's the thing."

"No o' course there weren't!" Jones said heatedly. "I only 'ad the bleedin' thing for less than an hour!"

"You got it from the landlord at the Triple Plea?"

"Yeah!"

"Can you prove that?"

"Well . . ." Jones suddenly saw a pitfall.

"What was he paying you for?" Tellman asked innocently.

Jones's mind raced; the reflection of it was in his eyes. Now the trap gaped in front of him.

Tellman waited.

" 'E owed me money," Jones said at last, a note of desperation in his voice. " 'E'll tell yer that!" he added, seeking to add a touch of defiance, brazening it out.

"For what?" Tellman asked.

"That in't none o' yer business." Jones was beginning to feel safer. He had very neatly avoided a nasty trap. "I done 'im a favor."

"Big favor, was it? You had twenty-seven pounds on you. Or had you done favors for other people as well, and just by chance they all repaid you that day?"

Jones saw the trap widening, but not how to avoid it this time.

"Or put it this way," Tellman suggested. "If I ask the landlord at the Triple Plea how much of a favor you did him, is he going to say 'five pounds worth,' or 'twenty-seven pounds worth'?"

"Er . . . 'ow do I know wot 'e's gonna say? 'E don't like ter talk about it!" Triumph gleamed momentarily in Jones's eyes. "Landlord feels like a fool if 'e's got ter admit as 'e borrered money from 'is customers."

"You lent him money?"

"Yeah!"

"Where did you get twenty-seven pounds to spare?" Tellman grinned. "Or was it five you lent him, and the rest was usury? Never mind, he'll tell me. And since you were so kind to him, he'll remember exactly when. I suppose you gave him back his note?"

Jones was sweating, it beaded on his upper lip. "Note?"

"Oh, Mr. Jones," Tellman said deprecatingly. "You're far too clever a man to lend money without a note for it. How could you collect? I'll ask him for it, and then the finny'll be his problem." He straightened up as if he were about to go.

"It weren't . . ." Jones began, swallowing hard.

Tellman stopped, turning back. "Yes?" He managed to invest the word with a certain menace, and was pleased with himself. He thought of the destruction in Scarborough Street and the fury he felt must have shown in his face.

Jones gulped. "It weren't for me . . . actual," Jones said miserably. "I fetch an' carry for someone as . . . lends . . . now an' again."

Tellman let the lie go for the moment. "I see. And who is this someone else?"

"I dunno as . . ." Jones stopped. He looked closely at Tellman and saw the rage and the steel inside him. "It were Mr. Grover o' Cannon Street," he said hoarsely. "As God's me judge!"

"I wouldn't be in too much of a hurry to call in judgment, if I were you," Tellman answered, but he felt a lift of victory over the admission. "Supposing I believe you, how will I get an ordinary law court judge to believe you too, since he isn't God, and doesn't know for himself."

"Law court judge!" Jones gulped again. "I din't do nuffin' wrong!" Now he was afraid, and for the first time he could not conceal it. "Yer mean a beak! Wot sits up there wi' a wig on 'is 'ead?"

"And puts people into the Coldbath Fields, or worse. Yes, that's exactly what I mean. There's a lot of money going funny places, Mr. Jones."

"Funny places? I dunno wot yer mean . . ."

"Do you do any other jobs for Mr. Grover? Nothing wrong if you do. He's a policeman. Works for Mr. Simbister, no less. It'd not be your fault if you thought it was all fair and right."

"No, it wouldn't!" Jones said with feeling.

"Any of these other jobs involve paying money out to people? For goods and work and the like?"

Jones blinked, his face full of doubt. Was he going to escape, or was Tellman playing with him? He plunged between hope and terror.

Tellman eased his body into a slightly more comfortable position, flexing his shoulders a little. "You're with me or against me, Mr. Jones. Somebody else may make things hard for you, or they may not. I come from near Scarborough Street." That was a slight stretching of the truth, but the difference was unimportant. "You should have smelled the stench of burning. They haven't got all the bodies out yet. Put you off a roast joint for the rest of your life, that would."

Jones blasphemed under his breath, his face white. "Yer wouldn't . . ."

"Yes I would." Tellman meant it. The anger inside him was like a hard knot of pain. "That money went to buy dynamite. Who did you take it to?"

"You can't n-never say I . . ." Jones stammered. "I din't . . ."

"Know what it was for?" Tellman finished for him. "Possibly not. If you're against bombing like that then you'll tell me where you took the money, who you gave it to, and everything else you know. Then I'll have proof that you aren't part of it, you just ran an errand for a man you thought was good. Right?"

"R-Right! I . . ." He gulped convulsively. "I . . ."

Tellman waited.

Jones looked at the high, barred window, at the steel door, then back at Tellman.

Tellman straightened up again to leave.

"I took a lot o' money down ter Shadwell," Jones said, his voice shaking with fear. "Ter New Gravel Lane."

"Where?"

"Second 'ouse from the end! I swear, as—"

"God's your judge," Tellman finished for him. "Who did you give it to? If it was a lot, you must have had very clear intentions. You wouldn't pass it to just anyone."

"Skewer! Big feller wi' one ear, called Skewer."

"Thank you. You don't need to swear anymore. Just remember the hangman's name if you've lied to me. You'll need to be nice to him, so he goes easy by you when the time comes."

Jones choked.

Tellman remembered Scarborough Street and felt no pity for him.

He left the prison and spent the next four or five hours checking all that Jones had told him. He could not afford to be mistaken. He went to the Shadwell Docks and found New Gravel Lane. It was bleak even in the summer sun and the wind whipped up off the water with a knife-edge to it. The river was busy with barges going from the Pool of London, lightermen, ferries, tugs, and cargo ships moored and waiting to dock. It would be an easy place to store dynamite. Loads of one sort or another were coming and going all the time.

He did not know enough to make a report yet to Pitt. They could afford only one search of such a place. Every trace of the dynamite would be moved long before they could mount a second. He had no choice but to risk asking the River Police for all the information they could give him. He would be oblique, as if asking a professional courtesy.

By midafternoon he knew that one of the old boats moored by New Crane Stairs belonged to Simbister, and it was due to be moved that night. It had not been as difficult to find, or to prove, as he had expected. Was it a double cross? Even a triple cross? He had no way of knowing, but it was time to find Pitt and tell him. He could no longer afford discretion.

"THE *JOSEPHINE*, AT New Crane Stairs in Shadwell Dock," Tellman said when he finally found Pitt in among the ruins of Scarborough Street. He had not known where to look for him, because he had no idea if Narraway even had an office, let alone where it might be. He was certain Pitt would not be at home, and he knew of no other investigation that would occupy him. He had tried Long Spoon Lane, but there was no one there, so he went to Scarborough Street next.

Pitt was tired and filthy, covered with ash from looking through the debris. Much of it had been removed. The houses still stood—their jagged, blackened walls showed skeletal beams the fire had missed. Splintered slate and glass lay scattered all over the cobbles. The smell of stale burning was still thick in the air. "Who does the *Josephine* belong to?" Pitt asked, pushing his hand through his hair and smearing more ash across his face.

"Simbister," Tellman replied. "The River Police say it's being moved tonight. We've no time to waste. What are you looking for here anyway?"

"Bodies that don't belong," Pitt replied. "We've found two so far that didn't live here, and nobody knows who they were. We might tie them in to the explosions." There was little hope in his voice.

"Anarchists?"

"Probably. On the other hand, they might just have been visiting someone who's not alive to say so." He straightened up. "If I find this boat and it has dynamite still in it, or traces left, will there be any proof of Simbister's connection with it?"

"Yes." Tellman told him briefly what he had learned from Jones the Pocket. "But I'm coming with you."

Pitt gave him a quick smile, which was the more startling because of the dirt on his face.

They were walking together out of the wreckage of the center house when they saw the elegant figure of Charles Voisey coming towards them, escorted by a constable. When he saw Pitt he increased his pace, barely glancing at Tellman.

"We can't wait!"

"They're reading the bill again tomorrow," he said simply, a note of desperation in his voice. In the setting sun his face looked tired. There were bruised-looking circles around his eyes. He was struggling against defeat. "God, this is awful!" He did not turn his head to see the ruins of the street around him, roofless chimneys jagged against the pale sky, the debris of people's lives strewn across the cobbles, pieces of furniture, pots and pans, clothes reduced to shreds of rag. The only things that had been removed were the dead bodies. It was plain in his expression that he had already seen them and did not want to mark it even more deeply into his consciousness.

"We've connected Simbister to the dynamite," Pitt told him, and felt Tellman stiffen with surprise that he should trust Voisey so far. "I'm going to Shadwell to see the boat where it's kept."

"When?" Voisey asked.

"Now."

"You can't go alone!"

"I'm not. Tellman's coming with me."

Voisey looked at Tellman for the first time, and with undisguised interest. He had barely had time to acknowledge him when another figure picked his way through the scattered rubble, from the other end of the street, and, after the briefest word with the constable, came straight to Tellman, who obviously recognized him.

"Mr. Tellman, sir," he said breathlessly. "You're needed back at the station, sir. There's bin a robbery, and Mr. Wetron sent me ter fetch yer. It's a big one, an' 'e says as it's too important ter leave ter Johnston. Seems they knocked the poor butler around summink awful, an' scared the lady o' the 'ouse 'alf out of 'er senses."

"Stubbs, tell . . ." Tellman began, then realized his predicament. Wetron had sent for him. Stubbs had found him with Pitt. He would not leave Pitt to go to Shadwell Dock alone.

"Mr. Tellman?" Stubbs said urgently. "It's already took me near an hour ter find yer!"

Why had he even looked here? Was Wetron so suspicious already? More likely he knew. There was a misery and defiance in Stubbs's eyes. Tellman remembered his family, dependent upon him, the one old enough to work. He could not return home emptyhanded, and Wetron would use that.

"It sounds ugly," Pitt said decisively. "You'd better hurry. I don't think we'll find anything to do with your forger here, but if we do, I'll let you know."

White-faced, Tellman followed after Stubbs, a stiff, angry figure disappearing into the lengthening shadows.

"Shadwell Docks," Voisey said with distaste. He glanced down at his elegant boots. "Still, Sergeant Tellman is right; it would be most unwise to go alone. I think this is one of those situations where cooperation would definitely be in our mutual interest. It's not far from here, is it?"

Pitt had no choice. Whatever he thought of him, Voisey could gain nothing by protecting Simbister and the dynamite. And the bill was being read tomorrow.

"Come on," he said. Please God it was not a fool's decision.

He knew his way to New Gravel Lane and the Shadwell Dock. It was close enough to walk if they had to, and the chances of picking up a hansom in this area were slight. It was a good two miles as the crow flies. Along the narrow streets with their dog-leg bends, it would take them the best part of an hour. He had no idea whether Voisey was used to such exercise.

"If we go up to Commercial Street, we might find a cab," he said dubiously.

Voisey looked at the mud in the street, then at the darkening sky. "Good!" He set off without waiting for Pitt to debate it any further.

They found a hansom, and in the event it took less than twenty minutes. They alighted some hundred yards from New Gravel Lane, and Voisey paid the driver. "Now what?" he asked, looking around at the vast warehouses and wharf buildings. The cranes were black against the sky, which was now completely dark except for the sulphurous glare from the patchy streetlamps. They could smell the salt of the river, and the damp of it filled the air and clung to the skin. They could hear water slapping against the stakes of old piers, sucking and splashing as it washed over the stone steps down to the river, and the bump of moored barges and boats against the bank.

"We go down to the water and find the *Josephine*," Pitt replied quietly. "This way."

"How are we going to see anything?" Voisey followed him gingerly. It was difficult to pick out more than outlines, and in the shadow of buildings nothing was distinct. Everything seemed to be moving very slightly, but it was an illusion carried by the light dancing on the water and the constant sound of creaking and dripping.

"Matches," Pitt answered, coming close to the old pier and the steps.

"We're looking for dynamite, for God's sake!" Voisey hissed.

"Then we'll have to be very careful," Pitt replied.

Voisey swore, and walked softly behind him to the steps.

"Tide's coming in," Pitt said after a minute or two. "We're lucky."

"What difference does that make?" Voisey was on his heels.

"Steps will be dry," Pitt answered. He fished in his pocket and pulled out a box of matches. He struck one briefly, sheltering it with his hand. It stayed alight just long enough for him to read the name on the stern of the nearest boat. "*Blue Betsy*," he said softly. "There are three more. Come on."

"I suppose you do know it's here?" Voisey asked.

"No. But I will in five minutes." Pitt went farther down the stairs. The water was only a couple of feet below him now. It looked solid, like molten metal, as if he could walk on it out to the moored ships a dozen yards away, their riding lights skittering brokenly across the ripples.

The second boat was not the *Josephine* either. They were obliged to board it, climbing with extreme care across its deck and crouching with another briefly flaming match to peer at the third.

"*Josephine!*" Pitt said with intense satisfaction.

Voisey said nothing.

Pitt led the way, moving with great care in case the wood of the deck should be slippery. A fall might injure him, or even send him into the water. Perhaps the worst risk of all would be that of raising the alarm, at least from one of the larger boats, which would have watchmen.

The *Josephine* was lower in the water, and they had a slight jump down onto the deck. Pitt moved forward, dropping to his hands and knees to be less conspicuous, and to make balancing easier as the boat tipped with his weight.

Voisey copied him.

They moved in silence, feeling for the hatch, and then for the way to open it. The boat was very old; there was a smell of rot in the wood and several planks were spongy to the touch. It was certainly not seaworthy; it was no more than a floating container in which to store things that would not be hurt by the damp.

The hatch opened easily. There was no lock on it, just a simple handle. Pitt was faintly disturbed by this. Had the dynamite gone already? Or was there some other way in which it was protected?

"What are you waiting for?" Voisey whispered.

Pitt wished it were Tellman with him. Reason told him Voisey could not afford to betray him now, but his instinct said he might.

Was he going, or not? Suddenly the glimmering lights of the

river and the sense of space, the salt and fish smells of the tide, even the stink of the mud, seemed like freedom. The air in the dark hold was stale, with a faint chemical odor.

In the shelter of the open hatch cover, Pitt lit another match and lowered it very carefully. Whatever happened, even if it burned his fingers, he must not drop it. He could feel Voisey only inches behind him.

The hold was almost empty. It was several moments before he saw the packages wrapped up and piled in the farthest corner. They could be dynamite, but they could also be any number of other things—even old newspapers, for all he could tell from here.

"I'm going down," he said quietly. "So are you," he added.

"Don't you want me to stay up here and keep watch?" Voisey asked, a trace of amusement in his voice.

"No, I don't!" Pitt snapped. "I need someone to hold the match."

Voisey gave a soft, nervous laugh. "I thought perhaps you didn't trust me."

"I don't."

"Well, we can't get through the hatch at the same time," Voisey pointed out. "One of us has to go first. No point in tossing a coin, couldn't see which way it landed anyway. Since I trust you, I'll go first." And he pushed past. After a moment's consideration of exactly how to do it, he dropped fairly lightly onto the floor of the hold.

Pitt followed him, and they went over to the corner where the packages were. Voisey struck a match and held it while Pitt examined them. It took only seconds to ascertain that it was dynamite.

"Simbister," Voisey said with intense pleasure and a very slight lift of surprise. The match went out. It was profoundly dark. It was impossible to make out anything at all, not even the paler square of sky through the open hatch.

Then Pitt realized that the hatch was not open. And he had not heard it slam!

Voisey was beside him. He knew it only because he could hear him breathe. He could see absolutely nothing at all.

"Did it fall?" Voisey whispered, although he already knew the answer. The fear was in his voice, almost steady, but with an overpowering effort. "Is there another way out?"

Pitt's mind was racing, trying to stop panic. Since Voisey was with him, this was not his doing. It must be Grover, or even Simbister himself. "No," he said, taking a deep breath. "Not unless we make one."

"Make one!"

There was a jolt, and then another, and Pitt heard a sound of water a little different from the slap and hiss of the tide. It seemed to be from the other hold rather than the hull on either side. He knew with sickening certainty what it was. They were flooding the ship. They were prepared to sacrifice the dynamite in order to kill their two most dangerous enemies. He should have seen it coming. He could hear Voisey's breath drawn in sharply between his teeth. He had realized it as well. The floor beneath them was beginning to tilt.

"All we've got is the dynamite," he said aloud. "But there are detonators with it. We'll have to blow the hatch off. And we'll have to do it fairly quickly."

Voisey let out a gasp. "How many matches have you got left?"

"Half a dozen," Pitt replied. "Unfortunately I did not foresee this."

"I have about three."

"Good. Well, start lighting them and hold them so I can see what I'm doing."

Voisey obeyed, and as soon as there was a flicker, Pitt started to work unwrapping the dynamite, looking for a detonator and molding the damp, slightly tacky substance into a strip that would stick to the edge of the hatch. Voisey lit match after match, first from his own box, then from Pitt's.

Pitt stuck the dynamite around the hatch and placed the detonator, left it and stepped back, pulling Voisey with him. The boat was now listing heavily and the sound of water running into the other hold was clearly audible.

Nothing happened.

"How long?" Voisey said quietly. "We're going down."

"I know. It should have gone off."

Voisey moved. Pitt grabbed at his arm and held him. "Don't! It still could!"

"That's not a lot of use if it doesn't do it in the next three or four minutes," Voisey pointed out.

"There are more detonators," Pitt answered. "We'll have to blow a hole somewhere else." His mind was racing. They were sinking by the stern. If they blew the bow, it would be into the air. Anywhere else and the water would rush in, carrying them back, not out. "Bow," he said, standing up. "Light another match. I need to see the dynamite."

"We've only got three more," Voisey replied, obeying. "You'd better make this work." There was no criticism in his voice, just a knife-sharp edge of irony, and fear.

Pitt did not answer. He was aware of all the nuances, and it was better to think of those than of Charlotte, his home, his children, or the cold, dirty water of the Thames only a few feet away. He worked as quickly as he could, intensely aware that too much haste, the smallest error, and they would not have another chance.

He pressed the dynamite onto the nearer wall of the hold, placing the detonator.

Voisey struck the last match and lit a cigarette, drawing the smoke into his lungs. The hold went dark.

Pitt could see nothing but the glowing end of tobacco. Words failed him.

"It will last longer than a match," Voisey said quietly. "Put the detonator in and get on with it!"

With shaking hands Pitt obeyed.

Voisey drew on the cigarette again, and again. The end of it shone red.

Pitt checked the detonator a last time. "Ready."

Voisey touched his cigarette end to the fuse. They stepped back as far as they could. The boat was listing so heavily it was hard for them to keep their balance. The fuse crackled. It seemed to take forever. Pitt could hear heavy breathing. He thought it was Voisey, then he realized it was himself. The river swirled and slapped outside, a couple of feet away in the darkness.

There was a sudden, violent noise and a rush of air. They were both hurled backwards, then ice-cold water struck them and the boat began to slide deeper.

Pitt thrust himself forwards, up towards the gaping hole in the bow. He must get there before the boat went down and the weight of water coming in forced him back. He reached the ragged edge and grasped hold of it. It was only a foot above the water. Any moment it would be too late.

He pulled with all his strength, and felt the air on his face and saw the lights of the river and the sky. He turned to reach back for Voisey and grasped his hand, heaving with all his strength.

Voisey emerged just as the *Josephine* slid into the river and disappeared. They were left to flounder to the steps, ice-cold, and free.

CHAPTER

NINE

Pitt sat in front of the stove in the kitchen. He was dressed in his nightshirt and a robe, but he was still shivering. Hot tea helped, but the cab ride in sodden clothes had seemed to go on endlessly, as if Keppel Street were twenty miles away, not five.

Neither he nor Voisey had spoken much after they were up the steps and on the wharf again. There was nothing to say; it was all understood. The dynamite had probably belonged, directly or indirectly to Simbister, but the point was that someone had deliberately tried to drown them, and very nearly succeeded.

The hansom had dropped Pitt at Keppel Street, before taking Voisey on to his house in Curzon Street. Charlotte had met Pitt at the door. She had been pacing the floor in anxiety and was ashenfaced.

Now she was standing in front of him, her eyes still shadowed with concern. He had already told her roughly what had happened—it would have been impossible not to, but apart from that he had had no wish to keep it from her. The dark hold, the sense of helplessness as the boat sank lower, and the sounds of water that seemed to be all around, was something he could never forget, even in dreams. He knew he would wake in the night grateful to see even a spark of light, the glow of the streetlamp through the curtains, anything at all. He had a new and terrible sense of what it would be like to be blind, attacked, and unable even to guess from which direction, until it was too late.

"Are you sure Voisey had nothing to do with it?" Charlotte asked for a third time.

"He doesn't care for any cause enough to die for it," he said with conviction.

She did not argue. "This time," she conceded. "What now? You don't have the proof of the dynamite anymore. It's at the bottom of the river."

He smiled. "I think it's quite safe there, don't you?"

Her eyes widened. "Will that do?"

"Sir Charles Voisey is a hero and a member of Parliament. I think his evidence will be accepted. And the records that the *Josephine* belonged to Simbister still exist."

"But what can you prove with that that could help defeat the bill?" she persisted. "Another explosion just looks like anarchists again, and will give Tanqueray even more fuel for his argument."

"If I take that proof of ownership to Somerset Carlisle, and tell him about the dynamite and Grover and Jones the Pocket, that may be enough to make a few people hesitate," he said slowly. Suddenly, in the warmth of the kitchen, he was overwhelmingly tired. Exhaustion seeped through every inch of his body and he could not think clearly. No decisions were clear-cut anymore.

"Don't trust Voisey," she said urgently. "He could still betray you." She was leaning forward a little, her hands over his.

"I don't need to trust him," he pointed out. "He wants the same thing I do: no police bill. For different reasons, but that doesn't matter." He yawned enormously. "Sorry."

She knelt in front of him, staring at his face. "You must go to bed. You have to keep warm." Her voice was thick with emotion. "I can't thank God enough that you're safe. I refuse to think how close you came to drowning, because I couldn't bear it. But Thomas, do you still have the proof that Voisey's sister was involved in killing Reverend Rae? Could you convict her of that, if you had to?"

"No." He struggled to keep some remnant of clarity in his mind. He looked at her earnest face so close to his, the soft hair and anxious eyes. He could feel the warmth of her skin and smell faint lavender and soap. He felt his emotions welling up out of control. He had so very nearly lost it all, this room with its smells of cooking and clean linen, the familiar china on the dresser, the scrubbed table, was home. Most of all she mattered overwhelmingly.

"You couldn't!" Charlotte was frightened, he could hear it in her voice. "Why not? What's wrong with the proof? You said it was all right at the time!"

"It is all right." He blinked, trying to stay awake. "I couldn't convict her, because I really don't believe she knew it was going to poison him."

"That isn't the point!" She was working very hard to keep her patience. "You wouldn't do it, but you could! The evidence is good enough. After all, she did give him the poison!"

"I don't believe she knew that." He was having difficulty keeping his eyes open.

She straightened up. "That doesn't matter. Where is it?"

"What? Where is—oh." He realized that she meant the evidence. "It's in the tallboy in the bedroom. It's perfectly safe. Don't be afraid. I won't tell Voisey where it is, or that I wouldn't actually use it." If he were honest, he did not believe Voisey was unaware of that, but he could not be sure.

"Go to bed," she said gently. "It doesn't matter tonight. Come on." She held out her hands as if to pull him to his feet.

He made an effort and stood up. He was warm now, and the idea of bed seemed exquisitely sweet.

PITT WAS LATE leaving Keppel Street in the morning. He did not even wake up until half past nine. He washed, dressed, had an extremely hasty breakfast, and was on his way to see Narraway by ten minutes after ten.

As soon as he was out of sight, Charlotte also left the house, but going in the opposite direction. She took a hansom to Curzon Street, giving the driver Voisey's address. She hoped he had not already left for Westminster, but the House did not sit until the afternoon, so there was a good chance he hadn't gone yet. Moreover, she was hopeful that the previous night's events on the river should have left him as exhausted as they had Pitt and herself. Of course it was possible he might have gone to Parliament early in hope of meeting with members before the sitting, but they also were likely to arrive later. It was only quarter to eleven, and she could not have come sooner.

She steeled her nerve so that when the manservant opened the door she appeared composed, even though her heart was lurching inside her.

"Good morning, madam," he said politely, with only the slightest lift of surprise in his voice.

"Good morning," she answered. "My name is Mrs. Pitt. Sir Charles knows my husband quite well. They were involved in a matter of great importance yesterday evening. It was very dangerous, in the end, and I am sure when Sir Charles arrived home he was cold and exhausted." She said it so the man would know she spoke the truth about her acquaintance with Voisey. "A situation has arisen which requires that I speak with Sir Charles before he goes to Westminster, if it is possible. I hope I am not too late."

The manservant's face was now clear of suspicion; in fact, he looked almost friendly. "Indeed, Mrs. Pitt," he replied graciously. "A most appalling event. I hope Mr. Pitt is recovered?"

"Yes, thank you."

"If you would care to come in, I shall inform Sir Charles that you are here. He is taking breakfast at the moment." He stepped back and opened the door wide so she could enter.

"Thank you," she accepted, following him across the hallway to a formal but very pleasant morning room.

She looked around with interest. Anything she could learn about Voisey might one day be valuable. There were photographs on the small mahogany table in the corner: a handsome man in military uniform, and a woman beside him—from the pose, his wife. They appeared to be in their mid-fifties or so, and from the fashion of their clothes, the picture had been taken in the 1860s. Voisey's parents?

She looked hastily at the books in the glass-fronted case. They were old single volumes, not sets, and some of the bindings were worn. She guessed they had been bought individually, to read, rather than en masse to furnish the room, as some people did. The titles were varied, mostly studies in history, especially Middle Eastern and North African, including the rise of ancient civilizations. There were histories of Egypt, Phoenicia, Persia, and what was once Babylon.

In the next case, she was surprised to see poetry and several novels, including translations from Russian and Italian, also German poetry and philosophy. Voisey's own books, or his father's?

How much did she know about Charles Voisey? What emptiness lay behind his hunger for power?

Not that it mattered to her. Nothing excused his threatening Pitt. She might even be sorry for him; it was not inconceivable. But she still would do anything within her ability to protect those she loved.

The door opened and Voisey came in. He looked pale and exhausted. He was shaved and neatly dressed, but there was something gone from his usual composure.

"Good morning, Mrs. Pitt," he said, closing the door behind him. There was a shadow of anxiety in his face now as he searched her eyes, her expression. She realized with an odd sense of irony that he was afraid something had happened to Pitt—he still needed him.

"Good morning, Sir Charles," she replied. "I hope you managed to sleep, after your ordeal?"

Something inside him eased a little. He had no idea why she had come, but it was obviously not with news of further tragedy. "Yes, thank you. How is Mr. Pitt?"

It was an absurd conversation of niceties. They were temporary allies in a cause, and underneath it bitter enemies. Pitt could destroy Voisey, be happy to see him in prison for the rest of his life, or even at the end of a rope. Voisey would not have hesitated to kill Pitt, with his own hands, if he could do it and escape the price. He had been behind what had seemed to be an attempt not only on Charlotte's life, but her children's as well, and Gracie's.

"Tired, but quite well," she answered his inquiry. "But I imagine he will not forget being trapped in that boat, with the water coming in. And I expect you will not either."

"No." In spite of his attempt at calm, he shivered very slightly. A flash of annoyance passed over his face, because he knew she must have seen it. "What may I do for you, Mrs. Pitt?"

She was not ready to be quite so direct, not for a moment or two. "How is your sister, Sir Charles? I remember her as being charming, and most individual."

There was a warmth in his face, a softening, in spite of his tiredness, and his concern as to why Charlotte was here. "She is well, thank you. Why do you ask, Mrs. Pitt? You did not come here, at this hour, to ask after my welfare, or hers."

She smiled. She had rattled him, just a little.

"Obliquely, perhaps," she answered. "My inquiry was not without purpose."

"Indeed." He was skeptical.

"I am very glad she is well," she continued. "And happy, I hope?"

His irritation was mounting.

Her smile vanished. "My purpose, Sir Charles, is to make it most clear to you that her welfare depends upon that of my husband. It is a trifle indelicate to put it so bluntly, but I can see that you are growing impatient with indirectness." She saw the surprise in his face, a momentary lack of understanding. "I hope you have not forgotten the Reverend Rae? He was a very fine man indeed, much loved." She held his eyes with a steady, unflinching stare. There was no pretense between them now. "His death was a tragedy," she continued. "I can imagine that the verdict of accidental death might be true, in so far as Mrs. Cavendish is concerned, at least morally. She did not intend to poison him. Nevertheless, the proof remains that she did, in fact, and in law. There are copies of the evidence, naturally. It would be most unwise for there to be only one. They will all remain quite safe, so long as Thomas is also safe, and my family, of course. That includes Gracie. But should anything happen to them, even if it should appear to be an accident, then the evidence will fall into the hands of whoever is most appropriate, and most certain to see that it is followed to the full length of the law."

He stared at her in astonishment.

"Do not imagine I would not use it. I have no vindictiveness towards Mrs. Cavendish. Actually, I think it more than probable she did not intentionally poison Reverend Rae, but she would find that hard to prove at trial, perhaps impossible. Then, of course, she would hang." She used the word deliberately, and saw the blood drain from his face.

"But I love my family, just as you love yours, Sir Charles. There are several copies of that proof, and I would use it without hesitation if you harm my husband, or any other member of my family." She met his stare levelly and unflinchingly.

The silence stretched out between them, cold and dangerous. She did not look away.

"I think not, Mrs. Pitt," he said at last.

"Oh, you're wrong!" she let all her passion and certainty spill into her voice. "I will!"

His smile was very slight, like sunrise on a glacier. "If I should hurt Pitt, and you destroy my sister, then what will you have left to protect yourself, and your children? And you will protect yourself, because without you they cannot survive."

Everything inside her froze, paralyzed.

"You may speak rashly, Mrs. Pitt," he said very softly. "But you are not a stupid woman. You will do what you have to, to protect your children. I don't for a moment doubt your courage, or your will. But neither do I doubt your perception of reality. You will not destroy my sister as long as you have anyone left to defend." He inclined his head very slightly. "May I show you to the door? Perhaps my footman can fetch you a hansom?"

She felt dizzy. He was right and they both knew it. It would be idiotic to argue. She must answer him, make herself speak, and move.

"No thank you. I can find my own, when I wish it." Should she add that there were degrees of damage? Whispers, rumors that could wound without killing? Or would that only make him think also of what he could do that would injure Pitt, or Daniel and Jemima. Or even Tellman?

He was waiting.

No. Better say nothing. She turned and walked out the door with him two steps behind her. It would be farcical to wish each other a good day.

She reached the door, went out into the sunlit street without looking back, and walked briskly away.

She found a hansom within ten minutes, and gave the driver Aunt Vespasia's address, then sat back. She was trembling in the aftermath of having faced Voisey, which she had no intention whatever of ever allowing Pitt to know. There were a few things, a very few, that it was both wiser and kinder not to share. Learning that was part of growing up.

She alighted at Vespasia's house, paid the driver, and went to ring the front doorbell. She intended to see Vespasia, or wait for her return, should she be out.

She was fortunate. Vespasia was not only in, but delighted to see her. Then when they were in the sitting room facing the garden, and the maid had left, Vespasia looked at her with concern.

"My dear, you are very pale. Has something happened?"

Charlotte would not tell her about the encounter with Voisey. She was frightened. A shield in which she had trust had melted away in her hand. She felt not only vulnerable but foolish. She had not yet absorbed the shock, nor formed any plan to deal with it. It would be sufficient to tell Vespasia about Pitt's adventure on the *Josephine*, which she did in as much detail as she knew.

"And is Thomas all right this morning?" Vespasia asked with concern.

"He may develop a cold," Charlotte replied. "And I am certain he will have nightmares about it for some time to come, but he is essentially unharmed. And Voisey also, which is fortunate, because we still need him." She hoped her voice did not shake as she said his name. "I understand there is to be another reading of the bill in the House this afternoon. It will have great support, after the Scarborough Street bomb."

"I am afraid you are right," Vespasia said grimly. "The best we can think is that Mr. Wetron is extraordinarily favored by events."

"The best?" Charlotte asked. "It seems bad to me!"

Vespasia looked at her steadily. "My dear, the worst is that he caused those events. That makes him very much to be feared. A man who would bomb an entire street full of people appears to know no moral boundaries at all. He will kill without thought—not only his enemies, but ordinary men and women who have no more connection with his ambition than that their extinction serves his purpose. Please heaven, Thomas is able to prove some connection between the boat and its dynamite, and ultimately Wetron himself." There was heartfelt emotion in her voice. She sat very straight, as always, but there was a painful tension in her.

"I have not spoken with Thomas in the last day or two," she went on gravely. "Is he closer to discovering who killed Magnus

Landsborough?" She asked as if it were of peripheral concern, but her hands were clenched on the delicate fabric of her skirt.

Charlotte realized with a surge of pity, even guilt, that Vespasia cared about this intensely. She had almost forgotten that Magnus had been the only son of one of Vespasia's friends, one who had been very close to her in her youth, and perhaps in later, less happy years.

"No," she said gently. "Except that he believes from the evidence that it must have been someone he knew very well. I suppose that means one of the other anarchists. It seems a bitter thing to do to someone fighting essentially the same cause."

Vespasia was silent.

Charlotte looked at her exquisite, high-boned face, and saw the fear in it. Would it be intrusive to ask, or callous not to? She would rather commit a sin of misjudgment than of cowardice.

"Are you concerned that it could have been one of his family?" she asked.

Vespasia turned to her, her skin bleached even paler. "Is that what Thomas thinks?"

This was a time for honesty, not false comfort. "He hasn't said. But it must have been someone who knew they used the house in Long Spoon Lane, because he must have been waiting there. And whoever it was shot only Magnus, when they could easily have killed all three of them. And whoever escaped."

Vespasia looked away. "That's what I am afraid of: that it was personal, not political, and not a struggle for power within the anarchists."

There was one glaringly obvious answer, and Charlotte could not honestly avoid it. "Could it have been his father who killed him?" she said in a little more than a whisper. They both understood the reasons why a man could do such a thing, the dishonor that would stain the whole family, the knowledge that the violence would only be worse the next time, and the time after that.

"I don't know," Vespasia admitted. "It is . . . a terrible thought.

And yet if I were a man, and a son of mine contemplated blowing up houses with dynamite, and the people in them, I would consider it my responsibility to stop him. I don't know what I should do. It is a long journey from knowledge to such fearful action. I don't know what lies along its path." A shadow crossed her face. "My children have certainly opposed me frequently, and I have disagreed with them, and disapproved of what they believed and again what they did, but I have never once feared they would embark upon a campaign of murder. If such a thing happened, and I knew it beyond doubt."

"Who else could it be?" Charlotte knew that retreating from the subject now would not help. It must be faced.

Vespasia frowned. "I have seen a deeply troubled emotion in Enid, Sheridan's sister, as if she were aware of something more tragic than Magnus's death."

"Enid?" Charlotte said with puzzlement. "But how would she be able to get to Long Spoon Lane, and actually have shot Magnus? Surely it isn't possible?"

"I have no idea," Vespasia admitted. "Cordelia is the one of whom I would have the least difficulty in believing would have the mind and the heart to do it, but I can think of no way in which she would have the ability, even if she were aware of Magnus's proposed actions. And he surely would not tell her."

"I'm sorry," Charlotte said gently. She made no excuses that Pitt would have to follow the truth wherever it led him, or whatever other tragedies it exposed. They both knew that too well for it to be anything but patronizing to observe it.

"Cordelia has invited me to call upon her again, within the next day or two," Vespasia said after a moment. "I think I shall go this afternoon, immediately after luncheon."

Charlotte was surprised. "Did she? Do you think perhaps she is fond of you after all?"

Vespasia's eyes filled with wry amusement. "No, my dear, I do not. Lady Albemarle is giving a dinner on Tuesday evening. I have been invited, although she will not expect me to accept. I imagine Cordelia has not, and wishes me to go, in order to exercise such influence as I have in favor of the bill. She will have to swallow a very large and awkward slice of pride in order to ask me. It will offer some wild entertainment to watch her." She said it lightly, but there was no pleasure in her face. Her words were of Cordelia, but Charlotte knew her thoughts were with Sheridan. "Would you care to stay for luncheon?" she invited.

"Yes, very much, thank you," Charlotte accepted without hesitation.

VESPASIA DRESSED IN the softest, very dark lilac gray. It was the sort of color that in silk resembles the edges of the evening sky. It became her extraordinarily well, of which she was naturally aware. It was not vanity. She was equally aware that there were colors that did not become her at all, such as all oranges, golds, and browns. The more difficult the task ahead, the more important it was to look one's best.

She arrived at the Landsborough's house unannounced, but the footman invited her to enter immediately. He must have had instructions to that effect. It was now early afternoon; a little soon for the usual caller, but it was a perfectly acceptable time for a close friend to come.

The family had just risen from their meal and were in the withdrawing room. Vespasia was not surprised to find Enid and Denoon also present. In the circumstances she had half-expected it. Sheridan Landsborough stood to greet her; the others murmured polite acknowledgments.

"Vespasia," he said warmly, but with a pucker of anxiety in his features. He still looked very drawn, and a glance at him was sufficient to know that he slept little. "How are you?" It was clear from his expression that he did not know Cordelia had asked her to come.

"I am quite well, thank you," she replied, allowing her eyes to express her concern for him. To have returned the inquiry would make her seem blind to his obvious pain.

Denoon rose to his feet, but only as much as courtesy demanded.

Cordelia came forward, her chin high. "How good of you to come," she said, trying to invest her tone with warmth, and failing. She was immaculately dressed in black silk with jet beads, so discreet one had to glance a second time to see them. Her hair was perfectly coiffed and dramatically streaked with white at the temples, but her skin was like dirty paper, smudged and too thin, stretched in all the wrong places. "I have a favor to ask of you."

Vespasia smiled. She knew this last remark was directed at Denoon, because his look of distaste to see Vespasia again so soon appeared to be an extraordinary breach of tact, even of decency, in the circumstances.

Denoon's eyes widened.

"It could be my pleasure," Vespasia said smoothly. She inclined her head towards Enid who gave her a half-smile in return, then she sat down in the large chair Cordelia indicated, and arranged her skirts with unconscious grace. "What may I do to help?"

"We need all the assistance we are able to raise," Cordelia said frankly. "Lord Albemarle would be listened to with great respect."

Sheridan moved slightly in his seat, the faintest gesture of discomfort.

Cordelia stiffened, but she did not look at him. Vespasia guessed that Cordelia had already asked him to speak in the House of Lords, use the extraordinary affection he had earned over the years by his honesty and his charm. If he changed his liberal views now, in the wake of his bereavement, he could carry scores with him, perhaps even most of the House.

She also knew that Sheridan would not do it. She did not need to see his face turned half away, the slight shiver of distaste, or her anger so thinly held in check. She despised him for cowardice. He followed his beliefs, indifferent to her. Neither loss nor outrage at injustice made him turn against what he held to be true.

Vespasia would like to have given words to her own feelings, but it would be a luxury she could pay dearly for, too dearly now. She must play the game as it was dealt her.

"Indeed he would," she replied, as if she had seen nothing of the emotion between them, nor Denoon's rising temper, or Enid's fury, which she did not begin to understand. That was the emotion that puzzled her the most. She kept her eyes on Cordelia's. "I have been invited to dine with them on Tuesday. I appreciate that in mourning you could not possibly go." That was a sop to Cordelia's vanity she would not have stooped to a month ago. Cordelia would never have been invited, and they both knew it. "Would you consider it helpful if I were to accept? I am sure that Lady Albemarle would permit me to change my mind. It came some time ago, of course, and I declined. I can give any of a number of excuses quite easily. We have been friends for years. She will probably not believe any of them, but neither will she care."

"Won't she?" Denoon said coldly. "You assume a great deal. I should be insulted if you declined an invitation to a dinner and then when it suited you, at the last moment, asked to be accepted instead. We cannot afford to offend her."

Enid blushed painfully red, her eyes reflecting mortification.

Vespasia looked at Denoon, her brows raised very slightly. "Really? Then perhaps it is a good thing that we are not friends, you and I—or you and Lady Albemarle."

Enid turned her back and sneezed—at least it sounded like a sneeze.

Denoon was furious. "I don't think you appreciate the gravity of the situation, Lady Vespasia! This is not some society parlor game. People's lives are at stake. More than six people were killed in the Scarborough Street explosions."

"Eight, actually," she told him. "I am glad you raised the subject, Mr. Denoon. Of course there are more than that who are now homeless. I believe the latest figure is sixty-seven, which does not include the twenty-three from Myrdle Street. I have begun a fund, much of which has already been dispensed, to provide them with shelter and food until they are able to make their own arrangements. I am sure you would wish to contribute to that, both personally and through the medium of your newspaper." She made it a statement, not a question.

Denoon drew in his breath.

"Of course we would," Enid said before he could speak. "I wish I had thought of it myself. I shall send my footman with my donation tomorrow morning."

"Thank you," Vespasia said sincerely. She could have liked Enid, had circumstances long ago been different. She had thought Enid disapproved of her, not catching even a glimpse of Vespasia's loneliness. She realized now how foolish that was, how self-absorbed to imagine she was alone in her sense of dreams frustrated, boundaries closing her in both physically and emotionally. Enid must have felt the same, perhaps worse. And she was still there, accustomed to the tethers perhaps, but hurting no less.

She found herself smiling at the other woman, as if for a moment there were only the two of them encompassing a hundred words.

Denoon cut across it abruptly, resenting his exclusion, although he was barely aware from what he was denied. "What do you propose to say to Lord Albemarle, should you have the opportunity to speak to him?" he asked. "I hope you are not going to ask him for money?"

Sheridan stood up. "Edward, you are being crass. What you say or do in your own house is your own affair, but in my house you will be civil to my guests, whether they are friends of yours or not." He sounded tired, hurt, and weary with an unutterable contempt.

Denoon turned on him, his face purple. "This is too important for aristocratic delicacy, Sheridan. We cannot afford to indulge whims and vanities, or the desire to be seen to do good. Donations are all very fine, and make us all feel better and be publicly admired. But they do not address the problem. They do not stop a single bomb going off or catch one anarchist. We need support in Parliament. We need stronger laws, and men of courage and decision in the places of power where they can do good.

He glanced at Vespasia as casually as if she had been a servant with a tray in her hands. "I have no desire to offend Lady Vespasia, but this is a serious business. There is no room for amateurs and dabblers. It matters too much. We need Albemarle. For that matter, we need you! For God's sake, put your oversensitivities aside and join the battle!" Perhaps without realizing it, he moved a step closer to Cordelia, allying himself with her sentiment, unspoken since Vespasia had arrived, but obvious in Cordelia's face from the beginning.

Sheridan looked back at Denoon, ignoring all three women.

"You are a fool, Edward," he said sadly. "And a stupid man with as much power as you have is dangerous enough to frighten anyone of wisdom. You seem to have no idea how political negotiations work. A word from Vespasia, and the doors of London will be open to you, or closed. A thoughtless insult, a callous gesture, and all the money you possess will avail you nothing. You need to be liked, Edward, and that is something you cannot force and you cannot buy."

Denoon's face was scarlet, but he could find no words to defend himself. As much as anything, he looked startled into silence by the fact that Sheridan had at last retaliated. It was obviously something he had not expected.

Cordelia was thoroughly out of composure. Anger darkened her face, but her first concern was for the cause.

"I apologize for my brother-in-law," she said to Vespasia. "It is ignorance that prompted him to be so rude. He cares too much about the danger of even worse violence to guard his tongue, which does not excuse him, of course."

Vespasia considered waiting in silence for Denoon to apologize. It would have had the desired effect. Sheridan would have done so, and forced it to happen. He would have understood, but he might not have admired her for it, justified as it was. More important than even the old affection, she would not have admired herself. It would be vanity, justice for herself. She was more concerned with her own cause, the defeat of the bill—and perhaps also having the kind of inner dignity that was above the need for collecting any debt.

"The need to be successful in this is far greater than our individual feelings," she said mildly. "We must overcome our differences of manner and do only that which furthers our aim. I believe that a quiet word with Lord Albemarle will bear fruit. His influence is much wider than is generally known. I will be happy to speak with him if you wish, or not, as your judgment dictates."

Enid looked at her with a puzzled expression.

"Thank you," Cordelia said with open gratitude.

Sheridan relaxed.

They waited for Denoon to speak.

"Of course," he agreed grudgingly. "As long as that is not all we do. The bill is down for a second reading this afternoon. The anarchists are still free, and growing more violent with every day. The police have not the power to stop them because we have not given it to them. Before Lord Albemarle can exert whatever influence he has, they may strike again. How many more people will be blasted to oblivion? How many more streets set on fire? The next time the brigades may not be able to extinguish it before it spreads and runs out of control. Have you considered that? Special Branch is useless. What have they achieved? A couple of minor men in prison, and one young man murdered! God knows why, or by whom."

Vespasia had not intended to, but she glanced at Sheridan, then wished she had not. In spite of all her wish to drive it out, the thought returned to her again. Could he have killed Magnus, rather than see him descend any further? Or even in order to pre-empt the hangman?

She could understand how one quiet shot to the back of the head would be immeasurably more merciful. Had he done that? Whatever Magnus's sins, Sheridan had loved his son. The pain of it was etched forever in his face.

"We don't know who they are, what connections they have, even what foreign allies these anarchists may have to draw on," Denoon was saying, oblivious of grief, or perhaps not caring. "The dangers are enormous. We cannot underestimate them. Whatever the embarrassment to ourselves, our duty is clear."

"You speak as if they had unity," Cordelia interrupted. "I don't think we should assume that is so."

He looked annoyed. "I don't know what you mean. I have no idea whether they have unity or not. I am only concerned with getting rid of them."

"My son was among them, whatever his delusions of purpose." Cordelia's voice was tight and thick with emotion. "Someone killed him. I wish to know who, and see him hanged."

Fear flared up in Vespasia again that it could have been Sheridan. It was more than just barely conceivable; it actually seemed possible. It raced through her mind. How could she protect him? How could she do something to prevent anyone knowing, even Pitt?

She saw Enid staring at Sheridan also, as if the same terror gripped her. What did she know? How could she know anything, unless he had told her? Would he do that, lay such a burden on her? Or had she simply guessed? Did she know him well enough that he could not have such a secret from her?

He must have changed from the man Vespasia had known. Would that man have killed anyone, for any reason? She did not know. Time, pain, and love change things. But she still believed Cordelia was the one who would kill to save herself, her honor, her reputation. She had the steel in her heart. But who could she use to actually pull the trigger? Who owed her enough, or was sufficiently afraid of her?

What did Enid know, or the footman she seemed to trust so much?

"We'd like to see all the anarchists hanged," Denoon said roughly. "I really don't care what for." He was looking at Cordelia, not Sheridan. "Knowing who is individually guilty is a luxury we may not have, satisfying as it would be."

"Possibly not," she said coldly. "But I shall still try!"

His face was bleak. "I advise against it. There may be things about Magnus you would prefer not to know, not to mention prefer were not made public in a courtroom. You should consider long and hard before you tear open issues of which you do not know the nature or the extent."

She looked at him with loathing, her face like stone. "Do you know something about my son's death that I do not, Edward?"

"Of course he doesn't!" said Enid desperately, half-rising to her feet. Deliberately she did not look at Sheridan. "That is absurd! I think grief has made you forget yourself, Cordelia."

"On the contrary!" Cordelia retorted. "Grief has made me remember a great deal that I should never have let slip from my mind!"

"We all know many things." Enid's look did not flinch. She faced her sister-in-law almost without blinking, her body stiff, her eyes hard. "Most of them are best kept silent, if we are to live in any kind of peace. I am sure if you consider it, you will agree with me."

Cordelia's face went scarlet, and then the color ebbed away, leaving her white. She turned to Sheridan, but it was impossible to tell from her expression if it were for help or any of a dozen other reasons.

He looked tired, almost indifferent. It seemed all old and stale to him.

Vespasia felt surrounded by pain and anger she did not understand. Perhaps if she remained she would learn more, but she felt impelled to end it. She rose to her feet.

"I agree with you," she said firmly. "Sometimes to forget is the only sanity left, otherwise the past imprisons us and makes the future impossible." She looked at Cordelia. "I shall accept Lady Albemarle's invitation, and do all I can to gain the fullest support." She straightened her skirts with a swift hand. "Thank you for your hospitality. If I hear more, I shall, of course, inform you. Good afternoon."

Sheridan stood also, and accompanied her to the front door. He stopped just inside, opening it himself so the footman retired out of hearing.

"Vespasia," he said gently.

She did not want to look at him, but now deliberately to avoid doing so would be worse.

"Enid is afraid that I killed Magnus myself," he told her. "She sent her footman to follow me. He is loyal to her and loathes Edward. He would not betray me if it were not her wish. I think perhaps you are afraid of the same thing. I can see it in your face."

There was no escape now. "Did you?" she asked.

He smiled very slightly, just a tiny curve at the corners of his lips. "Thank you for not denying it. Your honesty was always one of the things I loved about you most. No, I did not. I tried again and again to dissuade him from his path, but he would not listen. He was passionately sure that the corruption was too deep to cure except by violence. But I did not kill him, and I don't know who did. I am hoping your Mr. Pitt will find that out."

"Enid?" she whispered.

"I don't think so. But she could have had that footman do it for me. Enid has far more . . . passion than Denoon knows . . . or Cordelia. I pray not. It would be so terribly wrong of her to have dragged that young man into such a thing, whatever for."

"If she fears you did it, then she cannot know he did," she pointed out.

"I know that," he said with a bleak, agonized smile. "Perhaps I am just afraid of shadows. You were never afraid, were you." It was not a question.

"Oh, yes, I was!" she said with sudden honesty. "I still am. I just refuse to look at how much, or I might not have the nerve to stand."

He bent suddenly and kissed her, gently, on the mouth. Then he pushed open the door and she walked out to her waiting carriage.

CHARLOTTE WAS AT HOME in the late afternoon when the doorbell rang. Gracie answered it, and a moment later came to the kitchen, her eyes wide, to say that Mr. Victor Narraway wished to speak with her.

Charlotte was startled. "Here?"

"I put 'im in the parlor," Gracie said apologetically, her eyes wide. " 'E looks awful angry!"

Charlotte put down the iron, straightened her skirt, reached up automatically to make sure her hair was more or less tidy, and went to the parlor.

Narraway was standing in the middle of the floor, his back to the fireplace. He was dressed immaculately, his hair smooth and thick, his body rigid. His face was so tense; his voice, when he spoke, precise, sharp-edged.

"Mrs. Pitt, this morning you went to see Sir Charles Voisey at his home. Please don't embarrass us both by denying it."

His arrogance lit a sudden rage in her. "Why on earth should I deny it, Mr. Narraway?" she said hotly. Only the fact that he was Pitt's superior officer kept her from adding that it was none of his concern, and she considered him to be ill-mannered. "I do not know of any reason why I should account for myself to you, truthfully or otherwise."

"Have you forgotten who Voisey is?" he said almost between his teeth. "Have you put it out of your mind that he was responsible for the death of Mario Corena and Reverend Rae, and very possibly attempted to kill you, your children, and your maid?"

"Of course I haven't," she said tartly. "Even if I forget my own fear, I could not forget Mario Corena, for Lady Vespasia's sake." She did not mention Reverend Rae. In this instance, only Corena mattered.

"Why did you go to see him, Mrs. Pitt?" he demanded.

For a moment she considered telling him. Then her temper took control. "I thought you were against the bill to increase police powers to question people without reason, or to interrogate servants without their master or mistress's knowledge, Mr. Narraway?"

He looked surprised, temporarily caught on the wrong foot. "I am."

"Good." She stared at him. "So is Sir Charles."

"That is not a reason for you to see him, Mrs. Pitt! He is an extremely dangerous man . . ." His voice rose, getting sharper, angrier. "Do not go anywhere near him again. Do you understand?"

"I know that, Mr. Narraway," she replied icily, ignoring the fact that he was correct, Voisey's opposition to the bill was no reason for her going to see him. "But you appear to have forgotten that my husband works for you. I do not," she continued. "Or are you threatening me that if I do not do as you wish, you will somehow punish him for it?"

He looked startled. "Of course not!" His face was tight, his eyes burning. "But I will not allow him to be distracted from his work because he is worried that his irresponsible wife is endangering herself by meddling where she has no concern. I assume you care for his safety, and have learned, if not obedience, then at least loyalty?"

She was so furious she ached to be able to lash out at him, even physically, but she dared not, for Pitt's sake. "Mr. Narraway," she said, almost choking on the words. "I would like to tell you to mind your own business, and to ask how you dare to come here and ask me impertinent questions. But as you have pointed out, you are my husband's superior, and if I do such a thing I may be jeopardizing his position, so I cannot."

His face went white, stiff, his eyes very bright. "I am concerned for your safety, you stupid woman! If your husband cannot keep you in control, then someone else needs to."

It was on the tip of her tongue to tell him the real reason she had gone to see Voisey, but if she did then perhaps he would also see that no matter what happened to Pitt, she could not use her evidence against Mrs. Cavendish. She must keep it to protect herself and her children. She had more hostages to fortune than Voisey had. She should have known that. The threat would work for Pitt, if Voisey hurt the rest of his family, but not for her. She did not want Narraway to know that and see her defeat. She glared at him in intense, bottled-up rage.

"Your choice of language is becoming offensive, Mr. Narraway. I think you had better leave." She tried to say it with immense dignity, and was halfway through when it suddenly struck her that he had meant exactly what he said. He was frightened for her. There was emotion in his face, which was oddly vulnerable. He was so rigid because her safety mattered to him, and he was not used to caring. He felt naked.

Now she was aware of heat in her own face and she looked away.

"I assure you, I have no intention of seeing Sir Charles again," she said quietly. "I have no desire to impede your inquiries, or cause Thomas any anxiety for my safety. But I do believe the bill before Parliament is dangerous, and I intend to continue doing what I can to assist those who are fighting against it. Good day, Mr. Narraway."

"Good day, Mrs. Pitt," he said quietly. He allowed her to conduct him to the front door. She did not meet his eyes this time, because she was afraid of what she might see there, and be obliged to acknowledge. Then he would know that she understood, and it was better that that never happen.

She closed the door behind him, and stood still for a moment, breathing hard.

CHAPTER

TEN

I SUPPOSE I SHOULD consider myself fortunate you escaped with your life," Narraway said tartly when Pitt reported the *Josephine* incident to him late that afternoon. He had spent the intervening time tracing as much as he could of the connection between Simbister and the *Josephine*. He had found definite proof on paper and he was pleased with himself.

"Yes," Pitt agreed, remembering far too vividly the ice-cold darkness and the sound of water closing around him, shifting, gurgling, sucking the hull of the boat down, the only light that of the matches Voisey was striking one after another. It flickered through his mind to wonder what physical fear Narraway had known. He had never spoken of it. Was it because there had been none, or simply that it was a part of his life too woven into the core to attempt to describe it. And who would one share it with anyway? Those who had experienced it already knew. Those who had not yet tasted it, or never would, could catch nothing of the real terror merely in words. Pitt did not even try to explain it to Charlotte. What she knew, she guessed from his shivering body, the look in his eyes, and the fact that he did not try to tell her.

"Then I had better get someone to raise the *Josephine*," Narraway observed. He looked tense, pale-faced, as if containing his emotions with difficulty. Had he really been so concerned for Pitt's safety? "We would look foolish if we needed to find it and it had been discreetly removed," he added.

"Yes, sir." Pitt put the papers on the desk. "That ties it to Simbister, and to Grover."

"Who tried to drown you?" Narraway asked.

"Grover, I think. He was certainly there shortly before we were. I have witnesses to that. Three students are included." He tapped the papers with his finger.

"You seem to have been competent." Narraway stared at him, his eyes dark and hot. "You must have looked half dead when you arrived home last night."

Pitt was startled. "A bit wet," he agreed.

"A bit wet," Narraway echoed his words. "And what did you tell your wife? That you fell into the river?"

"That I was in a boat that sank, and I only just got out in time," Pitt replied, evading the truth.

Narraway's voice was colder than the Thames water had been. "Do you suppose that that was what sent her to see Charles Voisey this morning? Concern that he had caught a chill, perhaps?"

"She . . . she went to see Voisey this morning? Where?" Pitt was alarmed, caught off-balance. "At the House of Commons? He wouldn't be there so early . . ."

"Precisely," Narraway agreed scathingly. "At his home in Curzon Street. It seems I know rather more about your wife's comings and goings than you do, Pitt! From now on I suggest you keep better control of your domestic affairs. She is a willful woman greatly in need of a stronger hand than you have exercised so far. You obviously tell her too much, and her imagination does the rest." He looked truly and profoundly angry. His body was rigid, his shoulders high as if all his muscles were clenched. "She is going to get herself seriously hurt if you allow her to keep on interfering in things she has no grasp of, and no idea of her own danger. For God's sake, man, what's the matter with you? Can't you run your own household?"

Pitt stared at him, dumbfounded. He had had no idea Charlotte had gone to see Voisey, and could not think why she should want to. But one thing he was absolutely sure of was that she had not forgotten that he had killed Mario Corena, and the Reverend Rae, and that she would never trust him, no matter what he said or did. She had gone for a reason. There was nothing she could learn from him that Pitt had not already learned. She must have gone to tell him something. Then he remembered she had asked about the proof against Mrs. Cavendish, and he was certain he knew what she had said to Voisey, and why she had gone. He found himself smiling, even though it was shakily, with a mixture of fear and pride, and a strange oblique amusement.

"If you see something humorous in this, Pitt, I'd be delighted to know what it is!" Narraway said tartly.

Pitt straightened his face. He understood Charlotte, and with amazement and a flood of strange, fierce pity, he knew why Narraway was so angry. It was not Pitt or the success of Special Branch he was afraid for, it was Charlotte herself. He was moved to such irrationality because he cared for her. The emotion in him was personal. Pitt knew exactly what it felt like, the mixture of happiness and terror, the knowledge that you were not in control, like losing your balance, the feeling of helplessness and the waiting for a verdict that could hurt more than you would be able to bear.

He avoided Narraway's eyes, so that he would not know that Pitt had seen it. He knew about vulnerability; it was the price of investing part of yourself in anything. The only price greater was in not doing so. The cowardice of not caring was the ultimate defeat. It was a sharp reminder of his own vulnerability.

He changed the subject. "We have to connect the bombing to Wetron," he said aloud. "There's no good getting Simbister alone. Wetron will proclaim his horror, take credit for getting rid of corruption, and find someone else to put in Simbister's place, with a strict warning to be more careful about getting caught."

"I know that!" Narraway said abruptly. He was staring towards the window, his face turned in profile. "We need to use everything we have. We can't afford to protect those we like, or be squeamish about using those we don't."

"I know," Pitt acknowledged. "If I could think of an effective way to do it, I would."

"Who killed Magnus Landsborough, and why?" Narraway asked. "Was it in order to put one of their own in charge? The bombing in Scarborough Street was completely different from Myrdle Street. It wasn't amateur exhibitionism to make a point; it was a very professional, indiscriminate murder."

"It's possible," Pitt admitted. "From what I've learned of Magnus, he was an idealist, but neither vicious nor a complete fool. Whoever shot him was someone who knew their plans and expected them at Long Spoon Lane."

"Obviously," Narraway said bitterly. "Good name for it. Seems they have been dealing with the devil. Nobody's spoon is long enough for that. Be careful, Pitt. Use Voisey, don't trust him—not in anything!"

Pitt thought of the evidence against Voisey's sister. Would it be enough? Was Voisey's love for her greater than his hunger to have power again, and revenge on those who had robbed him of it once?

Pitt had made the mistake before of assuming that people always act in their own interest. It was not so. Passion, fear, rage prompted all kinds of acts that were stupid and self-destructive, and the perpetrators saw that only when it was too late.

"Pitt," Narraway interrupted his thoughts.

"Yes, sir. I'll be as careful of Voisey as I can."

"Good. Get on with it. And no more dips in the river. I can't afford to have you with pneumonia."

"Thank you for your solicitude," Pitt said sarcastically and went out before Narraway replied.

PITT ARRIVED HOME early that evening, and although he had considered for over an hour how he would confront the subject of

Voisey with Charlotte, and how much to say about the talk he had
with Narraway, he had still reached no satisfactory decision when
he walked into the kitchen.

Charlotte met him with a bright, innocent smile that pro-
claimed to him her total guilt. She knew precisely what she had
done, and had no intention of telling him. That settled it. At least
for the time being he would say nothing, because it required new
thought before he could decide anything in the changed circumstances.

Charlotte held out a letter to him. "This was delivered by hand
about an hour ago. It's from Charles Voisey."

"How do you know?" he demanded, taking it from her.

She opened her eyes very wide. "Because the messenger said
so! For heaven's sake, you don't think I opened it, do you?"

"I'm sorry," he apologized, tearing the flap. Narraway's face
with its raw emotion was sharp in his mind. "Of course you didn't."
He knew she was watching him as he read it.

> Pitt,
> Hope you are no worse for the ducking. I now know where
> there is the proof that we need. It is in the possession of the man it
> implicates, but there is no point whatever in getting the dog and leav-
> ing the master free. He will easily acquire another dog, so to speak.
> Of course there is a risk involved, especially to the only man in
> a situation where he can search his master's house! But I do not see
> any choice.
> Advise me.
>
> Voisey

Charlotte might have meant to control herself, but it was
more than she could manage. "What is it?" she said, her voice
sharp.

"I have to go and find Tellman," he replied, going to the stove,
opening the top with the bar, and dropping the letter onto the hot

coals. "Voisey says there is proof that Wetron is connected directly to Simbister in the bombing. We have to have it."

"It'll be very dangerous," she said a little huskily, but she too spoke half under her breath, afraid that Gracie might hear. There was nothing to be served by her knowing, and worrying. She knew too well what that fear was like to wish it upon anyone else, least of all someone she cared for. "What sort of proof is it?"

"I don't know."

"Maybe he's lying?" she said. "Maybe there's nothing at all, and what he wants is for Tellman to get caught. That would be a perfect revenge, and you couldn't even really blame him. There's . . ." She caught his sleeve as he stood in the doorway, already half-leaving.

He put his hand over hers. "I'm going to ask Voisey what it is before I speak to Tellman," he answered.

"And if he doesn't tell you?" She would not let go.

"Then I can't ask Tellman to look for it."

"You won't ask him just even . . ."

"No." He smiled. "No, I won't."

As it turned out, Voisey was quite specific. He simply was unwilling to commit it to paper, even sealed and in the hands of a messenger.

"I should have seen it before," Voisey said angrily. He and Pitt were in the small sitting room in his house in Curzon Street. It was a room of extremely pleasing proportions, painted in dark reds with white sills and deep windows that looked out onto a terrace. Climbing vines half obscured the tops of two of them, softening light and adding a touch of cool green to the warmth of the walls. The furniture was simple, the wood so well polished it reflected the grain as if it had been made of silk. He was surprised to note quickly that the pictures were pen-and-wash sketches of trees, exquisite in winter starkness.

"Seen what?" he asked, accepting a seat on a deep-red-and-gold-velvet armchair.

Voisey remained standing. "Police deal in crime. It's the obvious answer."

"To what?" Pitt asked, masking his irritation with difficulty.

Voisey smiled, savoring the irony. "The police detect crime, of all sorts, low and high. Then we assume they prosecute it in the courts, and the accused, if found guilty, are sentenced."

Pitt waited.

Voisey leaned forward a little. "What if they found a crime of which there is no proof, except to them? Or a crime where the victim is unlikely to speak? Then, instead of prosecuting, they quietly store this proof and blackmail the offender? I am surprised I have to explain this to you, Pitt."

Pitt felt a sharp stab of realization, like a knife in the mind.

"You have very carefully saved the evidence against my sister, in order to make me do as you wish," Voisey went on. "Why has it not occurred to you that Wetron may have done exactly the same thing? I would have, in his position. What's more useful than a cat's paw to do your bidding: buy dynamite, place it judiciously, ignite it at the right time, even murder Magnus Landsborough, if that's what you need?"

It was so incredibly simple they should both have thought of it. Pitt could never have concealed a genuine crime. He knew as well as Voisey did that Mrs. Cavendish had had no idea she carried poison in the food she gave Reverend Rae. If Pitt could have had Voisey condemned for it he would have, even had it included her part in it. As it was, to use the evidence would have condemned her and allowed Voisey to walk away—saddened certainly, lonelier, possibly even plagued by guilt, but still free.

And would Pitt have had Mrs. Cavendish hanged for her brother's crime, even if Voisey had hurt Charlotte? He did not know. The only thing that mattered was: Did Voisey believe that he would?

Of course Wetron was in the ideal position to find evidence of such a crime that he could use like that. "It could be anything, theft, arson, murder, anytime over the last . . ." he hesitated.

"Two or three years," Voisey answered for him.

"Why so short a time?" Pitt questioned. "He's been in the police all his adult life."

"Consider it!" Voisey said impatiently, stepping back till the sunlight fell from the window across the carpet between them. "When he was junior he wasn't in a position to keep secrets. It would have been far too dangerous. If he hid any, he'd have had to share them with others over whom he had no control. When he was promoted and could have done it successfully, wouldn't he have used whatever he had for the Circle? It would be the perfect way to gain favor and power. No, Pitt, this crime is only a year or two old, perhaps three at the most. And the perpetrator of it is someone who is vulnerable to disgrace, has no friends to defend him or to fight in his corner, and dares not face the consequences of whatever it is he has done. Which means it is not a man who makes his living in crime; it is someone who has committed one grave offense for which he is afraid to pay. And he is someone whom Wetron can use. That narrows it down a great deal."

Pitt was angry with himself for not seeing it before. It was galling to have Voisey, of all people, spell it out for him. But he was right.

"Wetron would have the proof of it somewhere safe," Voisey said grimly. "But getting it would in turn prove his complicity. We can't afford to be without it, Pitt, whatever it costs. Whoever we have to use." He was watching Pitt closely.

Pitt felt caught in a current too powerful to struggle against. It was foolish even to resent it. This at least was not Voisey's doing.

"Yes." He rose to his feet. He did not want to stay here. "I'll speak to Tellman. There's no one else we can trust."

Voisey stepped back. "Good," he acknowledged. "We must

move quickly. They're going to push the bill through as fast as they can."

Pitt forbore from making any comment about Voisey including himself, as if he were risking anything. His mind was already on finding Tellman, and what he would say to him.

THE FIRST PART proved easier than he had expected, the second more difficult. Tellman was at his lodgings and the landlady showed Pitt up without demur.

Tellman had taken off his boots and his stiff collar, and he looked completely comfortable. Pitt felt a twinge of guilt because he was going to shatter that.

"What is it? What's happened?" Tellman asked urgently, his voice already strained.

Pitt explained about the dynamite on the *Josephine*, and how he and Voisey had nearly been killed.

"Grover?" Tellman said miserably. It was not that he liked Grover, but that he was a policeman. The betrayal of what was good still hurt him.

"Yes," Pitt answered.

Tellman looked at him grimly. "I can't arrest him."

"I know. That is not what I'm here for. I told you because it's part of the story. I've just come from Voisey now." Pitt did not want to keep meeting Tellman's eyes as he said this, knowing what he was going to ask, but to look away seemed not only cowardly, but as if he were refusing to share it or to understand. "He says Wetron has proof of all kinds of crimes people have committed, which is obvious. It's his job. But his opportunity for blackmail is perfect for using someone to plant bombs."

For a moment Tellman's face was blank. Like Pitt, he had not even thought of using police information for that purpose. Then with a wash of grief he grasped it. His face changed; a light in it died. He did not say anything for several moments.

Pitt broke the silence. "Someone who committed a crime of impulse or desperation," he said, echoing the conversation he had had with Voisey. "Someone with a lot to lose. There's no blackmail without fear."

Tellman looked at him. "I'll find the evidence," he said grimly. "I'll look until I do. There can't be that many places to look. He'd keep it, so he could show the man, make sure he knew the power he had over him. Thing is, where? If it's at his home, how do we get to it? I don't fancy burgling! And if he thinks we're after it, he'll destroy it. If he's got the poor devil to let off bombs, that'd be enough to blackmail him with from now on."

Pitt felt a heaviness settle over him. Perhaps Wetron had destroyed it already? It was dangerous to keep. Surely he would have thought of that too? He must know Voisey was obsessed with revenge.

Tellman was staring at him.

Perhaps it was worse than that? He might have left the evidence in existence, with a trail that could be followed, precisely so Voisey and Pitt would send someone after it, and they would be caught. Pitt, at least, would do anything he could to extricate them, and be caught himself. He looked at Tellman quickly. "It's too dangerous. He must have thought of it. He'll be waiting for one of us to try. He'll . . ."

"He'll beat us if we don't," Tellman interrupted. "I'd rather be beaten trying than give up first."

"If we give up first, we'd be alive to go on fighting," Pitt pointed out angrily. It was not Tellman he was furious with; it was Wetron, the circumstances that brought them to this point, the corruption, the stupidity, the fact that he did not know who to trust.

"Not much purpose in fighting after you've lost," Tellman said with a sour smile. "Do you really think he's thought of us coming after it?"

"We can't afford to assume he didn't," Pitt said. "But that means there will be a trail of some sort drawing us in."

"What made Voisey think of it?"

"I don't know. But it's obvious, if you aren't blinded by loyalty, assumptions of decency that we made—and he didn't."

"Is that all, just a deduction that happened to come now?"

"I don't know."

Tellman contemplated it for a few more moments. It was dark outside now, no light through the crack in the curtains. "If whatever proof there is is in his home, then it makes it obvious that he's using it somehow. The other way, if it's in his office in Bow Street, it could be something he has innocently kept. He could say he'd just come across it, and was about to investigate it. He could blame anyone."

"And it could be far easier to find," Pitt added. "But it could be in his desk, where no one else would see it. The last thing he actually wants is for anyone else to see it and prosecute his man. He can't afford to have him questioned at all, let alone in court."

Pitt felt more and more sure the document, or whatever it was, had been destroyed. They would be caught searching without there ever having been a danger they would find it. And yet to be too afraid even to try was to admit defeat.

"I could look in Wetron's office," Tellman said. "There's only moderate danger in that. We've already proved the connection between the anarchists, the police and the bombings. It's reasonable for me to go looking for other names, suspicions, charges possibly unproved but still interesting."

"True. But if he wants to be sure he can keep on using it, it won't be where anyone in his station could find it," Pitt assumed.

Tellman considered that for a few moments. "No, but I'll start there."

"That's all!" Pitt warned. "Search there, then leave it!"

"Right," Tellman answered. "I'll do it tomorrow."

BUT EVEN AS HE said it, Tellman had no intention of stopping if he found nothing at Bow Street. Actually, he did not expect to find proof of any crime Wetron could use. What he did think possible was that Wetron would have left some clue as to where such proof might be, exactly as Pitt had said, so someone would get caught looking for it, preferably Tellman himself.

He lay in bed that night staring up at the wavering light on the ceiling. The scant traffic passed by, carriage lamps bright, and the boughs of the lime tree outside the window were blown back and forth across the streetlamp on the other side.

He would need help. There was no use asking any of his colleagues. Apart from the fact that they would not believe him, he dared not trust them, especially Stubbs. Even the honest ones could be hostages to fear and old loyalties. However, the first issue was that they would not have the skills that he was looking for. He needed a thief, a first-class housebreaker, someone who could go in and out without a soul being the wiser until it was too late. He needed a man who could break a window with the soundless "starglazing" method, climb in and find the right room in moments, not wake a domestic dog or light-sleeping footman, then open the safe with the manipulation of skeleton keys, and the careful use of a stethoscope.

He knew several such men, that was not a problem. The difficulty was to find one willing and able, and whose loyalty he could ensure, either by payment or some other kind of obligation. He did not like using fear; it gathered a harvest of dislike, and sooner or later some kind of revenge.

He slept only fitfully. At six o'clock, the summer daylight awoke him and he got up. If he were to find anyone, it would have to be before tonight. In fact, it would have to be before he went in to Bow Street for the start of the day.

He had two possible thieves in mind. Either would be difficult to find, and even harder to persuade. He dressed in his oldest clothes, in order to pass unnoticed among the labyrinths he would follow as he made his way east.

He bought a ham sandwich from a stall on Hackney Road,

then walked south to Shipton Street. He knew where to find Pricey, who had had that nickname for as long as Tellman had known him. He had no idea whether it was derivative or his given name, or a comment on his fees for the nefarious services he performed for his clients. Tellman had never arrested him—that was a satisfactory state of things between them—and they had a good relationship that he could now call upon.

Pricey, having been out all night, was still asleep when Tellman knocked on his door. His rooms were at the top of a narrow staircase up from a quiet, broken cobbled courtyard. Had Tellman been less urgent in his need of help he might have been nervous being here, even though it was now broad daylight out in the street.

After several minutes there was a disgruntled voice from inside demanding to know who was there.

"Sergeant Tellman!" he answered. "I need a favor, which I'm willing to pay for." There was no point in being evasive, nor was there time for it.

A bolt slammed back, then another, and the door opened slowly in well-oiled silence. Pricey was standing in his blue-and-white striped nightshirt, his feet bare on the wooden floor, a nightcap covering most of his lank, black hair. His sulky face was aquiline and lugubrious. On seeing Tellman dressed, not in his usual suit and white shirt but inconspicuous grays, his expression sharpened with curiosity.

Tellman pushed his way in and closed the door behind him. He had been here before and he knew his way to the kitchen, such as it was. It was the only place with chairs on which they could sit, and with luck Pricey might even offer him a cup of tea. The ham sandwich was making him thirsty.

"Well I never," Pricey said with interest. "Wot brings you 'ere at this hour, Mr. Tellman? It must be good."

"It is," Tellman replied, sitting gingerly on a wooden chair, which immediately rocked under his weight, little as that was. "I need a piece of evidence finding, and stealing. I expect it to be in someone's house, probably in a safe or a locked desk drawer."

" 'Ow'll I know when I see it, then?" Pricey asked, screwing up his face dubiously.

"That's the awkward bit," Tellman answered. "I'm going to find out more about that today, and I'll tell you before you go. I'll need to meet you somewhere convenient."

Pricey weighed it up, watching Tellman with hard, bright eyes. "Wot sort of evidence is this, then? Why are yer sneakin' it, then, instead o' goin' in an' takin' it, like reg'lar police? 'Oo's got it, an' wot d'yer want it fer? If yer asks me, it in't square, or yer'd be doin' it easier, an' cheaper. I don' work fer nuffin'. 'Oo's payin'? You or the police, eh?"

Tellman knew he would not escape with a lie to Pricey, and if he tried he would offend him. His pride mattered intensely.

"Yes, it's very dangerous," Tellman admitted frankly. "I don't want anyone else to know I have the evidence, especially the police."

Pricey looked startled. "You bent, then, Mr. Tellman? Go on! I never thought it. I'm disappointed in yer, I am."

"No, I'm not!" Tellman snapped. "It's a bent policeman I want it stolen from. It's proof of a crime, and he's blackmailing someone to go on doing worse things, with the threat of using it. At least that's what I think."

"Do you?" Pricey was dubious. "That's awful 'ard, Mr. Tellman, worse'n extortion, that is. Downright evil, I calls it."

"So do I," Tellman agreed. He thought of earning Pricey's personal involvement as an added incentive. "It has to do with the bombings in Myrdle Street and Scarborough Street, if I'm right."

Pricey let out a slow breath, and blasphemed carefully, emphasizing each syllable. "It'll still cost yer!" he warned.

"Be at the Dog and Duck at seven o'clock this evening, and wait for me, however long it takes," Tellman answered. "I'll have the information for you then. I'll keep the owner of the house busy somewhere else."

"Why? I never bin caught, not so as yer could prove it, Mr. Tellman! You know that!" He grinned suddenly. "Not that yer 'aven't tried real 'ard."

"Dog and Duck, seven o'clock," Tellman repeated, rising to his feet. It was later than he wished, and it was time he was at Bow Street.

TELLMAN HAD ONE OF the worst days of his career, which by now spanned over twenty years. He spent the morning with his mind racing over every possibility he could imagine, however far-fetched, for him to draw Wetron away from his home that evening.

But before he did that, he must search Wetron's office and see if the evidence was there, and Pricey's intervention would be unnecessary.

Fortune favored him in that Wetron went out to luncheon, and Tellman overheard him say that he would be gone for the best part of two hours. He was meeting with a member of Parliament to give his advice on the new bill being proposed to arm the police. It occurred to Tellman that the member in question could well also be one of the Inner Circle, recruiting more votes to support Tanqueray.

As soon as Wetron had gone, Tellman prepared his story in case anyone should ask him, and went into Wetron's scrupulously tidy office with its pictures of the Queen, and began his search. If questioned, he would use the forgery case involving Jones the Pocket, and his suspected connection with the Scarborough Street bombings. It was a subject the police should concern themselves with, since Special Branch was obviously not up to the job. As it turned out he was only questioned once, and received a broad grin of appreciation when he gave his answer.

"Somebody needs ter catch the bastards!" the other man replied. "Can I 'elp yer?"

"Could if I knew what I was looking for," Tellman replied, his heart pounding. "I won't know till I see it."

"Got an idea, 'ave yer?" the constable stood in the doorway curiously.

"Don't know," Tellman said, more or less honestly. "But if I'm wrong, I'll be in a hell of a hole. So let me get on with it before the superintendent gets back, eh?"

"Right! Yeh." The constable backed out quickly, not wanting to take any risks.

Tellman went back to searching the papers.

It was only another ten frantic minutes before, with shaking fingers, he held a sheet of paper up and read it. He went through it again before he was absolutely certain. It was an oblique reference to a crime committed roughly three years earlier, and a note that all action was pending. No further notice was to be taken of the event without Wetron's express direction. It was what he was looking for, and Wetron had left it where he could find it, not too easily, just with sufficient difficulty to be worth the effort, and allay suspicion. The proof would be in Wetron's house, as Pitt had thought.

The event had happened three years ago, in a rooming house off Marylebone Road. The address was supplied. Now he had something specific to give Pricey.

The next thing was to find a way to lure Wetron away from home.

Tellman went out of the office and closed the door behind him. He was surprised to find that his hands were sweating and he could hear the beat of the pulse in his ears. He walked quickly down the corridor to the stairs and to his own small room. He sat down, shaking a little, and thought.

What would be irresistible to Wetron? Tellman had to keep him out all night, or at least until three or four in the morning, to give Pricey the chance to find proof. Wetron wanted the police bill passed, above all things. It was key to his entire plan. Was there any way in which Tellman could use that? Wild and incoherent thoughts raced around his head, scraps of ideas, nothing whole. What could he offer Wetron? What would tempt him? Or frighten him? What could threaten to go wrong so seriously that he would be compelled to deal with it himself? Who mattered?

Slowly it began to come together, the desire and fear intermeshed. But he would need help. Someone must be in danger, someone Wetron needed and could not replace. Tanqueray did not matter. If he were killed, the bill could be sponsored by someone else. He would have been a martyr. It might even help!

But Edward Denoon was different. He was powerful and unique, the strongest public supporter of the bill, with a newspaper read by most of the men of influence in the south of England.

Who could threaten Denoon? Enemies of the bill. Voisey was obvious. And what would please Wetron more than to catch Voisey in a criminal act?

Tellman got to his feet. He must find Pitt or Narraway, someone to help make it believable. Wetron had to accept the plan and feel compelled to help implement it himself.

It worked. At least it seemed to. The weather was mild, a light wind rustling the leaves of the trees, the smell of chimney smoke in the air. A little after midnight Tellman stood by a hansom cab. It was drawn up twenty yards from Denoon's house, and to a casual glance he was a driver waiting for a fare. Wetron was on the footpath talking to one of his men, as if they were two gentlemen having a late-night stroll and conversation. They had been waiting for over an hour, and were growing restive.

Tellman kept glancing across at Denoon's house, hoping for a sign that Pitt was keeping his word. He could not hope to coerce Wetron to remain much longer. And trying to explain this tomorrow morning could be uncomfortable, to say the very least.

A dog started barking. Wetron stiffened. By the horse's head, Tellman hoped profoundly that something was about to happen.

Seconds went by. The horse stamped and let out its breath noisily.

Wetron spun around as a figure crept along the far side of the street, silent as a shadow, and disappeared down the areaway steps of Denoon's house. Five seconds went by, ten, then Wetron gave the signal to move.

"Not yet!" Tellman said sharply, his voice high and tight in his throat. Had he overplayed his hand, telling Wetron that Voisey meant to have Denoon killed. Now he was terrified it was Pitt in the shadows and Wetron would arrest him.

"We can't wait," Wetron argued furiously. "He might break in and set a bomb. We've only got minutes, maybe less. Come on!" He set off across the street, his footsteps sharp on the stones, the constable close behind him.

Tellman abandoned the horse and chased the constable, catching up with him in four strides. "Go that way!" he hissed, pointing to the farther side of Denoon's house. "If he went right around the back he'll come out there."

The constable hesitated, his face startled and undecided in the ghostly light from the streetlamps.

"We've got to get him," Tellman insisted urgently. "If he's put a bomb there, we have to know where it is."

"He won't tell us!"

"He bloody will if we take him back into the house!" Tellman swore. "Go now!" He gave the man a slight push.

The constable saw it with a sudden blaze of understanding, and sprinted across the street to the far end of Denoon's house.

Tellman caught up with Wetron, who was at the entrance to the areaway and starting to go down the steps. Tellman went down after him.

"There's no one here!" Wetron spat. "He must be inside already, and closed the door behind him. We're too slow, Tellman."

Pitt could never have picked a lock in those few moments, so he could not be inside. He must have gone on around the house. "Then we'll catch him inside, sir," he said aloud. "He can't have set a bomb already. He'll be red-handed. It'll be the most powerful argument anyone could make for the sake of the bill in Parliament. It's the worst outrage yet, far worse than Scarborough Street."

Wetron stared at him, his face for a moment gleaming with anticipation. Then it darkened, caution reasserting itself. They stood less than a yard from each other, the reflected streetlamp on the scullery windows making them seem even closer. Tellman felt his body shake as if his heartbeat were violent enough to choke him. Had Wetron seen through his trick? Was he even now having someone arrest Pricey in the act?

Had he allowed Tellman to bring him here in a double bluff?

"Yes, sir," Tellman said hoarsely. "Do you want to go in here, or the front door?"

"Front door," Wetron answered. "We'll take all night to rouse anyone here." And he pushed past Tellman and went up the steps, almost stumbling in the shadows.

The constable was in the lee of the house at the far end, almost invisible. If this was where Pitt emerged from the back, he might get caught, but there was no way to warn him. Tellman's whole body ached with tension, fear knotting his stomach, making him gulp for breath.

Wetron reached the front door and yanked the bell pull, waited a few moments, then yanked it again.

It was nearly five minutes before anyone came, by which time he was pale with rage.

"Yes, sir?" the footman said coldly.

"Superintendent Wetron," Wetron told him. "You have an intruder in the house who may have come to set a bomb. Go and call all the staff immediately, lock the doors, tell the women to stay together in the housekeeper's room. Immediately, man! Don't stand there like a fool! You could all be blown to smithereens."

The man went sheet-white, staring as if he barely comprehended the meaning of the words.

Wetron pushed past him, Tellman immediately behind him. The hall was large and the gas lamps were all out except for the one the footman had probably lit in order to find his way to answer the door. Tellman could barely see where he was going and cracked his shins against a low, oriental table as he went to turn up the main lamps.

Wetron turned around slowly, staring for any trace of disturbance. Everything was exactly as one would expect to find it: Chinese embroidered silk screen, pot of ornamental bamboo, long-case clock, chairs. Nothing moved. There was no sound anywhere. Tellman strained his ears, but heard not even the creak of wood settling. He prayed that Pitt was over the wall at the back, and far away by now.

"Wake everyone!" Wetron ordered in a low, tense voice, speaking to the footman. "But lock the front door first. If this man has set a bomb, I'm going to make sure he stays here with us!"

"Yes, s-sir," the footman stammered, moving jerkily to obey.

Wetron turned to Tellman. "You start over there!" he pointed to one of the large mahogany doors with a carved lintel. "Put all the lights on. We're going to flush this man out."

"Gas, sir," Tellman said, trying to sound afraid. "If there's a blast . . ." He left the appalling thought unsaid.

"If there's a blast, Sergeant, the gas already in the pipes will be enough to blow us all to Kingdom Come," Wetron replied. "Get in and find that man, before he can light a fuse to anything."

The next two hours were among the best and worst Tellman had ever spent. They woke all the servants, and of course Edward and Enid Denoon. Piers Denoon came blinking out of his bedroom, confused and obviously more than a little drunk. He seemed barely able to understand when Wetron told him that someone had broken into the house to plant dynamite.

Everyone was frightened. Several of the younger maids were in tears, the cook was outraged, even the male servants were visibly alarmed. The butler was so jittery, he knocked over a vase of flowers that fell with a crash of splintered china that sounded like a shot. That set off the thirteen-year-old between-stairs maid screaming until she was sick.

No intruder was found, nor any explosive device of any sort. By three o'clock in the morning, Wetron, white with fury and completely baffled, withdrew from the house, leaving Tellman and the constable on guard outside. He had some satisfaction climbing into the hansom as the rain started, and watching them begin to shiver with cold and exhaustion as he drew away, but it did not begin to compare with his embarrassment.

WHEN TELLMAN AT LAST returned to his lodgings, he was so cold he could not feel his hands and feet. Light rain had made the footpaths slick and the gutters gleamed wet and black. He found Pricey waiting for him. He looked warm, pleased with himself, and only his shoulders and the top of his hat were damp.

"I followed you," he explained, seeing Tellman's sodden appearance and dour expression. "You don' look 'appy, Mr. Tellman. Didn't catch anybody?"

"I was busy making sure you weren't caught!" Tellman said sharply. "Did you find anything?"

"Oh yes, oh yes indeed." Pricey rubbed his hands together. "A very valuable piece of information it is. Nice 'ouse, you might say. Bit new fer my taste. Like old stuff, got a bit of a story ter it."

"What did you find?"

"Statements, Mr. Tellman. Confession ter rape of a young woman. Not a good girl, but not a bad one neither. All got a bit out of 'and like. Witnesses all tied up proper. Would 'a made a nasty scandal, that. But nobody did nuffin'. 'Ushed up, it were."

"By whom?"

"That yer 'ave ter pay fer, Mr. Tellman. 'Oo done it, an' 'oo knows 'e done it, an' kept it ter their selves."

Tellman was shivering. "Come inside," he ordered, and turned to the door. Upstairs in his room, he went to the drawer where he kept all the money he could spare. "That's it, Pricey." He held out ten gold coins. He hated to part with it; had there been any other way he would not have. But if what Pricey had found could finish Wetron, it was a small cost to pay. "Now let me see it first."

"Ten pounds, eh?" Pricey looked at it with enthusiasm. "That yer own money, then, Mr. Tellman? Yer must want it real bad."

"You'll need a friend one day, Pricey, even if it's me not coming after you when I've a fair idea who's behind something. I'm a better friend than enemy, I can promise you."

"Are yer threatenin' me, Mr. Tellman?" Pricey said indignantly.

"This is too important for games," Tellman answered gravely. "I can get this easy, or hard. Friends or enemies, Pricey?"

Pricey shrugged. "I guess ten nicker clean is more'n twenty wi' dirt in it. 'Ere y'are." He handed over the papers. " 'Oo's 'ouse was it, then? Tell me that, eh?"

"You don't want to know that, Pricey. It'll give you bad dreams." Tellman looked at the papers Pricey had given him and unfolded them carefully. The top one was a witness's account of a girl flirting with, and then being raped by a young man too drunk and too arrogant to believe that anyone as ordinary as he thought she was could refuse him. It was a stupid, violent, and ugly scene.

The second paper was a confession to the rape, in detail, which made it obvious it was the crime described in the first paper. It was signed by Piers Denoon, and witnessed by Roger Simbister, superintendent at Cannon Street Police Station.

"Thank you, Pricey," Tellman said sincerely. "I'm warning you, for your own sake, you'd be better never to mention this to anyone at all, drunk or sober."

"I can keep a still tongue in me 'ead, Mr. Tellman."

"You'd better, Pricey. You stole this from Superintendent Wetron's home. Remember that, and remember what it would be likely to cost you if he ever found out."

"Gawd Almighty! Wot yer let me in fer, Mr. Tellman?" Pricey looked distinctly pale.

"Ten pounds, Pricey, and my gratitude. Now leave here, and go about your business. You were asleep in bed last night, and you know nothing about anything."

"On my life, I don't!" Pricey swore. "Don't take it personal, but I think mebbe I don't never want ter see yer agin!"

PITT HELD IT in his hand with a sense of blinding realization. He was in his own kitchen, where he had been all night since getting home from Denoon's house. He had spent half the time at least pacing the floor back and forth, worried sick about Tellman.

"Piers Denoon," he said slowly. "Wetron almost certainly black-mailed him into providing funds for the anarchists, and reporting back to him all their doings. He couldn't get Magnus Landsborough to bomb streets where people would be killed, so he got Piers to kill him, so a new man could take over, someone who would do as Wetron told him." He looked up. "Thank you, Tellman. You've done superbly."

Tellman felt himself blush. Pitt did not give this much praise lightly, and in spite of a desire to be modest, he knew that he had indeed done well. He had been profoundly afraid. He was still queasy when he thought of Wetron spending all night chasing a phantom bomber, getting Edward Denoon and his entire house-hold out of bed, for nothing. It was a pleasure for which he might yet pay very dearly. He had not told Pitt how it had been. Perhaps he should, while the pleasure of it was still unalloyed?

Pitt saw him smiling. "What is it?" he said softly, although the humor in his eyes suggested he knew.

Eventually and with too few words, Tellman described the night's events.

Pitt laughed. At first it was tense, a little high-pitched with nerves, then, as Tellman continued, with dour economy picturing the between-stairs maid's screams, the cook's fury, and the butler's jittering clumsiness, Pitt started to laugh from deep inside himself. He did so freely and with such delight that neither of them were aware of making so much noise that they did not hear Gracie come to the doorway, her hair tied up in a clean cap and her apron on already to clean out the stove.

They both apologized, like boys caught with their fingers in the jam pot, and sat obediently while she relit the stove and boiled the kettle to make tea.

It was nearly half past eight when Tellman finally left to go to work, hollow-eyed with tiredness, but with a good breakfast inside him. Pitt pondered on how much to tell Charlotte, and what to do next with the day. One thing he had already decided, the proof must be taken immediately to Narraway. He would not let it remain in his house where his wife and children were for even one more hour. Then he would go to see Vespasia. There was much to ask her, some of it acutely painful.

"Brilliant," Narraway said with deep satisfaction as he looked up at Pitt after reading the papers. He was elegantly dressed, but his face was pale. "You did superbly. But now Wetron will be more dangerous than ever. He will know that Tellman caused these to be stolen, and he will not have found last night's embarrassment amusing. He will never forgive either of you for that."

"I know," Pitt acknowledged. He was afraid for Charlotte now, not from any threat from Voisey, but from Wetron. He was even more afraid for Tellman, who had caused Wetron's discomfiture at Denoon's house. The fact that he had also witnessed it would be like pouring oil on the flames. "We must destroy him quickly . . ." He felt the urgency twisting inside him. "Can't we have him arrested today?"

Narraway's dark face was tight with emotion. "I'll send one of my other men to your house, armed, just in case. There's nothing I can do to protect Tellman. I assume Piers Denoon was the one who killed Magnus?" His mouth tightened. "His own cousin. I wonder if he hated him anyway, or if that was a further twist of the blackmail. This rape evidence connects Piers with Simbister, and Simbister with Wetron, but we need it all inextricably tied to the bombings before we arrest anyone. Or to put it more accurately, have the police arrest each other!"

"This is enough," Pitt insisted. "It damns both of them and Piers Denoon. It makes perfect sense." Tellman's danger weighed on his mind. Wetron would want him crucified! He would know the papers were gone by now, and he had to know Tellman was responsible, even though he had paid someone else to perform the actual theft. "Simbister owned the *Josephine*, where the dynamite was. Grover works for him. The circle of proof is complete."

Narraway looked tired and impatient. "This is a dangerous job, Pitt!" He said abrasively. "Ever hunted big game?"

"No, of course not."

Narraway's smile was sour. "There are some beasts you only get one shot at. You have to make sure that shot is fatal. Do no more than wound it, and it will turn and crush you, tear you apart, even if it dies afterwards. Wetron is an animal like that."

"You've been big-game hunting?"

Narraway looked straight back at him. "Only for the most dangerous creature of all—man. I have nothing against animals, and no desire to put their heads on my walls."

Pitt liked him better for that.

"Yes, sir!"

HE CALLED ON Vespasia briefly, only long enough to tell her about the night's doings. She responded with a mixture of laughter and grief, and a deep and troubling fear that there might be further tragedy yet to happen. However, she would not tell him of what nature she thought it, nor whom it would involve, although he felt certain she knew.

He left her house and went to St. Paul's where, at noon, he met Voisey at the tomb of the great Elizabethan and Jacobean clergyman, lawyer, philosopher, adventurer, and poet, John Donne. For once Voisey had little to say about him. A glance at Pitt's exhausted face, the haste of his step, and the fact that he was ten minutes early, took from him all desire to show off beyond the first remark.

"He entered Oxford University at the age of eleven. Did you know that?" he said wryly. "You look awful. Did you go back to the bombing?"

"No," Pitt said quietly, keeping his voice low so an elderly couple, also paying a passing reverence to Donne, could not hear him. "I was up most of the night, creating a diversion while a certain burglar took from Wetron's house a piece of crucial evidence, as you suggested."

Voisey's face lit up, his eyes bright. And wide open. "What?"

The eagerness in him had been so intense the elderly couple turned in surprise. The man had been in the middle of quoting perhaps Donne's most famous words: "therefore never send to know for when the bell tolls . . ."

"It tolls for them." The line finished in Pitt's mind. "Exactly where you expected," he said in little more than a whisper.

"For God's sake!" Voisey snarled. "Who?"

"Piers Denoon. An old charge of rape."

Voisey let his breath out in a sigh as if a long-held knot had at last unloosed itself. "Is it enough?"

"Almost. We need to be able to prove all the connections. We have the dynamite to Grover, Grover to Simbister, through that confession of Denoon's, Simbister to Wetron, but Wetron could still deny it. He could say he had only just found that, and intended to act on it when he was certain. It would destroy Simbister, and Wetron would merely replace him with someone else."

"I see, I see!" Voisey said impatiently. "We must tie Wetron to using Piers Denoon so he can't escape it. If Denoon shot Magnus Landsborough you can charge him with murder. He'll be happy to swear he was blackmailed into it. The papers are safe? Where? Not in your house!"

"Yes, they're safe," Pitt replied bleakly.

A half smile flashed on Voisey's face. He had not really expected to be told.

"Use your old Circle connections," Pitt went on. "We need the proof quickly. Wetron knows we have the papers."

The half-smile widened. "Does he indeed? I wish I'd seen that." There was regret in his voice, a hunger to take revenge: to roll it on his tongue, not merely be told about it.

Pitt felt faintly sick. A shiver passed over his skin, but there was no way around working with Voisey, and no point thinking about it as if he could escape. "Use them today," he said aloud. "Find the proof that Wetron knew of the rape and used it on Denoon to force him into funding the anarchists, then murdering Magnus Landsborough."

Voisey licked his lips. It was a slow, delicate gesture made without awareness that he was doing it. "Yes," he said, looking at Pitt. "Yes, I know just who to go to. I still have a few old debts to call in. You have a telephone? Of course you have. Be by it from four o'clock onward. You're right, there's no time to waste." He gave a very slight shrug, an inch, no more. "For Tellman's sake!"

Pitt gave him the number of his telephone, then turned and walked away, his footsteps rapping on the stone, before he gave in to the impulse to hit Voisey's subtle, smiling face. He was perfectly aware that they were on the brink of success, and it could all still go wrong. Voisey could betray him; destroy Wetron with the evidence, and Simbister; disgrace Edward Denoon through his son; and save enough from the ashes to step back into his old place in the Inner Circle. Perhaps he could even use the bill in Parliament to his own ends. And there was nothing Pitt could do to prevent that. He knew it, and he could see in his eyes that Voisey knew it too. Voisey was savoring it, as one does a hundred-year-old brandy: breathing the aroma, letting it dizzy your senses.

PITT WAS AT HOME at four o'clock, waiting, pacing the floor, starting at every sound. Charlotte was watching him. Gracie was banging around with a mop, muttering to herself, because she knew there was danger, and no one had told her what it was. She had not seen Tellman alone for two days. Pitt said Tellman had acted with extraordinary courage and intelligence, but would not elaborate, even to Charlotte.

At five o'clock they had tea, drinking it quickly, and too hot, wanting cake and then not wanting it.

It was quarter to six when the telephone finally rang. Pitt charged to the hall and picked the receiver off its hook.

"Yes?"

"Got it," Voisey said jubilantly. "But Denoon has been warned. He's at the docks already. Come as fast as you can. King's Arms Stairs on the Isle of Dogs, at Rotherhithe on the south. It's Limehouse Reach . . ."

"I know where it is!" Pitt snapped.

"Come now!" Voisey urged. "Fast as you can. I'll go ahead. If we lose him, we've lost it all."

"Coming." Pitt replaced the phone, swung around to look at Charlotte and Gracie staring at him. "I'm going to the King's Arms Stairs on the Isle of Dogs, to get Piers Denoon, before he escapes. Wetron must have warned him." And he started for the door.

"You can't arrest him!" Charlotte called after him. "You aren't police anymore. Let me call . . ."

"No!" he shouted. "No one! You don't know who to trust. Tell Narraway, if you can find him. No one else!"

She nodded. It was clear in her face she knew not even to try to reach Tellman. He kissed her so swiftly it was barely a touch, then went out of the house and sprinted to the end of the street. He hailed the first hansom that passed him. "Millwall Dock!" he called to the driver. "Then the King's Arms Stairs. Know it?"

"Yes, sir!"

"Fast as you can! I'll pay extra!"

" 'Ang on!"

The hansom lurched forward and increased speed as the light faded in the streets. Pitt hung on as they slewed around corners going south towards Oxford Street. They forced their way through the traffic eastwards, the driver yelling alternately praise and abuse. Oxford Street changed to High Holborn, Holborn Viaduct, Newgate Street then Cheapside. At the junction at Mansion House there was chaos. Two carriages were locked wheel to wheel.

The driver pulled up. Pitt was in a fever of impatience. All around people were shouting, horses backing and squealing.

Then they seemed to turn almost back on themselves, and down King William Street towards the river.

"You can't get through there!" Pitt shouted furiously. "You'll come up against the Tower!"

The driver shouted something he did not hear. It was darkening rapidly with a misty rain. They were picking up speed again, but it would do them no good. They could not get around the great bulwark of the massive eight-centuries-old Tower of London, built by William the Conqueror.

Then they turned again and were going north. Of course. Gracechurch Street, up Leadenhall Street, through Aldgate and Whitechapel, and on east. Pitt sat back, gulping, and trying to steady himself. He had miles to go yet. The gray air was full of rain, the road surface gleaming wet in the lights from carriage and streetlamps. The splash and hiss of wheels almost drowned by the sound of hooves.

Finally they pulled up at the King's Arms Stairs in near darkness. Almost immediately Voisey's tall figure came out of the gloom, solid black against the shifting glitter of the river, ships riding lights dancing on the ripples of the tide behind him.

Pitt leapt out, thrusting money at the driver—probably twice as much as he owed. He thanked him, and followed after Voisey over the quayside to the water's edge.

"He's on that barge," Voisey said huskily. "He's been hiding there. They'll take him out on the turn of the tide . . . about twenty minutes." He pointed out into the river. "I've got a boat. Borrowed it from one of the ferrymen. It's not much, but it'll get us out there." He started down the dark steps, balancing himself with one hand against the wall of the embankment.

Pitt could see the black shell of a boat riding in the water and the dripping rope that held it knotted to the ring in the stones. The oars were shipped, waiting.

Voisey clambered in and took the oarsman's seat. Pitt untied the rope, coiling it over his arm, and jumped into the stern. Voisey unshipped the oars, and slipped them into the rowlocks, and then threw his weight against them.

They pulled out into the tide, slithered around for a moment, righted, slewed the other way, then met the waves straight and the oars dug in. Voisey leaned forward, back, found his rhythm, and they sped away.

He slowed as they reached the moored barge, and swung the oars on board again. Pitt stood up carefully, balancing to reach out as they came around. He needed to stop them from bumping the hull of the barge and alerting whoever was there. Piers Denoon would not be alone. He reached forward, catching the side and holding on. Then he jumped and rolled, landing easily and regaining his feet, then dropping onto his knee not to make a high outline against the sky, if anyone were looking. He had a cudgel in his pocket, but at this moment he wished it were a pistol. Thank goodness Voisey was with him, with as much interest in catching Denoon as he had. Voisey was quite a big man, and both powerful and ruthless.

He crept forward and saw the lighted hatchway. There was only one man standing there. He looked about twenty years old, slender and angular. Beyond him there was the shadow of a second man, heavier, but bent forward a little. He did not appear to be armed, as far as Pitt could see.

He did not want to strike the younger man. He put his arm

around his neck instead and pulled him backwards. The other man jerked up, startled.

There was a movement on the deck. Pitt turned to look for Voisey, but it was a big man in a woollen hat. Beyond him, the boat with Voisey in it was pulling away, back towards the steps. It was the betrayal at last, at the one time he had not expected it.

CHAPTER

ELEVEN

Pitt watched the boat slide over the glittering water with a rage that almost choked him. How unbelievably, fatally stupid of him! But what clue had he missed? Voisey wanted Piers Denoon caught and charged just as much as Pitt did. It was the final connection between Wetron and the bombings. It was proof of police corruption that could not be denied.

The big man on the deck was coming towards him, hunched forward a little as if preparing to lash out. "Get outa my way, Mike!" he snarled at the fair young man struggling in Pitt's tightening grip. The only other person he could see was the older man inside the cabin.

Why had he believed Voisey that Piers Denoon was here at all? Because he had grown used to believing him. He had been swept away by the fever of the chase, the expectation of victory, and forgotten what Voisey was, what he had always been. Perhaps he even knew where Piers Denoon really was!

The big man stopped, momentarily confused by the fact that Pitt had the young man around the front of his neck, but it would be respite for a very short time. The other man was coming up the steps, an iron bar in his hand.

Pitt's only chance was to back away and hope to jump over the side without hitting himself too hard on any of the loose spars and boxes on the deck, or anything in the water. Even so he could easily drown. He was thirty yards from the shore; the current was high and pulling out to sea. The water was cold, and he had a coat and boots on. He would be lucky, very lucky indeed, to make shore, quite apart from the strings of lighters that went down the river and could strike him, knock him senseless, entangle him and drag him under. He needed only to catch a part of his clothing on a half-submerged spar, drifting wood, anything, and he would be trapped, sucked down.

He moved backwards carefully, dragging the man with him. He was struggling now, kicking and trying to gouge with his hands. Pitt was paying the price for his ultimate stupidity. Narraway had warned him, Charlotte had, even Vespasia. Why had Voisey taken the chance that Charlotte would not use the evidence against Mrs. Cavendish? Because if she did, she would have nothing left with which to defend herself, or the children! The thought twisted inside his belly till it was a physical pain.

"Jump!"

The sound startled him so abruptly that he slipped and stumbled, falling backwards and yanking the man off his feet as well, and letting him go. They both went clear together just as the big man struck, hit the furled sail and let out a yell of pain.

"Jump!" the cry came again.

This time Pitt scrambled awkwardly to his feet and threw himself over the side. He landed on his hands and knees on the bottom of a small rowing boat, sending it rolling so wildly it shipped water. It was lucky to right itself with considerable effort by the man working the oars.

"You clumsy oaf," he said, not very critically. "Keep your head down, just in case one of them has a pistol." He threw his weight against the oars, shooting farther out into the middle of the river and away from the lights. He steered between the moored ships into the current, pulling for the opposite shore.

Pitt climbed to his feet without straightening up, and sat in the stern now that they were beyond the light. "Thank you," he said sincerely, even though he had no idea if he was actually any better off.

"I'll collect," the man replied. "I'd have left you there if I didn't know you were the only one with a real chance of stopping the police bill."

Pitt was bruised and uncomfortable, but intensely grateful not to be in the water. "Who are you?"

"Kydd," the man replied, grunting as he put his weight to the oars.

"I was lucky you were passing," Pitt tried to steady his breath, and the beating of his heart. The air was damp on his skin. "Are you a ferryman, lighterman?"

"Anarchist," Kydd answered, irony in his voice, his face invisible in the darkness. "And I wasn't just passing. It's my job to know what's going on. If you weren't trying to stop police corruption, I'd have let them kill you. But as they say, politics make strange bedfellows of us. More strange than you and Charles Voisey! That was a mistake. But I imagine you know that now."

They seemed to be nearing the farther shore, because Kydd eased the boat around to go in stern first, alongside the steps. However, there was little that Pitt could see except the denser blackness of the unlit wharves and warehouses. They must be farther downriver than the Dog and Duck, where the public house lights would be clear.

"Where are we?"

"Saint George Stairs," Kydd answered. "By the railway yard. A little walk for you, and a swift brandy. Then you can make your way back. Cut along to Rotherhithe and get a ferry to Wapping, if I were you. I wouldn't get back on the water downriver of that."

Pitt received the advice in silence, turning over what Kydd had said. The boat was lashed to an iron ring and they climbed up the slippery steps, but the tide was only just turning so they were near the top anyway. Pitt followed the dark figure of Kydd across the open dockside. The wind was cold now and there was a slight fog settling, blurring the lights and making the damp air hang in little droplets. From farther down the river came the mournful cry of foghorns.

They walked for about ten minutes until, in an alley still close to the waterfront, Kydd stopped and opened a narrow door and immediately they were in a warm passageway. He closed it, setting a wooden bar across it, and they went on through a farther door into a startlingly comfortable and tidy room. It had three chairs in it, one wooden and two upholstered, and on the biggest one there appeared to be a cast-off hat, or rolled-together pair of fur gloves. At the sound of Kydd's footsteps it unwound itself into four legs and a tail, then yawned prodigiously and blinked. It started to purr. Pitt judged the kitten to be about twelve or fourteen weeks old.

Kydd picked it up with one hand, stroking it absentmindedly. "The brandy's over there," he pointed to a cupboard on the wall. "Let me give Mite something to eat first. She's been alone all day." He took a small piece of meat out of his pocket and tore it into pieces. The kitten snatched them from him almost before he had finished the task, purring so loudly now she sounded as if she rattled.

Pitt opened the cupboard and found the brandy. There were several glasses and cups. He chose two and poured mean portions into them, aware that there was not much there. He drank his in one gulp, and put the other on the small table for Kydd.

"Who were they?" he asked.

"On the barge?" Kydd put the kitten back on the chair and took his brandy. "River thieves, probably. What were you looking for, for God's sake?"

"How did you know I was going to be there?" Pitt continued.

Mite sharpened her claws, then climbed slowly up Kydd's leg and back and settled on his shoulder. He winced, but did not put her off.

"I didn't, but I knew Voisey was waiting for someone. It was an educated guess," he replied.

"You've been following me?"

Kydd looked very serious. In the light his face was high-cheekboned, blue-eyed. "I want to know who killed Magnus. I have to know it wasn't one of us. If it was, I'll execute him myself."

It was becoming clearer. "You were part of Magnus's group," Pitt said. "You are the leader who has taken over."

Kydd was unimpressed. "Who killed Magnus?" he repeated. "Don't you know yet? Someone betrayed him. Was it his father?"

"His father?"

"He came after him, several times. Tried to persuade him to go back to the establishment and give up his beliefs." Kydd had a savage amusement in his face, his voice was edged with pain as well as anger. Absentmindedly he put his hand up and stroked the little animal still perched on his shoulder. "Mite was Magnus's," he said irrelevantly. "He rescued her . . . or him. Actually I have no idea which it is. Hard to tell with kittens."

It was a sudden act of humanity, a gentleness that gave Magnus Landsborough a dimension infinitely larger than nameless idealism. Pitt found himself choked with fury that he should have been killed simply to provoke a public outrage and create the climate for a piece of monstrous legislation.

"No, it wasn't his father," he said harshly. "All he wanted was to change Magnus's mind. It was his cousin, Piers Denoon. That's who I was looking for on the barge, to arrest him before he fled the country. Easy to go downriver from here and across the Channel."

"Piers?" Kydd was incredulous. "What for? That makes no sense. I don't believe it." His eyes were bright and hard.

"Because he raised money for you?" Pitt asked.

"If you knew that, then you'll know why I don't believe it. Why would he kill Magnus?" Kydd unhooked Mite from his shoulder and sat down on the chair.

"For the same reason he did everything else to do with anarchy," Pitt replied. "Because he was being blackmailed. He couldn't afford to refuse, or he'd have gone to prison, where I doubt he'd have survived."

"We'd have helped him. As you pointed out, it's not hard to get across the Channel to France, or even Portugal."

"For anarchy, perhaps. Would you for rape?"

Kydd was stunned. "Rape!" he repeated. "Rape?"

"About three years ago. An ordinary girl. Mistook what she was, I think. But it was violent and nasty, and could have been made to sound even worse. Girl who could have been the sister or daughter of the kind of man he'd meet in prison."

Kydd's face showed his bleak understanding of what that would mean, and perhaps, momentarily, a bright shard of pity. Then it was gone.

"What are you going to do now? He killed Magnus. I suppose you're sure of that?"

"Aren't you! If you think about it?" Pitt asked. "It had to be someone who knew you would go back to Long Spoon Lane, because he was waiting there. He knew Magnus by sight, and killed no one else. He didn't even shoot at Welling or Carmody. Also he kept out of sight himself."

Kydd's face tightened. "All right, it must have been Piers. It's the only answer that makes sense. Poor devil. I suppose I want to see him on the end of a rope, but I'm not as sure as I was." He put his hand over Mite again and stroked her, being rewarded by an instant rattle. "Go and do whatever you have to. Turn left at the door. Follow the London Road to the Onega Yard, past the Norway Dock to where it goes into Brickley Road right to the Rotherhithe Pier. You'll get a ferry there." He did not get up.

Pitt nodded. "Thank you."

"Don't bother looking for me here again."

"I wasn't going to. As you pointed out, I owe you a favor." He stopped in the doorway. "I suppose you had nothing to do with Scarborough Street?"

The contempt in Kydd's face was unseen, but he spoke. "That's another one I'll see on the end of a rope with pleasure, if you can catch him. That's why I fished you out—I reckon you're the only one who's ever going to try."

VESPASIA WAS ABOUT TO set out for a late dinner with friends when her butler informed her that Mr. Pitt was in the hall.

"Have the carriage wait and show Mr. Pitt in," she ordered without hesitation. She went to her sitting room. The curtains were drawn because the evening was wet and she did not want to look at light reflected on dripping trees. She was barely there when she heard Pitt's voice thanking the butler, and then he was there, closing the door behind him. He looked pale and cold. His unruly hair was wet with the rain and curling wildly. There was a considerable amount of dirt on his face and his clothes.

"You were about to go out," he said, looking at her magnificent gown with its high, full-shouldered sleeves and the sheen of dove-gray satin under the falls of ivory lace. "I'm sorry." There was a finality in his voice and the short, shivering attitude of his body that canceled even the possibility of her wishing to leave.

"It is of no importance," she dismissed it with a tiny gesture of her hand, the diamonds on her fingers catching the light. "Shall I ask Cook to prepare us something? You look a little like a horse that has run a hard race . . . and lost."

He smiled. "Actually, I think I might have won. Yes. I'm cold more than hungry. I . . ." He stopped. He was trembling.

"Sit down," she ordered. "But for heaven's sake take that coat off!" She reached for the bell. When it was answered, she dispatched the butler to send the coachman with an apology for her absence at the dinner party. The cook was requested to prepare a meal for two, and the butler to bring back a hot toddy immediately, and, when he had time, to sponge clean and dry Pitt's coat.

"Now," she sat down facing him. "What has happened, Thomas?"

Briefly he told her, elaborating only when he came to the death of Magnus Landsborough, and what Kydd had told him. "I'm sorry," he said quietly. "It is going to be very hard for the Landsborough family, but I cannot let it go."

"Of course not," she agreed, her throat so tight she could barely swallow. She thought of Sheridan, then the instant after of Enid. They were so close to each other, and yet her son had killed his. How would they bear it? "I assume you would not have told me if there could be any doubt." That was not really a question. It all made an ugly and terrible sense. At least Pitt was safe, even if Voisey was still alive. "And this Kydd said that Magnus's father had been there, and tried to persuade him to abandon his anarchist beliefs?"

"Yes. That is a natural thing to do. Were it my son, I would have done so too. Kydd spoke of Magnus with respect, and I thought considerable affection. He had even adopted Magnus's kitten."

"Magnus's kitten?" she said. It was extraordinary. Surely Magnus was as sensitive to cats as the rest of the family? He would not keep a kitten. He would be sneezing all the time, scarcely able to breathe.

"Yes," Pitt answered. "A little black thing he named Mite. It can't have been more than a few weeks old. Not had its eyes open long."

"He must have been lying to you, Thomas. All the Landsboroughs are sensitive to cats."

"It seems a pointless lie," Pitt said thoughtfully. "It made no difference to anything. Are you sure?"

"I . . ." she began, about to say that she was, and then realized that she had assumed it, knowing that Sheridan and Enid both were. It had seemed that their father had been also, and so was Piers. Perhaps Magnus had escaped it. He resembled his mother more in some respects—the dark coloring for instance. With build, it was impossible to tell. Both Sheridan and Cordelia were fairly tall. He had remained spare, she had put on a little extra flesh. Magnus had not looked particularly like the Landsborough side when she had last seen him a few years ago. His coloring was different, the bones of his face. She remembered his smile, the strong teeth.

Then she remembered where once, very briefly, she had seen a smile that reminded her of Magnus, and a dozen impressions collided in her mind. One new, revelatory one emerged that replaced the passions she had felt below the surface of every encounter she had witnessed in the Landsborough house: Enid's hatred, Cordelia's fury, Sheridan's indifference. If that were true, it made hideous sense, even of the kitten.

Pitt was watching her, waiting.

She felt dazed, and overwhelmed with sorrow far from untouched by guilt of her own. She had liked Sheridan so much, found a companionship with him, a comfortable laughter, a friendship that had nothing of duty in it, nothing of expectation or advantage for either of them. It was a shared loneliness, an understanding of beauty missed, of infinite small pleasures that could not be fully savored alone. She had not even guessed at that love or loss. When had Sheridan known?

"What is it?" Pitt had to ask. The answer might be one he could not ignore.

She looked up at him. It surprised her how easy it was to tell him. Vespasia was an earl's daughter and Pitt's mother a domestic servant whose husband had been transported to Australia for poaching his master's game. There was an irony to it, and a value truer than most men would grasp.

"I believe Cordelia had an affair," she told him. "Magnus is not sensitive to cats because Sheridan Landsborough is not his father, Edward Denoon is. That is why Enid hates her husband, and her sister-in-law. It is why Sheridan has no feeling for his wife, and his indifference is the greatest insult she could imagine. It explains everything I've half-seen, half-understood before."

He said nothing. She could see in his face that he was weighing it, thinking of all the other things it meant, and how much it bore upon the murder, if it did at all. Had Piers Denoon known that it was not his cousin but his half-brother that he had been forced into killing? Had Wetron known, or cared? Probably not. It was just another, parallel tragedy.

"What will you do?" she asked him.

He looked tired. "I don't know. We have to arrest Piers Denoon and charge him, but Tanqueray's bill is more important at the moment." His face was tight, his skin pale and shadowed around the eyes. "At the moment Voisey is winning. He still has the proof of Simbister's guilt in the Scarborough Street bombing, and his connection with Wetron. That is, if he was telling me the truth about it, and I dare not assume he wasn't."

"No." Vespasia felt oddly empty inside. She had expected Voisey to betray Pitt if he could. One needed a very long spoon indeed to dine with the devil. Pitt was a man who had seen tragedy and all kinds of human selfishness, arrogance, and hatred, but he still encountered evil with surprise. He saw humanity where simpler and less generous men would have seen only the crime. There was no point in telling him that he should have been less trusting. He probably knew it. And anyway, she did not wish him to lose that peculiar quality that was his strength as well as his weakness. "There will be time to think of him later, perhaps." She smiled bleakly, but with intense gentleness. "But I am afraid it may require all the imagination and intelligence we have. Voisey does not yet know that you are still alive. He may well proceed tomorrow as if you were not."

"The bill?" His voice was tight. "Will he change sides, and back it now?"

"If I were he," she said slowly, "I would expose Simbister for the Scarborough Street bombing, and use that evidence of corruption to block the bill, at least for the time being."

"And after that?" His eyes told her he knew the answer.

"Destroy Wetron too," she answered. "And then take his place, unite the old Inner Circle again, and rule it as before. Knowing Voisey, he will exert a terrible revenge upon those who betrayed him." She told him the truth. He did not deserve less, nor could they afford evasions now.

He sat quite still. "Yes." He was thinking deeply, his face reflecting a desperate weariness.

She sat silent for some moments. "He will not forgive you, Thomas," she said at last.

He looked up. "I know. I still have the evidence implicating his sister in the murder of Rae. Should I use it? If I do, then I have nothing else left to protect Charlotte. And he knows that."

"Of course," she answered. "That is the trouble with the ultimate weapon. What is there left after you have used it?"

He looked at her with a searing honesty, his fear naked. A very slight smile at his own vulnerability softening his tiredness. "I expect Charlotte wouldn't use it either, even if I were dead in the river. She'd keep it to protect Daniel and Jemima. And he knows that. I wondered why he wasn't afraid to have me killed. I should have thought of that."

"There is no profit in what we should have done, my dear," she answered. "Let us sleep on tonight's events, and see what the morning brings. I shall call upon you at nine o'clock, when we see the newspapers. Now you must allow me to have my coachman take you home. Please don't argue with me."

He did not. He was grateful for it, and said so.

PITT SLEPT BETTER than he had expected. He had gone home not intending to tell Charlotte the details of what had happened. He not only wanted not to frighten her more than need be, but also he was aware how foolish he had been to take anything Voisey said as true, no matter how likely, or how rushed he was by circumstance.

In the event, she guessed too much for him to conceal it without deliberately lying to her, and he found her far more under-standing than he had feared. She was too relieved to criticize him. She even agreed that she would not have used the evidence against Mrs. Cavendish, precisely for the reasons he had supposed.

When he rose in the morning and went downstairs, he was con-sumed in domestic matters until the children had left for school. Then he, Charlotte, and Gracie opened the morning newspapers. They had read little more than the headlines when Vespasia ar-rived, closely followed by Tellman, and then Victor Narraway. They all looked deeply serious.

"Good morning, Thomas, Charlotte," Vespasia said briefly. "I took the liberty of calling Mr. Narraway to join us. It seems Sergeant Tellman must have had the same thought."

The *Times* was lying open on the kitchen table. All the other newspapers carried the same story. The only variations lay in which aspect of it they emphasized the most.

It had all happened yesterday evening, in time for today's press. Of course, Pitt thought ruefully. Voisey would have prepared everything he needed exactly so that should be the case. He could not afford to give Narraway time to react, or assume that Pitt was dead, and therefore could do nothing.

It seemed Voisey had gone directly to the home secretary him-self with the proof of Simbister's corruption. He had chosen to ex-pose not Piers Denoon's murder of Magnus Landsborough, but the systematic extortion from small businesses such as publicans, shop-keepers, and manufacturers—ordinary people dealing in pennies and shillings, who made up the vast majority of the population.

He had progressed from that through the finding of the explo-sives on the *Josephine,* proof that they were placed there by Grover, and his close connection with Simbister. He added a dramatic ac-count of Grover's attempted murder of Voisey himself, and an unnamed officer of Special Branch, whose identity needed to be protected.

It made exciting reading. The outrage at such an abuse of

power shone through it, lighting it with emotion and humanity. It was obviously a story that would unfold through the next days, perhaps weeks. Every reader would be purchasing the newspapers hot off the stands to follow it.

Denoon's paper carried it also, but with a more subdued note, sounding bewildered that such a tragedy could have come to pass. Surely it would be explained soon, and put right. It must be a single instance of criminality. That was the only credible explanation.

Even so, Tanqueray's bill to arm the police and give them greater power must be delayed. It was intolerable to allow a man such as Simbister to be in charge of an armed force.

"It will be a short respite," Narraway said grimly. "Without proof that it's connected to Wetron as well, it can be passed over as a single corrupt man leading astray one station."

Gracie had put on the kettle, and it was beginning to blow a light breath of steam. She stood with her back to it, having glanced at Tellman and met his eyes in a short moment of understanding. The cups were sitting on the kitchen table, a jug of milk from the pantry, a bowl of sugar if anyone wanted it, and the tea caddy had been brought down ready.

"It seems Sir Charles is a hero once again," Vespasia said drily. She was sitting on one of the hardback chairs.

Charlotte was standing by the dresser with its blue and white china. She was too tense to sit. She gave a sharp bark of laughter. "I wish we could think of a way to turn this against him too!" She was referring to the time they had outwitted him over Mario Corena's death.

Narraway looked at her. His expression was curious, unreadable. There was emotion in his face, but it was impossible to tell what it was. "I think he has turned our wit upon us this time," he said, first to her, but in a sense to all of them. If he thought that it was Pitt who had given him the opportunity, it was not implied, even in the tone of his voice. "I think he has used Special Branch as his cat's paw to pull out his prizes, then take them from us at exactly the right time."

"There must be something we can do!" Charlotte protested. She looked from one to the other of them. "If we haven't any power or any weapons, can't we turn their own against them somehow?"

Narraway stared at her. A tiny thread of a smile touched the corners of his mouth, but it was amusement, there was no joy in it.

Vespasia understood, Charlotte could see it in her eyes. She was a woman also, and grasped exactly the train of thought. If you are clever enough, know your opponent well enough, weakness can be turned into strength.

"Let us list everything we know of them," she said aloud. "Some combination of things may occur to us." She looked at Tellman. "Sergeant, you have worked for Wetron since Thomas left Bow Street. You must have made observations and formed judgments about him. What does he wish for? What might he fear? Is there anyone he cares about, other than himself? Anyone whose good opinion he either values or requires?"

When Tellman had recovered from his initial surprise that she should ask him, he thought hard. It was not his usual way of addressing a problem, and needed a little mental adjustment.

They all waited. The kettle boiled and Gracie made the tea, setting the pot on the table so it could brew before it was poured.

"Power," Tellman answered, uncertain if that was what Vespasia wanted.

"Glory?" she asked.

He was taken aback.

Pitt thought of covering for him, then bit his tongue.

"Does he like to be admired, loved?" Vespasia elaborated.

"I don't think so," Tellman answered. "I reckon he prefers if we're afraid of him. He likes to be safe. He's always playing careful."

"A brave man?" she said softly, a razor's edge of sarcasm in her voice, as if with a fine blade it cut almost without pain, until too late.

Tellman smiled very slightly. "No, Lady Vespasia, I don't think so. I don't think he wants to meet his enemies face-to-face."

Narraway nodded fractionally. He did not interrupt.

"If he is a coward," Vespasia said, pursing her lips slightly. "That may be of use to us. Cowards can be rattled, provoked into acting rashly, if they are given little time, and made to feel threatened." She turned to Pitt. "Is Sir Charles also a coward, Thomas?"

He knew his answer without having to weigh it. "No, Aunt Vespasia, he'd meet you face-to-face, if need be. In fact, I think he would rather enjoy it."

"Because he expects to win," Vespasia stated. "But he wants revenge, yes?"

It was a rhetorical question, and they all knew it.

"Yes," Pitt said ruefully.

"Does Wetron know that?" Vespasia asked, turning again to Tellman.

"I think so," he answered.

"If not, we could always tell him," Charlotte put in.

Narraway looked at her sharply, his brow furrowed.

"If we wanted to," she added quickly.

Gracie simplified the whole thing in a sentence. "Yer mean, like, set 'em at each other?" She poured the tea.

Vespasia smiled at her. "Admirably succinct," she said. "Since we appear to have no weapons, and they have, then we must use theirs, or let them win—a thought that sticks in my throat."

Narraway looked at Pitt, then at Vespasia. "Wetron has created a network of corruption where the police of several stations—we don't know the size of it yet—extort money from the ordinary people of their areas, using certain members of the criminal classes to do the ugliest of the work. As for example, Jones the Pocket. With the proceeds of this Wetron finances his empire. He has raised public feeling, with the help of men like Edward Denoon and his newspaper, to the pitch where they are willing, indeed eager, to arm the police and increase their power without giving any serious thought to the possibilities for abuse. The time for such legislation is ripe now, the bombings and the murder of Magnus Landsborough have seen to that."

Pitt understood, and he saw it in Charlotte also, and Vespasia. Tellman was frowning.

Narraway continued. He very pointedly did not look at Charlotte, as if he were afraid to meet her eyes.

"Apparently Voisey has the proof to destroy Wetron by connecting him irrevocably with Simbister and the Scarborough Street bombing, and the blackmail of Piers Denoon with the murder of Magnus." He faced Pitt. "Voisey still has this?"

"Yes," Pitt said unhappily. "We have the blackmail statements, but Voisey has the evidence that proves complicity in the Scarborough Street bombing. At least he said he has."

"Do you believe him?"

Pitt hesitated. "Yes."

Vespasia set down her cup. "Surely the point is, can Wetron afford to disbelieve him?"

A flash of appreciation lit Narraway's face. "Precisely, Lady Vespasia. If Wetron knows this, he cannot afford to allow Voisey to remain. Voisey is hungry to regain his old leadership and have his revenge upon the man who usurped him. He believes he has destroyed Pitt. He will now be turning his attention to Wetron, and he will lose no time."

"Wetron may know that, but, equally, he may not," Pitt pointed out. "His mind may be directed towards ensuring the bill goes through Parliament. And for all he says otherwise, perhaps Voisey would actually like it to, then quietly step into Wetron's place in the Inner Circle, and see that one of his own allies is appointed in Wetron's position, to keep on, far more discreetly, with the extortion. The bombing will stop and there'll be a big show of catching anarchists and trying and executing them. The people who have

power will be satisfied, and Voisey will reap Wetron's reward. And
be a hero. And make an advance towards being power minister
one day."

Tellman had said little since coming in. Vespasia regarded him
now, knowing that he was the only one in a position to tell Wetron
all these things, and assumed that he realized the urgency. She saw
in his thin, tense face that he understood it. Perhaps he also understood the danger, but what about the moral ambiguity? Wetron
and Voisey were both killers. If any of them here in this room were
going to interfere in their rivalry, to what degree were they necessarily implicit in the result?

She looked at Victor Narraway, and saw what she thought was
a conflict in his face. A decisive, almost ruthless, part of his nature,
used to the bitter choices of command, seemed to be warring with
something softer, and immeasurably more vulnerable.

Pitt saw it too, she knew that. What she had not expected was
the understanding in his eyes, a moment's pity, as if they were
equals in something.

Gracie sensed it in the air, the glances, the stiffness of bodies,
and was afraid. Instinctively she swiveled to Tellman. " 'A yer
gonner tell 'im, Samuel?" Her voice was a little shaky, caught in
her throat.

He looked at her gently, but there was no wavering in him.
"There's no one else who can do it," he told her. "He won't hurt us.
I didn't do it, at least not that he knows," he added ruefully.

"Don' be so daft!" she snapped. " 'E knows 'ose side yer on!
'E don' care about provin' it, 'e in't gonna charge yer, 'e'll jus' feel
like flattenin' someone, an' you'll be 'andy." She turned to Pitt.
"Mr. Pitt, yer gotta stop 'im. It ain't fair! Yer can't . . ."

"It's dangerous for everyone," Narraway cut across her. "Sergeant Tellman is the only one Wetron will believe. The alternative is to let Voisey win. And remember, Miss Phipps, if he does, he
has still not taken his vengeance on this family." His gesture in-

cluded her. "He will discover soon enough that Pitt is still alive, and there will be no one to stop him then."

Gracie glared at him, her protest dying on her lips.

"It'll be all right," Tellman assured her. "And we've got no choice. We can't leave Voisey with that kind of power. Mr. Narraway's right, next he'll come for us."

She smiled at him bleakly, pride and fear in her eyes, her lips pressed so tight it was impossible to see if they trembled.

Narraway nodded at Tellman. "I can't order you to, Sergeant, but, as you say, you are the only one of us who can do it."

"Yes, sir," Tellman acknowledged.

Vespasia stared at Narraway. "And when Wetron has disposed of Voisey, in whatever manner he decides—or he is inadequate to the task, and Voisey dispenses of him—what do you intend we shall do with the survivor?"

"That depends upon which one of them it is," he replied.

"That is not an answer, Mr. Narraway." Vespasia said it quite lightly, but her stare was inflexible.

He smiled. "I know."

Pitt moved his position slightly.

Vespasia turned to look at him. "Thomas?"

"Wetron cannot afford to have Voisey tried," he answered her, but he was speaking to all of them. "He'll find a way to protect himself and get rid of Voisey at the same time. Don't assume it won't be violent."

Vespasia looked at Charlotte, concerned for her, and saw the anxiety in her face. Then she looked at Narraway. He understood it. If he had deliberately avoided saying so, then it was for that softer part of him she had seen for an instant, and not recognized.

Narraway spoke to Tellman. "Report to Pitt immediately," he said. "But don't stay your hand because of it. Remember the dead in Scarborough Street, if you're tempted towards mercy."

Vespasia saw the distaste in Tellman. "Don't think of Scarborough Street," she amended. "They are already dead, or crippled. Think of the next street, and the one after."

Tellman filled his mind with that, and they parted soon after. He went out into the street and walked briskly along a couple of blocks to Tottenham Court Road, where he took the first hansom to Bow Street. If he gave himself time to think about it, he might lose the spontaneity, the high pitch of emotion he felt after sitting in the kitchen at Keppel Street. And as they had said, there was no time to lose.

He went in through the doors, past the duty sergeant with no more than a word, and up the stairs to Wetron's office. He had not asked anyone if he were in because he was not certain yet if he wanted anyone to know what he intended.

He knocked on Wetron's door. The answer was quick and impatient.

Tellman went in. "Good morning, sir," he said without hesitation, closing the door behind him. His voice was tight and a little high.

Wetron was standing at the window. He turned around, and saw Tellman with irritation. There was anxiety in his face, but an oblique kind of triumph also. "Morning, Sergeant. I'm sorry to hear about Pitt. Never liked the man, but I know you had a kind of loyalty."

Tellman's mind raced. Wetron must have been told that Pitt was dead. He had three choices—deny it, accept it as if he knew also, or pretend complete ignorance—and almost three seconds to decide which served his interests best. "Sir?" He played for time. He could not afford even the slightest mistake.

"Pulled out of the river this morning," Wetron said, watching him with malicious pleasure. "Seems the anarchists got him."

"Oh, that." Suddenly Tellman could see what he wanted to do. He had the chance to seize this as a weapon. "Looks a bit like Mr.

Simbister trying to defend himself, doesn't it? Last throw, as you might say."

Wetron's skin flooded with color. For an instant he was uncertain. He wanted to lose his temper and shout at Tellman, hurt him by playing on his grief. Then better judgment prevailed; he weighed his own needs and spoke calmly.

"You are aware of Simbister's corruption?'"

"Just what I saw in the newspapers this morning, sir," Tellman replied. "I know rather more about Sir Charles Voisey."

"Indeed?" Wetron raised his eyebrows. "How is that, Sergeant? I am not aware of any of your investigators taking you to ask questions about a member of Parliament."

Tellman shivered. It would be so easy to be overconfident, to say too much, or the wrong things. Now was the time for truth. "No, sir," he said meekly. "I'm courting the Pitts' housekeeper, sir. I happened to be there this morning."

"And yet you appear entirely indifferent to Pitt's death!" Wetron said in amazement. "Is there an entire dimension to your character of which I am unaware?"

"Not so far as I know, sir. Mr. Pitt was in good health. I don't know if some poor soul who looks like him was pulled out of the river. I should think, sir, frankly, that it is more likely Sir Charles told you a deliberate lie." He relaxed a little. "From what I know, sir, from Mrs. Pitt, and my own observation, it seems Sir Charles has some personal hatred towards you. He is the one behind Mr. Simbister's fall, if you want to put it that way."

Wetron was motionless. "What makes you think that, Sergeant?"

Now was the time to tell him what Narraway needed him to know. "He was the one who told Special Branch about Mr. Simbister using thieves and the like to collect money from the publicans, and he was the one who found out that the dynamite the anarchists used was kept in a boat down by Shadwell."

Wetron's eyes were glittering hard, his skin all but bloodless. "And how do you know this, Tellman? It sounds as if you have spent more time working for Special Branch than doing your job from the police who pay you. Just where does your loyalty lie? As if I didn't know!"

"Like I said, sir, I'm courting Mr. Pitt's maid. I happened to be there this morning, and I heard this from Mr. Pitt himself. Sir Charles tried to kill him last night, but he didn't succeed."

"Were you there?" Wetron demanded.

Tellman looked slightly aggrieved. "No, sir! I was on duty here!"

"What did you come for, Tellman?" Wetron said harshly. His lips were as thin as a knife cut.

"Loyalty to the police, sir." That was believable. He had spent all his working life in the police force, and Wetron knew that. "I think it's right that Mr. Simbister has to go. Seems he was rotten. But Mr. Pitt let some words slip out, and I can piece the rest together. Sir Charles plans to get rid of you too, sir, then get a man of his own in here, and spread the same kind of thing to Bow Street, but take the money himself. This is my station, sir. I'm not going to let that happen."

He drew in a long, deep breath. "I don't pretend I like you, sir, the way I liked Mr. Pitt, but I wouldn't see you done for something you had no part of. It's wrong. And I don't want one of Sir Charles Voisey's policemen running my station."

"Indeed," Wetron said softly. "And for what, exactly, does Sir Charles Voisey imagine he can have me 'done?' "

"Not sure, sir." Tellman was shaking and his stomach was knotted like a fist. "Something to do with blackmail, and the murder of a young man. Says he has a paper to prove what happened, and he'll lay it on you."

The silence in the room was like a growing thing, expanding to suffocate the spaces and take the air from the chest.

Wetron stared at Tellman, trying to control the rage inside him, trying to keep his brain cool enough to think. The truth of what Tellman had said was naked in his reaction to it.

Tellman could feel the sick fear grip him even more tightly.

"Will he?" Wetron said very slowly, his voice rasping. "Will he indeed?"

Tellman felt strangled. "Y-Yes, sir. I-I think perhaps he planned that all along. He's got a terrible taste for revenge. That's why he worked so elaborate, like, with Mr. Pitt, against the police bill—t-to set him up."

"But you said Pitt escaped!" Wetron challenged.

Tellman let his breath out. "Yes, sir. Just luck. Someone else was passing on the river. Rescued him."

"Mistake," Wetron said with satisfaction. "Always finish the job yourself. Well, if Sir Charles wants my place, the fruits of what I've built . . . he can have it! Very good, Tellman. Very good. In fact, I shall see that he has it—and the blame that goes along with it." He glanced at the clock on the mantel. "He will still be at home. Excellent. Just where the proof will be. I shall go and arrest him."

His voice was shaking a little with a sudden excitement. "You say he tried to murder Pitt? Then he is a violent man. I had better take a gun with me. He may resist." His smile was wide, mirthless, and filled with a savage pleasure. "Pitt is a fool, but his escape from last night's adventure may prove useful. He won't lie. If asked, he will say that Voisey tried to kill him." He walked to a locked cupboard, took a key off his watch chain, and opened it. He picked a revolver, loaded it, and put it in the pocket of his jacket.

"I shan't need you, Tellman," he said, straightening up. "This is between gentlemen. You've done a good job." He walked past Tellman and out the door, his back stiff, the gun invisible within the heavy fabric of his jacket.

Tellman waited until he was out of sight, then sprinted down the stairs and out the door. Pitt was waiting in an alley a couple of hundred yards away. They must follow Wetron and catch him at exactly the right moment, before he murdered Voisey. Then they would have them both, and all the evidence that was left. In their hatred, one would testify against the other.

He ran along the street, his boots echoing on the stones.

CHAPTER

TWELVE

Pitt was waiting in the alley, pacing back and forth, standing for a minute, peering around the corner, and then pacing again. He saw Tellman when he was still twenty yards away, his figure easily distinguishable in the momentary crowd on the footpath because he was running.

Pitt started out, then realized in the tangle of people they could miss each other, and stepped back again. The moment after, Tellman nearly collided with him.

"Wetron's gone after Voisey," he gasped. "At his house. He's got a gun. I think he's going to shoot him whatever, and say it was self-defense. No one'll argue with him."

"Voisey's house? Let's go. He can't shoot all three of us, and the servants." Pitt strode towards the main street, Tellman at his side, and hailed the first empty hansom to pass. He gave Voisey's address, and they both leapt in, shouting instructions to hurry.

"It's a matter of life and death!" Tellman added, his voice so sharp that passing drivers swiveled to pay momentary attention, but with disbelief.

The hansom plunged forward, fighting its way through traffic. Neither Pitt nor Tellman spoke. They were both trying to keep panic at bay, not allow their imaginations to race into all the things that could go wrong: the nightmare of Voisey winning, revenge feeding more revenge until there was nothing left.

And hope must be stifled too. They were not safe yet. They would arrest Wetron for attempting to kill Voisey, the proof of Wetron's guilt would be there, and Voisey would have it. The whole machine of corruption would be broken, the bill defeated. But Voisey would be alive, with all that that meant.

The hansom careered along a half-empty street and swung around a corner, throwing them almost on top of each other. Still, neither spoke. They picked up speed again.

It seemed an age before they slowed to a stop at last. Pitt handed the driver a fistful of coins—roughly what he thought the ride would cost, plus a generous tip. He and Tellman ran across the pavement and up the steps of Voisey's house. Pitt banged on the door.

A butler opened it with a look of distaste on his face. "Yes, sir?" His tone of voice conveyed his opinion of people who made loud and vulgar noise, whatever the circumstances. "May I be of assistance?"

"I must see Sir Charles immediately!" Pitt said, catching his breath. "His life is in danger."

"I'm sorry, sir, but Sir Charles is at the House. He customarily goes at about this hour."

"But he was here forty minutes ago," Tellman protested, as if it could matter now.

"No, sir," the butler said firmly. "Sir Charles left over an hour ago."

"Superintendent Wetron said . . ." Tellman insisted, his voice raised.

"I'm sorry, sir, but you are mistaken," the butler repeated.

Wild thoughts of conspiracy raced through Pitt's mind, before he realized the obvious answer. "He wasn't at home," he said aloud. "Wetron misled us on purpose. We must get to the House."

"He couldn't do anything in the House of Commons!" Tellman said incredulously.

"Yes he could, in a private office." Pitt started down the steps again in time to shout at the hansom. The driver had been giving the horse a few minutes' rest while he enjoyed the spectacle in the doorway, and was only just pulling away now. He heard Pitt's voice and stopped again.

"House of Commons!" Pitt ordered.

"I s'pose that's as fast as yer can make it too, eh?" the driver observed. "Don't you ever go nowhere at a normal speed like other fellers? More life an' death, is it?"

"Yes. Hurry! Or if this horse is exhausted, catch up with another cab and we'll change," Pitt replied.

The driver gave him a look of total disdain, and started forward again, picking up speed rapidly.

"We're going to be too late!" Tellman said between his teeth. "That bastard will have shot him!"

Pitt did not answer. He was afraid Tellman was right.

It seemed like another long, tedious, traffic-congested ride. All the impatience and sense of failure could not shorten it, or prevent what they now felt to be inevitable.

They finally reached the House of Commons. Pitt paid over nearly all the rest of the money he was carrying, with a request that it be spent on the horse, then sprinted to follow Tellman, who was already twenty yards ahead of him.

Once they had identified themselves they were allowed in and conducted up to Voisey's office. But as soon as they turned the corner of the long corridor they saw it was already too late. There was a grim crowd blocking the way. Voices were lowered, bodies tense, faces white and anxious.

"What's happened?" Pitt demanded, stopping as soon as he reached them, although he feared he knew.

"Terrible," one of the secretaries answered. He was a pale young man formally dressed. He clutched a bunch of papers in his hand and it was shaking, making a slight rustle as the sheets flapped together. "Absolutely dreadful."

"What is?" Pitt repeated urgently.

"Oh! Don't you know? Sir Charles Voisey's been shot. The superintendent of police is here. Man from Bow Street. To have a member shot dead in the House! What's happening to the world?"

Pitt pushed his way through, elbowing people aside until he reached the door, and found himself a yard away from Wetron who looked pale and shaken. However, the moment their eyes met Pitt saw the gleam of triumph, and knew he had been defeated.

Wetron gave nothing away. To all other onlookers he was a man startled and grieved by an appalling event.

"Ah! Superintendent Pitt," he said, as if Pitt still held his old rank. "I'm glad you've come. Dreadful thing. Irrefutable evidence, I'm afraid. Tragic. I went to question Sir Charles about it, hoping against hope that he had some other explanation, but he hadn't. Guilt overtook him. He lunged at me with a paper knife in his hand. I had no choice." His words were wrung out of him, harsh with shock and regret. His eyes burned with victory, and the hard, sweet taste of power. To those standing around, his expression could have meant anything, but Pitt read it for what it was.

"Evidence of what, Superintendent Wetron?" Pitt asked innocently, as if he had no idea.

Wetron's expression did not waver. "Of corruption, Mr. Pitt. Deep corruption, not only of serving officers of police. I regret profoundly to have to say it, but Sir Charles was in league with Superintendent Simbister of Cannon Street. Worse than that, it seems inescapably evident that he was also involved with the anarchists who bombed Scarborough Street so appallingly. He is tied indisputably to the dynamite used. I wish it were not so." He did not smile—there were too many others looking—but the victory shone in his eyes.

Pitt felt the taste of defeat as bitter as gall, but he could think of no weapon with which to strike back. There was no point in asking if Voisey had admitted any of it. Wetron would say he had, and Pitt would know it was not true.

"I shall tell Mr. Narraway," Pitt managed to say. "Proof of the Scarborough Street bombers' guilt will be very welcome." Would Wetron give up his accomplices, the men who had obeyed his orders? Possibly. If they had no idea and no evidence of where the orders had come from, he had nothing to lose, and perhaps much to gain. The thought of Wetron taking the credit for that too made him sick with anger at the injustice of it, and his own helplessness, but there was nothing whatever he could do.

"Of course," Wetron agreed slightly patronizingly. "I'll be happy to pass it to him, when my men have sorted it out. We must settle the matter of Sir Charles's death first, of course."

One of the several parliamentary secretaries nodded. "Naturally, naturally. Fearful thing. Very well handled, if I may say so, sir. Great personal courage to tackle the man alone. Grateful not to have a herd of uniformed men in the place. What a scandal. Terrible thing. Never suspected it at all."

"Years of experience," Wetron said modestly. "But I am still shocked, I admit. This is . . . crime of a terrible order, a tragedy for the country. I . . ." he gave a little shudder. "I am sure you understand that at the moment I prefer to say nothing further. It has all been deeply distressing." He glanced towards Voisey's closed office door.

"Of course," the parliamentary secretary agreed piously. He turned to the rest of the group around him. "Gentlemen, it is not appropriate for us to remain here when there is nothing we can do to help. This is the time for the sad duty of others. Let us return to our own offices, or wherever else we should be." He made a gesture half-ushering them away.

Pitt hesitated. He was oddly reluctant to go in and see Voisey's body. Was it his duty?

Wetron's hand gripped his arm, holding him back with some force. "It's a police matter," he said firmly. "You are Special Branch, remember?"

Pitt's mind was changed in an instant. "Did I mishear you, Superintendent? I thought you said Sir Charles was implicated in the Scarborough Street bombing, and that the money he had extorted from the tradesmen around the Cannon Street area went towards furnishing the anarchists."

Wetron was confused for a moment, caught on the wrong foot. At least one of the parliamentary secretaries was still within hearing.

"That makes it Special Branch," Pitt said with a tight, bitter smile. "That's what we're here for: anarchists and bombings. We are obliged to you for catching him . . . and of course for attempting to arrest him for us."

Wetron regained his balance, at least outwardly. "A pity I couldn't take him alive," he said bitterly. "That way he might have testified against others. Now, of course, he can't."

"No doubt that was in his mind also," Pitt said ambiguously. He shook his arm free of Wetron's grip and opened the door, leaving Tellman to follow or not, as he wished. In a way he hoped he would not.

He closed the door.

Inside the room it was silent in the morning sun, the closed windows kept out the sound of traffic below, and they were several floors up anyway. There was no sound of voices from the corridors, or from the walks by the river.

Everything was tidy. There were no signs of any struggle, as if whatever conflict they had had, it had been entirely verbal, a battle of wits rather than body against body.

Charles Voisey lay on the carpet between his desk and the window. He was half on his left side, his hand crooked, the neat bullet hole like a third eye in his forehead. There was no surprise on his face, only irritation. He had seen it coming, and knew his mistake.

Pitt stared down at him, wondering if Voisey had known that he had failed last night, and that Pitt was still alive. Was there some vision after death that would enable him to know it now? Or did whatever soul there was concern itself only with what lay ahead?

Would Mrs. Cavendish be distraught? Who was there to tell her? Her family, other friends? In all their conversations, Voisey had never mentioned other friends. Allies, people over whom he had power, but not anyone who would miss him simply because they had liked him.

Pitt had almost liked him. He had been clever, sometimes he had made Pitt laugh, he had been intensely alive, capable of passion, curiosity, and need. There was an emptiness because he was gone.

"You're a fool," Pitt said aloud to Voisey. "You didn't have to do this. You could have been . . . lots of things. You had the chance." He stared down at the body. "What the hell did you do with the proof . . . if you ever had it?"

Was it even worth looking for? Wouldn't Wetron have thought of it, and done all he could to tamper with it? He would have left only what incriminated Voisey rather than himself.

A deeper sense of defeat settled over Pitt, an anger and a sadness. He had fought against Voisey for a long time, and suffered intense loss at his hands. And yet he realized he still would not have had it end this way. What had he wanted? He realized with surprise that the answer was absurd. He had wanted Voisey to change. That was never likely to have happened. He was angry with him for it, angry with Wetron, and angry with himself for not having been clever enough to beat him.

There was a knock on the door. It would be people to take the body away. He could not keep them waiting. There was no debate over what had happened, Wetron had told as much of the truth as could be proved, so he had no reason to keep the body back as evidence.

"Come in," he answered.

AN HOUR LATER HE left the Houses of Parliament. Tellman had already gone with Wetron. He had had no choice: Wetron was his superior and had ordered him to. Pitt had searched Voisey's office as much as he could. Many drawers were locked, and he had been told they contained government papers to which he could be given no access. He had found nothing useful in the rest. The proof regarding the dynamite on the *Josephine*, Grover's involvement, and all the papers incriminating Simbister were already with the authorities. They were what Voisey had used to prove Simbister's guilt.

He went back to Keppel Street, going that way first almost without thinking about it. Then he realized that Narraway might still be there, expecting him to come back, and Charlotte and Vespasia certainly would be. He had to allow Tellman to do as Wetron commanded. That was just one other aspect of defeat. He dare not defy him, or Tellman would pay.

As soon as he opened the front door Narraway was in the passage. He saw from Pitt's face that they had lost.

"What happened?"

Pitt bent and took off his boots. "Stupid," he answered. "He telephoned Voisey at home, and apparently spoke to him, then he told Tellman he was going to see him there. We believed it."

"And?" Narraway snapped.

Pitt stood up, bootless. "He probably spoke to a butler, or maybe was just pretending to speak to someone. Voisey was at the House of Commons. By the time we got there he was already dead. Wetron was busy telling people he had gone to arrest Voisey, Voisey had resisted, attacked him with a paper knife, and in self-defense Wetron had had to shoot him."

Narraway swore, oblivious of the fact that Charlotte and Vespasia were both in the kitchen behind him.

"What can we do now?" Charlotte asked quietly, her voice sounding crushed.

Narraway turned around, and colored deeply. He seemed to debate whether to apologize or not. He drew in his breath.

Vespasia overrode him. "Gracie will make us tea, and we shall consider what choices we have," she answered.

"What are they?" Charlotte asked again, ten minutes later as they sat around the kitchen table, Gracie as well, eating thin-sliced bread and butter and drinking tea. Vespasia sat with them, exactly as if it were her habit to dine in the kitchen with friends, a maidservant, and the head of Special Branch.

"Denoon's paper will be full of Wetron the hero by midafternoon," Narraway said grimly. "On this tide, he'll be the next commissioner of police."

"We assume that was his intention," Vespasia agreed. "I must admit, there are few things that anger me as much as that. The man is vile, and he will harm this whole country irreparably."

"He's also still head of the Inner Circle," Pitt added. "And there is not even Voisey alive to challenge him. In fact, no one will dare to challenge him for a long time, I should think."

Gracie screwed up her face. " 'E still puts 'is trousers on one leg at a time, like anybody else. There must be summink as 'e's weak in, summink 'e forgets."

"He seems to have thought of everything," Narraway replied to her. It cost him a moment's surprise that she felt free to make a remark. "All the evidence anyone has could be attributed to Voisey as easily as to him. Simbister is totally discredited, and I imagine with Wetron's intelligence he has made sure there are sufficient threats in his hands to be certain that Simbister does not accuse him. Not that there is likely to be any proof. I know Voisey said he had proof, but no one has seen it, and if it exists, Wetron will have destroyed it by now."

"Piers Denoon's confession is no good. It only implicates Simbister, and he's finished anyway," Pitt added. "We can arrest Piers, but that doesn't implicate Wetron."

"Piers Denoon's confession to what?" Gracie asked, puzzled.

"He raped a young woman. Simbister got a confession from him and used it to blackmail him into supporting the anarchists, and then to shooting Magnus Landsborough," Pitt explained briefly. "Wetron took it over, but we can't prove that."

Gracie wrinkled her nose in disgust.

"We . . . removed it from Wetron's safe," Pitt said drily, "but we are not in a position to say so."

"All the same," Gracie persisted. " 'e's gotter 'ave suffink as 'e's scared of, or as 'urts 'im. Wi' Mr. Voisey it were 'is sister. In't Mr. Wetron got nobody?" She made a little noise of irritation. "We can't jist let 'im be! It in't right!"

"He has made himself very powerful indeed!" Vespasia said gently, looking at Gracie's small, stiff figure across the kitchen table. "And most of his power is secret."

"There must be someone as don't care!" Gracie protested. "If 'e's that wicked, 'e must 'ave 'urt someone bad enough. We just gotter find 'em."

An idea was beginning to form in Pitt's mind, but he did not like it. It helped very little, and it might take a long time.

Charlotte was watching him. "What is it?" she demanded. "What have you thought of?"

He rubbed his hand over his forehead. He was suddenly very tired. He did not seem to have had a restful night for weeks. The things in the world he believed in were crumbling around him; a decency he had taken for granted was not there. It was Wetron who was at the heart of the breaking, the sinking of good men and the betrayal of the people who trusted them.

"I think I'll go and tell the Landsboroughs that we know who murdered their son," he said, standing up slowly. "They have a right to know that. I can't arrest him until I know where he is."

"If you tell Lord Landsborough, they may warn Enid Denoon," Vespasia said reluctantly. There was intense pity in her face. "Or is that what you intend, Thomas?"

Charlotte looked from Pitt to Vespasia, and back again.

"I can't let him go, Aunt Vespasia," he spoke gently. The whole idea hurt him. "He raped a girl, he's been organizing the money for the anarchists who blew up Myrdle Street, and very probably Scarborough Street as well, but mostly he killed Magnus. And arresting him for that so his father knows how Wetron used him is the only way I have to trap Wetron himself at last."

"I see," she agreed. "I can think of no other way either."

He found himself almost choked with overwhelming sadness as he said it. "First mistakes are often not so big, and certainly not irreparable, if you pay for them at the time. He kept on making more, trying to avoid paying for the first. Until they became too big to pay for. I'm sorry."

Charlotte leaned forward and slid her hand over Vespasia's. It was a gesture of an intimacy she made without thinking. Had she thought, perhaps she would not have dared.

"Of course," Vespasia nodded almost imperceptibly. "My remark was made without consideration. How do you intend to arrest him, since according to Voisey he was planning to escape the country by sea?"

"There was no proof that that was true," Pitt pointed out, embarrassed still with how easily he had believed it. "I think I shall have some idea from Denoon's behavior whether his son has gone or not. I don't know for certain, but I believe Edward Denoon was providing at least some of the money Piers gave the genuine anarchists, either from his own sources or from Wetron's. Wetron probably allowed Grover to keep enough from his extortion to finance the Scarborough Street bombs."

"I see. You wish Denoon to be at Lord Landsborough's house when you tell him?" Vespasia made it a question, almost an offer.

He felt a tightening inside himself. "Yes . . . please."

"I see that you have a telephone in the hall. Perhaps I had better use it."

He offered her his hand.

She rose without it, giving him a dry, chilly look, but not without amusement. "I am grieved, Thomas, not incapable!"

Pitt turned to Gracie. "Thank you," he said sincerely. "I think Wetron may have a vulnerability after all, just a slight one."

Gracie blushed with pleasure.

Pitt looked at Charlotte. He did not say anything or offer explanations, simply met her eyes for a moment. Then he followed Vespasia out into the hall.

VESPASIA'S CARRIAGE TOOK Pitt to the Landsborough house before going on to take her back to her own. They did not say anything further on the subject along the short ride, but sat in a companionable silence. Pitt was still thinking about Voisey lying on the floor of his office, drained of the anger and greed, the wit and the hunger that had made him so alive. He did not know what she was thinking, but probably of Sheridan Landsborough and the grief that must fill him, and of Enid and the pain that so soon awaited her.

At no time had he asked Vespasia not to warn them. Such an idea was unthinkable, and to speak of it would be insulting to a degree she might forgive, but she would not forget.

"Thank you, Aunt Vespasia," he said quietly when the carriage stopped.

She did not answer, but smiled at him very slightly, her face filled with pity.

He wished there were something he could say or do, even a gesture, but he did not know what, and ended simply bidding his good-bye as he alighted, and closing the carriage door behind him.

The footman received him without surprise, or even needing to ask his name. Sheridan and Cordelia were waiting for him in the withdrawing room, Edward and Enid Denoon beside them. They all looked pale and tense, faces turned towards the door as soon as they heard his footsteps in the hall.

Landsborough came forward. "Good afternoon, Mr. Pitt. It is good of you to come in person to inform us."

"I thought you would wish to know," Pitt replied. "We now have sufficient evidence to arrest the man who killed your son."

Landsborough turned to Cordelia who let out a gasp, her face flooding with relief.

"Thank you!" she said with a crack in her voice. "It . . . it has been very hard waiting."

Landsborough kept his composure with difficulty. "I am deeply obliged to you, Pitt. It is a great burden lifted, especially among so much bad news. I see from the afternoon papers that Sir Charles Voisey is dead." His face looked pinched as he said it, the disappointment in his eyes profound. He looked at Pitt, desperate for some shred of hope to defeat the bill. His son was dead and the liberal, tolerant, enlightened world he loved seemed about to be submerged in a tide of corrupt tyranny. He knew of no way to fight it, let alone to win.

There was one last, terrible blow Pitt could not prevent. He could not even deliver it now, in front of Denoon. Wetron was too clever and too deadly a foe.

"Yes," Pitt said. "It appears that he was corrupted in a way we had no idea of."

"The newspapers are full of it," Landsborough agreed with acute distaste. "Superintendent Wetron is the hero."

"He's a good man," Denoon said sharply. "We owe him a great deal. He acted with supreme courage and decision. I admire a man who has the forthrightness of his convictions and goes to face the enemy himself, instead of sending his juniors to do it." He smiled bleakly. "Good thing he did. A lesser man might have ended in arresting Voisey, with injuries to everyone, and then a messy trial with a lot of scandal coming out. This way he's unmasked Simbister and gotten rid of Voisey as swiftly and surgically as possible. We can begin to recover. Get rid of the corruption and suppress the anarchy."

Cordelia looked at him icily. "Mr. Pitt came to tell us that he is about to arrest the man who murdered Magnus, Edward, not to praise Wetron for shooting Sir Charles Voisey, much as we may have disagreed with him politically."

"I didn't disagree with him politically," Enid said, staring at Cordelia. "Personally I thought he was a fearful man, cruel and greedy and careless of people's welfare, but I thought politically he was absolutely right."

"For heaven's sake, Enid, you don't know what you are talking about!" Denoon retorted. "He was against the Police Bill! Now we know why; he was totally corrupt, and he had corrupted Simbister as well."

"That isn't the reason," she argued.

Denoon's face was dark with anger.

"Of course it is. He couldn't afford to have the police investigated, he was in it up to his neck." He turned to Pitt. "Isn't that what you've come to say?"

"Were you investigating the police corruption?" Landsborough asked Pitt.

"Yes," Pitt replied. "And it didn't at any point implicate Sir Charles Voisey."

"Then you are incompetent," Denoon snapped back. "Superintendent Wetron's evidence shows that Voisey was in it, in fact he was behind it. If you were any good at your job you would have known, and proved it, not had to have Wetron do it for you."

Sheridan Landsborough froze. "Edward, Mr. Pitt is a guest in my home," he said stiffly. "And as such you will treat him with courtesy, or if that is beyond you, then at least with civility. He has come here to tell me he is about to arrest the man who murdered my son. Will you at least respect my wife's feelings, and mine, if you cannot respect the fact that you also are a guest here, even if you are family." He invested the last word with such a desperate irony that Pitt had a sudden, agonizing certainty that Landsborough knew the truth about Magnus's birth.

Denoon saw Pitt's face and flushed scarlet. There was rage, and now fear as well in his eyes.

Cordelia glared at her husband, but she also said nothing.

Enid stood with her head high, eyes direct.

"I apologize for my husband's lack of manners," she said very clearly to Pitt. "I wish I could think of a reasonable excuse, but I cannot. Would you be good enough, in spite of our lack of grace, to tell us what you have observed. Sheridan, at last, would like to know. He loved Magnus deeply, and did all he could to bring him back from the path of anarchy."

Pitt found her compassion almost unbearable. It even raced through his mind to wonder if there was any way at all that he could spare her from her own son's arrest, and almost certainly his trial and death.

"Well?" Cordelia broke the silence.

There was nothing Pitt could do. It was not the first time he had hated catching someone, and many he had understood better than Piers Denoon.

"It is one of the other anarchists," he said in answer. "I am not sure if I can arrest him, but I am going to do all I can. I regret it, very much. I wish I could say it was Voisey, and put an end to it, but I can't."

"Why on earth would you wish that?" Cordelia demanded. "We all want whoever it was! Go and arrest him. Don't waste time standing here. Tell us when it is done."

Pitt felt a flicker of anger at her bluntness. It passed in an instant. "I regret it because it was someone Magnus knew and trusted," he answered. "Possibly even cared for. I am not telling you until I arrest him, because if I do, I may cause unnecessary pain, and make a charge I cannot prove. One way or another, I believe it will be over by this time tomorrow. Good day."

Landsborough went with him to the door, and just short of it he stopped.

"Is it true, Pitt? Do you know who it was?" he said urgently.

"There seems to be only one possible answer," Pitt replied.

"But you needed something from us, which is why you came."

"You went after Magnus and tried to dissuade him?" Pitt made it a question, although he knew the answer.

Landsborough's face tightened, bleak with misery and a drowning sense of failure. "Yes."

Pitt felt brutal, as if he were cutting a man apart while he was still alive. Apologizing would only make it worse.

"Did you see two men, one with pale skin and red hair, the other thin with a mass of dark hair, curling?"

"Yes?" Landsborough was confused.

"They said they were friends of Magnus's. Is that true?"

"Yes. I saw them with him several times. They seemed to be quite . . . close. Does it matter now?"

"Yes. I want to use them to catch the man who killed him." Pitt felt guilty that he could not warn Landsborough of the fearful pain to come. But he was so close to his sister that he might very easily betray the truth to her, even if he did not mean to. He might even do it intentionally, to save her some tiny portion of the grief. In fact, Pitt was almost certain he would do so. It was his nature. "Thank you," he added. "I thought they were telling the truth, but if they were involved, they would lie."

Landsborough frowned. "You said it was someone he trusted," he pointed out.

"It was. But it couldn't have been either of them. We know where they were standing at the time. Thank you, Lord Landsborough. Now I must go and do what I have to." It seemed absurd to say "good day." He gave a brief smile and left.

HE WENT STRAIGHT TO the prison where Welling and Carmody were being held. He told the jailer to put them in the same cell, then he went in himself.

Both men stared at him. The change had disconcerted them and they were afraid of what it might mean. It was as he had intended, but only part of his reason for doing it. He had a plan to trick Denoon, and hoped that he could be driven to testify against Wetron in order to save himself. At the very least he might betray himself in a way that would give Pitt a wedge to drive into the smallest crack, and eventually begin Wetron's destruction.

Welling and Carmody were staring at him and waiting.

"I want you to give a message to Piers Denoon," he said bluntly.

There was a sneer on Welling's face. "You mean like, post a letter?" he said sarcastically. "Post it yourself."

"I mean like go and find him," Pitt replied.

"Oh yeah? And then come back obediently to prison, so you can lock me away for the rest of my life?" His look said that he would like to have wished Pitt in hell, but did not dare say so, in case Pitt revoked the few privileges he had, or even his promise not to charge him with Magnus's death.

"You know," Pitt said coolly, "if you would be quiet and let me put the offer to you, you might find it was a much better one than you seem determined to frame for yourself."

"Be quiet!" Carmody snapped at Welling. "Yes, Mr. Pitt?"

Pitt acknowledged it with a tight smile. "I want one of you to go and find Piers Denoon and persuade him to go home. Choose whatever manner you know will work. He shot Magnus, and I can't let him get away with that." He saw the emotion in their faces, the anger and the hurt. "And if that is not sufficient for you," he went on, "he also helped finance the dynamite that blew up the houses in Scarborough Street that killed seven people and injured many more, for which anarchists in general are being blamed."

"Why would he kill Magnus?" Welling said doubtfully. "They were cousins, family!"

"Because he was being blackmailed into it," Pitt replied with the truth. "He may not even have wanted to be involved with anarchists at all, but he had no choice. He committed a rape three years ago. I've seen his confession to it, and the supporting statements. The police kept them, and used them to force him to do what they wanted."

Carmody used an obscene word about the police, his face twisted with revulsion and hatred.

"He still shot Magnus, rather than face his own punishment," Pitt reminded him.

"It seems like a betrayal," Carmody bit his lip.

"Of whom?" Pitt asked. "Piers? Or Magnus?"

"What if we don't come back, whichever one of us goes?" Welling asked.

"I don't expect you to come back," Pitt replied with a very slight smile. "If you do what we agree, the other one goes free as well. If you don't, then he stays here and faces the charges on the Myrdle Street bombing. And considering how many people were killed in Scarborough Street, I don't think juries feel good about bombers at the moment." He added that because he could not afford to lose, nor could he tell them all that could be won or lost on their decision.

"I'll go," Welling said with decision.

Pitt looked at him, then at Carmody. "No," he said flatly. "Carmody will go. Do it straight away. If you fail, Welling pays the price, and I'll make very sure indeed that Kydd knows about it."

Welling jerked his head up, his eyes sharp.

Pitt smiled. "You thought I didn't know Kydd?"

Welling let out his breath silently.

"Are you coming?" Pitt said to Carmody.

Carmody straightened up. "Yes . . . sir. Yes, I'm coming."

I T W A S A L O N G and miserable wait, watching the house, not only because of the time involved, or the possibility that Carmody would fail, but that he deliberately might not even try. Pitt had threatened to charge Welling if that were so, but he was reluctant actually to do it. There was an injustice in punishing one man for another's weakness or cowardice that he found repellent. Worse than either of these was the knowledge of what success would mean: the arrest of Piers Denoon in his home, in front of his father. It was the only way to turn Edward Denoon against Wetron. It was not Edward Denoon's feelings Pitt cared about—he was not proud of the pleasure he would take in inflicting some injury on such an arrogant man, one who might even take over Wetron's leadership of the Inner Circle, if he were not prevented. But he grieved already for Enid, and for Landsborough, even as he stood stiff in the areaway of the house opposite, Tellman beside him. The latter was off-duty, but Pitt still needed a policeman there to make an arrest possible. Besides, Tellman deserved to be here.

Narraway himself had taken his turn, and was now waiting only a hundred feet away.

It was after six. The morning was bright with a slight wind coming up from the direction of the river when Pitt realized with a jolt that Tellman was poking him in the side.

"That's him!" Tellman whispered as a deliveryman with a bag on his arm went quickly down the areaway steps of the Denoon house. Instead of knocking on the scullery door, he let himself in.

Pitt went up his own steps, calling a warning to Narraway. He took Tellman quickly across the street and knocked on the Denoons' front door.

It was opened by a downstairs maid with an apron on and hands smutted with ash from cleaning out the withdrawing room fireplace.

"Yes, sir?" she said doubtfully.

"Police," Tellman said, and pushed past her.

"You had better waken your master," Pitt added.

Tellman was already on his way towards the kitchen. Pitt followed him, passing a bemused boot boy who was half-awake and a scullery maid with a bucket of coals.

They found Piers in the kitchen itself, pouring a cup of tea from the pot the staff must have made for themselves.

"Don't bother trying to go out the back door," Pitt said quietly. "There's someone waiting if you do."

Piers froze. The cup dropped out of his hand and slopped over onto the kitchen table. Closer to, his face was gaunt, his cheeks darkened with stubble, his eyes hollow, haunted. Terror mixed with a kind of strange, desperate relief as if at last the chase were over and he could resign himself to the worst.

"Piers Denoon," Tellman said stiffly. "I arrest you for the murder of Magnus Landsborough. You'd best come without trouble, sir. Sake of your family."

Piers remained as if unable to move. Tellman was confused as to whether to put manacles on him or not.

"Go through to the front of the house, Mr. Denoon," Pitt told him. "There's no need to do this in front of the servants."

As if he were an old man, Denoon began to walk out to the corridor and through to the front, Tellman half a step behind him.

They came through the green baize door almost together, and found Enid Denoon standing at the bottom of the stairs. She was wearing her night attire with a gown wrapped around her. Her hair was loose, still luxuriant despite her haggard face.

"What has happened?" she asked Pitt.

He had a terrible feeling that perhaps she guessed.

"I'm sorry, Mrs. Denoon." He meant it intensely. He would have given a great deal to have had it differently. It would have hurt him far less if it could have been Edward Denoon. But Denoon was too careful of himself and his ambitions to have done such a thing personally, and perhaps she knew that. He was a man who used others, as Wetron did, in all but the most desperate circumstances.

Piers looked at his mother, but it was not for help. He knew there was nothing anyone could do. "I couldn't face it, and I thought I could get away," he said simply.

Enid looked beyond him to Pitt.

She deserved an explanation. He made it as simple as he could. "Three years ago he committed a crime," he said. "The police kept his confession and the witness statements. They used them to blackmail him into acting for the anarchists, obtaining money for them. They wanted the bombings to provoke public feeling to the point where the vast majority would be willing to arm the police and give them greater powers."

Her face was ashen; she knew what was coming next. "And Magnus knew?"

"I don't know," he admitted. "Magnus was killed in order to raise public outrage and get it in all the newspapers. A lesser man, someone without a famous family, and it might not have mattered so much."

"Police?" she repeated. "Who? The man Simbister? Or the leader who just killed Voisey? No, you don't need to answer that. It must be Wetron, or you wouldn't still care so much. You do. I can see the anger in you." She looked at her son. "I shall inform your father. I doubt he can help you, but I am sure he will try. I will do what I can." She looked back at Pitt. "Please see yourself out. I have duties to fulfill. I understand that you have done what you had to, now so must I." And she turned and climbed the stairs slowly, her hand on the banister rail as if it were all that held her upright.

Pitt followed Tellman and Piers Denoon outside where Narraway was waiting. There was a cab also. Tellman put the manacles on Piers Denoon, just in case he should suddenly panic and run, or even try to throw himself out of the cab once they were moving. Narraway got in beside them.

"Well done, Pitt," he said without pleasure. "You'll have to get another cab. Sorry."

"Yes, sir," Pitt replied. "But after I've been to see Lady Vespasia. I think Mrs. Denoon needs all the comfort she can be given."

"It's not yet seven in the morning!" Narraway protested.

Pitt was determined. His own distress demanded an earlier balm for Enid than at eight, or nine. "I know. If I have to wait, then I will do." He did not wait to hear what Narraway would say, but turned and strode towards the nearest cross street where he might find a hansom. If there were none, then he would walk. It was not above a mile and a half.

In the event, when he saw a cab he was within ten minutes of his destination, and he ignored it.

Naturally Vespasia was not up, but her maid answered the door and invited Pitt to wait in the drawing room while she woke Vespasia.

"Please tell her that Mrs. Denoon will need her comfort as soon as possible," Pitt added.

"Yes, sir. And I'll have the scullery maid bring you tea and toast, shall I?"

"Oh, yes, please," Pitt suddenly realized how empty he was, how clenched with unhappiness. He had found the truth, but Piers Denoon was only a pawn. Wetron was still free, still winning. That Edward Denoon would somehow stop him was a gamble, and a very long one. It was far more likely that Wetron would buy him off by using his power of corruption to obtain some kind of pardon or escape for Piers. Maybe he would even find a way to blame someone innocent, at least of that particular crime, like Simbister!

The tea and toast came, and he welcomed it. He had just finished when Vespasia appeared. It had been barely twenty minutes but she was fully dressed in outdoor clothes and obviously ready to leave.

"What has happened, Thomas?" she asked, dread in her voice as if she already knew, although she could not have.

He rose to his feet immediately.

"I just arrested Piers Denoon for the murder of Magnus Landsborough," he answered. "Wetron blackmailed him into it, but that doesn't alter the facts. And no. I can't prove it was Wetron. It was Simbister who began it, and it is his name on the papers."

Vespasia lost the last trace of color in her face. "And Enid knows?"

A tightness inside him clenched like a locked fist. "I meant it to reach Denoon first. I sent the servant for him, and she woke Enid instead."

"I daresay she is frightened of Denoon," Vespasia said, walking to the door. "My carriage is waiting." Her voice was hoarse with emotion. "Piers is her only child. Hurry, Thomas. We may already be too late."

He did not ask for what, but did as she requested, dreading that Enid Denoon might have taken her own life, unable to bear the shame and the grief. He should have made sure her husband was there to care for her, or at the very least a strong, capable servant—the butler, or a long-serving ladies maid. He had been stupid. Now he cursed himself for it. He had been so occupied with his loathing of Wetron he had not thought to see that she was coping with the initial shock.

But it was not Enid's address Vespasia gave her coachman, it was Wetron's, and she climbed in without waiting for Pitt to give her his hand.

"Wetron?" he exclaimed.

"Hurry!" was all she said.

The coachman obeyed, urging the horses forward. In the almost deserted morning streets, where there was no trade but domestic deliveries, they careered through the silent avenues and squares as if there were almost no one else alive.

There was no opportunity for speech and Pitt was glad of it. Thoughts raced through his mind, but they were too hectic to make sense. They pulled up and he threw the door open, swiveling to hand Vespasia out, almost catching her in her urgency to follow him. Enid's carriage stood silently on the far side.

Together they sped across the pavement and up the steps. It was the second time this morning he had banged on a front door and had a startled servant open it to him.

They pushed past him just as the shot rung out. Vespasia gave a cry and turned to the morning room just as Wetron appeared at the door. He looked gray-faced, his hair tousled, and there was a small pistol in his hand.

"She's insane!" he gasped, staring wildly first at Vespasia, then at Pitt. "She came at me like a . . . a . . . a mad woman! I had no choice. It's . . ." He looked at the gun in his hand as if he were almost surprised to see it there. "This was hers. She was going to shoot me! Her son has been arrested. It . . . it unhinged her mind . . . poor creature."

Vespasia pushed past him as if he had been a servant in the way, and went into the morning room, leaving the door wide open behind her.

Even from where he stood Pitt could see Enid on the floor, lying on her back, blood welling scarlet from a wound in her lower chest.

Vespasia bent to her, cradling her in her arms, oblivious to the blood now covering her also.

Pitt took the gun from Wetron. It was surprisingly small, a woman's weapon.

Enid was still alive, just.

"She's mad!" Wetron said again, his voice thin and high. "I had no choice!"

Vespasia looked up from where she was kneeling, her arm now

around Enid's shoulders. "Rubbish!" she said with savage, glittering triumph. "The bullet is in the carpet under her!" she shouted hoarsely. "She was lying on the floor when you shot her. You struck her and she fell and dropped the gun. You picked it up and used it in cold blood. The police surgeon will be able to prove that. You've made your one final mistake, Mr. Wetron. You destroyed her nephew, and her son. But she has destroyed you. It is the end of the Police Bill, and I think at last it is also the end of the Inner Circle. Voisey is dead and Edward Denoon will be ruined."

She looked down at Enid and the tears filled her eyes. "I hope she knew what she had achieved," she whispered, letting go of her at last. "You had better use the telephone to have someone come and take the wretched man away, Thomas. You must have people for such things. I will then tell Lord Landsborough what is lost, and what is gained."

Pitt remembered that among all the collected things in his pocket he had a set of manacles. He took them out and locked Wetron to one of the brass posts on the magnificent club fender around the fireplace, obliging him to sit on the floor a yard from Enid's body.

"Yes, of course," he said. "I'm . . . sorry."

Vespasia looked at him, ignoring her tears. "Don't be, my dear. This was what she chose, and I think perhaps there was no other way."

"Thank you, Aunt Vespasia," he said, swallowing hard, and went to obey.

PHOTO: © JONATHAN HULME

ANNE PERRY is the bestselling author of two acclaimed series set in Victorian England: the Charlotte and Thomas Pitt novels, most recently *Treason at Lisson Grove* and *Buckingham Palace Gardens*, and the William Monk novels, including *Acceptable Loss* and *Execution Dock*. She is also the author of the World War I novels *No Graves As Yet, Shoulder the Sky, Angels in the Gloom, At Some Disputed Barricade,* and *We Shall Not Sleep,* as well as nine Christmas novels, most recently *A Christmas Homecoming.* Her stand-alone novel *The Sheen on the Silk,* set in the Byzantine Empire, was a *New York Times* bestseller. Anne Perry lives in Scotland.

www.AnnePerry.com